R0061587945

02/2012

D1376448

The Mechanical Messiah and Other Marvels of the Modern Age

Also by Robert Rankin:

The Brentford Trilogy:
The Antipope
The Brentford Triangle
East of Ealing
The Sprouts of Wrath
The Brentford Chainstore Massacre
Sex and Drugs and Sausage Rolls
Knees Up Mother Earth

The Armageddon Trilogy:
Armageddon: The Musical
They Came and Ate Us
The Suburban Book of the Dead

Cornelius Murphy Trilogy:
The Book of Ultimate Truths
Raiders of the Lost Car Park
The Most Amazing Man Who Ever Lived

There is a secret trilogy in the middle there, comprised of:
The Trilogy That Dare Not Speak Its Name Trilogy:
Sprout Mask Replica
The Dance of the Voodoo Handbag
Waiting for Godalming

Plus some fabulous other books, including:
The Hollow Chocolate Bunnies of the Apocalypse

And its sequel:
The Toyminator

And then:
The Witches of Chiswick
The Brightonomicon
The Da-Da-De-Da-Da Code
Necrophenia
Retromancer
The Japanese Devil Fish Girl and Other Unnatural Attractions

The Mechanical Messiah and Other Marvels of the Modern Age

Robert Rankin FVSS*

*Fellow of the Victorian Steampunk Society

with illustrations by the author

GOLLANCZ

London

The right of Robert Rankin to be identified as the author
of this work has been asserted by him in accordance with the
Copyright, Designs and Patents Act 1988.

First published in Great Britain in 2011 by Gollancz
An imprint of the Orion Publishing Group
Orion House, 5 Upper St Martin's Lane, London WC2H 9EA
An Hachette UK Company

A CIP catalogue record for this book is available
from the British Library

ISBN 978 0 575 08635 7 (Cased)
ISBN 978 0 575 08637 1 (Export Trade Paperback)

1 3 5 7 9 10 8 6 4 2

Typeset at The Spartan Press Ltd,
Lymington, Hants

Printed and bound by
CPI Group (UK) Ltd, Croydon, CR0 4YY

The Orion Publishing Group's policy is to use papers that
are natural, renewable and recyclable products and
made from wood grown in sustainable forests. The logging
and manufacturing processes are expected to conform to
the environmental regulations of the country of origin.

www.thegoldensprout.com

www.orionbooks.co.uk

THIS BOOK IS DEDICATED TO

YVETTE AND VERITY

AND TO THE MEMORY OF

JAMES STUART CAMPBELL

1965–2010

The universe is a machine
In which everything happens
By figure and motion.

René Descartes

I'd like to be a machine.
Wouldn't you?

Andy Warhol

1897

1

he foyer of the Electric Alhambra was lit to a pretty perfection.

One thousand vacuum bulbs, brought to brilliance by Lord Tesla's latest innovation, the wireless transmission of electricity, illuminated a scene of lavish enchantment. Just so.

The foyer was crafted to the Moorish style, with a high central dome and surrounding arches. And all throughout and around and about, mosaics of turquoise and gold sparkled in the dazzling luminescence. These mosaics were wrought with cunning arabesques and details of intricate geometry. Here a hexagram, picked out in oriental amethyst and lapis lazuli. There a pentacle, in heliotrope and aquamarine. So rich and complex were these ornamentations as to baffle the eye and stagger the senses. To inspire both wonder and awe.

The foyer was furnished with settles and settees, copious couches and diverse divans. These were upholstered with sumptuous swan's down, moleskin and marmot and pale astrakhans. Towering torchères with filigreed finials, tables of pewter and copper and brass. Inlaid and overlaid, fiddled and diddled, fantastic fittings and glittering glass.

But all of these wonders – and wonders they were – served only as an architectural hors d'oeuvre to the great banquet of gilded glory that was the auditorium. For beyond tall doors of embellished enamel, which rose like hymns in praise of pleasure, were Xanadu and Shangri-La made flesh in wood and stone. In bronze and in ormolu, travertine and tourmaline, crystal and silver and glittering gold.

The auditorium boasted seating for three thousand people in the most exquisite surroundings imaginable. Electrically lit and lavishly appointed, it was truly a marvel of the modern age.

But—

There were certain folk who expressed certain doubts.

The Society columnist of *The Times* newspaper, for instance. He had coined a new term to describe the interior of the Electric Alhambra: 'Architectural Sesquipedalianism'. Words such as 'grandiloquent', 'overblown', 'ostentatious' and, indeed, 'intemperate', flowed from his steam-powered fountain pen and figured large in his repertoire of damnation for this 'Monstrous Testament to Bad Taste'.

For 'The Thunderer's' columnist was a titled toff of the esoteric persuasion and the Electric Alhambra, a *Music Hall*!

Now this was not to say that the gentry did not frequent the Music Hall. Not one diddly bit of it. But even those adventurous aristocrats who favoured titillation above temperance entered the portals of such establishments furtively and in heavy disguise, thereby perpetuating the belief that the Music Hall was really just for commoners – the hoi polloi and *not* the hoity-toity.

Upon this particular evening, a warm summer's evening in early July, the hoi polloi held sway. Certain swank events here in the British Empire's capital had drawn most of high social standing to the company of their own and the Electric

Alhambra was the almost exclusive preserve of the down-trodden masses. Or at least those members of the lumpen-proletariat as could scrape together the price of admission: three fine, bright copper pennies.

But there were others present upon this summer's evening. Others whose undeniable *otherness* distinguished them. Marked them out as *different*. Other men from other worlds were these. Beings from the bloated planet of Jupiter, or the cloud-girt world of Venus.

It was now twelve years since the Martian invasion of Earth, as recalled in that historical memoir of Mr H. G. Wells, *The War of the Worlds*, and two since Worlds War Two. Happily the Martians had been mercilessly destroyed and happier still the British Empire now extended to Mars. But the alliance and state of peace that existed between Earth, Venus and Jupiter was an uneasy one. There was a singular lack of trust and at times acts of open hostility were directed towards off-worlders who walked the streets of London.

But not *here*. Not here in the Music Hall. Whatever happened outside remained outside. Within, the Music Hall justly considered itself to be the very exemplar of egalitarian-ism. All were welcome and all were treated equally. Al-though those with more than three pennies to spend *could* occupy the better seats.

So, what of the Alhambra's patrons this evening? What of their looks and their manners and styles? Mr Cameron Bell, that most private of private detectives, was known (by those in the know) to be capable of discerning a man's occupation merely by the study of his boots.

The boots of those who now shuffled about upon the mosaic floor of the foyer spoke of many occupations. As indeed did their distinctive attire.

Here were the piemen and those who offered for sale upon the thoroughfares of the great metropolis such tooth-some viands as mock-plum duff, straw muffins, mud pies, sawdust puddings and cardboard cakes. Shirts, once white, found favour with them, as did long, pale smocks of antique design, as worn by bakers in bygone days. When bread was oft-times made out of bread and rarely, as now, out of chalk.

Mingling amongst these fellows were to be seen the cockney street sellers of flypapers, beetle wafers and wasp traps, cockroach castles and sea-monkey sanctuaries. These were men of the 'pattering class', who plied their wares with silken tongues and honeyed words. Displaying a tamed spider or two, with which to garner interest from Samaritans. They sported suits of rough-cut plaid with patterns in beige and taupe, echoing those of Lord Burberry.

Many and various were the trades of London's working class. Trades that had persisted since the dawn of recorded history and would no doubt prevail for ever, resisting all future trends. Crossing sweepers conversed with rat-catchers, bone-grubbers and those who gathered the Pure.* Mole-stranglers and ferret-stretchers shared jokes with horse-sniffers and donkey-punchers, the men who point at poultry and those who untwist dogs into the shape of balloons.

The owners of dancing ducks and industrious insects exchanged banter with characters who bruised peaches for public entertainment and others prepared to scrape tortoises in private, once a proper price had been agreed upon.

And here also were the folk of London's underworld. The men 'who would not be blamed for nothing'. The coiners

* Canine excrement used in the tanning process for the manufacture of kid gloves.

and card sharps. The purloiners of parrots. Burglars of bunnies and budgerigars. Kidnappers of kittens. Procurers of poodles. Pimps of Pomeranians. Loudly dressed and loudly spoken were they, and in the company of women.

Women of easy virtue these and of boisterous disposition. Brightly frocked, given to the downing of gin and the employment of fisticuffs and foul language. And such im-moderate laughter as to rattle light bulbs and set upon edge whatever teeth any possessed.

But not all women here were such as they. Others were decent working girls. Those ingénues, poor but honest, clean and well turned out. Girls in service to the houses of the great and the good. Parlour maids and linen-folders. Respectable spinsters who laundered lavender bags, pam-pered pillows and fluffed up the muffs of their mistresses. In corsets and bustles, best gloves and bonnets, out for a night at the Music Hall.

And what a night this would prove to be for those who thronged the foyer upon this summer's evening. Cooled by conditioned air that wafted from the patent ice grotto, yet warmed by anticipation for all that lay ahead.

Tonight they would thrill to the best that Music Hall had to offer. The topmost of all top turns. The greatest comics and songsters, dancers and novelty acts of this or any other age. And topping the topmost of the bill, none other than England's best-loved entertainer, Mr Harry 'Hurty-Finger' Hamilton. Four billings up from the now legendary Travel-ling Formbys and three above the remarkable Lovell's Acro-batic Kiwis, Harry bestrode the London stage as a colossus, admired by men, adored by women. *A smile, a song and a damaged digit* – how could it get better than *that*?

Tonight, Harry, all dapper in tailcoat and topper, would sing his heart out and raise the crowd to a standing ovation.

And having done so, he would return to his six-star dressing room to toast his triumph with champagne and sherbet. In the company of ladies skilled in those arts which amuse men.

Or at least such was his intention.

But even the best of intentions can occasionally come to naught. And tonight things would not go quite as Harry had hoped that they would. Tonight an event would occur at the Electric Alhambra. An event that was definitely not listed upon the playbill. It would prove to be a tragic and terrible event. The first in a series of tragic and terrible events. Tragic and terrible events that would threaten not only the Music Hall, but London, the Empire and all of the Solar System.

Tragically.

And terribly.

They would involve, amongst others, a man and a monkey, as can sometimes be the case.

2

n a crowded communal dressing room, which owned to no stars upon its door but an abundance of kiwi birds flopping foolishly about, a man and a monkey sat and scowled.

Neither was speaking to the other.

That a man might have nothing to say would appear reasonable enough. Most ordinary men have the choice of speaking words when they wish to and withholding them when they do not. But not so monkeys, which are generally assumed to be wordless, at least in human terms. This, however, was no ordinary man and certainly no ordinary monkey.

The gentleman's name was Colonel Katterfelto.

The monkey's name was Darwin.

Now Colonel Katterfelto had a tragic tale to tell and would tell it at the dropping of a sixpence. Late of the Queen's Own Electric Fusiliers, he had distinguished himself in the Martian campaign and been awarded several medals for valorous deeds above and beyond the call of duty. Sadly the colonel no longer sported these medals, for he had been forced to pawn them. He did, however, cling to his dignity, though this was oft-times perilous.

Although age had brought a bow to his back, Colonel Katterfelto still retained his military bearing. The greying whiskers of his mustachios were tinted a steely blue and twisted into martial spikes. His pale grey eyes were clear and alert, though in them sadness showed.

For the colonel had fallen upon hard times and been reduced to the status of Music Hall bill-bottomer. A precarious position at best and one to be dreaded at worst. The worst being the volatile crowd's aptness to greet those first up on the evening's bill via the medium of hurled rotten fruit and vegetables.

It was a tradition, or an old charter, or something.

But the colonel would give of his best this evening, for he knew of no other way. Had he not laid down fire upon Martian tripods? Rescued wounded comrades-in-arms? Marched across the dusty landscape of the red planet, letting loose at anything that moved with his back-engineered service ray-gun revolver (which now sadly lay in the pawnshop next to his medals of honour)? Yes he had, he most certainly had.

A rough crowd held no fear for Colonel Katterfelto, though he fretted for the staining of his uniform. It had been for him a sad and sudden decline into penury and it had not been of his own making. The colonel knew just where the blame for it lay.

The blame lay with Darwin the monkey.

Darwin the monkey's tale was equal in sadness to that of the colonel's. Perhaps more than equal, in fact, because it involved the loss of not one but *two* fortunes. And Darwin the monkey had no one to blame but himself.

He had once been employed as monkey butler to Lord Brentford. When his lordship came to a sorry end aboard the ill-fated airship the *Empress of Mars*, Darwin inherited the Brentford fortune. The Great House at Sion Park, along with extensive grounds, which Darwin soon converted into England's biggest banana plantation, and a good many golden guineas besides. Some of these guineas Darwin had invested most wisely; others most surely he had *not*.

Upon a May morning in the year of eighteen ninety-six, a gentleman caller at Sion Park had presented his card. Known only as Herr Döktor, he had a unique proposition to put to England's most moneyed monkey.

It was Herr Döktor's conviction that it was possible to teach monkeys to read, write and speak the Queen's English. This, he considered, would advance their evolutionary progress, enabling them eventually to catch up with our own. This was *not*, he was careful to stress, in any way a heretical idea. On the contrary. Herr Döktor was doing God's work. His goal was to bring enlightenment and understanding to Man's hairy cousins, that they might save their souls through knowledge and worship of the Almighty.

Naturally it was difficult to put a price upon the benefits of such an offer. The benefits that would present themselves to the world's first talking ape. But Herr Döktor was nonetheless willing to name a sum, which although on the face of it sounded over-excessive to the point of whimsy, he considered suitable. A labourer being worthy of his hire, as the scriptures so aptly put it.

Darwin, who had a basic understanding of English – for how otherwise might he have served as a monkey butler? – warmed immediately to the prospect of articulating human speech. He forked out the most considerable sum, in cash (for render unto Caesar those things which are Caesar's) and engaged in a six-month programme of intense tutorage.

It was not, however, without incident and Darwin, who had yet to eschew the basic ways of monkeydom, had not been above the occasional flinging of dung to enforce a point when he felt it necessary.

But he met with success and half a year later had mastered the basic rudiments of the Queen's English. He then shook hands with Herr Döktor and in all but perfect 'Man' thanked him for his lessons and bade him farewell.

Herr Döktor bowed and turned away, struggling down the drive, bow-legged beneath the weight of golden guineas.

Three days later, cleanly shaven of face and presenting himself as an English country gentleman, Darwin settled down before a gaming table at Monte Carlo and within several hours had gambled away his entire remaining inheritance. Big house, banana plantation, a spaceship and all.

Very sad.

There was probably a moral to be learned there, but whatever it was, it was lost upon Darwin. Who now found himself gifted with speech, though quite without funds.

He could of course have chosen to exhibit himself before a paying public, but this he had no wish to do. Knowing something of the showman's life, he harboured no longings to be presented as a freak of nature. Rather he wished for comfort and stability and so chose once more to accept the position of monkey butler. But not, it must be said, without a slight degree of bitterness towards humankind.

Colonel Katterfelto had, like most gentlemen of his time, always yearned for a monkey butler. A servant who would work for bananas, be ever obedient and not answer back. He had lately come into an inheritance of his own and this coupled with his army pension, which he chose to take as a cash sum, would, he felt, enable him to achieve his life's ambition. To build a certain something, with the aid of a monkey butler.

The certain something that the colonel had in mind was a something of almost infinite magnitude. Its genesis had come about with a book the colonel had read when still a child. A book of considerable age entitled *Treatise upon the Establishment of a New World Order, through the Construction of the New Messiah.* As curiosity might have it, and here it might be said that curiosity was piled upon curiosity to form an all-encompassing coincidence, the author of this ancient tome was one Herr Döktor.

The gist of this treatise was that the New Messiah would not come down in glory from the skies, as was popularly touted about in scripture. The New Messiah would be a modern messiah, behaving in the ways of modernity. The New Messiah would require a little help from his friends to manifest himself. He would in fact need to be constructed from modern materials. The author argued convincingly that human anatomy was far too complicated, and that a good engineer could create a man of greater simplicity and greater efficiency. A man that would last far longer than three score years and ten. A man who might be as a God. Included in the treatise were the plans for such a man. A mechanical man that would be designed as 'a magical magnet used to attract divine energies'. A Mechanical Messiah to be imbued with the presence of God. Heaven's last and best gift to Mankind.

And all it required was finance.

In the communal dressing room, Colonel Katterfelto tapped distractedly upon his ray-gun holster, wherein lay the ancient tome. Somewhat scuffed and charred about its edges. Where had it all gone wrong? he wondered, and then he recalled well enough.

He had engaged the services of his monkey butler. He had drawn out his fortune from the bank. He had purchased tickets to America, where a family property had been bequeathed to him, and had sailed upon *The Great Eastern** in the company of Darwin, striking port in New York and heading off to Wormcast, Arizona.

Here, in a simple shack on the edge of town, the colonel had set up his Spiritual Laboratory and begun his Great Work. Things had gone well. Up to a point. The actual construction of the Mechanical Messiah had been reasonably straightforward. A local blacksmith shop, a light engineering company and an airship construction works had shared in the manufacture of parts. Each working upon separate, seemingly unrelated items and no one but the colonel knowing of the intended whole. Secrecy, the colonel considered, would be for the best, until the Great Day dawneth. The parts had been expensive, but how could one place a monetary value upon the salvation of Mankind? It was beyond price.

It took six months to construct the Mechanical Messiah. It took the townsfolk of Wormcast, Arizona, less than an hour to destroy it.

It had all been such a sad misunderstanding. It had all been the fault of Darwin the monkey butler. The colonel had not one inkling as to his servant's skills in the field of human speech. And then, upon having made his tenth attempt to bring life to the Mechanical Messiah by drawing into it the electrical ether, in a manner which had hitherto only been

* *History asserts that* The Great Eastern *was broken up in 1889. But what does history know!*

attempted (with some success, it is recorded) by a certain Victor Frankenstein, the misunderstanding had occurred.

The colonel considered that if the lightning rod had been correctly aligned by Darwin, the experiment might well have proved a success. But instead of the lightning darting down the rod to engage with the terminals upon the shoulders of the Mechanical Messiah, it jumped these terminals and bounced about the Spiritual Laboratory, striking Darwin and setting fire to his tail.

Which caused the monkey to cry out *the Name of God's Son*.

Colonel Katterfelto had fallen back in amazement. And then rushed forwards to extinguish his burning butler.

'It is a miracle,' cried the colonel. 'You have become a Vessel of God. The voice of the angels speaks through you.'

Darwin, still smouldering slightly, turned a bitter, although thoughtful, eye upon the colonel.

'The angels require that you should furnish this vessel with a bunch of bananas and a large gin and tonic,' he had said. Most eloquently.

And from thereafter all had gone terribly wrong.

The angels made many demands of the colonel. Many demands that did not seem even remotely connected with bringing life to the Mechanical Messiah. Most seemed more directly concerned with the vessel's welfare in the form of culinary requirements and bottles of vintage port. At times the colonel questioned these demands.

'To what end,' he enquired, 'did the New Messiah need to have the front garden converted into a banana plantation?'

But who was he to argue with the angels? Who would do such a thing?

The end came swiftly and in the form of fire. Darwin, somewhat bloated of belly from an over-surfeit of bananas and far gone in drink through the imbibition of too much vintage port, had taken it into his hairy head to borrow the horse and trap (a surrey with a fringe on the top) and drive into town to purchase some chocolates from the general store.

It had been an ill-considered move. For where Colonel Katterfelto discerned the voice of angels speaking through Darwin, the plain folk of Wormcast, Arizona, saw something altogether different. They saw a demon employed by the Antichrist. For rumours in Wormcast were rife that Colonel Katterfelto was up to something altogether unhealthy at his shack. And this, if proof were needed, was all the proof there needed to be.

That night the God-fearing folk of Wormcast, Arizona, marched upon the Spiritual Laboratory in the company of blazing torches.

And that was that was that.

The man and his monkey fled Arizona. They returned to London, where Colonel Katterfelto hocked his medals and his ray gun and invested the last of his money in a set of battered clockwork minstrels.

He was down, was the colonel, but not entirely out. He would rise again. But for now he certainly wasn't speaking to Darwin, who had remained with the colonel for reasons of his own. And Darwin was *not* speaking to *him*.

So the two sat wordlessly and glowered at one another, as kiwi birds flopped foolishly, and the five-minute bell rang a kind of a death knell in the crowded communal dressing room.

3

n evening at the Music Hall quite suited Cameron Bell. He needed something to exercise his mind. The challenge of another complex criminal case would have been the first choice of the man known by those in the know to be the world's greatest detective. But if such was not forthcoming then an evening of frivolous entertainment. Especially if it came in the comely form of the enchanting Alice Lovell, whose acrobatic kiwi birds were presently causing some annoyance to Colonel Katterfelto.

Cameron Bell was a most private man, and although history would remember him, it would do so under two quite separate names. And neither of these his own. Amongst Cameron's many friends was a pair of literary types and each chose to immortalise him in print. Charles Dickens based the look of Mr Pickwick* upon Cameron Bell. And Arthur

---

* *History records that* The Pickwick Papers *was originally published in 1837 and that Charles Dickens died in 1870, the year of Cameron Bell's birth. No further references to the inaccuracy of recorded history will be made in this tome.*

Conan Doyle based the skills of Sherlock Holmes upon those of this real-life detective.

Cameron Bell was greatly tickled by his friends' depictions of him. The only drawback being that folk did tend to stop him in the street to enquire whether they could join The Pickwick Club, and how was Sam Weller* doing these days?

Upon this particular evening, this early summer's evening in July of eighteen ninety-seven, Cameron Bell had chosen to fork out the full half-crown for a box seat near to the Electric Alhambra's stage. There were others in that box upon this evening and Mr Bell doffed his silk top hat towards them as he entered and settled into his numbered seat.

These others were Venusians. A male and a female so it seemed, although a debate still raged amongst those who were not in the know, yet wished to be, as to exactly how many sexes Venusians had. Some said three: male, female and 'of the spirit'. Others contested that Venusians were trimaphrodite, embodying all three sexes in a single being.

Cameron Bell knew the truth, but this truth he kept to himself. From the corner of his eye he viewed his fellow patrons of this most expensive box. They were certainly magnificent creatures. Tall and stately, with skin of an ivory paleness. High snowy plumes of hair, teased into intricate spires and intriguing curlicues. Eyes of gold and angled cheekbones. Fingers delicate and fine. They exuded a subtle perfume. Artificial? Or bodily odour? Cameron Bell did not know *that*.

The Venusians spoke one to another in hushed tones, and in their native tongue. The meaning of their words was lost to Cameron Bell. For although he had made numerous attempts to learn Venusian – no simple matter, as Venusians

---

* *Mr Pickwick's famous valet.*

were not at all forthcoming – he had concluded that without the aid of a willing tutor, the task was nigh impossible.

Why, it would be easier to teach a monkey to speak the Queen's English. And such an idea as that was clearly ludicrous!

The most private of private detectives placed his silk top hat between his feet and divested himself of his white kid gloves. Perching his pince-nez upon his nose, he gazed out across the brightly lit auditorium. And certain words which he had recently read in *The Times* Society column returned to him. He tended to share the columnist's opinion: the interior of the Electric Alhambra was really much too much.

The ceiling, so very high above, beyond the six tiers of balcony seats, was frescoed in the style of Michelangelo. With Queen Victoria, the Royal Sovereign, pictured as Empress of the Solar System, throned in glory and presiding benignly over her realm. Her subjects, of every colour, race and hue, including some that looked suspiciously Venusian in origin, knelt before her, gazing up in adoration. Cherubim and seraphim fussed and fluttered around and about, smiling with love upon Her Majesty.

The walls that climbed to meet this travesty of Renaissance genius were of the rococo persuasion. Fussed and made fancy with a frenzy of gilded ornamentation. Fairies and phantoms, satyrs and sprites, fabulous figures and mythical heroes, scrambling over one another. As if seeking to reach, and no doubt offer praise, to the Queen Empress Goddess on high.

But at least those who were made giddy from the gazing upwards did so in a cool and healthy climate. For the temperature and quality of the air was managed by intricate electrical systems, pneumatic, hydrostatic, magnetical and hydraulic in nature. Driven through the patent ice grotto and all linked to a self-governing nexus designed by Sir Charles Babbage.

No matter one's feelings for this Music Hall's aesthetic, it truly was a marvel of the modern age.

Mr Cameron Bell leaned back in his plush red-velvet-covered chair, delighting momentarily at simply being here and taking in the din of the restless crowd.

Raucous cries and cockney oaths and all over general hubbub.

Then—

The dimming of the house lights, the crowd noise gone to murmurs, now to silence.

Then—

The striking up of the band. Tonight the world-famous Titurel de Schentefleur would conduct Mazael's Mechanical Musicians. A single tap of the baton and the overture began.

This overture consisted of several popular Music Hall songs of the day and the crowd enthusiastically sang along with these.

The first to have the patrons in full voice was Tommy 'the Teapot' Tompkinson's famous audience-pleaser, 'A Nice Cup of Tea for the Baby Girl'.

Which went after this fashion:

> *A nice cup of tea for the baby girl*
> *It don't get better than that.*
> *You can keep all those gents*
> *With their sweet-smelling scents,*
> *Those toffs in their toppers*
> *And fine opera hats*
> *Because my wife's a regular diamond*
> *She's pure as an emerald or pearl.*

If I'm down on my uppers
I'm still brewing cuppas
For my sweet baby girl.

A time would come in the future when folk would look back upon lyrics such as these and say, 'They don't write songs like *that* any more.' And they would clearly be right.

Cameron Bell sang what words he knew and hummed along with the rest. He had a good view of the mechanical musicians. Scarcely manlike, more a number of mahogany cases filled with complicated gubbins that squeezed bellows to power the woodwind section, or drew complex bows across curious violins. It was said that a professor from Brentford in Middlesex was working on a more compact system, which might be installed in drinking houses for their patrons to sing along with. But whether anything would come of Professor Karaoke's musical machine was anybody's guess.

The first song came to an end and the second began. A sad one, this, as could tease a tear from the eye of a potato. The plaintive ballad that was 'Me Mammy's Wooden Foot'. A song of maternal love and accidental amputation.

And so it went on, but not for *too* long. The secret has always been knowing when to stop, and when faced with a crowd armed with rotten fruit and veg, it is better to err upon the side of caution.

Titurel de Schentefleur turned and bowed to the audience and then he and Mazael's Mechanical Musicians descended at speed beneath the floor of the auditorium via a system of hidden hydraulics. Doors closed over the orchestra pit. A spotlight stabbed at the stage. Struck the great curtain to form an illuminated disc.

And into this swaggered the master of ceremonies and

interlocutor for the evening, 'Lord' Anthony Spaloney (the King of the old Baloney). In turquoise tailcoat and topper, he cut a considerable dash. The crowd cheered as he bowed extravagantly towards them, before, as he put it, 'enunciating the gamut of delicious delectations that would gloriously grace the stage upon this eventime'.

And as no one as yet had thrown anything, he went on to speak of tonight's star 'turns'. He showered syllables of sophistry upon the skills of the Scandinavian Saxophonists. Poured paeans of praise over Peter Pinkerton, the Piebald Prestidigitator. Eloquently extolled the exceeding excellence of Elmer Ellington's Electric Eels. Affected an amorous appassionato whilst addressing amatory attention to Acton's Aphrodite Alice Lovell. She of the Acrobatic Kiwis. And then, for here was a man who, through long experience in his line of work, had certainly learned that the secret was in knowing when to stop, hastily introduced the first star turn and exited the stage without a single missile being thrown.

He inclined his head towards Colonel Katterfelto, waiting stage left, made the sign of the cross and then made away to the bar.

The chords of a hidden harmonium heralded the arrival of Colonel Katterfelto. The great curtain rose to reveal the ample stage, bare of theatrical properties, but made gay by a colourful backdrop in the form of one vast Union Jack.

This backdrop had been hung at the instigation of Colonel Katterfelto. The old soldier reasoning, quite rightly, that this might prove a deterrent against the flinging of foul fruit and veg. For no Englishman or woman, in the rightness of their minds, would ever think of besmirching the Union Jack.

The hidden harmonium struck up a military march and Colonel Katterfelto strutted onto the stage. Polished boots and swagger stick and goggled helmet perched upon his head.

The crowd, recognising at once the distinctive blue and silverly braided uniform of the Queen's Own Electric Fusiliers, applauded the colonel and viewed the stage with quizzical expressions. Katterfelto's Clockwork Minstrels were still an unknown quantity.

The old soldier gazed towards his audience. But naught could be seen of them beyond the glare of the footlights. A tactical error, the colonel considered. One should always see one's enemy before one's enemy sees one.

The colonel raised his hands slowly and lowered his goggles over his eyes. This brought some mirth to the crowd, who now, entertaining the idea that this might be a *mime* act, readied their soft-skinned weaponry, Union Jack or no Union Jack.

Colonel Katterfelto switched on his goggles. Night-vision mode, Martian technology back-engineered by British boffins for soldiers in service of the Crown. The crowd became visible.

Ugly, thought the colonel, affecting a gap-toothed smile.

'Ladies and gentlemen,' he began, 'it is my pleasure to present for you this evening an entertainment that embodies the very spirit of our age. An age of enlightenment and progress. An age—' The colonel saw the movement, gauged the arc, watched as the turnip reached its apogee, stepped smartly aside as it swung down onto the stage.

This evasive manoeuvre most impressed and somewhat baffled a crowd that was used to having the element of surprise on its side. A cabbage was launched towards the stage; the colonel nimbly sidestepped this. Fruit followed on and the colonel dodged this, too.

In his box, Cameron Bell opened his umbrella. When

fruit and veg were being thrown, there was a tendency for some of it to 'accidentally' strike home amongst the sitters in the expensive boxes. It was better to be safe than to be sorry.

Then there came a temporary lull in the bombardment. For without warning something short and shiny-looking tottered onto the stage. It was a tinplate manikin, some three feet in height. Its face wore smiling painted features, its body a painted red suit and a painted bow tie. A large key revolved slowly in its back as it made its precarious way towards the colonel, wobbling uneasily with every metal footfall.

The crowd applauded the tin man's entrance and Colonel Katterfelto, with hope in his heart, twirled his swagger stick, bowed low towards the automaton, then made a number of expansive gestures that none could fathom the meaning of. Then bit upon his upper lip as the clockwork walker toppled.

The bombardment that followed was given equal distribution between Colonel Katterfelto and the fallen tinplate figure. Two heavy swedes struck home against the latter, causing a turn towards the unexpected. Seams split and a monkey, now suddenly revealed to be the hidden operator of the clockwork minstrel, leapt out, baring his teeth.

The crowd jeered and bellowed and flung everything it had.

Darwin, now gibbering in the tongue of his ancestors, did as his simian forebears would have done: produced dung and heaved it in joyful retaliation at the audience.

The curtain fell.

4

olonel Katterfelto returned to the communal dressing room.

To receive a standing ovation.

Somewhat taken aback and drop-jawed by this unexpected applause, the old campaigner gratefully received the penny cigar that Peter Pinkerton, the Piebald Prestidigitator, pushed into his mouth. And sucked greedily upon it, once lit.
Surely these artistes had made some mistake. The colonel was rightfully bewildered.

'It is this way, sir,' said Alice Lovell, made lovelier by the white ringmaster's uniform that hugged her where a lady should be hugged. 'No bill-bottomer has ever before stepped from that stage utterly free of besmirchment.'

'Ah,' said the colonel. And nodded his elderly head.

'And what is more,' continued Alice, coquettishly cocking her head upon one side, 'you have spared your fellow performers, having caused the mob to exhaust its supply of mouldy fruit and vegetables.'

'Ah,' said the colonel once more. And he once more sucked upon his cigar.

'Sorry about your monkey, though,' said Alice.

Colonel Katterfelto gazed down at his erstwhile monkey butler, now bedraggled stage assistant. Darwin, with no night-vision goggles to enable him to view 'incoming', was a monkey greatly in need of a bath. A sad and sorry sight.

A shadow of a smile appeared upon the colonel's face, but sensing a retribution for such an expression that was likely to come in the form of faeces, he turned far down the corners of his mouth and said, 'Poor fellow indeed. Perhaps, dear lady, you might assist in bathing my hirsute companion. Your hands being smaller than my own and better suited to so delicate a task.'

'Well . . .' went Alice Lovell.

The colonel displayed his hands and caused these to tremble somewhat. 'The shock of it all,' he said. 'Perhaps I should retire this night forever from the stage.'

It was now Alice Lovell's turn to say, 'Ah.' Followed by, 'Not a bit of it, sir. You must complete the season with the rest of your fellow performers.' Adding that she would gladly cleanse the ape upon this occasion.

Darwin viewed the attractive young woman, scarcely a head higher than himself. Slim and sleek, with the prettiest of faces. Certain thoughts passed through the mind of Darwin the Music Hall monkey. Certain thoughts that are best left unrecorded.

Alice Lovell took Darwin by the hairy hand and led him to the patent water closet.

Onstage, the Travelling Formbys were singing a song that extolled the virtues of a washed bottom and a clean handkerchief. The crowd, most of whom owned to neither of these, sang along with vigour. Whilst making a mental note that next week they must bring *more* fruit and veg.

Cameron Bell put his finger to the servant-call button and

when the liveried menial arrived at the box, ordered a bottle of champagne. 'With three glasses, if you please.'

And then he settled back once more in his comfortable seat and longed for Alice Lovell.

Cameron Bell had scarcely known a woman's touch since the death of his mother. For he was a man driven, a man consumed by his occupation. Not for him the pleasures of the flesh, or indeed the deeper joys of female companionship. His was a solitary and cerebral existence. To match his wits against master criminals and to succeed. To unravel the seemingly inextricable conundrums that foxed the fellows of Scotland Yard. To prove that he was the best, nay, better than the best.

Mr Carl Gustav Jung had already coined a term to describe the mental condition of subjects he examined who displayed the obsessive nature of Mr Cameron Bell. Mr Bell had no time for such nonsense. And no time for Carl Gustav Jung.

In truth there was really only one being in the whole wide world that Mr Bell had any personal time for, and that was the adorable Alice. Cameron Bell was in love with Alice Lovell.

But could this angel made flesh ever share such feelings for a young man who bore an uncanny resemblance to Mr Pickwick? Cameron Bell supposed it unlikely, but he could always dream.

The liveried menial brought the champagne; Cameron Bell uncorked it. What could a man such as himself offer a woman such as Alice? he wondered. He had money, if money she wanted. He was well paid at times for the exclusive and discreet services he offered to clients of the wealthy upper classes. Though somewhat portly, he dressed well and both his bottom and his hankie were clean. And beauty *was* in the eye of the beholder. The lovely Alice might take to him immediately. He might be just what she was looking for.

'Tall and spare,' said Alice Lovell, lathering Darwin in the water closet, 'with a head of curly black hair. An Italian songster, perhaps. There is Señor Voice, the singing horse-tram driver of the number twenty-three to Hammersmith. He has a certain swarthy charm.'

Exactly why she was describing the man of her dreams to a monkey, Alice wasn't certain. He just looked like a good listener.

Darwin, somewhat cross-eyed and gaga from the delicate and at times intimate bath he was receiving, picked up on the words 'spare', 'curly hair' and 'swarthy'. A fair description of himself, he supposed.

'Five minutes, Miss Lovell,' called a voice, as knuckles knocked at the water-closet door.

'You'll have to dry yourself,' said Alice to Darwin. 'And please stop doing *that*, my dear, it really isn't decent.'

Alice Lovell's act could justly call itself unique.

Certainly there were many other bird and animal acts to be seen. Upon the stage and also on the streets.

But acrobatic kiwis? Not another.

There were many dancing ducks, of course, displayed along the thoroughfares. These inevitably danced upon the tops of biscuit tins. It was said, and not without good cause, that these biscuit tins generally contained a lighted candle.

Chicken baiting was, as ever, a popular sport. And women were thrilled to an excess of excitement watching a healthy young man, stripped bare to the waist and armed with nothing more than a butcher's cleaver, matched against as many as five ferocious fowl in a backstreet chicken pit.

Ranked also high in popularity were the predictive parrots and prophesying penguins, birds so trained as to convincingly cast tarot and foretell the future. And here it has been justly stated (by those who hath the wisdom to discern trickery in the shape of the candle that heateth the biscuit tin) that a client seeking knowledge from such birds might find a far better future for five guineas than five shillings.

Acrobatic kiwis, though? Well, that was another matter.

They had come from New Zealand, of course, conveyed to these shores by Alice's father, Captain Horatio Lovell. The good captain brought back with him a number of natural curiosities, many of which he exhibited before paying clientele. Amongst these was a mermaid. A shrivelled leathery item, quite unlike the glamorous creature pictured upon the printed handbills the captain distributed in the East End street markets.

Those discerners of candles in biscuit tins and the dubious credibility of feathered prophets concluded that Captain Lovell's mermaid was a skilfully constructed chimera. Its top half being that of an ape, its lower, that of a codfish.

Captain Lovell argued with conviction that this was *not* the case. Conceding that perhaps his exhibit was not actually a mermaid as the creature was popularly imagined, but was, nonetheless, the genuine article.

It was a hitherto undiscovered species of aquatic ocean-going monkey.

Aquasimius Lovelli was the name he suggested to the curator of the Natural History Museum.

His kiwi birds met with a more sympathetic audience.

Especially when presented by his delightful daughter.

The theatre-going public, always on the lookout for unusual amusements, had warmed to the acrobatic kiwis.

Alice had patiently trained her wingless charges to ride specially constructed tricycles, tread tightropes, form avian pyramids, unfurl a Union Jack and bow their knobbly knees before a framed lithograph of Queen Victoria. They were really quite this season's thing.

The audience that night at the Electric Alhambra adored Alice and cooed and ahhhed at her kiwis as one might at a bonny baby in its crinoline bonnet. They had naught to throw, but would not have thrown it if they had. As the kiwis were put through their entertaining paces, ladies crooned and gentlemen cheered and Cameron Bell's heart fluttered.

The private detective toasted the trainer of kiwis. The Venusians sharing his box having declined to share his champagne, Mr Bell, somewhat flushed now of face, raised high his glass and to each acrobatic perambulation of the kiwi birds cried, 'Bravo,' and, 'Well done,' and, 'God bless you, sweet lady.'

The performance concluded with a bijou re-enactment of the Battle of Waterloo. A kiwi dressed as Wellington, the Iron Duke, engaged in beak swordplay against another clad in the uniform of Napoleon. This was a great crowd-pleaser, as was indeed anything that involved the trouncing of the unsavoury Johnny Frenchman. It was patriotism, really.

Alice Lovell left the stage to rapturous applause, her kiwis on her fine high-booted heels.

And so the evening progressed. Act followed act. Turn after turn. Each receiving a warm reception.

Then came the top of the bill.

Harry 'Hurty-Finger' Hamilton. Darling of the Music Hall. Harry presented himself this evening in the military trappings of that now-legendary regiment the Queen's Own Third Foot and Mouth. The terrors of Johnny Afghan in the Khyber Pass. Pith helmet rakishly angled, regimental waist-coat firmly buttoned, kilt a-sway as he gambolled to and fro, flourishing a sporran, a dirk and puttees.

From the start to the end the audience loved him. Harry held each of them in the palm of his hand. He sang the song that had made him famous. The song that the audience loved so well, for they had part in it, too.

HARRY: I've got a hurty-finger and it has me feeling sad.
CROWD: He's got a hurty-finger.
HARRY: I've got a hurty-finger and I think it's rather bad.
CROWD: He's got a very hurty-finger.
HARRY: I've got a hurty-finger and I think it's getting worse.
         I've got a hurty-finger, please will someone call a nurse?
         It doesn't help when folk like you sing—
CROWD: Stick him in a hearse.
ALL: I've got a really hurty-finger.

HARRY: I've got a hurty-finger and it makes me want to cry.
CROWD: He's got a hurty-finger.
HARRY: I've got a hurty-finger and I think I'm going to die.
CROWD: He's got a really hurty-finger.
HARRY: I've got a hurty-finger and it has me feeling glum.
         I've got a hurty-finger and I really want my mum.
         It doesn't help when folk like you say—
CROWD: Stick it up your b*m.
ALL: I've got a really hurty-finger.

Harry bowed, the crowd cheered wildly.

29

Harry waggled his kilt suggestively.

Washerwomen swooned and a frog-fondler clutched at his heart.

Harry bowed once more and then, without warning of any kind whatsoever, that certain event that was not listed upon the playbill, that certain event that would rightly be described as a tragic and terrible event occurred.

All of a sudden.

And just like that.

Fire seemed to fall from the Heavens.

Or did it rise from Hell?

There was a whoosh and a ball of flame.

And Harry Hamilton exploded.

He was gone in the twinkling of an eye. In a million flaming fragments.

And naught was there left to be seen of him at all, but for a single bandaged finger.

The crowd looked on in slack-jawed amazement. Was that part of the act? they asked themselves. Some spectacular finale? Those in the front rows, spattered with blood, agreed not. In terror and panic the crowd took to a collective decision. Chaos reigned as those in the stalls made a mad rush for the exits.

In his box and with only the minimum of blood-splatter soiling the silk lapels of his evening jacket, Cameron Bell looked on. He viewed the crowd and he viewed the stage and he nodded. Thoughtfully.

'Well now, indeed,' said he.

5

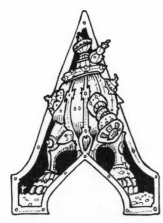n unnatural silence descended.

It all but popped the ears of Mr Cameron Bell, now all alone in the great auditorium. The private detective gazed about and cocked his ear to this silence.

Distant sounds *were* to be heard. A soft purring of revolving cogs, meshing gears, spinning ball-governors. Cameron Bell identified these sounds to be those of the Music Hall's mighty central nexus – the advanced Difference Engine, designed by Sir Charles Babbage, which managed many aspects of the Electric Alhambra's day-to-day running.

Clearly the air-cooling system was compensating for the sudden rise in temperature caused by the incendiary destruction of the star turn. The phrase 'went out in a blaze of glory' momentarily entered the hairless head of Mr Cameron Bell.

But what *had* happened to hapless Harry Hamilton? Some natural disaster? Which was to say something *not* caused by the hand of Man? Mr Bell recalled that in *Bleak House*, his friend Charles Dickens had written of a character by the name of Krook, a rag-and-bottle merchant and hoarder of papers. Krook met his demise in a ball of fire, in what was described as a case of spontaneous human combustion. The scientific community debated over the reality of this phenomenon. But was this what had happened here, witnessed by an audience of thousands?

And if not?

Cameron Bell did strokings of his chin. If not, then this was a rare one indeed. In that it represented a most singular occurrence. A murder committed in plain sight of the detective who would set about its immediate investigation.

'Please, sir,' came an urgent voice, stirring Mr Bell from his reverie. 'You must vacate the premises. You may be in danger, please, sir.'

Cameron Bell glanced over his shoulder towards an anxious-looking liveried menial who danced nervously from one foot to the other.

'We should all flee *now*,' implored this person.

'I think *not*.' The private detective picked up his hat and perched it upon his head. He handed his champagne glass to the liveried menial, then upon second thoughts retrieved it from his trembling fingers and snatched up the champagne bottle. 'Waste not, want not,' he said with a smile. 'Now take me to your master.'

Lord Andrew Ditchfield, owner of the Electric Alhambra, was a man who liked to be on his premises. Though he owned to a town house in Kensington and a country manor in Ruislip, he all but lived at the Electric Alhambra. High in the building's uppermost towering turrets, he lodged in apartments that he had nicknamed the Eagle's Nest. With swank office and living accommodation, including a modern bathroom with shower arrangement and a marble bathtub into which jets of water might be introduced at the touch of a single button. This particular marvel of the modern age was the invention of a professor of hydraulics from Brentford in Middlesex by the name of Doctor Jacuzzi.

Lord Andrew's bedroom in the Eagle's Nest had electrically driven doors that opened onto a roof garden of surpassing beauty. Topiaried hedges surrounded this most private garden. Hedges shorn into the shapes of steamships and railway engines, dirigibles and spaceships. Fountains played and rare flowers bloomed upon this London rooftop.

Lord Andrew Ditchfield was not pleased to see Mr Cameron Bell. Lord Andrew was in something of a lather.

'I will not be blamed for this,' he cried, upon introduction to the Pickwickian personage who had somehow slipped past his personal guard and used his private lift. 'It is not my fault. I will not take the blame.'

'Well now, indeed,' said Mr Cameron Bell, viewing the Alhambra's owner. An exceedingly handsome young man. Straight of back, broad of chest and narrow of waist. He wore a quilted red silk dressing gown that reached to his monogrammed slippers and a matching smoking cap with a dangling golden tassel. He was in a state of some distress and his voice had a certain quiver.

'They will blame it upon the theatre. I know it,' he said. 'Upon the electrical system. They will, I know it, I know it.'

Cameron Bell placed champagne glass and bottle upon an inlaid ivory side table, crafted in the manner of Dalbatto. Removed his hat from his head and slid it onto the hat rack next to the entrance door. Then took up the champagne bottle once again.

'Would you care for a glass?' he asked.

Lord Andrew perused the label. 'Not *that* muck,' he said.

'Quite so.'

'You—' Lord Andrew now perused the calling card that

Cameron had presented to him. 'Bell.' He nodded. 'I know of you – you have a slight reputation.'

'*Slight?*' said Mr Bell.

'You dealt with a delicate matter concerning Lady Karen Pender. A personal friend of mine. She said you did an adequate job.'

'*Adequate?*' Cameron Bell took in the opulent apartment and the titled owner, who bobbed about in the nervous fashion affected by at least one of his liveried menials. 'How sad,' he added.

'Sad?' asked his lordship. 'What mean you by this?'

'To lose so much,' said Cameron Bell. 'Should the responsibility for Mr Hamilton's most tragic and *public* demise fall upon your shoulders. Do they still employ the silken rope for the hanging of aristocrats?'

Lord Andrew Ditchfield came all over pale. 'Silken rope?' he said.

'Progress,' said Cameron Bell, as if musing aloud. 'Such a vexed question. Is it good, is it bad? All around us miracles of new technology. But are we losing ourselves, our own identities? Is this progress a blessing or a curse?'

Lord Andrew Ditchfield flapped his hands about.

'This wireless transmission of electricity, for instance. The latest piece of genius from *Lord* Nikola Tesla—' Cameron Bell paused to observe the grinding of Lord Andrew's teeth. The old aristocracy had not taken kindly to Mr Tesla's elevation to the peerage. Although he had been rightly rewarded for his services in the Second Worlds War, he was still to the minds of Lord Andrew and company just one more Johnny Foreigner.

But *very* good with electrical systems. Hence his employment here.

'We might blame Tesla,' said Lord Andrew hopefully.

Cameron Bell just shook his naked head. 'I regret to say,' he said, 'that if Mr Hamilton died through some malfunctioning of the electrical system, it is you who will do the dance for Jack Ketch, silken cord or not.'

Lord Andrew buried his face in his hands and began to sob.

'If only,' continued Cameron Bell, as if once more musing aloud, 'there was someone possessed of investigative skills to a degree that could justly be described as *above adequate* who could look into this matter on your behalf. Who could possibly present plausible evidence to support an argument that the electrical system of this elegant and *successful* establishment was in no way to blame, then—'

'*How much?*' cried Lord Andrew. 'How much do you want? You are hired, just tell me how much.'

Mr Cameron Bell made a thoughtful face and offered a thoughtful nod. In business, as in life, he tended to adhere to something known as the Vance Principle, a universal overview which posited that nothing in the universe was stable. All was constantly changing, evolving, all was mutability.

Mr Cameron Bell's fees were in harmony with this cosmological axiom and so varied according to the anxiety and financial standing of his clients.

This was in no way dishonest, for Cameron Bell was a most honest man. This was merely business. And it also had to be said that Cameron Bell was not one who could be 'bought'. He would never knowingly attempt to prove the innocence of any he knew to be guilty. No matter how much they paid him.

And he had already made up his mind that Lord Andrew Ditchfield was *not* guilty of this crime, if crime it really proved to be. Neither through negligence nor intent, no guilty man was he.

This Mr Bell *instinctively* knew, with an instinct based upon reason.

Cameron Bell named a figure as a daily retainer and another as a final remuneration upon satisfactory closure of the case. Lord Andrew, aghast at the enormity of the figures concerned, took to a wilder flapping of his hands.

'What luck,' said Cameron Bell.

'Luck?' queried Lord Andrew Ditchfield, who could see no luck at all.

'That I am already on the scene, as it were. Even now the London bobbies will have been alerted and will be on their way. Commander Case of Scotland Yard will probably take immediate charge of this one. A thorough fellow he is, to be sure. Although perhaps at times too thorough. He would no doubt wish to preserve the crime scene for as long as possible. Days, weeks, months, who can say? The Electric Alhambra would have to remain closed throughout this protracted period.'

Lord Andrew groaned dismally.

'What joy,' said Cameron Bell.

'Joy?' queried his lordship, throwing up his flapping hands.

'What joy will be seen upon the face of Commander Case when he finds that there is an aristocrat involved. He is presently flirting with this new political fashion known as *Bolshevism*. What was it I recently heard him say? Oh yes – "Come the revolution, aristocrats will be first up against the wall." A foolish fellow at times. But a great friend, and one who will *take my advice*.'

'I will write out a contract,' said Lord Andrew, 'employing you from this very moment.'

'As luck would have it,' said Cameron Bell, producing a cream vellum envelope from an inner pocket, 'I have one of my own with me. I will just fill in the financial details and then you can sign it.'

Commander Case took command of the situation. He arrived at the Electric Alhambra minutes later. In the company of numerous police constables and several members of the press. Including the Society columnist of *The Times*.

He was greeted in the foyer by Cameron Bell.

'Ah,' puffed Commander Case, a lean and wiry individual with the looks of a whippet and a love for utter control. 'You, Bell, who invited *you* here?'

'I witnessed the entire event,' said Cameron Bell. Who once more held a champagne bottle in one hand and a glass in the other. It was not, however, the same champagne bottle. Rather it was a magnum of superior vintage, fresh from the electrical refrigerating cupboard in Lord Ditchfield's suite of rooms. 'Care for a swift glass or two of the bubbly stuff, before you depart?'

'I suspect that I shall remain here for some considerable time,' said Commander Case. 'And, as you know full well, I *never* drink on duty.'

'Duty?' Cameron Bell made a certain face. 'I see the hacks of Grub Street are hard upon your heels once more. I recall, to our shared horror, the liberties they took with you regarding the pronouncement you made in the case of Doctor Hill, the Putney Poisoner.'

Commander Case turned bitter eyes upon Mr Cameron Bell. 'You got me out of that one, right enough,' he conceded.

'And this one also, if you will allow me to conduct the investigation in my own manner, unhampered—'

'*Unhampered?*' Commander Case raised his eyebrows.

'Slip of the tongue,' said Cameron Bell. 'Naturally I meant *unassisted*.'

'Naturally you did.'

'I saw the whole thing happen,' said the private detective, sipping upon his champagne, 'and I will be pleased to conduct the investigations entirely alone and with only the minimum of expense to the Metropolitan Police Force.'

'Minimum expense?'

'Travel costs and other sundries. Trifling fancies, really.'

'And—'

'I will report my findings directly to you and when the case is successfully concluded, you may take full credit. What say you to this?'

There was a moment. A significant moment. And both men knew the significance of this moment.

Commander Case put out his hand and Cameron Bell then shook it. The nature of the handshake was also significant.

'Champagne?' said Cameron Bell, with a smile.

'Certainly,' said the commander.

6

he clinking of champagne glasses was not to be heard in the unstarred communal dressing room. The chattering of teeth and the knocking of knees and the rattle of pewter hip flask's neck against the plywood dentures of Peter Pinkerton. Surely.

But *not* the clinking of champagne glasses.

The turns were in a state of some distress.

Jugglers jiggled nervously and kiwi birds, exhibiting that mysterious sixth sense that their kind are noted for, discerned a palpable danger and used their chameleon-like skills to blend in with the fixtures and fittings. The sounds of chattering teeth, knocking knees and juggler jigglings were interspersed with cries and curses as folk tripped over the kiwi birds.

There was chaos, there was fear and there were theories.

'I saw it happen from the wings,' wailed one of the Travelling Formbys. 'He was consumed by the fire of the Almighty.'

''Tis true as my brother tells it,' his brother agreed. ' 'Tis punishment for the sins of all the artistes.'

Another Travelling Formby, although exactly which one it was — as they all looked so alike — none could say, put in his three-pennyworth, too.

'Let us pray for salvation,' he cried, 'for which of us sinners will be next?'

Peter Pinkerton advanced another opinion, no less apocalyptic, but perhaps a tad more optimistic. He had recently become a Jehovah's Witness and so knew with utter conviction that the world was due to end in a matter of months.

'It is the Rapture,' he intoned, 'when the good will be taken up.'

Tony Spaloney waggled his fingers and wobbled a bit on his heels. He was now somewhat gone with the drink and as such he had plenty to say. 'Murdering Martians,' he began. 'Bombed out me pie, eel and mash shop, they did. And me poor Aunty Doris was strewn to the four winds. Nothing left but 'er stays and 'er old battered bonnet.' He was a cockney, was Tony.

Peter Pinkerton said, 'All the Martians are dead.'

'I'll not argue with *that*,' cried Tony Spaloney. 'But think on this. We all knows there's ghosties, don't we? Anne Boleyn, as walks the Bloody Tower, with 'er 'ed tucked underneath 'er arm.'

Peter Pinkerton nodded. Where was this going? he wondered. And shouldn't *he* be going? Far away from here?

'Martin ghouls!' shouted Tony Spaloney, making the camouflaged kiwis more restless. 'The ghosts of dead Martians, exacting a 'ideous revenge upon all 'umankind. What we needs 'ere is an exorcist, not no ruddy policemen.'

Some heads nodded, some shoulders shrugged.

''Tis the wrath of God,' bawled a Formby. 'The wrath of God is upon us.'

'Please calm yourself, young sir.' Colonel Katterfelto

finally rose from his seat to take command. 'It was *not* the wrath of God. You may have my assurance on *that.*'

A wailing Formby squared up before the colonel. But the old campaigner had twenty-five years of military service and the command of men to his account. He fixed the Formby with a baleful eye.

'I'm sorry,' the Formby snivelled. 'But how can you know for sure?'

'Because *I* know how he was killed,' said the colonel.

This brought a sudden silence to the communal dressing room.

A silence that was almost all-consuming. Broken only by a rhythmic crunching sound. Of Darwin munching peanuts.

'I know how he was killed,' said the colonel once more.

'Then I would very much appreciate it if you would enlighten *me.*'

Colonel Katterfelto turned at the sound of this voice, to view a fellow standing in the open doorway.

'Cripes alive,' said Tony Spaloney. 'It's only Mr Pickwick.'

Cameron Bell sighed softly. 'Cameron Bell,' said he. 'I am the investigative officer assigned to this case. I was making my way to the scene of the crime when I overhead this heated conversation.'

'Wrath of God,' a Formby whispered, and merged amongst his brothers.

Cameron Bell would have doffed his top hat, but he had left it, for reasons of his own, along with his umbrella, in Lord Andrew Ditchfield's lofty apartments.

'Any help that anyone can offer in this tragic affair will be very much appreciated. And well rewarded, too,' said the private detective.

'The ghosts of Mars,' said Tony Spaloney. 'You can have that for a quid.'

Cameron Bell smiled politely. 'I would be interested to hear what Colonel Katterfelto has to say.'

'Ah,' gruffed the colonel. 'You know me name. Assume you caught me act.'

'An unappreciative crowd,' said Cameron Bell, diplomatically. 'You certainly foxed them with your—' The private detective gestured with his champagne glass towards the goggles that adorned the colonel's headwear. 'I would dearly love to purchase a pair of those.'

'I'm keeping *mine*.' The colonel added a huff and a puff to his gruffing.

'Quite so.' Cameron Bell offered up the warmest of smiles. 'But I would be grateful to hear your theory regarding the untimely death of Mr Harry Hamilton.'

'Gun,' said the colonel. 'He was shot.'

'Gun?' said the private detective, his warm smile sinking away.

'Space gun.' The colonel tapped at his holster. '*Ray* gun, man. I should know, I've fired a few in me time. Hunted big game on the Martian steppes. Used to lead safaris for the gentry, after the Martian Menace was brought to an end. Bagged great three-legged beasties. But *zap* and *blat*—' The colonel mimed cocking and shooting. 'Reduce a man to atoms in the twinkling of an eye. It was a ray gun took poor Harry Hamilton. Take my word as a fact.'

'Interesting.' Cameron Bell raised bottle to glass. And then became aware that all stares that were aimed in his general direction had now specifically affixed themselves to the magnum of champagne.

'Would anyone care to join me in a glass of bubbly?' asked Mr Bell.

But then he caught his breath. For from behind the curtain that screened off the female artistes' area stepped the lovely Alice Lovell. She wore a black silk kimono, smothered in floral motifs, and a cloche cap of the very latest fashion.

'Did I hear someone mention champagne?' she asked.

The champagne didn't really mend the artistes' shattered nerves. But it *did* go down very well and it did give Cameron Bell the chance to breathe in Alice Lovell's beauty at close quarters.

'Do you work at Scotland Yard?' she asked him, as he poured champagne into her out-held enamel cup. *Very* slowly.

'I am a *private* detective,' said Cameron Bell. 'A consulting detective.'

'Like Sherlock Holmes?' said Alice. 'My cup is now completely full,' she added.

'*Just* like Sherlock Holmes,' said Cameron Bell.

'He is dreamy,' said Alice and she sighed. 'He's a *real* man. Tall and slender and *so* intelligent.'

Cameron Bell dwelt upon the words *man* and *intelligent*. Both *certainly* applied to himself, he considered.

'They should call in Sherlock Holmes,' said Alice.

'He is fictional,' said Cameron Bell, toasting Alice with his glass.

'Of course he's not.' Alice laughed a most enchanting laugh. 'I have a good friend, a decent, honest working girl, employed to pamper Lady Windermere's pussy. Such a friendly little cat. She says that Sherlock Holmes took care of a very delicate matter for her ladyship.'

'Ah now, well, indeed,' said the most private detective.

★

Cameron Bell was enjoying himself most deeply and the artistes of the communal dressing room were most deeply enjoying his champagne. For he had ordered two more magnums be brought down from above by the trembling liveried menial, whom Lord Andrew had ordered *not* to leave the building. The private detective knew, however, that he should hasten to the scene of the crime to begin his investigations.

He thanked the artistes for their theories and their company, then took and kissed the hand of Alice Lovell. An act of daring that he would certainly never have accomplished sober. He then told all and sundry, man and woman, kiwi and monkey alike, that he would do everything in his power to bring this sorry matter to a speedy conclusion. Then bade his farewells to all.

'And give my regards to Sam Weller,' called a Formby, who had not previously spoken and was altogether uncertain as to what was actually going on.

The footlights were off, but the stage was still well lit. Cameron Bell stepped gingerly onto this stage. It was as if he was making his entrance. And although the great auditorium was now empty and all was still and silent, he felt that *he* was now the star turn and that *this* was somehow his moment.

Cameron Bell took deep and steadying breaths. Brought out his pince-nez, perched them on his nose. He strode to the centre of the stage, then paused. And mused for just a moment more. One could not help but be overwhelmed by this. The scale and splendour of it all and that special something that all true performers sense when they tread the boards. It is passion and reality, it is fear and excitement, it is all that show business in its many forms embodies. And it touched the very soul of Cameron Bell.

For he was in his way a performer, and he could understand.

The private detective shrugged off with difficulty the feelings that pressed upon him and applied himself to his profession. For it was not sufficient that he should merely see the aftermath of what had happened. He should see *more*.

He stood now where Harry Hamilton had and gazed all around and about. He squinted up to darkness and dwindling perspective. Much machinery was there to be seen. Cogs and pistons, ratchets and chain-wheels. Mechanisms for raising and lowering backdrops, shifting scenery and 'flats'. There were lighting gantries and complicated gadgetry. Much that could possibly pour down electrical death upon an unlucky performer. *Was this but an accident?* wondered Cameron Bell. But no, he had *sensed* otherwise. He had discerned purpose behind this killing. This was *not* the whim of fate. This was murder most foul.

Cameron could feel it in his bones.

But how?

The ray-gun hypothesis held to a certain charm. An assassin with some terror weapon, hidden somewhere—

Cameron peered through his pince-nez. Any one of many many places. It would be necessary to search every box and every balcony and seat for a clue.

However. Cameron turned his gaze to the stage before him.

An all-but-circular scorch mark, with an outer ring of spattered blood. A far from pretty sight.

Cameron Bell affected a satisfied smile. 'Ah,' said he. 'From above, then, and not from before. That makes sense.' And so it did to him.

'And you,' said Cameron Bell. To something that had caught his attention. 'You, I feel, will have very much to tell me.'

He stooped and withdrew from within his jacket his silver cigar case. A present from a grateful head of state, for sorting out yet another delicate matter. Cameron emptied its contents into his hand, then thrust the three cigars into his top pocket. 'Let us be having you, then,' he said to the something.

This something lay just beyond the scorch mark and the horrid ring of blood. This something was the bandaged 'hurty-finger'. All that remained of the late, great Harry Hamilton.

Cameron Bell now brought out a small leather wallet that contained a number of enigmatic-looking tools. Removing a less-than-enigmatic-looking pair of tweezers from this, he plucked up the remaining remains of the famous artiste.

Something fell and struck the stage, rolled a little, then came to rest. Cameron Bell placed the bandaged finger into his cigar case, then reached out with the tweezers and picked up—

A golden signet ring.

Examining this closely, he thought to observe a queer and complicated sigil.

'Ah indeed,' said Cameron Bell. 'Ah now, yes indeed.'

7

olonel Katterfelto had engaged theatrical diggings.

Which was to say that he had rented accommodation in a house that catered to actors and artistes. Its style had been represented to him as 'shabby genteel', which as the colonel knew was a euphemism for 'rough but with running water'. As he was now in reduced circumstances and had roughed it out in far worse upon Mars and in other theatres of war, the colonel considered it comfortable enough and adequate to his needs.

Not so, however, Darwin, who felt himself to be a monkey of superior requirements, fit for far better than *this*.

The house itself had once been part of a proud Nash terrace that swept from Piccadilly to the park. But now it stood all alone, its neighbours hacked from it by the bombings of Worlds War Two. Great raking shores of timber supported its side walls, which appeared perilously close to collapse. Within, the floors were no longer level and the doors of the guest rooms had been cut to trapezoid shapes to accommodate themselves within their buckled frames. Windswept nights were made sleepless by the shudderings of this failing house. By the creakings and groanings and terror-stricken prayers of its tenants.

The landlady's name was Mrs Emily Marsuple. Widow of the parish. A toothless, bearded hag who would one day be immortalised in popular song by Messrs Jagger and Richards.

She was rather taken with the colonel, who put her in mind of her dear departed husband. A purveyor of frog-skin waistcoats and toad-pelt toppers to a discerning clientele, he had come to an untimely end whilst engaged in a tadpole-eating tournament at the Royal Amphibian Club in the Mall.

The colonel never lacked for ersatz tea or brick-dust biscuits whilst in the company of Mrs Marsuple. But he kept the door to his room well locked at night.

He and Darwin were not the only tenants of this room. A policy of *sharesies* existed at Mrs Marsuple's. As many beds as could be were crammed in every room. The colonel and the monkey shared their room with the brothers Britain, who specialised in being the front and rear ends of a pantomime horse.

It was nice work if you could get it and the brothers Britain could.

These two were identical twins who shared not only the same bed, but evidently the same dreams, for both were given to talking in their sleep and called out strange phrases in unison. And although Colonel Katterfelto snored through these uncanny utterances, Darwin the monkey gibbered to himself, for he found such speakings fearful.

It was approaching midnight as the colonel trudged up the cockeyed staircase towards his shared accommodation, Darwin riding piggyback, somewhat tiddled by champagne. Moonlight fell upon him through an out-of-kilter casement and but for the muffled rumblings and hoof-falls of horse-drawn conveyances, the occasional drunken ejaculation of a home-bound reveller and the distant *thrubbing* of engines as a dirigible passed through the night sky bound for the spaceport at the Crystal Palace, Mrs Marsuple's boarding house was near to silent.

The colonel eased open the door to his room, entered, struck a lucifer, lit a candle, closed and locked the door behind him. He removed the monkey from his back and placed him tenderly into the child's cot that served Darwin as a bed. Tousling the hairy head of the sleeping simian, for the colonel was at heart a kindly man.

Giving a tired flex to his creaking shoulders, the old soldier took off his headwear, his uniform and boots. The uniform he neatly folded and laid out upon wax paper beneath his bed. The boots he buffed on the counterpane, then stood them to attention before his uniform. In naught now but his ragged vest and long johns, Colonel Katterfelto drew back the counterpane, shook away the bedbugs, blew out the candle and settled down to sleep.

'We know we're in the future as we're wearing metal beards,' murmured the brothers Britain.

The colonel was already snoring.

Alice Lovell had slightly better theatrical diggings.

Hers were a suite of elegant rooms in Bayswater. An elderly patron of the arts, a man of means with an eye for a well-turned ankle, had established her there. But, like Cameron Bell, Alice Lovell was not a person who could be 'bought'. And so she had made it known to her sponsor that although she appreciated his generosity in granting her rent-free occupation of these delightful diggings, this appreciation did not extend to furnishing him with sexual favours.

The elderly sponsor had mulled this over, complimented

Alice upon being a fortress of moral rectitude and then given her three weeks to vacate the premises.

These three weeks were almost up and Alice Lovell fretted.

It would have to be said, however, that had the ageing admirer of a well-turned ankle actually been granted entry to the apartment after Alice moved in, he would probably have demanded that she leave immediately. Fortress of moral rectitude or otherwise notwithstanding. For the damage being wrought upon the fixtures and fittings of this Bays-water *nid d'amour* by the acrobatic but scarcely house-trained kiwi birds was of an order above and beyond the endurance of most but Alice.

The keeper of kiwi birds released her troublesome charges from their travelling cage and slipped into the bathroom that was hers for now, locking the door behind her.

This room was frescoed after the manner of Prince Giulio Pezzoli's famous vestry in the church of Saint Maria in Trastevere. The style was that known as *fête galante*, with rose-wound arbours where romantic chevaliers in extravagant uniforms offered chocolate lovelies to the ladies of their hearts.

Here Alice ran hot water into the huge marble bathtub, scented it with crystallised lavender, stepped from her clothes and slid, deliciously naked, into the fragrant depths.

Here she sighed, but smiled a little, too.

Her first night at the Electric Alhambra had lacked not for excitement. And although poor Harry Hamilton had come to an end that was both terrible and tragic, the audience had loved *her*. She would enjoy a successful season there, she felt sure. Although it would probably be for the best if tomorrow she began the search for new accommodation.

But now was for now and she splashed in the scented water.

In the home where he had been born and brought up, Cameron Bell sat alone. His shuttered study had a scholarly aspect, with its countless leather-bound books, precisely catalogued and impeccably preserved, filling numerous glass-fronted cabinets of mellowed mahogany inlaid with tropical woods.

It was also a room that contained many items of rare beauty. Exquisite Chinese porcelain and Japanese lacquer work. Ancient Mayan bronzes, bright Parisian glass and ornate objects fashioned in gold by Peter Fabergé.

Here too were curiosities, queer things that to some might seem grotesque. A shrunken head, fashioned not by natives of the Jivaro tribe, but by a Londoner known as the Bermondsey Butcher, whom Cameron Bell had brought to the hangman's rope. Similarly a necklace made of human teeth and gloves of human skin. Grim trophies these for those who would hunt the biggest game of all. And who in turn would find themselves brought low by Cameron Bell.

The most private of private detectives poured ruby port into a cut-crystal rummer that had been in his family for three generations and brought it to his lips. This night had been one of double excitement for him. In that it had led him to embark upon a most challenging case of murder most foul. Which in turn had allowed him to meet and kiss the hand of the woman who filled his dreams and offered the prospect of enchantment to his waking hours. A promise, perhaps, but at present no more than that.

Cameron Bell adjusted his pince-nez, took up a magnifying glass and examined the object that lay before him upon the tooled-leather top of his writing desk.

The signet ring of Mr Harry Hamilton. Deceased.

The curious sigil engraved upon it offered up nothing but mystery. Masonic? Not as such, the detective supposed. The symbol of some secret order? That was a possibility. Secret societies and magical orders were all the rage in London at the present. Cameron Bell had knowledge of Aleister Crowley. The two had been at Trinity College together. Crowley was presently making a name for himself as a mystic, having recently wrested leadership of the Hermetic Order of the Golden Dawn from Samuel Liddell MacGregor Mathers.

Taking tea with Aleister Crowley was always an enlivening experience, although not one that Cameron relished. But upon this occasion it might prove invaluable as Crowley's knowledge of matters metaphysical far exceeded that of Cameron Bell.

The private detective turned the ring upon the palm of his hand. It was weighty for its size. Then was it gold? Cameron Bell took out those items from his desk which he required to test the authenticity of gold and went about the business. The ring was *not* of gold. Cameron Bell performed further tests and further tests, too. The ring was of no metal known at all to him.

'A mystery indeed,' he said. Then smiled a bit and yawned.

Then, finishing his port, went off to bed.

And so the night moved on towards the morning.

Colonel Katterfelto snored rhythmically, his sleeping head filled with curious alliterative visions: magic, mayhem, mechanical marvels, messianic madness and the Music Hall.

Darwin the monkey dreamed oft-times of bananas. Sometimes cooked but mostly on trees which grew in his own plantation. His dreams were briefly interrupted by a line from a Music Hall song: 'I tend to find fish disappointing, they always tail off at the end.' Sung in perfect harmony by the sleeping brothers Britain.

Alice Lovell, pretty-pink and pampered by her bath, slept beneath a silken sheet and dreamed of men who were tall and dark and handsome.

Cameron Bell cuddled up to his teddy and dreamed of Alice Lovell. Tonight, as upon many previous nights, he dreamed of their marriage. Tonight it was being held at Westminster Abbey, the wedding officiated by the Archbishop of Canterbury. Alice looked radiant in a dress that was a facsimile of the one worn by Queen Victoria at her marriage to Albert. So far these dreams of he and Alice had never reached beyond the actual ceremony. Never to the actual wedding night. And tonight would be no exception, with the wedding turning into chaos when the archbishop flung aside his ecclesiastical robes to reveal himself to be a giant kiwi bird.

Others all over London slept, curled against their loved ones, or alone.

But there were those who did not sleep, or would not sleep. Those who prowled the gaslit alleyways, moving from one dark space to another. Stealthily and quiet as you please.

One lean figure crossed a cobbled yard, dressed as would a gentleman with high top hat and trailing cloak and black malacca cane. His gloves were of the finest kid and at times his gloved fingers rose to adjust the black silk mask that offered disguise to his face.

There was a strange vitality evident to this figure.

Something almost electric. A violet light appeared at times to flicker all about him. As an aura.

There were psychics in London who claimed to be able to view the auras of men. There were also psychics who claimed to possess sanctified goggles through which fee-paying clients might perchance view all manner of marvellous sights.

But had a genuine psychic, one possessed of powers of inner vision, been present upon this night and in this cobbled yard to view the gaunt figure in the high top hat, this psychic would surely have grown pale and turned away. Turned away and run for all of their life.

For this unhappy psychic would have discerned an aura of pure and palpable evil cloaking the being in the mask.

For this being, whose identity was known to but a very few, bore the distinction of being the most evil creature who had ever walked the Earth.

He never slept, but dream he did, of terrible, terrible things.

8

'o what thou wilt shall be the whole of the law.' The fussy nasal voice that intoned this Rabelaisian dictum belonged to Aleister Crowley. 'I have been expecting you,' he continued.

Cameron Bell knew Mr Crowley well enough. Knew of his bravado and the high opinion he had of himself. Crowley's calling card announced him as *To Mega Therion*, the Great Beast of Revelation, whose number is six hundred and sixty-six.

Crowley was at present a man of wealth, a traveller, a noted mountain climber, a published poet and a magician. In his personal opinion, the greatest magician that ever there was.

Physically there was nothing special that signalled him as different from the rest. He was tall and well muscled, given to premature balding, expensively dressed and carried himself as would an English gentleman.

Cameron Bell put his hand out for a shake. Mr Crowley raised a blessing finger. 'Hurry inside,' he said to his old university friend. 'Problems with the landlord, at the present.'

Cameron Bell made his entrance, smiling as he did so. Crowley always caused him a chuckle or two. Here was a man of independent wealth who would skip off a horse tram without paying his fare, if the opportunity arose. Crowley was of that order of being who 'offer the world their genius, expecting only in return that the world should cover their expenses'.

The door slammed shut upon the outer world and Cameron Bell stood in the lair of the Beast. It was all rather cosy and nice. Crowley had clearly rented these rooms in a furnished condition. The homely furniture with its colourful coverings, the chintzy curtains all floral and sweet, were hardly what he would have chosen. They did not cultivate a sufficient air of drama and mystery.

'What charming antimacassars,' observed Cameron Bell, gesturing towards the embroidered items which graced the chairs and settees.

'Breakfast?' asked the Beast of Revelation.

'Not for me, thank you.' Cameron Bell removed his brown bowler hat and hung it on a peg amongst a most curious collection of headwear. Things of a magical nature, he supposed. 'I have already eaten,' he continued. 'At the London Hospital. I had to drop off a certain something to my good friend Sir Frederick Treves. Before it, how shall I put this, *went off.*'

Cameron Bell was of course alluding to the hurty-finger of Harry Hamilton, but Aleister Crowley did not know this, and Cameron Bell did not intend to enlighten him.

'So,' said Crowley. 'I perceive that you are having no luck with your latest case.'

Cameron Bell sat down upon a settee. 'Your perception does not enter into it,' said he. 'I observed this morning's *Times* newspaper upon your side table there, its pages thoroughly thumbed. I have already read it myself. It offers a vivid account of the tragic event that took place last night at the Electric Alhambra. It names Commander Case as investigating officer. You are aware of my relationship with Commander Case. But then you know well enough that I am *always* on a case.'

Aleister Crowley smiled. 'I was expecting you,' he said. 'I perceived *that*.'

'I glanced up at your window as I crossed the street,' said Cameron Bell. 'I saw you skulking behind the net curtains. I note the pile of unpaid bills upon the side table next to the newspaper. You are expecting the imminent arrival of the bailiffs, I perceive.'

'Basic stuff,' said Crowley. 'But you *are* here and you are not a man who makes too many social visits. If you are here regarding that twenty guineas I borrowed from you back at Trinity, then—'

'Not that,' said Cameron Bell.

'Then as I thought, you seek to learn something from me. You suspect, and correctly, I do have to say, that *I* know something, many somethings in fact, that *you* do not.'

Cameron Bell nodded his naked head. 'You are correct,' said he.

Aleister Crowley flung himself into an armchair opposite Cameron Bell and fixed him with a stare. It was a practised stare, Crowley's eyes focusing upon a point somewhere to the rear of Cameron's head. On first encountering the Beast, folk were generally most perturbed by this stare, as it seemed as if the mystic was looking right through them. Cameron Bell would have none of it, though.

'Let us take a morning pipe,' said Aleister Crowley. Producing from the pocket of his quilted red velvet smoking jacket (he wore also a matching smoking cap to cover his balding pate) an opium pipe and a rather large bag of opium.

'Somewhat early in the day for me,' said Cameron Bell. 'But do not let me stop you.'

'No one stops *me*.' Aleister Crowley took to the filling of his pipe. 'And it is not so early for me. I have not slept for three nights. I am engaged in a complex magical ritual.'

A series of thumps occurred at this time, coming from an adjoining room. The Inner Sanctum perhaps, where magical rituals were performed? Or the bedchamber?

Muffled cries were added to the thumping.

Mr Crowley excused himself from the presence of Mr Bell and made off in the direction of these sounds.

The detective then heard a loud slap and the voice of Crowley calling out for silence. The mystic returned; the conversation continued.

'You are not a believer in magic, are you?' asked Aleister Crowley.

Cameron Bell gave shakings of his head. 'I am more a man of science, I suppose.'

'The two are interlinked in more ways than you might imagine.' Aleister Crowley lit his pipe, drew in lungfuls of smoke.

'I would not scorn any man's belief,' said the private detective. 'But I deal in fact, and not belief.'

Aleister Crowley laughed a wicked laugh. 'Folderol,' said he. 'You are a man of inspiration. Of intuition. These things cannot be quantified or brought to scientific measurement. These things are aspects of magic.'

Cameron Bell made a thoughtful face. He wasn't sure about that.

'Once you have experienced the power of real magic—' the mystic focused his eyes once more to the rear of

Cameron's head '—there is no going back. And there is no question as to its reality.'

'The young lady you have bound and gagged in your bedroom is what, then?' Cameron asked. 'A sorcerer's apprentice? An acolyte?'

'No, she's a whore,' replied Crowley. 'And I perceive that you are already out of your depth in this conversation and so seek to make light of my words and change the subject.'

Cameron Bell nodded thoughtfully. There was some truth to *that*.

'And magic *is* a science,' continued the Beast. 'It has to be performed with precise exactitude. It is formulaic, it responds to the laws of cause and effect. A mistake is not rewarded by failure, it is rewarded by a disastrous consequence.' Crowley drew deeply once more upon the stem of his opium pipe. 'Trust me,' he said. 'I know these things. *I* am a magician.'

'And one of increasing reputation.' Cameron Bell fanned away at the opium smoke Crowley was pointedly blowing in his direction. 'I hear that the Hermetic Order of the Golden Dawn is now under your leadership.'

'Buffoons to a man of them,' quoth Mr Crowley. 'That second-rate rhymester Yeats.* That clown Mathers. Do you know what he once told me after nothing but a single pint of laudanum? "The Sun is not a star," he said. "It is a lens that focuses the brilliance of God onto the Earth." Priceless, don't you think?'

'Priceless,' the private detective agreed. 'Might I open a window?' he continued.

'No,' said Crowley. 'They are all nailed shut.'

---

* *William Butler Yeats, 1865–1939. An Irish poet and dramatist, who would go on to win the Nobel Prize for Literature in 1923.*

'A glass of water, then?'

'I have absinthe.' The mystic smiled as he spoke.

Cameron Bell shook his head politely. 'Again somewhat early for me,' said he.

'So,' said Aleister Crowley. Leaning back in his chair and making all-inclusive gestures with his pipe-free hand. 'Let us continue with the discourse. Let me explain to you exactly what magic is and what exactly it does. And when I have explained these matters to you, you will place five guineas in my hand, kneel before me and address me as Master.'

Cameron Bell considered this to be unlikely at best.

'I do seek enlightenment,' he said, 'but only in a small matter. One perhaps beneath your dignity. I think I should leave you to your Great Work.'

Cameron Bell rose slowly.

Aleister Crowley said, 'Not one bit of it.'

Cameron Bell reseated himself.

'You carry an item upon your person that baffles you,' said Crowley. 'I perceive.'

The private detective was prepared to concede that one to Crowley. Although it might have been nothing more than a lucky guess. Either way he wanted an answer and it would be better to get it now, if it existed, rather than attempt it a little later, when Crowley would either be stupefied by opium or fast asleep in his chair.

'Take it out, then,' said Crowley. 'It is in your right-hand waistcoat pocket.'

'Ah,' said Cameron Bell, suddenly aware that he had been distractedly tapping at the pocket throughout the conversation. He brought the ring into the smoky light and handed it to Crowley.

The Beast of Revelation perused it on his palm. And Cameron Bell observed a most intense expression momentarily cloud the young man's features. It was an expression that could justly be described as 'covetous'.

'Humph,' went Crowley. 'A trinket, a gewgaw.'

'As I suspected,' said Cameron Bell. 'Hand it back, if you will.'

'It has a certain garish charm,' said Crowley. 'I have a young nephew it might amuse. How much do you want for it?'

'I was hoping you might give me a valuation.'

'Perhaps five shillings,' said Aleister Crowley. 'I have a ten-shilling note, if you have change.'

'Return the ring,' said Cameron Bell. 'I will waste no more of your valuable time.'

'A pound, then,' said Crowley. 'Two pounds, three. Five pounds, then. Guineas rather than pounds.'

'You would appear to be bidding against yourself,' said Cameron Bell. 'I suspect that you have imbibed too freely of your pipe. I feel certain that this gewgaw, as you describe it, could not possibly be worth, how much did you say?'

'*Six* guineas,' Crowley suggested. 'Seven if you will.'

'*Seven guineas?*' said Cameron Bell. 'I would be stealing your money. But I will tell you what. I have a close friend, a Yiddisher jeweller at Hatton Garden. I will have him appraise the ring. It might well prove to your advantage.'

'Oh *no!*' cried Aleister Crowley, clawing his way up from his chair. 'You must not do that.'

Cameron Bell smiled up at his host. 'I will be back within the hour,' he said.

'Certainly you will *not*,' said Aleister Crowley.

'Your magic enables you to predict the future?'

'On this occasion absolutely yes.' The magician now jigged from one foot to the other. After the manner of Lord

Andrew Ditchfield, whom Cameron Bell had observed performing similar nervous jiggings the previous evening.

'The ring,' said Cameron, stretching out his hand.

'Not as you value your life.'

'And what of this?'

'Should you take this ring into the Jewish quarter and display it to a jeweller there,' said Aleister Crowley in the gravest of tones, 'you will not return alive.'

'Come now,' said Cameron Bell. 'I have many friends in that neighbourhood.'

'Friends or no,' the mystic said, 'they will murder you where you stand.'

9

'eturn the ring,' said Cameron Bell, 'or I will shoot you dead.'

The young magician looked perplexed, then stared at his friend. Cameron Bell displayed a small but deadly looking revolver, aimed at the heart of Aleister Crowley.

'The ring,' he said. 'And now.'

The mystic grudgingly parted with the ring, which Cameron returned to his waistcoat pocket.

'And now reseat yourself and we will discuss the matter in the manner of gentlemen.'

'With a gun held upon me?' Aleister Crowley made the fiercest of faces.

'And replace the poker,' said Cameron Bell. 'The poker that you surreptitiously took up when you rose from your chair. The one you meant to strike me down with in order to steal this ring.'

A poker dropped from the sleeve of Crowley's red velvet smoking jacket. Crowley now made a guilty face and returned once more to his chair.

'I will do a deal with you,' said Cameron Bell. 'A deal to be struck between gentlemen. You will tell me everything you know about this ring and in return I will give it to you as a present.'

'A *present?*' The mystic's eyes widened.

'Once the case I am working on is satisfactorily concluded. But only if you are completely honest with me.'

'You *swear* that you will give the ring to me?' Crowley was once more on his feet.

'I *swear* and we can shake hands upon it.'

Cameron Bell transferred his gun to his left hand and with his right hand shook that of Aleister Crowley. It was a significant handshake. And both men were aware of its significance.

Crowley once more seated himself and stared at Cameron Bell.

'Tell me *all*,' said the private detective.

'It is a valuable ring.'

'*All*,' said Cameron Bell, with a sigh.

'And you *promise* the ring will be mine?'

'You have my word upon it. Now tell me all that you know.'

Aleister Crowley put his hands together, made steeples with his fingers and spoke. 'It is a magician's ring,' he said. 'A ring of enormous power.'

'You have several there upon your fingers,' said Cameron Bell. 'What is so special about this particular one?'

Crowley now took to sighing. 'It is a *real* magician's ring,' he said. 'A *magic* ring, do you understand?'

'I will once you have explained it all to me.'

'It is this way,' said the mystic. 'Many books of magic exist, but few of them are genuine. The original magic book, the original grimoire, dates to the time of Moses. It is said that when he descended from the holy mountain in the company of the Ten Commandments, he also brought down other tablets that God had caused to be engraved with magical texts. *Heaven's First and Best Gift to Mankind*. The magic was a gift from God to his chosen people, that they might use it for good in the glory of his name. In the absence of Moses, however, the children of Israel had created a golden calf and taken to drunken revelry. Moses cast down the tablets of stone on which were engraved the Ten Commandments. As biblical history records. And also the tablets containing the magical texts. As biblical history does *not* record. These were gathered up and put back together by certain evil men, who sought to use them for their own advantage. The first black magicians.

'When Moses returned to the Holy Mountain, God gave him a replacement set of Commandments. But *not* a replacement set of the magical texts. Although he did give Moses something else. Something to compensate for the loss of the magical texts.'

'And so,' said Cameron Bell, 'it is your contention that these magical texts were the genuine article, given to Man by God. And that copies of these texts still exist and that they can be used to bring *real* magic into being?'

Aleister Crowley nodded. 'Here be wisdom.'

'Here be *fiction*,' said Cameron Bell. 'I read that tale in a penny dreadful, I recall.'

'Because it is *partly* fiction,' said Aleister Crowley. 'And I will explain to you why in just a moment. When I reveal to you a Great Truth. I do not believe that any Englishman other than myself would know that ring of yours to be the thing it truly is. And neither do I believe that it was simply *chance* that brought you here today. And brought that ring to *me*. It was fate. It was destiny. I am not some bogus popinjay posing as a magician. I am Crowley, the Logos of the Aeon. I sensed the magic upon you the moment you entered my rooms. I could smell it on you, as could any Cabbalist. The Oxford English Dictionary defines the word *Cabbala* as 'an ancient Jewish mystical tradition, based on an esoteric interpretation of the Old Testament'. It is a most fashionable movement amongst the Jewish community at present.'

'Are you suggesting that the Jews are black magicians?' asked Cameron Bell.

'Quite the opposite, you fool!' Crowley's voice was raised in pitch, but Cameron Bell did not flinch. 'My apologies,' said Crowley. 'I am no enemy of the Jews. Their magic is white. It is the purest of all magic. Because it stems from the genuine source.'

'From God and from Moses?'

'I will explain all to you, if you listen. Your jeweller friend would have had no option other than to have killed you, or had you killed, had you shown him the ring. Because even by touching that ring you commit a supreme blasphemy. What I am going to tell you now, I tell you because you have given me your word as a gentleman that you will give me that ring and I take you at your word.'

'As indeed you can,' said Cameron Bell.

'The ring in your pocket is a magic ring. It is *the* magic ring. The ring that Cabbalists have sought for six thousand years. It is the Ring of Moses.'

'The Ring of Moses?' said Cameron Bell.

'That is the something that God gave Moses to compensate him for the loss of the magical texts. That is the Ring of Moses. A direct gift from God.'

Cameron Bell now found himself speechless. This ring was a present from *God*?

'You must pardon me,' he said, when he could find his voice, 'but *that* is a lot to take in and as a rationalist I would be forced to dismiss it as fanciful at best.'

'Indeed,' said Crowley. 'And I would expect nothing more. But as you have promised the ring to me, it is neither here nor there whatever you choose to believe.'

'But you believe it to be genuine?'

'With all my heart. Although I had doubts of my own regarding its existence. Might I enquire as to how you came by it?'

'You may,' said Cameron Bell. 'But for now I would prefer not to answer you. I would ask you a question or two more, however. If this *is* a magical ring, what powers does it possess?'

Aleister Crowley laughed and said, 'Now that indeed would be telling.'

'Touché. Then answer me this. You agreed that the Moses story was partly fiction. Yet you believe in the authenticity of this ring. Explain this seeming contradiction.'

'Magic,' said Aleister Crowley, 'or magick, as I prefer it to be called, is by nature unworldly. It enters our world from another realm. It does not come willingly. It has to be persuaded. There are, however, other places where magic, it would appear, is treated as commonplace and used in an everyday manner.'

'Only in fairy tales,' said Cameron Bell.

'On the contrary,' said the magician. 'There is one specific place I know of. One specific world.'

'Go on.'

'I speak, of course, of Venus. It is believed – and on most scientific grounds, I understand – that the denizens of that cloudy world employ magic to power their aether ships through space. Their spaceships are referred to as Holier-than-air craft – they move through the power of faith alone.'

'I have read of this,' said Cameron Bell. 'Few men have

walked upon Venus. The native population there discourages tourism. They are certainly a secretive race.'

'And not without good cause. You see, upon our world there are few things capable of *carrying* magic. Magic is almost at times like electricity. It has to be conducted along the right channels. Things are different upon Venus.'

'I see,' said Cameron Bell.

'Of course you do not see,' said Aleister Crowley. 'You do not see because you do not believe. Do you think that I would have told you all that I have told you if I had for one moment thought that you would actually believe it?'

Cameron Bell shrugged his shoulders.

'Because if you actually believed it, you would hardly be likely to part with a ring that you knew God had given to Moses, now would you?'

'Probably *not*,' said Cameron Bell.

'So let us leave it at that.'

'Not quite. I believe you are withholding something most pertinent. And as you do not believe that I will believe, so to speak, there can surely be no harm in you confiding in me.'

'All right, fair enough,' said Aleister Crowley. 'But allow me to ask you a question or two. I would estimate that you have had that ring in your possession for at least eight hours.'

Cameron Bell nodded at this.

'And I would wager that you have examined it thoroughly.'

Cameron Bell nodded once more.

'And I would further wager that you tested it, when you noted just how heavy it was for its size.'

'Bravo,' said Cameron Bell and he nodded again.

'And so you were greatly puzzled when you found that you could not identify the metal,' said Crowley, with triumph in his voice.

'Go on,' said Cameron Bell.

'The Great Truth I now reveal to you is this,' said the mystic. 'It is difficult for Man to engage in magic because Man is far away from God. There was a time when Man was close to God. When God regularly visited the Earth. But those days are gone and God is far from Man. How far?' Crowley laughed. 'I gave you the answer earlier, when I gave it to you in jest. Magic exists upon Venus, because Venus is nearer to God. The Sun really *is* a lens that focuses the brilliance of the Almighty upon the planets. And Venus is far closer to the "Sun" than is Earth. The Great Truth, however, is *this*.

'Moses ascended the holy mountain and there met with God, who made him a gift of that ring. But Moses and the mountain were not of this Earth. Those marvellous events did not occur on *this* planet. They all took place upon Venus. That ring is made of Venusian metal, handed by a Venusian God to a Venusian holy man named Moses.'

Aleister Crowley's eyes flashed fire and he shook from his smoking cap down to his carpet slippers.

Cameron Bell displayed his gun once more.

'I am leaving now,' said the private detective. 'Do not try to stop me.'

10

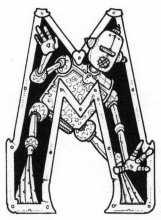

agic was to Alice Lovell not a matter for doubt.

She greatly feared it and she had good cause.

It had all begun some years before, when she was still a child, on a visit to her jolly Uncle Charles.

Uncle Charles was a big merry fellow who smelled strongly of tweed and tobacco smoke and Sunlight soap and who liked nothing more than to dandle tots upon his knee and coo into their ears. As he and his wife had never been blessed with children of their own, he was greatly taken with Alice and showed her much affection.

Uncle Charles was an author by noble trade and at that time lived modestly from the proceeds of his labours. But he was a restless man and sought ever to know more. To find some truth. *The Truth*. A truth that he believed might possibly be found through the study of mystery religions and occult teachings. As such he spent what spare time he had at the British Library, leafing through ponderous tomes in the hope that some truth or another might be printed on their pages.

His researches, however, were coming to nothing and he

had almost reached the point of giving up and settling for a life of writing, interspersed with the wearing of tweed, the smoking of tobacco, the bathing of himself with Sunlight soap and the dandling of tots upon his knee, when he chanced upon a paper flyer that some previous seeker after truth had placed in one of the ponderous tomes as a page marker.

It advertised a book entitled

THE LATHER OF LOVE

produced by an author named only as

Herr Döktor

and went on to extol the esoteric virtues of this work with such high praise as to thoroughly intrigue Uncle Charles. Having discovered that this book was out of print, he took to scouring the stalls of the Charing Cross Road until he eventually turned up a copy. It was a grubby and battered item that at first glance, or indeed at second or third, would not have appeared to be of any apparent value. In fact the stallholder was using this book to prop up the uneven leg of his stall.

But looks can oft-times be deceptive, particularly, it would appear, in the second-hand book trade. For Uncle Charles's cries of, 'Heaven be praised for at last I have found the thing that I seek,' were followed by the stallholder naming a price for the book that all but had Uncle Charles swooning away on the thoroughfare.

The seller of books made some attempts to explain a phenomenon known as 'the Vance Principle' and its application to commerce. But Uncle Charles merely flung the requisite number of five-pound notes in his direction and bore away his prize with a giddy head.

The principles propounded in *The Lather of Love* were an extension and expansion of those propounded by all good parents to their children. Namely, that *cleanliness is next to Godliness*.

The book explained that the way to Heaven could be found through the power of soap. And here again coincidence and curiosity pile upon coincidence and curiosity, for the book offered the same Great Truth that Aleister Crowley offered to Cameron Bell: that the Sun was not a star at all, but a lens that focused the brilliance of God onto the Earth. Mankind, it went on to explain, had fallen from the grace of God and could no longer *experience* God because Mankind was dirty and had taken to the wearing of clothes.

It all began in the Garden of Eden, when our first parents ate the forbidden fruit of the Tree of Knowledge and realised they were naked. When God expelled his errant children from Earthly paradise, they clothed themselves and no longer knew his love. And so it had continued to the present day. The Victorians, so said *The Lather of Love*, were particularly notable for the over-abundance of clothes that they wore, the amount of flesh that they covered. They were also notable (especially in the case of the Godless working class) for their dirtiness. As such they had lost all physical contact with the brilliance of God that shone down upon them. They were shielded from it by clothing and grime. They could no longer feel and experience his presence.

The answer was simple, or so said the book. Cast off your clothes, scrub yourself to righteous cleanliness, step out into the radiance focused on the Earth and feel once more the power of the Almighty.

At the time when this Great Truth was made known to

Uncle Charles he was living in Tunbridge Wells. The community there was a middle-class community and not one given to tolerance of those who expressed their beliefs in a manner that lacked for a conservative ethic.

When, upon a fine summer's morning, Uncle Charles took a stroll to the shops sporting nothing but sandals and a smile, jaws dropped, eyebrows rose and the law took him firmly in hand. After that Uncle Charles restricted his naked commune with the Godhead to areas of his garden that could not be seen from the road.

But, to his mind, there was certainly no doubting the efficacy of the system. Uncle Charles felt himself to be twice the man he had been before. He felt *healthy*. He felt *free*. He felt *alive*. And he was developing a lovely tan. His wife, it did have to be said, was a woman of sensitive disposition and modest behaviour and she resisted his attempts to convert her to what she considered to be nothing less than primitive pagan Sun worship. She also insisted that whenever tots came round for him to dandle, he should always wear his trousers.

Now Alice had been a well-kept child, cleaner than some, less dirty than most. But her father, Captain Horatio, was often away on his adventurous voyages and her mother, a 'seaman's widow', was apt to alleviate her pangs of loneliness with frequent applications of gin. As such Alice did become a little grubby at times.

So when Uncle Charles offered to take care of his niece throughout the school summer holidays, her mother made no objections. She packed a suitcase for Alice, dressed her in her best bonnet and frock then packed her off by train to Tunbridge Wells.

Uncle Charles was fully dressed when he met her at the station. But had it not been for the consequences of the aforementioned naked stroll along the high street, the holiday in Tunbridge Wells would probably have been very different for Alice. And not led to her greatly fearing magic.

As it was, the tradesmen of Tunbridge Wells had taken against Uncle Charles and refused to deliver his groceries. His wife, with no small degree of resentment, now did all the shopping and more than once she 'forgot' to purchase soap for Uncle Charles. So when Alice arrived, the well-scrubbed, well-tanned uncle was down to his last two bars of Sunlight. So, as Alice would be encouraged to wash, he did that thing that the British are so noted for: he *improvised*.

Uncle Charles understood the basics of soap. That it acted as an emulsifying agent and was mostly composed of animal or vegetable fat or oils. Uncle Charles set out to make his niece some special soap of her own. As a base he used lard from the kitchen and then to add fragrance he gathered and ground together flowers and herbs and suchlike from his garden.

Amongst the *suchlike* that he chose to gather was a substantial quantity of rather prettily coloured mushrooms. Unknown to Uncle Charles, these were of the genus *Psilocybe*.

These were *magic mushrooms*.

At the time of Alice's arrival in Tunbridge Wells, the local horse and carriage drivers were still in dispute with Uncle Charles, having joined pretty much everyone in the vicinity in a general boycott. Charles and Alice were therefore forced to walk a considerable distance. Although Uncle Charles did enliven the walk with details of the Great Truth he had learned. And how Alice would benefit from this Truth.

Alice got very hot and dusty during this walk.

Once her aunt had welcomed her, she wasted no time in popping Alice into a nice hot bath and lathering her up with the soap that Uncle Charles had prepared. And little girls can at times make quite a fuss in a bath and get a lot of soap in their mouths when they are being naughty.

During that summer Alice experienced a series of intense and dramatic psychedelic experiences. Emerging from these in terror and dismay, she related the details to her uncle. And he, being quite unaware that he was literally doping up his niece with massive doses of hallucinogens, imagined that the ultimate breakthrough had occurred and that she must be in direct contact with God. Thus he wrote down everything that she told him, no matter how absurd, believing it to be a new Revelation. An angelic dictation that came in the form of two gospels.

At length he would publish these two gospels as separate works, entitled *Alice's Adventures in Wonderland* and *Through the Looking-Glass and What Alice Found There*. Uncle Charles of course changed his name to Lewis Carroll and found fame and fortune through the publication of these two gospels.

It was clearly the Will of God and Uncle Charles was glad to be spreading God's word. And glad too was he for the money, some of which he spent on building very high walls around his garden.

But Alice was never quite the same again. The experiences had been so intense that she had no reason to believe that they had not actually occurred. They had truly been magical experiences, of this she had no doubt.

From that day forth she harboured fears, not only of magic. But also of mirrors and rabbit holes.

In the present day and the morning after the night before, Alice applied her make-up whilst viewing herself in a very small looking glass. When powdered and primped to as near perfection as might be achieved, she pondered on the day that lay ahead.

She would have to make efforts to find new accommodation. And she would do well to leave her present home by dead of night, before her wealthy patron arrived to discover the full extent of the mayhem wrought upon his premises by the unruly kiwi birds.

Alice had copied down a number of names and addresses of theatrical diggings gleaned from the backstage notice board at the Electric Alhambra. She would breakfast and then set out in search of a room.

After kedgeree and coffee, both supplied by her patron and neither composed of sawdust or toenail trimmings, she fed her kiwi birds, placed a purple fascinator on her head, her best gloves on her hands, took up parasol and handbag and went out to face the day.

The streets of Bayswater were busy and bustling. Horse trams rattled and hansoms clattered by. One of those brand-new flying landaus powered by Lord Tesla's wireless transmission of electricity purred above the rooftops. Cries of Old London filled the air and newsboys bawled the news. Much of this bawling concerned the untimely death of Harry Hamilton. Ladies and gentlemen took the air. Alice hurried onwards.

The first boarding house on her list was in Pimlico. The rooms were pleasant, the landlord charming, tall and dark and handsome. The terms, however, were ludicrous and not open to any negotiation. Not that Alice offered any.

The second was that owned by Mrs Marsuple. Alice viewed the teetering establishment, which quivered slightly as a steam dray rumbled past. *No*, decided Alice, *not in a month of Good Fridays.*

The third on the list, however, proved interesting. It was

only a ten-minute walk from the Electric Alhambra and had a handwritten sign in the window which read

One room suddenly available —
Would suit cultivated young lady

Alice Lovell tapped with the knocker and stood on the red-leaded doorstep. Presently the door was answered to her knocking and she was ushered inside by a slender lady. This fragile being had a curious hairstyle that resembled a helter-skelter. Tiny flowers had been inserted into it, as to resemble children's faces peeping out. This lady enquired of Alice's name, then introduced herself to be Lucy Gladfield, the proprietress. As she led Alice up pleasantly carpeted stairs she named the sum required for weekly rent. Which Alice did not consider excessive as long as the room proved sound. And as she tottered up the stairs on delicate heels, Lucy Gladfield extolled the virtues of her establishment. Its cleanliness, which she considered next to Godliness. Its freedom from any kind of infestation. Its warmth in winter due to a fireplace in every room.

She then placed great emphasis upon certain matters that were clearly dear to her heart. The keeping of regular hours by her boarders. The absolute prohibition of gentlemen from visiting the rooms of ladies. The prompt payment of rent. The turning off of taps after use and the necessary flushings of toilets. There were plenty more of these besides and Alice took all of them in.

She did note, however, that the proprietress neglected to mention anything about boarders keeping kiwi birds in their rooms. So Alice did not raise the subject.

The room she was shown was really quite grand, affording a fine view of the street through a high double casement.

There was a single brass bed, covered by an embroidered quilt. A bedside table, with a brand-new candle in a copper holder. A pitch pine wardrobe and a single chair. A large rag rug smothered the floor and a brass-bound portmanteau stood in a corner next to a pile of clothes.

Could Alice furnish a week's rent in advance?

Alice could.

When would Alice care to move in?

Tomorrow, if that was convenient.

It was.

Alice shook a fragile hand and glanced about the room and nodded gently.

'Do not worry about the portmanteau and the pile of clothes,' said Lucy Gladfield. 'A gentleman will be calling later today to collect them.'

'The previous tenant?' Alice asked.

Lucy Gladfield shook her narrow head. The helter-skelter bobbed from side to side. 'I regret that the previous tenant will not be returning,' she said. 'The previous tenant met with a terrible accident. Not here of course. Not in this room. But at a Music Hall. Perhaps you read of it in the newspaper today. His name was Harry Hamilton.'

11

'ow listen to me, my dear fellow,' said Colonel Katterfelto. 'I know that we have our differences, but it would be to our mutual advantage were we to work together.'

His words were addressed to Darwin the monkey. The two sat in a Soho coffee house taking breakfast. They sat in a shadowy corner. The two were not observed.

'The angels command—' began Darwin.

'I think we might dispense with *that* guff,' the colonel suggested.

'The power of Christ compels you.'

'And that I believe to be somehow blasphemous. But please do listen to me. I seek to complete the Great Work that was denied me in Wormcast, Arizona.'

Darwin almost made a guilty face. Almost, but not quite.

'You seek comfort and, er—'

'Bananas,' said Darwin, and he poked a hairy finger at his breakfast. There were eggs and there were bacons, but there were no bananas.

'Precisely, we both have our wants and our needs. And if we both work together, surely we might accomplish these.'

Darwin scratched at his hirsute head. He was not exactly sure how that was going to work. *He* yearned for comfort, good clothes, good food and pretty much good everything. The colonel sought to build a Mechanical Messiah, infuse life into it and hasten on the End of Days.

The two did not appear compatible.

'I have a plan that will benefit us both,' continued the colonel, in a somewhat conspiratorial fashion. Which involved a hunching of his bowed shoulders and harsh stage whispers behind the hands. 'It is not strictly honest, but it would furnish us with much-needed monies.'

'Fifty-fifty,' said Darwin the monkey.

'Pardon me?' said the colonel.

'Fifty-fifty we split up the profits.'

'Ah,' said the colonel. 'I see.'

Darwin stuck out his hand for a shake. He knew at least that the colonel was a man of honour. Although perhaps it might have been wise to ask just what the colonel's plan entailed before agreeing to *anything*. But Darwin was, after all was said and done, a *monkey*, and as such he did tend towards the mercurial, even in his most thoughtful of moods.

'Allow me to explain,' said Colonel Katterfelto.

Now a Gaming Hell is a Gaming Hell, no matter how you dress it. You can dress it grandly, as in the casino at Monte Carlo. Or you can clothe it in rags, as in the back-alley dives of old Shanghai. In London there were many ways of dressing it. And many many ways there were of gambling. From the whelk pits of Whitechapel, where East Enders of the sporting persuasion would lay bets upon the fortunes of a single man of sterling bravery who would match himself against as many as twenty wild whelks (that's *twenty wild whelks!*) with nothing to defend himself but a three-pound brickie's club hammer . . .

. . . to the swank casinos of Mayfair.

Somewhere in between was The Spaceman's Club.

Colonel Katterfelto was a member of The Spaceman's Club. An honorary member was he. Due to his medal-winning bravery, not amongst the wild whelks of Whitechapel, but the murderous Martians from Mars. The colonel had not only blasted the blighters in Battersea during the Second Worlds War. He had later led his regiment across the wastes of the red planet to mop up any Martian survivors. Not that there had been any Martian survivors to mop up. But there had been plenty of big-game hunting and this takes bravery, also.

The Spaceman's Club shared something with the Music Hall in that it, too, was egalitarian. As long as you had travelled in space and could prove it, you could become a member. Assuming of course that you could afford the membership fees.

Jupiterians, or Jovians as they were more popularly known, were known to be big spenders at the gaming tables. Unlike the svelte, aloof Venusians, who drifted about rarely speaking to others than their own, Jovians were boisterous, gregarious, rumbustious (although this is very much the same as boisterous) and always up for a wager, no matter how mad it might seem.

Many Jovians frequented The Spaceman's Club, and as they did not subscribe to the Earthly hours of eating and sleeping, they tended to gamble all around the clock.

'Good morning, Colonel Katterfelto,' said Mr Cohen of Cohen Brothers Pawnshop, from his seat behind the counter. 'Have you come to redeem your ray gun and medals? I've kept them all polished and safe.'

Colonel Katterfelto sadly shook his head. 'Regretfully, no,' was his reply. 'I still find myself lacking in necessary funds. I am forced to pawn more of my valuable possessions.'

Mr Cohen rubbed his hands together, as any pawnbroker might. And as any pawnbroker *did*, he rubbed them together beneath the counter and out of sight of his client.

'That is indeed sad,' said he. 'But if I were not here to help out gentlemen such as yourself when they are in need, what indeed would be my purpose on this planet?'

There were elements of disingenuousness in this statement. Although not in as obvious a way as might be supposed. Mr Cohen *did* have a purpose upon this planet, but it was *not* to help out fallen gentlemen. It was indeed to seek the lost Ring of Moses, as Mr Cohen was a practising Cabbalist. Small world!

Colonel Katterfelto smiled upon Mr Cohen. 'It is a *very* delicate matter,' he said, 'and a most private matter also.'

'Go on,' said Mr Cohen. Leaning forwards towards the bars of the steel cage that separated himself from his grateful clientele.

Colonel Katterfelto made as if to affect a thoughtful disposition. He gazed all around and about the pawnbroker's shop. The sad and sorry array of items told their sad and sorry stories as they might. Here hung the tools of artisans and the instruments of musicians. The pewter and silver plate of the once wealthy. The meagre bits and bobs that were precious to the poor.

'I have a great treasure,' said Colonel Katterfelto. 'Perhaps one of the greatest treasures of this age. I am forced to part with it, but only for a single day. Just one single day, do you understand me?'

Mr Cohen viewed the speaker. 'No, I don't,' he said.

'I need to borrow one hundred pounds,' said Colonel Katterfelto.

'*One hundred pounds?*' Mr Cohen sank back into his seat.

'I have a treasure worth far more than that.'

'Please speak of it,' said the man behind the bars.

Colonel Katterfelto leaned forwards and whispered hoarsely. 'It is a talking monkey,' he said. And he pointed to the monkey at his side.

Mr Cohen rose from his seat, leaned forwards and stared.

'Get out of my shop,' said he.

'No,' said the colonel. 'Please hear me out. I have a system. A gambling system. It is infallible. But I need the readies, do you understand me? So I must part with the old talking ape. Wonder of the age and all that kind of business.'

Mr Cohen sighed and said, 'Get *out.*'

'One moment more.' Colonel Katterfelto raised a calming hand. The hand of Mr Cohen was moving towards the colonel's pawned ray gun. 'Let me ask you one question. You are a businessman. If you were in possession of a monkey that could speak the Queen's English, what price would you put upon him?'

Mr Cohen shrugged extravagantly. 'Do you think I'm a schmuck?' said he. 'A real talking ape would be worth at least a thousand pounds. A shrewd showman could make that kind of money back in a week.'

Colonel Katterfelto cast a brief yet bitter glance towards his companion. So much he had suspected. But Darwin stubbornly refused to exhibit himself. He had only agreed to operate the clockwork minstrel because he would not be seen.

'Say something to the nice gentleman, Darwin,' said Colonel Katterfelto.

'Would'st thou sell thy fellow man into slavery?' said Darwin, who had clearly been exercising his reading skills. 'Cut me, do I not bleed?'

'Oh, very good,' crowed Mr Cohen. 'A fine ventriloquist's act you have on the go there. But enough of such larks, I have work to be doing.'

Colonel Katterfelto sighed. 'I will exit the premises,' he said. 'Leave you to converse, as it were. Smoke a pipe outside. Return in five minutes.'

And when five minutes had passed, Colonel Katterfelto returned to Mr Cohen's business premises. Inside he discovered Darwin to be no longer before the counter, but behind it, in the company of Mr Cohen.

'Well now,' said the colonel. 'What of this?'

'One hundred pounds,' said Mr Cohen, counting money notes onto the counter before him. 'That was the sum we agreed on, I believe.'

'Indeed.' The colonel nodded sagely. 'And I will return within twenty-four hours to redeem my loquacious companion.'

'No hurry,' said Mr Cohen. 'The loan is yours for a week.'

Colonel Katterfelto noted that Mr Cohen now appeared to be packing things into a small suitcase. As if he was going away somewhere, perhaps? Was thinking to give up the pawnbroking trade, perhaps? Intending, mayhap, to join a travelling sideshow? Perhaps?

'Going somewhere?' asked the colonel, counting and recounting money notes.

'Just tidying up,' said Mr Cohen.

The colonel nodded, then said, 'Whilst I have money in

my hand, perhaps now would be the time to redeem my medals and my ray gun.'

'I will tell you what,' said Mr Cohen. 'As a gesture of good will, I will return both medals and ray gun to you without charge.'

'I say, that really is most generous.' The colonel huffed and puffed in a gracious manner. 'Damned fine fellow that you are. Many thanks. Many thanks indeed.'

Colonel Katterfelto folded the money notes into the inner pocket of his dress uniform. Repinned his medals onto his breast, reholstered his ray gun. Saluted the man behind the iron cage. 'You are a gentleman, sir,' said he.

'Indeed, indeed,' said Mr Cohen. 'Now don't let me keep you any longer. You get off about your business. And good luck with the gambling system.'

'I'm sure it will pay off,' said the colonel.

And with that left the pawnshop.

But Colonel Katterfelto did not go immediately to The Spaceman's Club. Rather did he take himself a little way off from the pawnbroker's shop, to an alleyway, where he merged into shadows and took once more to the smoking of his pipe.

He was not far gone with this endeavour when there came to his ears a terrible crying and caterwauling, as of someone in great pain and distress.

And these dreadful sounds suddenly increased in scale as the door to Mr Cohen's establishment burst open and the proprietor staggered out into the street, vainly attempting to beat off the violent assault that was being visited upon him. By Darwin the monkey.

The beleaguered businessman called for help from passers-by. But given the fury of the beastly attack no gentleman of sterling bravery stepped forwards to aid Mr Cohen.

Darwin bit Mr Cohen's right ear, then leapt from his shoulders and bounded over the road.

Mr Cohen clutched at his bleeding ear, sank down onto his bottom, fainted and fell backwards through the doorway of his pawnshop.

The passers-by went passing by and there was peace once more.

'Nice work,' said Colonel Katterfelto, patting his accomplice upon his hairy head. 'And that is a rather nice waistcoat you are sporting. A gift from Mr Cohen?'

'So I might look smart for the packed houses, during the European leg of our world tour.'

'Splendid,' said the colonel. 'And now I don't feel quite so bad about our bit of duplicity.'

Darwin the monkey stuck out his hand.

The colonel took and shook it.

'No,' said Darwin, baring his teeth. 'My share of the booty, please. Fifty pounds, if you will.'

12

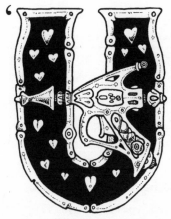‘Unusual, to say the very least.’ These words belonged to Sir Frederick Treves, surgeon general to the London Hospital and private physician to Her Majesty Queen Victoria. He spoke these words to Cameron Bell as they stood in the hospital's morgue.

'I have seen some queer things in my time,' Sir Frederick continued. 'In fact, they do not come much queerer than that chap over there.' Sir Frederick took up a severed human arm from the dissecting table and pointed with its fingers.

The object of this pointing turned away. His name was Joseph Carey Merrick, better known to Londoners as the Terrible Elephant Man. 'Up yours,' he was made out to mutter.

The surgeon general winked at Cameron Bell. 'Joseph and I are not presently seeing eye to eye,' he said. 'He wanted me to take him to the Electric Alhambra last night, but I had an appointment at a society event. He is sorely miffed that he missed the spectacle of Mr Harry "Hurty-Finger" Hamilton being reduced to ashes on the stage.'

'It was not an edifying experience,' said Cameron Bell.

'I suspect it to be on this occasion a Roman plebeian sort of thing,' the great physician went on. 'The Roman plebs taking great delight as the Christians were cast to the lions. The joy being that at least *someone* was worse off than they were.'

'It wasn't that at *all*,' mumbled Mr Merrick. 'I wanted to see the acrobatic kiwis.'

'I will be going to see them myself, tonight,' said Cameron Bell. 'Perhaps you might care to accompany me.'

'Oh yes.' Joseph Merrick turned, offering the full force of his hideousness to the private detective. 'You are so very kind, my friend. Would you care for a cup of tea?'

'Indeed I would,' said Cameron Bell. 'But please do not put any laudanum in it, as you did last time. I nearly fell under a hansom cab and I could not tie my shoelaces for days.'

'His sense of humour, like laudanum, can be something of an acquired taste,' Sir Frederick Treves said to Cameron Bell as Joseph Merrick turned and hobbled away.

'But as to the hurty-finger?' asked the most private of detectives. 'Might I ask what conclusions you have reached?'

'You might ask, my dear chap, but I have little to offer you in return.'

'My interests lie in chemical residues,' said Cameron Bell. 'As of some accelerant, perhaps, that might have set off the combustion.'

'I found no immediate evidence of such. But it is the finger itself that presents us with an enigma.'

Cameron Bell asked, 'How so might this be?'

'Well.' Sir Frederick Treves drummed the fingers of the severed arm onto the dissecting table. 'You are certain that it is *actually* a finger?'

'The famous hurty-finger, yes.'

'As you are probably aware,' said Sir Frederick, 'it was

88

myself who performed the first post-mortem examination of a dead Martian. The first *Alien Autopsy*, as the papers put it. What I learned of the Martian anatomy I wrote up in a lecture that I presented to the Royal Society. Martian and Mankind have few similarities. The beings upon this planet that are the closest to Martian would be certain sea creatures. The shark, certain cephalopods.'

Cameron Bell nodded thoughtfully. 'Where is this leading to?' he so enquired.

'The finger is not Martian,' said Sir Frederick Treves.

Cameron Bell made laughter. 'I never thought that it was.'

'But neither is it human,' said Sir Frederick.

'Ah now then,' said Cameron Bell. 'Ah now well indeed.'

'Examining the cell structure of this "finger", it would appear to exhibit more in common with the vegetable kingdom than the animal. It is almost like a branch, or sapling. The nail resembles a fingernail, but beneath the microscope appears more to be bud-like. This is not some prank that Merrick has put you up to, by any chance?'

'I swear to you, no,' said Cameron Bell. 'And please don't do *that* with the severed arm.'

'My apologies,' said the surgeon. 'I have been working late and have not seen my wife for several days.'

'Might I ask you a question, then?'

'Regarding my wife?'

'Regarding the finger. Do you suppose it could possibly be that of a Venusian?'

'Interesting question.' Sir Frederick laid the severed arm aside. 'I would love to examine the carcass of one of those strange fellows. Certain parts of their anatomy would be of surpassing interest.'

'But do you believe it possible?'

'I, like yourself, am a man who deals in facts. I rarely speculate. I test each hypothesis through intense study and strenuous experimentation. Present me with a dead Venusian and I will present my findings. But let me say this to you. I have seen Harry Hamilton perform upon the stage. To all intents and purposes he certainly looked human. We know of four distinct species in our Solar System: our own, the Martian, the Jovian and the Venusian. I have examined specimens of the first three and we can rule them out. If the finger is not of a Venusian, then I am at a loss to suggest just what it might be. But do not quote me on this.'

'Quite so.'

'And I might ask that you leave the finger with me for the present – I would like to conduct further tests. I have it preserved in formaldehyde; it will be safe for now.'

'As you wish,' said Cameron Bell. 'I have no other lines of investigation to follow. Mr Hamilton becomes more mysterious by the moment. This will prove to be a challenging case.'

Mr Merrick returned with a nice cup of tea held in his good hand. Cameron Bell noted that he had something of a smirk upon the mouth parts of his face.

'Your tea,' said the Elephant Man.

'I regret that I am in something of a hurry,' said Cameron Bell, 'but I will return in a cab at seven-thirty and take you to the Music Hall.'

Joseph Merrick bowed his bulbous head. Then placed the cup of steaming tea in the hand of Sir Frederick Treves.

The surgeon general gave the tea a sniff.

'*Cascara*,' he said. 'A powerful laxative. Why do you do these things, Joseph? The nice gentleman is taking you to the Music Hall.'

★

Having mildly admonished the Elephant Man, and thanked Sir Frederick Treves for his assistance, the nice gentleman left the London Hospital and hailed a hansom cab.

'Carlton Road,' said Cameron Bell. 'Number ninety-five.'

The cabbie climbed down from his perch, aided Mr Bell into the cab proper, closed the waist-high door upon him and returned to his perch. 'How would you like it, guv'nor?' he called down to his fare through the little hatch just above Cameron's head.

'How would I like what, exactly?' replied Mr Bell.

'The journey, guv'nor. Would you care for it all nice and sedate? Or should I whip the 'orse into a frenzy and go orf like a batsman out of 'ell?'

'The former,' replied Cameron Bell. 'It is but a five-minute journey at best.'

'I can make it more like 'alf an 'our.'

'I'll only pay a shilling either way.'

'Right, as you like then, guv'nor.' The cabbie stirred his horse into a gentle trot, then sought to engage his fare in conversation.

'Lovely weather we're 'aving,' he said.

'Delightful,' said Cameron Bell. His mind upon other matters.

'We had a mild winter.'

Cameron Bell just nodded his head.

'But things'll liven up when we've summer all year round.'

'I suppose they will,' mused Cameron Bell. Then, 'What do you mean?' he asked.

The cabbie called down to him from on high. 'The End of the World,' quoth he.

Cameron Bell said, 'Perhaps, on second thoughts, you might drive just a bit faster.'

'Don't want to spoil our conversation,' called the cabbie. ''S'not often I get into a the-o-ma-logical discussion.'

Cameron Bell said nothing.

'It's technology to blame,' called the cabbie, 'techno-flipping-nonology. All this elec-ti-ma-tricity buzzing about in the hatmosphere.'

'Right,' said Cameron Bell.

'You know what they 'ave now?' asked the cabbie, but he did not wait for a reply. 'A flyin' platform, so they 'ave. More of that Johnny Yugoslavian Tesla's fiddling with the elements. They say it's the size of Piccadilly Circus and can 'ave upwards of an 'undred toffs parading about on top of it as it sails through the sky like a flipping artichoke.'

'Artichoke?' asked Cameron Bell.

'Airship,' said the cabbie. 'Don't mind my pro-nunce-if-ic-cation. I've been up 'alf the night drinkin' gin. I can 'ardly speak, let alone steer this flipping 'andcuff.'

'Hansom,' said Cameron Bell.

'Well, I do take care of meself,' said the cabbie.

There was a brief pause there, possibly for applause, before the cabbie continued, 'Them's messing with the natural laws,' he continued. 'Wireless trans-mis-if-ic-cation of elec-trickery through the sky. If man was meant to be fluttering around in the 'eavens, the Good Lord would 'ave given 'im wings on his back like the flipping angel that Zeus sent to care for Castor and Polly Parrot.'

'Pollux,' said Cameron. 'Pollux.'

'Language, please, guv'nor, this is a public thoroughfare.'

'I think I'll get out and walk from here,' said Cameron Bell.

And so he walked the rest of the way. Stopping only at a headwear emporium to purchase a straw boater. Having left his top hat at Lord Andrew Ditchfield's and his bowler at Aleister Crowley's. He had left them there for reasons of his own, but a gentlemen should never go hatless.

Carlton Road wore fine and pink-bricked houses to its either side. They were capped by London slate, with chimneys tall that offered smoke no matter whatever the weather.

Cameron Bell stopped before number ninety-five. A movement at a window caught his eye. A slim hand withdrew from sight a sign that read

One room suddenly available –
Would suit cultivated young lady

'The room of the late Harry Hamilton,' said Cameron Bell, to no one but himself. 'Having gleaned his address from Lord Andrew Ditchfield last night, I sent a telegram first thing this morning to the proprietress of this establishment, to inform her that a gentleman in an official capacity would be arriving today to remove the late Mr Hamilton's goods and chattels. And I am now here to present myself as this very gentleman.'

Having concluded this discourse to an imaginary audience, Mr Cameron Bell stepped up to the front door and tap-tap-tapped with the knocker.

Shortly thereafter the slim and delicate form of Lucy Gladfield opened up the door.

'No hawkers and no circulars, sir,' she said.

'Neither hawker nor distributor of circulars, I, fair lady,' said the gallant Mr Bell. 'I sent a telegram earlier regarding the worldly goods of Mr Harry Hamilton.'

Lucy Gladfield made a puzzled face. Cameron Bell found fascination in her curious hairdo.

'Did you receive the telegram?' he asked.

'Oh yes I did.' The helter-skelter bobbed about, and the lady looked more puzzled.

'Well, I have come to pick up the goods,' said Cameron Bell.

'But you already have.'

'Please pardon me, fair lady, but I do not understand the meaning of your words.'

'Well, not you. But your representative. A tall, very striking gentleman. He said he was authorised to collect the effects of the late Mr Harry Hamilton.'

Cameron Bell now made a puzzled face.

'Why, there.' The lady pointed with a pale slim hand. 'Getting into the four-wheeled brougham over there. Mr Hamilton's portmanteau is strapped upon the top, as you see.'

'I do,' said Cameron Bell. And he stared aghast as he watched the tall and indeed striking individual enter the brougham and rap his malacca cane against the roof to hasten up the driver. And call out, 'As fast as you can,' in a curious high-pitched voice.

'Hold hard there!' cried Cameron Bell, making his way through passing passers-by. The driver of the brougham cracked his whip above the horses, which reared and took off as fast as might be.

'Damn!' cried Mr Bell. Then viewing an approaching hansom hailed it down.

Without further ado he climbed swiftly aboard and called up to the cabbie. 'Follow that brougham!' he cried.

The cabbie grinned down at him through the little hatchway.

'Well, ain't it a small world,' he said. 'Do you want as I should follow on all nice and sedate? Or should I whip the 'orse into a frenzy and go off like a batsman out of 'ell?'

13

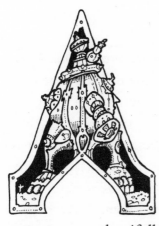

s requested, the cabbie took off like a batsman out of 'ell.

The brougham took a sudden left and knocked a passing cleric from his penny-farthing bicycle.

'Damnable icon-o-mo-clast!' cried the cabbie, stirring up his horse to even greater frenzy. Not that they were making any particular headway, or indeed speed, as the streets were plentifully crowded with hansoms and horse buses, pedestrian passers-by, new electric 'wheelers', bawling newsboys, beggars and those picking up the Pure.

But as that was the way in which such chases were conducted, Cameron Bell leaned back in his seat and reached for his silver cigar case.

'No smoking in the cab, sir,' the cabbie called down to him.

'What the dickens?' cried Cameron Bell, rightfully appalled.

'Only joking,' returned the cabbie. 'Just imagine that if you will, though. A gentleman not being allowed to smoke in a cab. A sad and sorry world that would be, to be sure.'

'Were such an unlikely event ever to occur,' said

Cameron Bell, 'I would expect all right-thinking Englishmen to load their pistols, march to the terrace and take the gentleman's way out.'

The cabbie made laughter. 'Hello,' he called. 'The brougham's turning into the Strand. We'll be able to catch him up by going down the bus lane.'

'*Bus lane?*' queried Cameron Bell. Leaning forwards to stare.

''Orse bus lane, guv'nor. A new in-o-va-cation to ease London's traffic. The next thing you know they'll be charging folk to drive into the capital.'

'Enough of this biting satire,' called Cameron Bell. 'Take to the bus lane or whatever, but do catch up with the brougham.'

The private detective returned his cigar to its case and replaced this in his pocket. From another pocket he removed his handgun, checked it for ammunition and cradled it in his lap.

'Blimey,' called the cabbie, glancing down. 'I 'opes you're not meaning to fire that thing in my cab.'

'I have a special licence to use it,' called Cameron Bell. 'And,' he added, 'I believe the gentleman in the brougham to be a murderer.'

'Even so,' said the cabbie, who had his reservations.

'And *French*,' said Cameron Bell. Knowing full well how all right-thinking Englishmen harboured especial distaste for the unwholesome Johnny Frenchman.

'Then fair enough!' The cabbie now steered his hansom into the bus lane and cracked his whip at the horse. Cameron was thrown back in his seat as the cab gathered speed.

The brougham swerved out from the crowded public lane and into that reserved for horse buses, hansoms and the like.

'Must be a damned Frenchie!' cried the cabbie. 'No law-a-ma-biding son of this Sceptical Isle would behave like *that*!'

'There's a sovereign in it, should you bring him to a halt,' bawled Cameron Bell. Clutching his pistol in one hand and holding on tight with the other.

''E does 'ave two 'orses to my one,' the cabbie replied. 'But we'll catch 'im, don't you fret.' He cracked his whip above the horse's head. 'Giddy up, Shergar!'* he shouted.

The chase was on, the horse's hooves thundered, the hansom rattled fearfully and Cameron Bell held on tight. All was relatively safe and secure along the Strand and down into Pall Mall. Sporting toffs, who shopped in this fashionable area, raised their top hats and cheered as brougham and hansom rushed by. 'Jolly good fun,' they remarked.

Things took the first big turn for the worse when the brougham, up upon two wheels, turned right into St James' Street. Here a steam-pantechnicon was parked, with removal men unloading a grand piano. The brougham crashed back down onto four wheels and the driver dragged the horses to the right, but the brougham's rear end struck the grand piano, scattering removal men and hurling the piano through the glazed facade of a pharmacy. One of several such pharmacies, owned by a physician from Brentford in Middlesex named Professor Superdrug.† This particular pharmacy specialised in volatile nostrums of an unstable nature.

'*Boom!*' went the explosion.

The hansom cab, now hard upon the brougham's heels,

---

* *Scientists have recently been considering the possibility that the missing racehorse Shergar entered a black hole and was transported into the past. This would tend to confirm that proposition.*

† *They can't all be winners.*

took much of the force. Cameron Bell suddenly found himself engulfed in flames and choking fumes and battered by a downpour of surgical appliances.

'Oh my dear dead mother!' The private detective hung on to his hat as a truss caught him full in the face.

'Wah!' wailed the cabbie. 'Me bowler's blown off and me barnet's on fire. I'm proper angered now!'

Billowing smoke and bawling invective, the cabbie stepped up the pace.

The brougham had now turned left into Piccadilly and was heading past Green Park.

Normally, when passing this delightful area of pastoral beauty, the cabbie would become melancholic and often find the muse upon him and recite either Gray's 'Elegy Written in a Country Churchyard' or William Words-worth's 'I Wandered Lonely as a Cloud' (otherwise known as 'Daffodils').

'******* French *******!' swore the cabbie, beating at his smouldering topknot and whipping further life into Shergar.

It was at Hyde Park Corner that things took a second and decidedly worse turn for the worse.

'We'll 'ave 'im in all this 'ere 'ubbub,' roared the cabbie, as in amongst a great slow-moving whirligig of traffic went the brougham. 'I can ease alongside and you shoot Mr Froggy dead, if you will, guv'nor.'

I hope it will not come to that, thought Cameron Bell.

But it *did* come to something like *that*. Of a sudden.

Above the considerable 'ubbub of traffic was heard a loud report and an almost simultaneous whine as a bullet of high calibre ricocheted from the roof of the hansom cab.

''E's firing first!' The cabbie ducked and thrust his head

through the hatch above Cameron Bell. '****** unsporting *****.'

The scream of a woman rang out. Atop a nearby horse bus a gentleman clutched at his chest. The ricocheting bullet had struck an innocent soul.

'There,' cried somebody, pointing at Cameron. 'There is the man with the gun.'

'Not *I*.' Cameron rose to protest his innocence. But then dropped back as further gunfire raked about the hansom.

Passengers atop the nearby horse bus, where the innocent soul had been hit, were now delving into their handbags and morning coat pockets, depending upon the gender, and tugging out an assortment of weaponry. The blades of swordsticks were being unsheathed; derringers attached to hydraulic contrivances sprang into the hands of gamblers.

A lady in a straw hat, who steered a pony and trap, cocked a bulky-looking parasol which housed a flame-throwing cannon. And several soldiers of the Queen's Own Electric Fusiliers, home upon leave and crammed into the rear of a steam-powered charabanc, unholstered their ray guns and prepared to lay down fire.

The cabbie atop the hansom dragged out his blunder-buss.

There had not been a substantial shoot-out at Hyde Park Corner since that memorable day in eighteen twenty when the Duke of Wellington, somewhat far gone in his cups and in the company of regimental colleagues equally far gone in theirs, opened fire upon a party of nuns, believing them to be Black Watch highlanders in the service of Napoleon Bonaparte. An easy enough mistake to make and one which George IV, then Prince Regent, considered a just cause for awarding the Iron Duke the Order of the Garter. Two posthumous medals for bravery were also awarded to three officers in Wellington's regiment who tragically fell when the nuns returned fire.

Cameron Bell ducked in his boater as pistols were drawn and potshots were taken and murder and mayhem ensued.

The drivers of hansom cabs, whom the drivers of horse-drawn buses believed to be members of a secret underground Masonic association, opened fire upon the drivers of the horse-drawn buses, whom they believed to be members of a secret underground Masonic association.

A regiment of Royal Horse Guards, who were taking their morning constitutional along Rotten Row, overheard the sounds of gunfire and took to the drawing of their sabres and the diggings of their boot spurs into the flanks of their stallions. '*Charge!*' cried their commander.

A blackly clad anarchist pulled from his cloak something that resembled a cannon ball and lit its fuse.

Cameron Bell called up to the cabbie, 'The brougham is getting away.'

And indeed the brougham was. Its driver was steering it through the thick of battle. Beams of energy sliced at the sky as fine ladies in upholstered carriages pressed their gloved fingers to the ivory triggers of miniature jewel-encrusted ray guns that were the very latest fashion accessory. Horses reared and panicked and the death toll rose. The cabbie shouted, 'After 'im, Shergar.'

The brougham emerged from the war zone and plunged forwards into Hyde Park, narrowly avoiding the onward charge of the Royal Horse Guardsmen.

These gentlemen in their uniforms of red with emblazonments of golden braid rushed to either side of the hansom cab, causing the cabbie to shout out, 'Rule Britannia!'

Along beside the Serpentine streaked the brougham, on the straight and drawing ever away from the hansom cab.

'Faster, Shergar,' screamed the cabbie, but Shergar was doing his best.

'We're losing him,' called Cameron Bell. 'Can't you go any faster?'

'We could if you'd care to get out,' the cabbie suggested. 'You are somewhat weighing us down.'

Cameron Bell spoke through gritted teeth. 'What is *that* up ahead?' spoke he.

'*That*—' the cabbie was shaking the reins about, having given up on the whipping '—*that* is the flying platform what I told you about. As what floats into the air like a flipping 'air cut.'

'*Airship*,' said Cameron Bell. 'And we don't have time for any more of *that*.'

'Quite rightly too, guv'nor. All this careering about the streets 'as fair sobered me up any'ow.'

In the distance Cameron could observe a lot of colourful bunting and a goodly crowd of people. The brougham was no longer to be seen.

'We've lost him.' Cameron Bell made a fist at the cabbie.

'We've not lost 'im, guv'nor. I can see 'im in the crowd. 'E's down from the brougham and making for the platform. And 'e's carrying a ruddy great portmanteau on 'is 'ead.'

The cabbie brought the hansom to a halt, poor Shergar all sweaty at the flanks and foamy-faced.

'Best settle up now,' the cabbie called down. 'And I'll want a least a guinea for all this fuss and bother. Not to mention the— Oi there, 'old on—'

But Cameron Bell had left the cab and shouting, 'I'll be back,' fought his way into the crowd. Ahead the flying platform stood. A truly magnificent creation of burnished brass and polished steel, one hundred feet in diameter with surrounding guardrail and central dining salon. Beneath the promenade deck were the powerhouse and electric turbines, which received their driving force through Lord Tesla's wireless transmission of electricity. A marvel of the modern age.

Cameron Bell elbowed his way through the surrounding crowd. Ladies and gentlemen elegantly dressed in the latest finery. Tots in sailor suits. Little girls in bonnets.

'Pardon me,' puffed Cameron Bell. 'Important delivery coming through.'

Ahead he could just make out the portmanteau. It was rising now. Up the gangway to the flying platform.

'Pardon me, *please*.' Cameron Bell pressed forward.

But now his way was blocked by a chap in a uniform.

'Have to stop you there, sir,' said this fellow. 'All full up for this trip. Have to wait your turn.'

'I am an officer of the law,' puffed Cameron Bell. Now short of breath from all of the excitement.

'I recognise you, rightly enough,' said the chap in the uniform.

'Then let me pass. The suspect in a murder case has boarded the flying platform.'

'Why, you're a card and no mistake,' said he of the uniform. 'Come on now, Mr Pickwick.'

Cameron Bell waved his pistol. 'Let me pass,' he shouted.

But it was all too late.

The flying platform rose silently from its moorings, drifting up to tree-top height in a manner not unlike an airship. Folk were cheering and waving up at it. Folk aboard were calling down and waving back at them.

As Cameron looked up in dismay he saw a tall, lean and most dramatic figure lounging at the guardrail. The face was lost in the shadow of his high top hat, but a gaze swept down at Cameron Bell, as if a palpable thing.

There amidst the cheering and waving of the crowd upon this bright summer's day, Cameron Bell felt an awful chill. And it was as if everything became momentarily silent and he was all alone in the presence of a terrible evil.

The moment passed. The shock of it remained.

The flying platform gathered speed and swept away through the sky.

Cameron Bell made a bitter face and returned to the hansom cab.

14

he doorman of The Spaceman's Club waved as the flying platform passed him by.

It passed him by at quite close quarters and at an elevation of one thousand feet.

The Spaceman's Club occupied extravagant and unique premises. The luxuriously appointed gondola of an airship nearly fifteen hundred feet in length, which hung in the sky above London. Moored to a wheelhouse in the pleasure gardens at Battersea Park.

Although perhaps not the most exclusive of all London's clubs (the award for this surely going to The Bill and Roger Club in Dean Street, which boasted only two members, Bill and Roger Club), The Spaceman's Club was undoubtedly the most novel and owned to the very finest views.

It had always been a matter for debate, amongst those who choose to debate such matters, as to whom The Spaceman's Club actually belonged. A certain faction believed the owner to be a member of the royal household. Others subscribed to the belief that it was a foreign potentate or even an off-world conglomerate. But folk more circumspect in nature would point to the brass plaque above the entrance doors, on which were engraved in letters bold and bright the words: LICENSEE AND PROPRIETOR: MARK ROWLAND FERRIS, FIFTH EARL OF HOVE.

This circumspect minority put forward the proposition that this might well be the same Mark Rowland Ferris, property developer and industrial millionaire, noted sportsman and airship aficionado, who was regularly to be seen in the company of his three French bulldogs, Ninja, Yoda and Groucho, welcoming members to The Spaceman's Club.

But where at all would life be without mystery?

In order to reach The Spaceman's Club, members and their guests had to ride 'The Upper': an electrically driven chairlift affair, operated from the ground-located wheelhouse. Double seats, somewhat resembling those of a fairground big wheel and linked to never-ending chains that ran from the wheelhouse to the elevated Gaming Hell, hoisted members aloft. Affording fine vistas of the capital, weather permitting.

The weather was glorious upon this summer's day, but only one double seat of the electrically driven chairlift affair was actually occupied.

And this by a man and a monkey.

The man sat up as straightly as he might and inhabited the uniform of the Queen's Own Electric Fusiliers.

The monkey bounced excitedly, as monkeys will when raised to any height, and sported a rather fancy waistcoat.

'So,' huffed Colonel Katterfelto, who was reverting more and more to the clipped martial manner of speech so favoured by those of his military rank. 'Up to club. Carry out campaign according to plan. Pocket winnings. Withdraw to base.'

Darwin the monkey was almost paying attention. He was

greatly enjoying the exhilaration of elevation. Although this was coupled with a small degree of regret. As it put him in mind of the *Empress of Mars*, upon whose ill-fated maiden voyage Darwin had travelled, two short years before.

'Born down there,' the colonel said suddenly and he pointed to the west. 'Ealing. Rural community then. All changed now. All changed. See those, my dear fellow?' A sweeping gesture included several of the tall steel towers that rose above the rooftops of London to all compass points. Tall steel towers topped by huge metallic spheres that sparked and crackled with electrical energy.

'Tesla towers,' said Colonel Katterfelto. 'Springing up everywhere. Transmit electricity, they do. Without wires or cables. Revolutionise everything. Transport, communication. New world, it is. Damned clever. Damned very clever indeed.'

Darwin turned his face towards that of the colonel. 'Regarding this infallible gambling system that you claim to have masterminded,' he said. Most eloquently.

'Not a system as *such*,' the colonel puffed. 'More a strategy. Means to an end. Take two to pull it off, though. Fifty-fifty all the way, as agreed.'

'I mastered Snap some years ago,' said Darwin, 'but I have no knowledge of other card games.'

'No need,' went the colonel. 'Simple matter really. Just require you to look over the shoulders of the other players, then report back to me what cards they hold in their hands.'

Darwin's eyes and mouth widened simultaneously. 'What?' he exclaimed. 'What are you suggesting?'

'All fair in love and war,' quoth the colonel. 'Require cash for Great Work. Means to an end and all that. Folk will thank me for it one day soon.'

'No,' said Darwin, shaking his head. 'I do not have qualms

regarding the acquisition of funds through means that are not wholly honest. However, such a scheme as this is open to exposure. It will mean jail for you and the zoo for me. Should not some overzealous henchmen of the proprietor choose to simply fling me from the airship.'

'Don't fret, old chap.' The colonel tousled the top of the monkey's head.

Darwin bared his teeth.

Colonel Katterfelto withdrew his tousling hand. 'No need for anyone to suspect,' he assured his business associate. 'Your secret is safe with me. No one else knows you can talk. A quick shufti over a shoulder or two. A whispered word in my ear. Job done. You can take trays of drinks around. You are good at that kind of caper.'

Darwin made a doubtful face.

'Fifty-fifty,' said the colonel. 'You might have yourself fitted out with a new wardrobe of clothes.'

Darwin's face became thoughtful.

'Nice top hat, kid gloves. Cane with your initial on the silver top.'

Darwin's face took on an eager look.

Chains purred upon cogwheels and finally they reached the gondola.

The doorman who had so recently waved to the flying platform saluted the colonel and offered politely to aid him from his seat.

'I can manage,' gruffed the old soldier, rising stiffly, but affecting a certain sprightliness. 'Come on, Darwin, if you will.'

The doorman now barred the colonel's way.

'Terribly sorry, sir,' said he, 'but you must observe the dress code.'

'Wearing my dress uniform, you damn fool,' the colonel was heard to remark.

'Oh, sir, please pardon me. I was not alluding to yourself. You are the very proprietorial exemplar of sartorial elegance. Naturally I was referring to your companion.'

'He's a bally monkey,' said the colonel.

'He is wearing no—' The doorman did whisperings behind his hand. 'No trousers, sir.'

Colonel Katterfelto offered the doorman what he considered to be a most formidable and intimidating stare.

The doorman merely smiled and said, 'No trousers, no admittance. Sorry, sir.'

Colonel Katterfelto made huffing, puffing, grumbling sounds and for one moment actually toyed with the idea of flinging the doorman from the gondola. Reason, however, prevailed and he prepared instead to strike the fellow down and have done with it.

'We can supply trousers,' said the doorman.

'*Monkey* trousers?' queried the colonel.

'We have trousers for most species,' said the doorman. 'Although I regret that those for okapi are presently at the cleaners. You know how it is.'

Colonel Katterfelto shook his head. 'Yes?' he said.

'I would say your companion would be a size fifteen.'

'Is this some kind of joke?' asked Colonel Katterfelto. 'Monkey trousers? Okapi trousers? Elephant trousers, too, do you have?'

'Now *sir* is joking,' said the doorman. 'Elephants would hardly need to be supplied with trousers, would they?'

'Not to *my* way of thinking,' huffed and puffed the colonel.

'Because elephants are denied entrance anyway, due to weight restrictions on The Upper.'

'Are you married?' the colonel asked the doorman.

'Married? Me, sir? Only to my work.'

'Unfortunate,' said the colonel. 'Nothing like a good wife to dress a husband's wounds. When he has received a sound thrashing for his impertinence.'

'No impertinence intended, sir. Come, let me show your companion to the dressing room.'

Colonel Katterfelto took to the taking of deep and calming breaths. The air was fine and clear up there. He and Darwin followed the doorman into The Spaceman's Club.

Its interior was certainly something to behold, being all decked about with inlaid woods and silks and finest lacquers. The style was oriental, though with touches of moderne. The air was sweetly scented by the lily and the fern. There were kilims, there were carpets, there were paintings most eclectic. There were crystal candelabra, though the lighting was electric. It was tasteful, it was elegant, exquisite and effete. And it offered entertainment to space-travelling elite.

The doorman led Darwin away to the dressing room. The colonel made his way to the bar and ordered a gin and tonic. The barman, a chappy of foreign extraction who no doubt wore trousers beneath his floor-length robes, bowed a head burdened by a turban of extravagant proportions and set about his task with a will. The colonel's gaze strayed towards a large cage hanging behind the bar counter. It contained a parrot. The parrot wore a pair of turquoise trousers.

'I know what you are thinking.'

Colonel Katterfelto turned at these words to view the young man who had spoken them. He was tall and lean and elegant, with the dashing good looks of some hero of the Empire. A head of lush black hair and the bluest eyes the colonel had ever seen.

'Mark Rowland Ferris,' the young man introduced

himself. 'Fifth Earl of Hove and owner of The Space-man's Club. And you, if I am not mistaken, are Colonel Katterfelto.'

'Your servant, sir,' said that very fellow. 'But how do you know my name?'

'I am blessed with a total recall of events,' said the young man. 'I say blessed, but at times it is a terrible curse. But what I see, what I read, what I hear – I recall all. I observed your photograph in *The Times* newspaper of—' Mark Rowland Ferris named day and month and year correctly '—being awarded that very medal that adorns the breast of your uniform by our grateful monarch, Queen Victoria, God bless her.'

'God bless her,' echoed the colonel.

'Our paths have not crossed before,' said Mark Rowland Ferris, 'but I regularly peruse the visitors' book and it is more than five years since your presence has graced my establishment.'

'Been away.' The colonel cleared his throat. 'In the Americas. Don't wish to dwell upon the matter.'

'Quite so. The privacy of members is to be respected at all times.'

Trouser humour? wondered the colonel. *Of course not!* he concluded.

'Sorry about the trousers,' said Mark Rowland Ferris. 'Some new Government ruling, thrust upon entrepreneurs such as myself who only seek to go about their business, unfettered by needless regulations. A health and safety executive, it is called.' Mark Rowland Ferris turned up the palms of his exquisitely manicured hands. 'Please have this drink upon the house. And see – here comes your pet in the most stylish of trousers.'

Colonel Katterfelto agreed that the trousers which

adorned Darwin were indeed especially stylish. He hoped, however, that his simian business partner had *not* overheard the word *pet*.

'Would you care for a sherbet, little fellow?' asked Mark Rowland Ferris. Darwin bared his teeth at Hove's Fifth Earl.

'He does not really understand English,' lied Colonel Katterfelto. 'Responds well to a cuff around the ear with a swagger stick, though.'

'Splendid,' said Mark Rowland Ferris. 'Well, I must be leaving you now. I just wanted to welcome you to the club. Not very much going on at this time of day, I regret. Apart from a party of Jovians in the Snap salon.' Mark Rowland Ferris now spoke conspiratorially from behind a manicured hand. 'Very big spenders,' said he. 'And very *slow* Snappers.' And he winked at the colonel, clicked his heels together, bowed his head and said farewell and strode away from the bar.

Accompanied by his three French bulldogs, Yoda, Ninja and Groucho. All of whom wore trousers and berets.

'What a strange fellow,' mused the colonel to the monkey. 'But polite enough in his manner. Hop up onto a stool here and take a glass of sherbet.'

The turbaned barlord decanted a sherbet for Darwin and then removed himself to a respectful distance. The colonel muttered whispered words to the monkey.

'Damned near impossible to – how shall I put this – *gain an advantage at Snap*,' was what he had to say.

Darwin whispered words of his own to Colonel Katterfelto.

Armed with one hundred pounds' worth of gambling chips (there had been some unpleasantness from Darwin regarding the handing over of his fifty pounds, but reason had finally prevailed), Colonel Katterfelto and his trousered companion took themselves off to the Snap salon. The room was dressed up as a traditional gentleman's club, with oak-panelled walls and mahogany gaming tables. The house Snapper sat to one side of the only occupied table. Two girthsome Jovians sat to the other.

The colonel had always been rather taken with Jovians. He had led several parties of them on big-game shoots upon Mars. There had been some fatalities, but the Jovians took that, as they seemed to take everything else, in good humour. There was much more of the human to the average Jovian than there was to the average Venusian. But for their overall size and their natural grey skin tone, which they tended to humanise with pink make-up when visiting London, they might well have been taken as sons of the British Empire. The two at the Snap table were laughing now. They seemed in the best of spirits.

The house Snapper spied Colonel Katterfelto's entrance and called out to him, 'Sir, would you care to join us in a game?'

'Not I,' said the colonel, 'but my nephew here.'

'Your *nephew*?' The house Snapper viewed Darwin the monkey. 'Your *nephew*, did you say?'

The colonel approached the house Snapper and whispered down at him, 'The boy is somewhat backward,' he explained, 'and somewhat deformed, as you can see. He suffers from hypertrichosis, a medical condition of all-body hirsuteness that was recently exhibited in the sideshows *The Missing Link* and *Half-Man, Half-Monkey*.'

'*Really?*' asked the house Snapper, wondering over Darwin's tail.

'He has managed to master the word "Snap",' continued Colonel Katterfelto, unabashed, 'and has some of the basic rudiments of language at his command. I trust you would have no objection to him sitting in upon a round or two?'

The house Snapper thought to smell, if not a monkey, then perhaps *a rat*.

'He has a daily allowance of one hundred pounds to spend at the table,' said the colonel.

'I will fetch him a couple of cushions to sit on,' said the house Snapper with a smile.

15

ithout further incident, but also without further progress in the case, went the day for Cameron Bell. The flying platform had skimmed away at speed towards Sydenham Hill and the Crystal Palace. Forcing Mr Bell to give up the chase and fume in the London traffic.

He dined that evening at his club in the Mall. A club that did not permit the admittance of monkeys, trousered or otherwise. Drank perhaps a trifle too freely of the port and then returned home to don his evening wear and prepare himself for another night out at the Electric Alhambra.

The walk to his home had not been enhanced by the bawling of newsboys hawking the evening editions. *Many Dead in Hyde Park Corner Massacre* was a popular cry of the early evening. As was *French Spies Suspected*. Cameron Bell took no joy whatsoever in the hearing of these cries.

The arrival at his home had not been enhanced by the discovery of a black envelope that lay upon his front door mat. Within this he found a brief note printed in a Gothic font. Which read:

Do What Thou Wilt Shall
Be The Whole Of The Law

My dear Bell,
I must insist that the Ring of Moses
be placed <u>at once</u> in my safe keeping.
I will dispatch an acolyte to
you later. In the interests of your own
safety you would do well to comply
with my words.
                    Yours in Godliness

Aleister Crowley

Love Is The Law
Love Under Will

Cameron Bell digested the contents of this missive. Then filed it in his correspondence cabinet within the folder labelled *Threatening Letters*.

Taking a small brandy to settle his stomach, he bathed, dried, dressed and departed by hansom to the London Hospital. There to collect Mr Joseph Carey Merrick.

The Elephant Man was dressed in his finest apparel, all tailor-made to flatter his *outré* physique. His white winged collar could easily have encircled an average fellow's waist. And his top hat, upturned, could well nigh have served as a dustbin. His good hand was encased within a white silk glove and in this he held up and before his face a lady's modesty fan upon which had been whimsically painted, in a fullness of colour and a lifeness of size, the face of ex–Prime Minister William Ewart Gladstone.

'Most droll,' observed Cameron Bell.

The journey to the Electric Alhambra was enlivened,

although in the opinion of Cameron Bell not *enhanced*, by examples of Joseph Merrick's boyish brand of humour. Mr Bell suffered the initial dignity of the *squirty flower* with stoicism. Declined the offer of chocolate that smelled strongly of the Pure. Politely refused to slip his hand into Mr Merrick's trouser pocket to feel 'a certain surprise'. And kept his buttocks firmly on the seat, thus thwarting the Elephant Man's attempts to introduce a whoopee cushion beneath them. It was, however, when offered a tipple from a hip flask reeking of chloroform that the private detective finally displayed his pistol and promised to shoot the prankster dead if he did not immediately affect the demeanour of a Trappist monk.

Chastened, but unabashed, Joseph Merrick took to a sulking silence.

Presently they arrived at the Electric Alhambra.

Performing artistes were already assembled there and many were crammed into the communal dressing room.

Colonel Katterfelto, lately returned from a most successful day's Snap, was smoking a cigar. Darwin the monkey now wore a silk shirt and bow tie to go with his waistcoat and trousers. The sum of five hundred pounds' worth of winnings had been split fifty-fifty.

There had only been a small amount of unpleasantness.

Darwin had concluded that as he did all of the Snapping he deserved a bigger share of the winnings. Also that as they were now both substantially *in pocket*, they should *not* return to the Music Hall, but book straight into a swank hotel and review their plans for a prosperous shared future.

Colonel Katterfelto had put the monkey straight. They had shaken on the fifty-fifty agreement, he explained. A handshake was a bond of trust, no matter the species that took it. And as to the matter of the Music Hall, yes, it was regrettable that they must return to suffer more from the hurled fruit and veg of the mob. But the colonel *was* a man of his word. And he had signed a six-week contract to play at the Electric Alhambra.

The monkey had bitten the colonel.

The colonel had kicked the monkey.

And now they both sat glowering once again.

Lovely Alice Lovell, accompanied this evening by, it appeared, all her worldly goods in carpet bags and cases, said, 'Do you know who is topping the bill?'

Conversations focused as the artistes dwelt upon this.

'Smelly Charlie Belly,' said one of the Travelling Formbys. 'Greatly overrated, in my opinion.'

Alice Lovell sighed and said, 'He's dreamy.'

Peter Pinkerton said, 'I heard that Lord Andrew literally bought him from Henry Irving at the Lyceum. Paid Irving one thousand pounds.'

'Well,' said another Formby, the one to the right of the rest, 'the Alhambra was going to need the best now that Harry Hamilton is gone. And no matter what my brother thinks, Belly really is the best.'

Heads nodded in agreement at this. Smelly Charlie Belly was top of the tree and no mistake about it. Probably the best-loved Music Hall turn of the day.

A smile, a song and an acrid stench.

It did not get better than *that*.

'I have also heard tell,' said Peter Pinkerton, 'that Mr Belly's smell is prepared for him by a Parisian perfumer.'

'I heard it was a professor from Brentford in Middlesex,' said yet another Formby. 'Professor Chanel, I heard.'

'You heard *wrong*,' said Peter Pinkerton. 'Ten guineas per fluid ounce he pays for that particular pong. It contains musk, ambergris and civet and has an aphrodisiac effect on the ladies, I'm told.'

'Dreamy,' said Alice Lovell once more. 'Tall and dark and handsome too, with lovely long eyelashes.'

'No chance that I've been moved up the bill, I suppose?' asked Colonel Katterfelto.

'No chance at all!' the artistes replied, as one.

'Then best be sprightly on my pins, I suppose.' The colonel rose and did limberings-up, whilst puffing upon his cigar.

Cameron Bell was puffing a cigar. With an extraordinary vigour. He and Mr Merrick sat in the luxurious box that the private detective had occupied the night before. Cameron Bell was somewhat red in the face.

'That was outrageous behaviour,' he told the Elephant Man. 'Fondling that lady in the foyer. Whatever were you thinking?'

Joseph Merrick was idly flicking peanuts onto people in the stalls. 'Please do not raise your voice to me,' he said.

'You are a monster,' said Cameron Bell. 'No wonder Sir Frederick Treves declines to take you out to the Music Hall.'

'A *monster*?' The Elephant Man now took to an exaggerated high-pitched wailing. 'He calls me a *monster*,' he cried to all that were in earshot. '*I* who have suffered so much.'

'Shame!' came calls from the orchestra stalls. A cabbage flew in Cameron Bell's direction.

'Stop it at once!' the detective told the wailing Mr Merrick. 'Or I will suggest to Mr Treves that a month or two in Bedlam might serve you well.'

'Mr Treves is my friend,' said the Elephant Man. 'He would not do that.'

'He told me he was thinking of having you moved on,' said Cameron Bell.

There was not one single word of truth to this, but it did have the desired effect upon the unruly Elephant Man.

'Can I have some popcorn, please?' asked Mr Joseph Merrick.

There was a full house at the Electric Alhambra upon this summer's evening. Smelly Charlie Belly could really pull the crowds. And of course there was that thing about morbid curiosity. Wanting to see whether there were any traces of Harry 'Hurty-Finger' Hamilton still to be seen upon the stage.

There were *not*, as it happened. The stage had been thoroughly scrubbed.

The Elephant Man enjoyed the evening performances. He had neglected to bring any fruit or veg to throw and so had to content himself with flinging popcorn and peanuts at the elusive Colonel Katterfelto, who, aided by his goggles, left the stage once more completely unscathed.

Mr Merrick was entranced by the jugglers, the acrobats, the magician and the singers of the songs. And as the enchanting Alice Lovell put her performing kiwis through their paces, he and Cameron Bell leaned forwards in the expensive box and sighed their separate sighs for her en-chantments.

Finally, and to the kind of applause that most performers could do nothing more than dream of, Smelly Charlie Belly took the stage.

There was no doubt that this chappie had charisma. He was tall and dark and handsome and the rest. He wore a purple suit with matching topper. And he really was the bestest of the best. His voice was deep and mellow, his buttonhole was yellow, he was a jolly fellow. And all were most impressed.

And when it came to the singing of his famous song, the crowd joined in with gusto.

With my seafood antipasti I'll be strolling along.
Everyone knows my name.
People, they come up to me, say, 'Cor, what a pong,'
They know that I'm to blame.

Now you might think I stink
Just like a fishmonger's boot
Or something's crawled and died
Inside my best Sunday suit.

But every single day it's the same
For Smelly Charlie Belly is my name.

It was a triumph and there was a standing ovation.

Smelly Charlie Belly wafted his personal fragrance towards the ladies in the front row and took bow after bow, receiving a bunch of roses thrown from the Royal Box.

He smiled and he waved.

And then he exploded.

In a great big ball of flame.

16

'am closing the theatre,' said Commander Case. 'One public murder was too much. I do not possess sufficient words to express my feelings now that *two* have occurred.'

'It *is* an unfortunate circumstance,' said Cameron Bell.

'*Unfortunate circumstance?*' roared the commander. 'No, sir. That does *not* cover it. Not one little bit.'

The two stood once more in the otherwise deserted foyer of the Electric Alhambra. The time was close to midnight. Tensions had been raised.

'I would appreciate it very much if you did *not* close the theatre,' said Cameron Bell. 'It would impede the course of my inquiries.'

'Ah,' said Commander Case. 'Clearly I have not expressed myself in a manner that you can understand. I do not wish you to make any further inquiries. You are dismissed from the case.'

Cameron Bell was clearly rattled by this. Words momentarily failed him. He removed his hat and ran a handkerchief over his naked scalp to mop at sudden perspiration.

'I have a theory,' said Cameron Bell, when words returned to him.

'You always have a theory.' Commander Case turned his nose up. 'But I have two men dead on a London stage.'

'You will not solve these cases without me,' said Mr Bell. 'You do not know what I know.'

'Do you wish to share what you know with me?'

'Should I do so, would it lead to reinstatement?'

'No.' Commander Case folded his arms. 'It would not.'

Cameron Bell made the saddest of faces. 'You *are* making a terrible mistake,' he told the commander. 'I feel confident that I can break this case within the next few days. And believe you me, we are dealing with something here that is beyond the realms of anything that the Metropolitan Police Force have ever dealt with before.'

'Oh really?' said Commander Case in a tone of some sarcasm. 'A magical mystery is it, then?'

'*Magical?*' asked Cameron Bell. 'Why would you use such a word?'

'There seem to be a lot of queer things happening lately. Around and about Whitechapel. There's been scrawlings on walls. Magical symbols, I'm told. Certain superstitious young bobbies have been getting themselves all in a lather and—' Commander Case ceased his discourse and then said, 'Why am I telling *you* this? You are off the case, Bell. If you have any information to offer me, it is your duty as a gentleman of the realm to offer it. Is there anything you wish to say?'

'You are making a terrible mistake.'

'Then this conversation is at an end. Kindly leave the premises.'

'But I have—' Cameron Bell almost said, *Things that need doing here. A crime scene to investigate.* But he did not. Instead he said, 'I must then fetch my hat and umbrella. I left them in the apartment of Lord Andrew Ditchfield.'

'I will have one of my chaps accompany you,' said Commander Case.

Cameron Bell did *not* retrieve his hat and his umbrella. After all, he *was* wearing a hat and he *was* carrying an umbrella. He did, however, speak with Lord Andrew Ditchfield, sharing with him the appalling news that the Electric Alhambra was to be closed whilst police investigated the two murders. Then making the suggestion that should Lord Andrew continue to employ him in the capacity of personal private investigator, he felt confident that he could solve the cases and have the theatre opened in a very short time.

Lord Andrew Ditchfield had engaged in considerable flustering and flapping around. But he had at least agreed to retain the services of Cameron Bell. Including the 'incentive bonus' the private detective suggested might help to grease the cogs of cogitation and ensure an early and satisfying outcome.

Cameron Bell now left the Electric Alhambra.

As he stood before the Music Hall awaiting a hansom cab, he mused upon the doings of the day. It had certainly been a *full* day and he felt he was making some progress. Although he had *not* been expecting Smelly Charlie Belly to go up in a cloud of smoke.

'Do you think you might assist me, sir?'

Cameron Bell turned at this voice. It was one that he recognised.

'Oh,' said Alice Lovell. 'It is you, Mr Bell. I am thankful for a kindly face in my moment of need.'

'Moment of need, dear lady?' asked Cameron Bell.

'I am moving to new lodgings. I can manage most of my bags, but the kiwi birds as well . . . It's rather difficult.'

'It will be my pleasure to assist you, Miss Lovell.'

The kiwi birds were quiet in their carrying cage.

'Sleeping?' asked Cameron Bell as he lugged the weighty cargo through the stage door and out into the gaslit alleyway.

'Chloroform,' said Alice Lovell. 'They make such a fuss otherwise.'

Cameron Bell was now burdened down not only by kiwis, but by hatboxes, carpet bags and Heaven knew what else.

Alice Lovell carried nothing but her handbag and her parasol.

'Perhaps we might share a hansom,' she suggested.

'Oh indeed, fair lady. Oh yes indeed.'

It was all too much for a hansom and so they had to wait for a four-wheeled 'growler' to come rolling by. This was one of the new electrically driven horseless carriages, low-slung, high-wheeled and comfortable within. The driver sat before them, working controls and humming a Music Hall tune.

'We will drop you off first,' said Cameron Bell. 'What is the address of your new lodging house?'

'Ninety-five Carlton Road,' said Alice Lovell.

'Oh my dear dead mother,' said Cameron Bell.

A full moon hung in the sky above and London dreamed in its glow. All seemed to be at peace in the great metropolis. Cameron Bell looked up at the sky, then stole a glance at his travelling companion. She was *so* beautiful. And so near. He could smell her perfume. Her elbow was nearly touching his knee. *If only it could be*, dreamed Cameron Bell.

'Wasn't it terrible about Mr Belly?' Alice's words broke the spell.

'Terrible,' said Cameron Bell.

'I thought you were supposed to be solving the case.'

'I was,' said Cameron Bell. 'I *am*.'

'I bet no one will want to top the bill tomorrow night.'

'Oh dear,' said Cameron Bell. 'Were you not informed? The theatre is to remain closed whilst the police go about their investigations.'

'Oh no!' cried Alice Lovell. 'Then we shall not be paid.'

'You *will* be paid,' said Cameron Bell.

'Not if we do not perform.'

'I spoke earlier with Lord Andrew Ditchfield,' said the private detective. 'I insisted that the performers must be paid during the time the theatre is closed.'

'You did?' asked Alice Lovell. And leaning over she kissed Mr Bell, right on the side of his cheek.

'I did,' said Mr Cameron Bell. Who knew full well that he had done nothing of the kind. But concluded that he really *must* tomorrow.

'You are a wonderful man,' said Alice Lovell. And she kissed him again.

Cameron Bell blushed rosy pink. And then he said, 'Dear me.'

'Is something wrong?' asked Alice Lovell, giving his arm a squeeze.

'I have just remembered,' said Cameron Bell. 'I was supposed to be escorting Mr Merrick back to the London Hospital. But with all the excitement, I left him sitting in the expensive box we occupied together.'

'Serves him right,' said Alice Lovell. 'He is a dreadful man. I went to visit him once in his rooms. It used to be a very fashionable thing to do. He dropped his handkerchief and when I bent down to pick it up, he pinched my bum.'

Cameron Bell fought with hilarity and chewed upon his bottom lip. Perhaps there had been some justice after all this evening.

'Carlton Road,' called the driver of the growler.

And Carlton Road it was.

Cameron Bell unloaded the worldly goods of Alice Lovell and paid off the cabbie. 'I will help you to your lodgings,' he said. 'Then I will engage another cab.'

'You are most kind, Mr Bell.'

'Oh, do please call me Cameron.'

As Cameron struggled and Alice Lovell tottered lightly in her heels, they approached the theatrical diggings of number ninety-five.

'You took the room so recently occupied by the now late Harry Hamilton,' said Cameron Bell as he staggered beneath his load.

'You really *are* a detective,' said Alice Lovell. 'Now we must be very very quiet when we enter the house. We would not want to wake anybody, would we now?'

Nor, suspected Cameron Bell, announce the arrival of a flock of kiwi birds that no landlady in her right mind would ever agree to have upon her premises.

'I will be mouse-like,' said the private detective. 'Which floor is your room upon?'

'The very top. You can see the two windows up there.'

Cameron Bell peered upwards. 'So is the room presently unoccupied?' he asked.

'There was a portmanteau that a gentleman was to collect.'

Cameron Bell made a bitter face. He well remembered *that* portmanteau. 'But no one should be in the room *now*?' he whispered.

'Not at this time, no.'

'I saw a flash of light at a window, as of a bullseye lantern. There.' Cameron Bell, having nothing other to gesture with, gestured with his chin. 'See it again. Someone is moving about in the room.'

'Most curious,' said Alice Lovell.

'Someone who should not be there,' whispered Cameron Bell, 'for otherwise they would have lit the gas mantle.'

'Curiouser and curiouser,' said Alice.

Cameron Bell relieved himself of his burdens. 'Give me the front-door key,' he said, softly. 'And please wait here until I return.'

For a heavyset fellow, Mr Cameron Bell could move at times with the delicacy of a Siamese cat. His footfalls on the stairs hardly registered in the silent house. And though he was caused to halt upon the second landing and draw his breath, the journey up was achieved with admirable furtive speed.

He paused before the door he sought, noted a brief flash of light flicker beneath it and engaged upon an inner dialogue.

Beyond this door, said Cameron Bell, to no one but himself, *someone moves about. Doing what? Searching for something, would be my considered opinion. Searching for what? Something that the searcher did not find in the portmanteau he stole? Perhaps. Something that has been represented as being the lost Ring of Moses, perhaps?*

Satisfied with the logic of these propositions, Cameron Bell drew out his pistol, checked it, cocked it, put his free hand to the handle of the door. Turned it gently.

Then flung open the door.

'Officer of the law,' cried Cameron Bell. 'Drop any weapons and raise your hands, if you will.'

The beam of a bullseye lantern caught him full in the face.

The roar, as of some savage beast, brought fear to Cameron Bell. Something leapt towards him from the darkness.

The private detective shielded his face and fired his pistol blindly into the room. Again and again and again and again until he ran out of bullets.

17

here was chaos in the theatrical diggings.

Artistes in various states of undress filled the halls and crowded the stairs. Lucy Gladfield pushed her way amongst them.

There was much light now, for all mantles were lit.

Cameron Bell called down from the topmost landing. 'There is no cause for alarm,' he called. 'Everything is under control.'

'Everything is far from *that*,' cried Lucy Gladfield. 'And what are *you* doing in my house?' And spying the pistol added, 'And who have you shot?'

'A burglar and I suspect a murderer, too,' the private detective called down. 'But everything *is* now under control.'

'Let me get up there.' Lucy Gladfield, proprietress of the establishment, forced her way to the top of the stairs.

Cameron Bell said, 'Madam, if you please—'

'Let me pass,' demanded Lucy Gladfield. 'I want to see just what went on in one of my finest rooms.'

'I really do feel it best that you do not.'

Lucy Gladfield glared at Cameron Bell. 'How *did* you get in here?' she wanted to be told.

'The front door was unlocked.' Cameron Bell was never too far from a necessary untruth. 'I suspect the burglar picked the lock. After we both observed Harry Hamilton's luggage being stolen this morning, I felt it prudent to keep a watch on the house this evening, in case the villain returned, seeking even more.' He paused here to gauge the reaction of the landlady.

Lucy Gladfield bobbed her head. It was enclosed by a tight and laced night bonnet. Clearly the helter-skelter hair-do was a wig.

'Is he dead, this burglar?' Lucy Gladfield squinted into the darkness.

'It would probably be for the best if I went in alone to find out.'

'Yes, probably.' The wigless woman offered her box of lucifers to the private detective. 'There is a mantle to the left of the door,' she said.

'My thanks.' Cameron Bell struck a lucifer, held it before him. Entered the room.

He turned up the mantle and lit it.

The room welled into light. It had been thoroughly ransacked. Bed linen cast to the floor. Pillow torn open. Wardrobe overturned. But all done evidently in silence so as not to awaken the household.

Lucy Gladfield fell back in alarm. 'You have shot a child,' she cried and fainted dead away.

In the middle of the untidy room, the toppled and extinguished bullseye lantern by his side, lay a small, slight figure. Face down in a spreading pool of blood.

Moving on the lightest of feet, the private detective approached the fallen figure. It did appear to be a child. An awful chill passed into Cameron Bell.

What have I done? he demanded of himself. *Irresponsibly*

fired off rounds into a darkened room, was the answer to that. But he had heard a fearful sound. As of a ferocious animal. *A dog, perhaps? Some beast that still lurks in the room?*

Cameron Bell stepped warily and took to reloading his pistol.

The smell of carbide tainted the air. And another smell also. Of something unidentifiable. Strange.

Mr Bell ducked down and peered beneath the bed. Nothing but a chamber pot. The beast had somehow departed.

With a heavy heart the private detective approached the small and slender body. Slowly he stooped to examine it. And here he saw something that caused him concern. The child was shaven-headed.

Cameron saw more.

From the crown of the head to the nape of the neck ran a line of raised ridges, not unlike the dorsal spines of a fish. Cameron Bell took hold of a shoulder, gently turned the body onto its back. It seemed all but without weight. And then he saw the face.

It was not the face of any child that ever walked this Earth.

It was not the face of any human being.

The breath caught in Cameron's throat. He stared in fascination at the thing that lay before him. It was certainly *not* a human being. But then what, exactly, was it?

Some trained animal dressed in human clothes?

Cameron knew of trousered apes, but this was no such thing.

Which left . . . ?

'Not of this planet,' said Cameron Bell, gazing down at the face.

There was something of the reptile to the features, the nose parts consisting of two small holes, the mouth being wide and lipless. The eyes were all-over black, lustreless now; they put Mr Bell in mind of a pair of shark's eyes he had seen preserved in a jar at the London Hospital. Part reptile? Part fish? Part mammal?

Cameron set to searching the corpse for some identification.

The sounds of commotion, of shouting, pushing and shoving, came to him through the open doorway. A voice shouted, 'Return to your rooms.' Another shouted, 'Now.'

Cameron Bell made haste with his search. Discovered something, slipped it into his pocket.

'Step away from the body now, sir, if you please.'

It was *not* a request, but a clear command. Cameron rose and turned to face the speaker.

Two men stood in the doorway. Two men these and very much alike. They wore identical black morning suits, with black wing-collared shirts and black bow ties. Each wore a pair of pince-nez specs. The lenses of these were black.

'We will have to ask you to leave now, sir,' said one of these gentlemen in black. 'There is nothing to see here.'

'Quite the contrary,' said Cameron Bell.

'I repeat,' said the blackly clad figure, 'there is nothing to see here. Please return to your room. We will speak with you presently.'

Cameron Bell opened his mouth to protest. But thought better of it. 'I saw nothing here,' he said. 'I will return to my room.'

'There's a good gentleman,' said a fellow in black. 'Cut along now, we will correct this untidiness.'

'Yes,' said Cameron Bell.

He had to squeeze between the two gentlemen in black and this was not easy as they chose not to stand aside—

'Remember,' whispered one of them. 'You saw *nothing* here.'

'Nothing at all,' said Cameron Bell, politely taking his leave.

He stepped carefully over the unconscious body of Lucy Gladfield, made down stairs that were now deserted. Opened the front door and passed into the street.

A Black Maria was parked next to the kerb. One of those new electric police vehicles for housing criminals during transportation. This one, however, was unusual in that it did not bear the distinctive crest of the Metropolitan Police Force upon its sides. It was all-over black. A driver sat in the forward cockpit. He was dressed in black, with matching pince-nez.

Alice Lovell called to Cameron Bell from across the street.

The private detective sighed. He had actually forgotten about *her*.

She sat upon her luggage and the sound of waking kiwi birds was irksome in the otherwise silent street.

'Some very unpleasant men dressed all in black said I was to sit over here and not move until they returned,' said Alice Lovell. 'What happened in there? Did I hear gunshots?'

'Well now, dear lady,' said Cameron Bell. 'Well now, well now indeed.'

Alice Lovell looked up at Cameron Bell. Fixing him with her big blue eyes. 'I am homeless, am I not?' she asked.

'Regretfully, yes,' said Cameron Bell. 'It would certainly not be prudent for you to gain occupation of your new room at this time. There has been — how might I put this? — an incident.'

Tears filled Alice Lovell's eyes. She began to weep.

'Oh, weep not, fair lady,' said the gallant Mr Bell. 'I have of course organised other accommodation for you this night.'

'You have?' asked Alice Lovell. 'Where is *this*?'

Cameron Bell thought hard for a moment. 'At *my* house,' said he.

The sounds of wheels upon cobbles reached the detective's ears. It was *not* the arrival of a four-wheeled growler. Rather it was another unmarked Black Maria.

'I feel it best if we start walking *now*,' said Cameron Bell. 'We can hail a cab on another street, I am thinking.'

Even though struggling beneath a load that was now made ever more difficult due to boisterous kiwi birds, Mr Bell enjoyed the walk. For it was a walk *away* from the gentlemen in black and one in the company of the beautiful Alice Lovell.

'You really are my protector,' said she, skipping at his side.

'It would be ungentlemanly not to aid a lady in distress.' Cameron Bell was growing breathless, but he plodded on.

'Is it far to your house?' asked Alice.

'Not too far, as it happens. But flag down a cab if one comes.'

Sadly no cab came in their direction, so Cameron kept on walking. His enjoyment tempered now by near exhaustion.

'You shot someone, back in Carlton Road, didn't you?' asked Alice, skipping backwards before the detective. Fixing him with those eyes.

'Shot a person?' The voice of Mr Bell had a certain distance.

'Shot a person. Yes.'

'I did *not* shoot a person,' he said. And this was strictly true.

'I'm glad,' said Alice. 'Shooting people is horrid. Do you know who killed Mr Belly? It was the same one who killed Mr Hamilton, I suppose.'

'Undoubtedly,' said Cameron Bell. And then a thought struck him most forcefully. That the person who murdered

Mr Harry Hamilton was *not* the person who had stolen the portmanteau. The person who had escaped upon the flying platform and who had dispatched the whatever-it-was to search the room that Alice Lovell sought to occupy was *not* the murderer. If Harry Hamilton had been murdered by someone who sought to acquire the Ring of Moses from him, he would never have been done to death in such a manner that might well have destroyed this treasured item. The murder of Harry Hamilton and the murder of Charlie Belly were undoubtedly the work of the same evil hand. But it was *not* the same hand that sought to gain possession of the ring.

There were certain flaws in this train of logic and Cameron knew this. He would deal with them when the time was right. But for now he was certain that he had made some kind of breakthrough. He was looking for two criminals. And it was more than just possible that neither of these were human.

'You are suddenly smiling,' said Alice Lovell, still skipping before him. 'What has made you smile? Please tell me, do.'

'Your company,' said Cameron Bell. 'I find you – how shall I put this? – inspirational.'

'Am I to be your muse, then?' Alice affected a most coquettish expression.

Would that it were so, thought Cameron Bell.

Presently and with Cameron now feeling that he was surely upon his last legs, they reached the home of the detective.

'What a beautiful house,' said Alice. 'Is it *very* old?'

'It is Georgian,' said Cameron Bell, 'and has been in my family ever since it was built.'

'How lovely.'

'But just one thing.' Cameron Bell lowered bags and boxes and the kiwis' travelling cage onto the doorstep before his home. 'Regarding your kiwi birds,' he said to Alice.

'They are very well behaved,' said Alice Lovell.

'They are nothing of the kind and you know it. There is a wash house in the yard to the rear of the premises. I must insist that the birds be lodged there and *never* enter the house. Do you agree to these terms?'

'Are they the *only* terms?' asked Alice.

'What other terms might there be?' came the reply.

Alice smiled upon Cameron Bell. 'None whatsoever, I am sure,' said she.

Cameron Bell took out his house key and raised it to the front door. To his horror the front door swung open before him.

'You forgot to lock your door,' said Alice Lovell.

Cameron Bell drew out his pistol. 'That is something I *never* forget,' he said. 'Wait here.'

Moonlight, streaming in through the open front doorway, lit the hall to an eerie perfection. Cameron noted with some relief that there were no immediate signs of ransacking. He edged forwards and then threw open the door to his beautiful study. All was as it had been. All was neat and nice. Cameron Bell turned up the gas mantle.

Someone *had* been here. His desk chair had been moved.

'Oh my dear dead mother.' Cameron Bell swiftly crossed the study floor. Took himself to the rear of his writing desk, tugged upon the lowermost left-hand drawer. The drawer opened to reveal neat piles of paper. Cameron reached inside, tapped upon a hidden button. A secret compartment slid open from beneath the drawer revealing a small black box.

Cameron Bell lifted the box from its hiding place. But even before he opened it, he knew that it was empty.

His secret drawer had been discovered.

The Ring of Moses was gone.

18

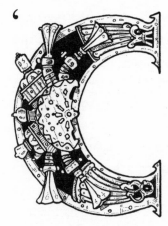

'rowley did it,' said Cameron Bell. 'Crowley has taken the ring.'

Alice Lovell appeared in the open doorway. 'Is everything all right?' she asked. 'Has anything been taken?'

The private detective dropped into his chair. 'A precious item has been stolen,' he said. 'But I know who the culprit is and will pay him a visit in the morning.'

But Mr Bell had certain qualms regarding this. Crowley had entered the house with seeming ease. He had known exactly where to find the Ring of Moses. Nothing else had been tampered with. Nothing else was stolen. Crowley's claims to magical powers were not, upon this evidence, without some foundation. Cameron Bell felt most uneasy – magic was hardly within his province. Commander Case had let slip that magical doings were afoot in Whitechapel. Was there a connection, or connections?

Mr Bell had had quite enough for one day.

'Let us bring in your belongings,' he said to Alice. 'Settle your kiwi birds in the outhouse and then I will show you to your room.'

Alice Lovell yawned most prettily. 'I am rather tired,' said she.

Colonel Katterfelto was an early riser. Always had been, always would be. In his present theatrical diggings it paid to be first out of bed. First man up could take advantage of what little hot water the copper geyser in the communal bathroom managed to produce. First man up had unhurried access to the Thomas Crapper. First man up received breakfast.

Colonel Katterfelto enjoyed a good breakfast. And he did enjoy being fussed over. He would naturally have preferred of course to have had his breakfast served and himself fussed over by an attractive young lady rather than a toothless bearded hag.

But such was life, and who was he to argue?

'I heard about poor Charlie Belly,' said the hag as she served the colonel porridge. 'He lodged here in the past, you know. We had to open all the windows to let out the pong. But a very pretty fellow was Mr Charlie Belly. He liked a little sugar on his porridge.'

Colonel Katterfelto wondered whether that was some kind of sexual innuendo. The very thought that it might be set his teeth upon edge.

'I will have to ask you for next week's rent in advance,' said the hag, out of the blue and whilst pouring tea.

'You will?' asked the colonel. 'But why?'

'Because of the Electric Alhambra being closed for at least a week.'

'What of this?' asked Colonel Katterfelto. 'I have heard nothing of this.'

'It's in the morning paper,' said the lady of the land. 'That

Commander Case intends to search every single inch of the theatre.'

'Thorough enough, I suppose.' The colonel perused the newspaper that had been thrust before him.

WORLD'S GREATEST ENTERTAINER
HORRIBLY MURDERED

ran the headline.

'Fellow wasn't *that* good,' puffed the colonel. But he read on. Commander Case had apparently granted the newspaper's editor an interview. And had stated a number of things. That he suspected that the unwholesome Johnny Frenchman might be at the back of it. Johnny Frenchman being the number-one suspect in yesterday's HYDE PARK CORNER MASSACRE.

Colonel Katterfelto nodded approvingly at this. Like all good Englishmen he always had his suspicions about exactly what Johnny Frenchman might be up to.

Commander Case had gone on to make vague references about a magical connection. Possibly Masonic.

Colonel Katterfelto shrugged his shoulders.

Commander Case had ordered that the Electric Alhambra be closed for an indefinite period, until investigations within it were concluded.

Colonel Katterfelto smiled hugely at this. It could not be more convenient. He had matters that needed attending to. Serious matters centred about his life's quest, to create and energise the Mechanical Messiah. A week or two without the nightly dread of hurled cabbages and tomatoes would suit the colonel perfectly.

'You look happy,' said the toothless hag. 'Would you like me to butter up your muffin?'

Cameron Bell did not awaken Alice Lovell. There was no need to, he would let her sleep. As he attended to the minutiae of his morning ablutions, his thoughts took a turn towards the amorous. She was actually here. Right here in his house. The woman he adored. It could not have gone better if he had planned it himself.

Cameron Bell took stock. He *had* planned it himself. In a way. But she *was* here and if he was careful, polite, gallant, charming, protective, sympathetic and all the rest, who knew how things might progress?

However, he had a case – no – *cases* to solve. And the all-consuming passion of his life was solving such cases.

And now he had a breakfast appointment with Mr Aleister Crowley.

He should not have been surprised by what occurred. It was obvious really and had he not been distracted by the lovely Alice, it would have made itself obvious to him as soon as he had discovered the ring to be stolen.

Policemen milled before the door to Aleister Crowley's lodgings. Several burly fellows bearing sheaves of paper muttered to these policemen.

Cameron Bell turned down his eyes to their boots. *Bailiffs,* he concluded. *Debt collectors, too.*

The private detective pushed towards the door, but his way was amply blocked by large policemen.

'Sorry, sir,' said one of these. 'We're asking folk to form an orderly queue.'

'He has absconded, hasn't he?' said Cameron Bell. For this was the obvious thing. 'Mr Crowley, he has done, as they say, a midnight flit.'

'Hardly *that*,' said the policeman. 'He's dead.'

Cameron Bell took stock of this. 'He is *dead*?' he asked. 'But *how*?'

'Spondacious combusturan,' said the policeman.

'Spontaneous combustion?' said the private detective.

'Went up in a ball of flame, apparently. A big poof and he was gone.'

Cameron Bell had no comment to make upon that.

'Detective Bell,' said Cameron Bell. 'Commander Case sent me to examine the crime scene.'

The policeman saluted Detective Bell. 'Go up then, sir,' said he.

There was a most unpleasant odour in the sitting room of the Beast. As of pork left too long in the oven. The private detective brought out his hankie, held it over his nose. A number of young bobbies inhabited the rooms of the late Mr Crowley. Touching things they should not, contaminating the crime scene. Behaving as policemen will, always have done, always will do, too.

Mr Bell announced himself. The bobbies came to attention.

'Don't 'alf stink, guv'nor, don't it?' said one, who hailed from the East End of London.

'A fitting end for such as he,' a God-fearing bobby said.

'What have you to report regarding the garden?' asked Detective Bell.

'The garden, sir?' asked a bobby whose mother had taught him the meaning of politeness.

Detective Bell said, 'Surely now.'

'I do not quite understand,' said the bobby and all of them shook their heads.

'Oh dear,' said Detective Bell. 'Commander Case is going to be most displeased when he finds out that you have not examined the garden for clues. He does have this thing about gardens. "Show me the garden and I will close the case," he often says.'

The bobbies made doubtful expressions.

'Well, hurry along, then.' Cameron Bell did flutterings of his fingers. 'I will not tell the commander that you have been lacking in your duties. I will tell him that I arrived to find you hard at work in the garden.'

With much spoken thanks, which even included the well-brought-up policeman shaking the hand of Cameron Bell, the bevy of bobbies left the detective alone.

Cameron Bell made haste with his investigations.

In the very centre of the room there yawned a hole. The private detective approached and peered into this. A circular section of floor had been burned away and he could see clear through to the room below. On the ceiling above, a circular scorch mark. The room was all-over black with a layer of soot.

Cameron Bell was on the point of making an allusion to his dear dead mother. But time did not permit and he instead did searchings for the ring.

But it was an impossible task and footsteps upon the stairs announced the untimely (at least to Cameron Bell) arrival of Commander Case.

'Well now then,' said this very fellow. 'What do we have here?'

'A possible case of spontaneous human combustion,' said Cameron Bell.

'You misunderstand me,' said Commander Case, squaring up before Mr Bell. 'I mean, of course, what in the name of all that I find holy are *you* doing here?'

'I was paying a social visit to Mr Crowley. We were students together at Trinity. I lent him a book. I came here to collect it.' Cameron Bell smiled politely. 'If you will permit me a couple of hours or more, I feel sure that I can find it.'

'Out!' cried Commander Case. 'Out, or I will run you in for loitering with intent, illegal occupation of private premises and any number of trumped-up charges as might take my fancy.'

'I have a theory regarding this!'

'Get out!' bawled the commander.

Colonel Katterfelto left his diggings. A big breakfast under his belt and a confident stride in his steppings. Under his arm was the daily newspaper the hag had thrust in his direction. On the very back page of this was a list of

PREMISES TO BUY OR RENT

The colonel marched along.

He was going to need a base of operations. A *private* base, this, and one kept secret from potential flaming-torch carriers. A discreet workshop tucked away in a back alleyway, or in amongst premises that were given over to light engineering or the manufacture of goods.

And once settled in—

The colonel smiled once more. He would begin the Great Work. He had perhaps been a little too hasty last time. Choosing America had been a bad idea. Here was where it needed to be done. Right here in the heart of the British Empire. It had to be, really. Any Mechanical Messiah worthy of its name must be created here. Must have

MADE IN ENGLAND

engraved upon its back.

The colonel marched on, whistling a popular Music Hall tune.

Cameron Bell left the rooms of the late Great Beast of the Apocalypse. He was greeted – not kindly – by several bobbies in the street. Bobbies who had discovered that the premises owned to no back garden. Bobbies who had been shouted at by Commander Case. They jostled Cameron Bell and one made threatening gestures with his truncheon.

The private detective crossed the street and pondered on his lot. London had once more come to life. Horses clipped and clopped. Wheels clattered over the cobbles. Newsboys cried out the name of Charlie Belly. An airship passed across the sky, casting a mighty shadow.

Crowley dead? thought Cameron Bell. And made dead in a manner that closely, if not identically, resembled those of the two star turns. Perhaps there was only *one* murderer. Perhaps. Perhaps. Perhaps.

The private detective dug into his trouser pocket. Brought out a certain item that he had acquired the previous night. An item that he had transferred from the trousers of his evening suit to those that he wore of a morning.

The item he had plucked from the pocket of the thing that he had shot dead.

'This is the lead that I shall follow,' said Mr Cameron Bell.

19

‘ow pleasant to see you again,’ said Sir Frederick Treves. He stood once more at the dissecting table in the morgue of the London Hospital.

Cameron Bell smiled back at the surgeon. ‘I see you have a fresh one there,’ he said.

Sir Frederick Treves nodded. ‘Brought in from—’ Then he paused. ‘But why do not *you* tell *me*,’ he suggested.

‘Indeed,’ said Cameron Bell. ‘Might I see the clothing and shoes of the deceased?’

The famous surgeon gestured to a sorry-looking pile of clothing and a pair of shoes that lay upon a table not too far distant. The private detective took himself over to these, examined them closely and said—

‘In her late teens, unmarried and a virgin. Employed for the last three months as a seamstress, but prior to that was engaged as a ladies’ maid in a Great House. In Knightsbridge, I believe. Dismissed due to dishonesty, although this was not proved. Domiciled in Whitechapel. In Naylor Street, to be precise. And murdered, by means that I confess I am not yet able to tie down with precision, a mere few hundred yards from her doorstep.'

Cameron Bell took himself over to the corpse. Placed his hands upon it. 'The murder took place at three-fifteen a.m.,' he said.

'Extraordinary,' said Sir Frederick Treves. 'I will not ask how you came to these conclusions.'

'Through observation,' said Cameron Bell. 'Allied with a considerable knowledge of London and its population. *I* specialise.'

'Well, you were certainly correct about the location where she was found and I would agree with you regarding the time of death. You would not care to take the Gold Cup by telling me the victim's name?'

Cameron Bell shook his head. 'If you wish to know that, I would suggest you interview the constable who found the body. I have reason to believe that it was *he* who stole her purse and not the murderer.'

'Uncanny,' said Sir Frederick Treves. 'You are a regular—'

'Do not say it,' said Cameron Bell.

'Sherlock Holmes,' said Sir Frederick Treves. And he grinned.

'Everything I told you is plainly to be seen upon the clothing, the shoes and the body,' explained Mr Bell. 'But were I to point it all out to you, you would simply nod your head and say, "It's all so simple, there is really no trick to it." And then where would my mystique be?'

Sir Frederick Treves nodded. 'Your mystique would be safe with me,' he said.

'No matter.' Cameron Bell smiled. 'But I do confess to puzzlement. There is a great deal of blood upon the clothing, yet I see no obvious wounds. And I do not believe she was stabbed in the back. Do you know how she was killed?'

'Strangulation, I believe.'

Cameron Bell looked hard at the victim's face. He lifted an eyelid, stared into the lifeless eye. 'She was partially strangled,' he said, 'but that was not the cause of death. I see you were about to open the victim's chest. You would have no objections if I were to watch as you do so?'

'None whatsoever.' Frederick Treves took up the *big* bone saw. Put it down, rolled up his sleeves, picked it up again.

Cameron Bell backed away.

'Squeamish?' asked the surgeon of the Queen.

'Not as such,' the detective replied. 'Let us just say *cautious.*'

'There is nothing to fear from a corpse.' Sir Frederick Treves held high the saw, then went to work with a will. The sounds of cracking ribs were simply frightful and Cameron Bell had cause to cover his ears.

The surgeon whistled a Music Hall song, then ceased to whistle mid-verse.

'There is something queer here,' he observed.

Cameron Bell uncovered his ears. 'You had best be careful,' he said.

'There is nothing to fear from a— *Waaaaaaah!*' There was a muffled explosion and Sir Frederick Treves found himself literally doused from head to waist in the contents of the corpse. 'By the grace of God,' cried he, flailing about in the gore.

'I suspected something of the sort,' said Cameron Bell. 'I did counsel caution.'

★

Cameron Bell waited patiently in the office of Sir Frederick Treves whilst the great surgeon took himself off to the shower room and acquired a change of clothes.

Cameron Bell did not waste his time, however. He spent it gainfully going through the surgeon's private papers and filing drawers to acquaint himself with everything that might prove pertinent to the case, or cases. Which now might in fact number several.

Cleanly scrubbed, lightly pomaded, dressed less than comfortably in one of Joseph Merrick's suits, Sir Frederick Treves eventually appeared. His face no longer smiling.

'If that was some kind of prank,' he said, 'I will do for Mr Merrick.'

'He is not to blame upon this occasion.' Cameron Bell took himself over to the sideboard. 'Should I pour us both a whisky?' he suggested.

Sir Frederick Treves nodded grimly and sat himself down behind his desk. Cameron Bell fought once more with hilarity as he handed the surgeon a glass of whisky, whilst noting the bizarre effect the weirdly shaped suit created upon him.

'Don't you smirk at me,' said Sir Frederick Treves.

'Of course not.' Cameron Bell raised his glass. 'To Her Majesty the Queen,' he said.

'Her Majesty the Queen.' Glasses clinked and whisky went its way.

'Regarding Mr Merrick,' said Sir Frederick Treves. 'You seem to have made a friend there, Bell.'

'Really?' said Cameron Bell. 'That is pleasing to my ears, I suppose.'

'Yes, he was greatly taken by your jest of leaving him alone and penniless at the Electric Alhambra. Thought it the funniest thing ever. I never actually considered playing pranks on him myself. Odd what pleases some fellows, is it not?'

The private detective nodded. 'As long as he got back here safely,' he said.

'Ah, that.' Sir Frederick Treves raised an eyebrow. 'We do not allow Mr Merrick to prowl the streets of Whitechapel at night, as a rule,' said he. 'It can be dangerous, you know.'

'For whom, I wonder?' mused Cameron Bell.

'And what do you mean by *that*?'

Cameron Bell did shruggings of the shoulders. Took Sir Frederick's now empty glass from him. Took himself to the sideboard and refreshed both glasses. 'Rumours persist,' he said.

'And I know of them.' Sir Frederick Treves made the face of fierceness. 'That Joseph was implicated in the Ripper killings of eighteen eighty-eight.'

'Not publicly,' said Cameron Bell. 'And the Ripper murders were before my time as a detective. It is of course interesting to note that all the murders occurred within walking distance of the London Hospital, yet no staff or patients at the hospital were ever questioned. How would you account for that?'

Sir Frederick Treves offered Cameron Bell a most un-expected wink. It was a *certain* wink. Allied to a *certain* handshake. Cameron Bell, as a Brother Under the Arch, knew well the meanings of both wink and handshake.

'*Not* Mr Merrick, then,' said he.

'We all make mistakes in our youth,' said Sir Frederick Treves. 'But some of us atone for them with good works once we are older.'

'Let us speak of other matters,' said Cameron Bell. ' "The regrettable affair of the exploding corpse", as it might be chronicled in the memoirs of Mr Holmes.'

'Odd,' said Mr Frederick Treves. 'Post-mortem gases generally form in the stomach as the digestive juices begin to eat into the body. As to why the lungs would erupt in such a fashion I have absolutely no idea.'

'I will put a proposition to you,' said Cameron Bell. 'You may tell me whether you believe it to be sound.' He handed the surgeon his refilled glass. Clinked his own against it. 'Your victim, I believe, died through inhaling a noxious gas of some sort. The gas was introduced through the victim's mouth. The throat was closed through partial strangulation. The gas within ate into the windpipe, sealing it shut. As it ate into the lungs they expanded, but were locked against the ribcage until you cut through it.'

'This is a theory I would have liked to have heard before I did the actual cutting.'

'I regret that up until the explosion it *was only* a theory. I would suggest you test the lung tissue, it might yield up interesting results.'

Sir Frederick Treves supped further whisky. 'You have not yet told me why you came here,' he said. 'I assume you did not visit on a purely social basis.'

'What luck have you had with the hurty-finger?' asked the detective.

'It is a finger of *something*. But at present I can tell you no more than that.'

'I have *something else* that I think might interest you.' Cameron Bell took this something from his trouser pocket and handed it to the surgeon.

Sir Frederick Treves held it up to the light. 'A crystal?' he said. 'From some chandelier?'

Cameron Bell shook his head. 'Run it about your whisky glass,' said he.

'Like *this*, do you mean?'

The detective nodded. There was a high-pitched grating sound. The top of the glass fell down to the desk, cleaved neatly away from the bottom.

'*A diamond?*' said Sir Frederick Treves. 'And surely the biggest I have ever seen. What of this, my friend? Have you added Grand Larceny to your achievements? Is this part of the Crown jewels?'

'No such gem has been reported stolen. But peer a little closer, if you will.'

Sir Frederick Treves squinted at the glittering gem. 'Well, I will be damned!' was what he said.

'Intriguing, is it not?' Cameron Bell leaned over the desk and peered hard into the gemstone. 'There would appear to be something going on in there. Movement of some kind. As if something lives within.'

'A foetus?' the surgeon suggested. 'Is this some kind of an egg?'

Cameron Bell shrugged hopelessly. 'I am unqualified to say. Show me a gentleman's bow tie and I will tell you which public school he attended. Show me a sock and I'll tell you his religion. But once again I am out of my depth. This is something unworldly. Something not of this Earth.'

'I am a man of Earthly medicine,' said Sir Frederick Treves. 'I will put this unusual object beneath the micro-scope. But I am at a loss to know what else can be done.'

'Amongst the patients here,' said Cameron Bell, finishing his second glass of whisky, 'might there be any who have travelled in space?'

'Ah, good point. You think they might recognise the mysterious item?'

'It is a possibility.'

Sir Frederick Treves leaned back in his chair and tugged

upon a velvet bell pull whose upper end vanished through a hole in the ceiling.

Presently there came a knock upon the door.

'Come,' called Sir Frederick Treves.

A young nurse entered, her head bowed low in modesty.

'Nurse When,' said Sir Frederick Treves, addressing the young and most attractive nurse, 'do we at present have any patients here who have travelled in space?'

Nurse When raised a pretty face and made a thoughtful expression. 'Not at present,' she said. 'We do have an out-patient, though. A retired military gentleman. He comes in regularly to renew his prescription for Mercury Vapour, to relieve his back pain. I believe he was in—'

'The Queen's Own Electric Fusiliers,' said Sir Frederick Treves. 'I recall him now. Colonel somebody-or-other.'

'Colonel Katterfelto,' said Cameron Bell. Who had recognised the name of the sprightly bill-bottomer whilst rooting through the filing cabinet of Sir Frederick Treves. 'I have other lines of investigation to pursue for now, but I'll speak with this fellow soon enough.'

20

 ZZ MANUFACTURING LTD ran the sign above the door. A sign that was weather-worn and going all to seed.

'Just needs a little lick of paint,' said the managing agent of the property. He was a sharply dressed young gentleman with an educated accent who carried himself with a confident air that the colonel did not warm to.

The managing agent took out a ring of keys and applied one to the padlock securing the door. Rotten wood crumbled and padlock, hasp and all went tumbling to the rubbish-strewn yard that lay before this property.

The young man made a pained expression, then brightened as he said, 'You will find the interior deceptively spacious.' Putting his shoulder to the door, he added, 'We'll soon have this open.' But the door remained shut.

Colonel Katterfelto added effort and with a rather sickening crunch the door fell from its hinges.

Colonel Katterfelto gazed down at the broken door, then squinted into dusty, fusty darkness.

'Smells like a damned latrine,' said the colonel. 'Don't think I'll bother with this one.'

'Sir.' The managing agent made a face of exasperation. 'This is the sixth property I have shown you.'

'And each of less suitability.'

'Would you care to see the first one again, sir?'

'No, I would not.' The colonel flicked away at the dust that was beginning to settle upon his shoulders. 'Have to try some other part of London.'

The managing agent wrung his hands. The thought of a potential tenant slipping through his fingers irked him mightily.

'It does have to be an *industrial* premises, does it?' he asked.

The colonel, who had so far disclosed absolutely nothing at all to the managing agent regarding the use he intended to put the property to, shrugged his shoulders. 'I own a set of clockwork minstrels,' he said. 'Need somewhere to store 'em. Somewhere to fix 'em up when they break down. Somewhere private. Somewhere secure.'

'We do have one property that might interest you.' The managing agent smiled pathetically. 'You might consider it quirky, but the rent is reasonable.'

'Go on then,' said the colonel. 'Tell me what you have.'

'It is an abandoned chapel,' said the managing agent. 'In Whitechapel.'

'Whitechapel, you say?' The man behind the high clerk's desk looked down upon Cameron Bell. 'All sorts of reports come in from Whitechapel. We take most with a pinch of salt.'

The private detective nodded his head and gazed about at the office. It was the office of the *Daily Rocket*, one of the capital's more sensational news-sheets. Its walls were papered with *front-page exclusives*. The high clerks' desks held tottering towers of papers. The rhythmic thrashing sounds of the letterpress had the room in a constant vibration. Newsboys came and newsboys went. There was an air of much busyness.

'There are rumours about some kind of magical goings-on.' Cameron Bell had to keep his voice raised to be heard. 'Commander Case gave an interview to your editor last night.'

'Would not know anything about it,' said the clerk.

Cameron eyed him carefully. 'Magic seems to be all the fashion nowadays,' he said. 'All manner of magical societies flourish here in the capital.'

'People don't believe in magic,' said the clerk. 'There's no news in magic.'

'So the business about magical goings-on in—'

'Whitechapel, yes, you said, and no, I do not know anything about any such thing.'

'Perhaps I might speak with your editor, then.'

'He has taken leave,' said the clerk. 'Gone away on a trip to the continent. He will not be back for some time.'

'Then whoever is standing in for him.'

'*I* am standing in for him.'

'And you have not heard—'

'Please, I will have to stop you there, sir. We are very busy, as you can see, preparing the evening edition. How do you like this for a headline?' He displayed a rough proof of a news-sheet front page:

LITTLE TICH
ATE MY
HAMSTER

'Splendid,' said Cameron Bell.

★

Outside, Fleet Street seemed almost peaceful by comparison. The open-topped horse buses with their colourful advertising signs, the gay parasols of the ladies, the glitter and sparkle of London alive. Cameron Bell loved it all.

'Excuse me, guv'nor.' A ragged-looking urchin tugged his trousers.

'On your way, my boy,' said Cameron Bell.

'No, guv'nor, I work for—'

Cameron Bell made observations of the ragged lad. 'The *Daily Rocket*,' said the detective. 'What do you want of me?'

'It's what I has to offer money-wise,' said the lad. Rubbing together the thumb and forefinger of his right hand in a suggestive fashion. 'I has something as you might want.'

'Go on then,' said the detective.

'I has the file,' said the lad.

Cameron Bell said, 'Go on then,' once more.

'When they took 'im away,' the ragged lad continued. 'They said as I was to dump the file in the furnace. But I didn't dump it, I hid it.'

'Enterprising boy,' said Cameron Bell. 'But who are *they*? And what are the contents of the file?'

'The *they*—' The grimy boy did furtive glancings to the left and right, then beckoned Cameron Bell to lower his head. 'The *they*,' he whispered, 'was two gentlemen in black. They took away the editor this morning.'

Cameron Bell took in this intelligence. 'And the file?' he asked in a measured fashion.

'What you was talking about with George the chief clerk. The magical goings-on in old Whitechapel.'

The large and ornate key turned in the chapel door with a satisfying click. The door did not even creak upon its hinges. Colonel Katterfelto breathed in the smell. Of incense and of candle wax, of ancient wood and mellow stone. Of prayer books and hassocks. As only a chapel can smell.

The colonel breathed it in again and nodded in approval.

'All it needs is a lick of paint,' said the managing agent. 'And as you can see it is deceptively spacious.'

Your remarks are certainly specious, thought the colonel. And gazing up at a stained-glass window that vividly depicted the martyrdom of Saint Sebastian, he asked, 'How much is the rent?'

'Five guineas per week,' said the managing agent.

'*Five guineas?*' roared the colonel. 'Damn it, man, I could lodge at the Ritz for less.'

'It has potential, you see,' said the managing agent. 'As a dosshouse. You could cram maybe one hundred in here of a night. At three pence a pop, you would come out with a clear two pounds profit a week. I worked it out myself upon a piece of paper.'

'Hmmph,' went the colonel, huffing and puffing away.

'There is other interest,' said the managing agent. But he knew and the colonel suspected that this was naught but a lie.

'Four pounds,' said the colonel, 'and not a penny more.'

The managing agent thought about this. 'We will call it four guineas,' said he.

'Four guineas a week, then, it is.' The colonel put his hand out for a shake. The managing agent shook it.

'Four shillings then, sir, and it's a deal,' said the ragged boy. Cameron Bell shook the grubby hand, then examined his own for cooties. The lad slipped into an alleyway beside the offices of the *Daily Rocket* and presently returned with something bundled up beneath his rags.

The exchange was made in silence and Cameron Bell took his leave.

In a nearby alehouse he ordered a pint of porter. That the sole contents of his stomach this day consisted of the two large whiskies that he had taken in the company of Sir Frederick Treves did not concern Cameron Bell. He had a hardy constitution and although of Pickwickian proportions tended to eat little more than one meal a day.

Taking himself, in the company of porter, to a quiet corner of the saloon bar, Cameron Bell began leafing through the contents of the file. Interesting contents they were.

There were written reports by 'concerned citizens' that Cabbalistic practices were rife in the East End and that these involved the sacrifice of Christian babies. Cameron Bell turned his nose up to this. Anti-Semitic nonsense, he considered. There were several photographs, which showed a number of curious symbols that had been scrawled upon walls. The late Mr Crowley could probably have interpreted those. Then there were the reports of missing persons. And as he slowly went through these, Cameron Bell found a creeping chill a-moving up his spine. Four young women had vanished. All of reported good character. All – Cameron Bell considered the word – *virgins*, he supposed. And a suspect had been seen lurking about near the locations where each of the young ladies vanished. A *suspect*? This suggested kidnapping. The suspect was described as tall, slim and well dressed in a high top hat and carrying a malacca cane. Witnesses agreed that there was an indescribable *something* about this fellow that 'fair put the wind up them'.

Cameron Bell removed his hat and applied his handkerchief to his naked pate. The figure who had escaped upon the flying platform fitted well the description.

The private detective swallowed porter. Tried to steady his nerves. He had felt that indescribable *something* and it had fair put the wind up him also.

'Whitechapel, then,' said Cameron Bell. 'Whitechapel it must be.'

'*Whitechapel?*' screamed Darwin the monkey. 'You've taken us rooms in Whitechapel?'

'Not rooms,' said Colonel Katterfelto. 'Not rooms, my dear fellow. An entire property. Deceptively spacious.'

Darwin the monkey shook his head. 'We should take lodgings in Mayfair,' was his opinion.

'When we both have accrued sufficient funds,' said Colonel Katterfelto, 'then we will dissolve our business partnership. You may go your way and I will go mine. But for now we must work together.'

Darwin made as thoughtful a face as he was capable of making. He did not really in his heart of hearts believe that the colonel would actually be able to energise his Mechanical Messiah. It was just the mad scheme of an otherwise good-hearted and basically sane individual. And *sufficient funds* would be *goodly funds* and Darwin yearned to live once more a life of luxury and excess.

'All right then,' said he. 'If Whitechapel it has to be, then Whitechapel it is.'

But in Whitechapel something evil lurked.

Something shaped as a man, but *not* a man.

Tall and slender and wearing a high top hat, it dwelt now in the deep shadow of an alleyway that led to Miller's Court. Where nine years earlier Mary Kelly, the last recorded victim of the infamous and uncaught Jack the Ripper, had been cruelly done to death.

Soundless and sinister, lost in the shadows, this thing of evil offered up strange sounds in a language that no human knew.

21

eturning to the Electric Alhambra
upon this morning had not been
one of Cameron Bell's original
intentions. But as he found himself
in need to do so for two specific
reasons, he did so.

Lord Andrew Ditchfield put on a
hopeful face at his appearance. 'You
have good news?' he implored, a-
wringing of his hands.

'In that a breakthrough is imminent,' said Cameron Bell,
'indeed, yes indeed.'

'In that my theatre can be reopened today?'

Cameron Bell made a so-so face at this. 'Two matters,'
said he. 'I need you to supply me with the address of Colonel
Katterfelto's theatrical diggings.'

'I suspected him all along,' said Lord Andrew. 'Seedy
fellow and that monkey of his is always up to no good.'

'He is not a suspect,' said Cameron Bell.

'The monkey might have done it.'

Cameron Bell did rollings of the eyes whilst Lord Andrew
Ditchfield sought the box file in which he kept the artistes'
P45s and personal details.

'I would ask,' said the private detective, 'that throughout

the duration that the theatre is closed you pay the wages of the artistes.'

Lord Andrew Ditchfield literally froze. 'Are you completely insane?' cried he, when he had found a voice to cry with. 'You are not one of these Bolsheviks that we've been reading about in the press lately, are you?'

'Certainly not,' said Cameron Bell.

'Then let us have no more of *that* nonsense.'

'Perhaps you might make an exception for *one* of the performers.'

Lord Andrew Ditchfield looked long and hard at Mr Cameron Bell. 'I am not a detective,' said he, 'but I would be prepared to wager that you allude to the glamorous trainer of kiwi birds.'

Cameron Bell flushed somewhat at the cheeks.

'The answer is no,' said Lord Andrew Ditchfield. 'And if you have made some promise to that flirty little dolly-mop, it will have to be raised out of your own pocket.'

Cameron Bell reddened somewhat at the cheeks.

'I face ruination!' cried Lord Andrew, similarly red. 'If the theatre is shut down, my creditors will close in upon me like a pack of wolves.'

'Perhaps you might hire another theatre in the interim,' suggested Mr Bell. 'You have the performers, you only need the premises.'

'No such available theatre exists in London. However—' Lord Andrew made a thoughtful face and rushed away, returning in the company of the morning's newspaper. Ignoring the front page, which had many sensational things to say about the death of Smelly Charlie Belly, he leafed through it until he found—

'Eureka!' cried Lord Andrew. 'Concert season cancelled due to sudden death.'

'Not another?' said Cameron Bell. 'Tell me not another ball of flames.'

'Old age,' said his lordship. 'Karol Mikuli, the famous concert pianist and conductor. He was booked for a season at the Crystal Palace.'

'The Crystal Palace?' said Cameron Bell.

'I will hire the Crystal Palace and move the Earl Grey Whistle Test show there. Music Hall at the Crystal Palace, it will be a sensation.'

'Then all is well that ends well, and meanwhile you can pay the performers—'

'No!' bawled Lord Andrew Ditchfield.

Cameron Bell said farewell and left without his hat.

As he left the lift at the ground-floor level he overheard the excited voice of a young bobby saying, 'But he said he was working on the case with you, Commander, which was why we let him in.'

Moving once more upon the lightest of feet, Cameron Bell slipped away.

Commander Case fumed quietly. He was after all a high-ranking officer of the Metropolitan Police Force and those who played silly blighters with him were wont to come to a grief that ended in Strangeways.

Commander Case had recruited the services of a young and impressionable constable to assist him with his investigations. A foil for the commander's wit. A whipping boy when things went poorly. The fellow to blame when things went terribly wrong. The young and impressionable constable had not been aware that such unhappy roles awaited him and had jumped at the opportunity of working with so exalted a figure as the commander.

'Constable Williams,' said Commander Case, as he and

the young constable strode in step down the centre aisle of the auditorium, 'fetch me a cup of tea, if you will, and bring it to wherever I happen to be.'

'Sugar?' said the constable.

'Don't be familiar,' said his commanding officer.

A church bell rang the midday hour. A dog howled in the distance.

The constable did scuttlings-off and the commander strode to the stage. Having assured himself that he was all alone, he let out a bit of a sigh. 'What can there be to this stuff?' he asked himself. 'This "show me a fellow's cufflinks and I'll tell you what he has for breakfast" stuff? It is only observation. There is no real trick to it. If Cameron Bell can do it, I am damn sure I can, too.'

He ran a finger along the brass rail that surrounded the hydraulically driven orchestra pit. 'The answers are all here somewhere,' he continued to himself. 'It is just a matter of rooting them out. And if a little fat man with a baldy head can do it, then—'

A little fat man with a baldy head raised his baldy head from the orchestra pit and grinned at Commander Case. 'Someone alluding to yours truly?' he asked.

'Oh my dear sir, no.' A somewhat rattled Commander Case stepped back in surprise.

'I know you,' said the baldy-headed fellow, wiping his hands upon an oily rag and sticking out the right one for a shake. 'You are the famous Commander Case. My name is Babbage, Charles Babbage.'

'Mr Babbage, *sir*.' Commander Case did bowings of the head and mighty handshakes also. 'Indeed a pleasure,' he continued. 'You are certainly a famous fellow, to be sure.'

'I have coined the term "backroom boffin",' said Mr

Babbage modestly. 'Chaps like you do the valiant stuff, I just tinker about.'

'It is most fortuitous that I should find you here.' The commander took out his cigarette case and selected from it a light blue cocktail cigarette that was the very latest thing. Slotted it into his mouth, offered the case to Mr Babbage, who declined it with the words, 'I'm a snuff man myself,' lit the cigarette and continued, 'I need to know all about the electrical gubbinry of this theatre and you are the man who can put me straight.'

A painful smile appeared upon the face of the backroom boffin. 'Rumours have reached my ears regarding the two horrible incidents here,' said he. 'That some kind of electrical malfunction might be the cause. You can accept my word as a gentleman that this is *not* the case.'

'One must never overlook any possibility.' The commander puffed upon his cigarette. Mr Babbage coughed and fanned at his face. 'Excuse me. But this is a very pickle of a case. Two star performers identically struck down in a most dramatic fashion.'

'Ray gun,' said Charles Babbage. 'If you were to ask my opinion, I would say that they were literally reduced to atoms by a ray gun of the Martian persuasion. They function through a transperambulation of pseudo-cosmic anti-matter, which causes a cross-polarisation of beta-particles resulting in—'

'That's easy for you to say,' said Commander Case, now coughing too upon his cigarette and viewing it with suspicion.

'New brand, is that?' asked Charles Babbage.

'Tastes appalling.' The commander made as to fling down the cigarette prior to stamping it out.

'Oh, please *don't*!' cried Mr Babbage, taking it carefully

from his fingers. 'You would not want to burn the carpet or spoil the polished floor, now would you?'

Commander Case gave his head a minor shake. 'Some kind of ray gun?' said he.

'To reduce a human being to ashes—' Mr Babbage carefully extinguished the cigarette in an appropriate receptacle '—requires an extremely high temperature and a prolonged period. These new electric crematoria take at least half an hour to consume a corpse. I understand that the unfortunate events here were all but instantaneous. Something beyond the everyday occurred, Commander Case. Something most unworldly.'

Alice Lovell woke to a world of sunlight. It fell upon her pretty face and on her golden locks. Alice Lovell gave a little yawn and then a stretch. Became momentarily startled by her new surroundings and then remembered all the events that had happened the previous night.

'I must do something nice for dear Cameron,' said Alice.

She peeped about the room that was now hers. It seemed slightly smaller than she remembered it. And the colours of everything now appeared so much brighter. The pastels of the bed cover were now all primaries. The formerly drab wallpaper fairly shone a vibrant yellow.

'Sunlight rather than gaslight, then,' said Alice.

Throwing back the covers and swinging out her legs, she was momentarily surprised by what she was wearing. The blue flannelette nightdress that she had worn as a child. She always carried it with her, but she had not worn it for years. She was surprised that it still fitted. She must have slipped it on the previous night without thinking.

'I must have been *very* tired, then,' said Alice.

Her bare feet touched a carpet which had a mossy feel and

her waking thoughts now turned towards her kiwi birds. She had slept long into the day and they would be wanting their breakfast.

'Something from Cameron's kitchen, then,' said Alice. And, 'A nice cup of tea for the baby girl,' she sang.

'I have a nice cup of tea for you,' said Constable Williams. 'But they did not have any sugar or milk, I'm afraid.'

Commander Case received the cup. 'Nor saucer either,' he said.

'Nor tea, I'm afraid, sir, so it's mostly water.'

Commander Case put the cup to his lips. 'It is *cold* water,' he said. 'This is a cup of cold water.'

'It is a mineral water,' said the constable. 'Full of goodness and loveliness too, I was assured.'

Commander Case was not one of those officers who allow life's vicissitudes to raise too many sighs. He drank the water, returned the cup, then smote the young constable.

'Ouch!' went Constable Williams.

'Clown,' said Commander Case.

'Would you care for me to show you the Nexus?' asked Charles Babbage, with much pride in his voice. 'So that you can see how very safe the electrical workings of this theatre are?'

'I would like that very much.' The commander turned to his young companion. 'And you will take notes,' he said.

They travelled with Mr Babbage inside the orchestra pit. Hydraulics hissed, cogs purred together, down and down they went.

'The Nexus is housed in a secure chamber to which only I have the key,' said the backroom boffin.

'And why so might this be?' Commander Case asked.

'A matter of national security. As all technical innovations are. Can't have foreigners finding out our secrets,' confided Mr Babbage. 'Between you, me and your young constable here, the Nexus is the most advanced and sophisticated piece of apparatus in all of the British Empire.'

'In a *Music Hall*?' asked Commander Case. 'Why in a Music Hall?'

'It seemed like the perfect environment.' Mr Babbage led his two guests along an electrically lit corridor towards a huge and imposing metal-bound door. 'The system is virtually self-regulating.' The backroom boffin took out a large key. 'It is a development of my Difference Engine. It automatically governs temperature, lighting, the condition of the air within the auditorium and can be programmed—'

'Programmed?' queried the commander.

'Issued with a series of commands, upon strips of punched paper. Made to perform a sequence of tasks without the need to be overseen and constantly managed by a human operative. You will find that when it comes to failures in mechanical technology, these failures are almost always the result of human error. A properly programmed machine will not make mistakes. It will simply perform its pre-programmed routine, step by step by step.'

Step by step, Alice descended the stairs. There really did seem to be a lot of them. Far more than she recalled from the previous night. But she had been *very* tired. At the foot of the stairs, Alice found herself confronting a number of doors. Rather too many doors? Alice spotted one that had the word PANTRY stencilled upon it in lively orange paint. She turned the handle and pushed the door before her.

★

Charles Babbage turned his key and pushed his door before him. Commander Case and Constable Williams gaped in undisguised awe at what lay beyond.

Alice stared into the pantry and awe appeared on *her* face.

Before the three men arose a vast and intricate machine.
   'Gentlemen,' said Charles Babbage, 'allow me to introduce you to the Harmonising Arithmetical Logisticator.'

Before Alice, and apparently doing some washing-up in the butler's sink, stood a large and well-dressed kiwi bird. Alice was too stunned to say anything.

'Good day, Mr Babbage,' said the Harmonising Arithmetical Logisticator.

'Good day, Alice,' said the kiwi bird.

22

'h no!' cried Alice, in much dismay. 'I am off with the fairies once again.'

The kiwi bird ceased its attempts at the washing-up. It was making no progress. What with having no hands and the most rudimentary of wings.

'I am sorry to startle you,' it said with politeness, 'but there are matters of great importance that I need to speak with you about.'

'Which way is the exit?' Alice Lovell asked. 'By rabbit hole or looking glass, I wish to return to my world.'

'And so you shall,' said the kiwi and it smiled.

Alice had never seen a kiwi bird smiling before and she thought it the prettiest thing.

'I could stay and talk to you for a short while,' said she. 'But I cannot stay long, for I must return to *my* kiwis.'

The kiwi bird nodded and said, 'Walk with me, Alice, and I will tell you why I have come to visit.'

'You have brought gentlemen to visit me,' said the Harmonising Arithmetical Logisticator. 'I see by the elder fellow's shirt cuffs that he holds a high rank in the London Police Force.'

Commander Case tucked in his cuffs. He was not having *that*.

'What trickery is this?' he asked Charles Babbage. 'Some stage magician's folderol, like the Mechanical Turk?'

'The Mechanical Turk,' said Charles Babbage, wistfully. 'That takes me back. Do you know that I saw that illusion when I was a child. A clockwork figure in the shape of a Turk that could beat all-comers at chess. I did not know at the time that the operator's assistant lurked within, moving the pieces. I thought it to be real. I then reasoned that if a machine could be made to play chess, another could be made to perform mathematical calculations. And so was born the Difference Engine.'

'Fascinating,' said Commander Case, his voice implying that he considered it otherwise. 'But a *speaking* machine – that is surely the province of Far-Fetched Fiction.'

They had entered the room now that housed the Great Nexus, and what a Great Nexus it was. There was much of the vast pumping engine at Kew to this construction. Much more of the workings of a musical box, hugely magnified. And there were a great many whirring brass ball-governors, pistons moving up and down, networks of cogwheels rattling round, belt-drives whirring endlessly. And atop all a brazen head that somewhat resembled its creator. The eyes in this head appeared to focus upon the visitors. The animated jaw moved rhythmically as the automaton spoke.

'So, fine joke,' said Commander Case. 'But how is it done, Babbage? Chap inside at the controls, I suppose.'

The backroom boffin shook his baldy head. 'It is fully automatic,' he said.

'Incredible,' said Commander Case.

Constable Williams said, 'Sir?'

'What is it, lad? Cannot you see I am talking with this gentleman?'

'I think the gentleman is not being entirely honest with you,' said the young constable.

Commander Case gave Mr Babbage a very hard look indeed.

The backroom boffin said, 'Much of it is electrical, of course. I have designed something I refer to as a logic circuit, which—'

'Honesty?' asked Commander Case, with his face very close to that of the famous inventor.

'I think the Harmonising Arithmetical Logisticator wants to say something,' said Charles Babbage, pointing towards the brazen head.

'By the looks of the young constable's elbows,' said the Harmonising Arithmetical Logisticator, 'he has all the makings of a French spy. He should wait upstairs whilst I engage in conversation with his handsome superior officer.'

Commander Case gave his shoulders a shrug.

'Please, sir,' said Constable Williams.

'Perhaps you should go and wait upstairs, lad.'

'No, sir, please. Mr Babbage is pulling the wool over your eyes, sir. He has some kind of speaking tube concealed in his sleeve and he is making the automaton's jaw move by pressing a button on the floor there with the toe of his right boot.'

'What of this?' cried Commander Case.

The backroom boffin made a guilty face.

The kiwi's face looked very jolly. Alice patted its head.

'Let us walk over the rooftops,' he said. 'Hold on to me tight and we'll fly.'

Alice put her arms about the bird's neck and held on ever so tightly. The kiwi bird, with no wings really to flap, simply rose from the pantry floor and floated from the room hauling Alice with him. They drifted up the staircase, with Alice observing that things were becoming 'curiouser and curiouser', then out through a fanlight and onto the roof.

'You can let go now,' said the kiwi bird, 'for you are all but throttling me.'

'Sorry,' said Alice. 'But why have we come up here?'

The kiwi bird shook its feathers about. 'Just look at that sky,' said he.

Alice looked up towards the sky. It was indeed a beautiful sky. But then, was it a *real* sky? And was she really on the rooftop looking up at it?

'Look,' said the kiwi, 'an airship.'

Alice looked up and saw it. 'What a pretty thing,' said she.

'Would you like to travel on it, Alice?'

'Oh, indeed I would,' said Alice. 'And if I ever marry some dashing young gentleman, I will have him take me away upon such an airship for our honeymoon.'

'What about a spaceship, then?' asked the kiwi bird.

'He would have to be a very rich gentleman indeed to pay for our passages aboard a spaceship.'

'Can you imagine what it would be like?' asked the kiwi bird.

'Oh yes,' said Alice. 'I have seen photographs in ladies' journals. There are cushioned seats in rich blue velvet. A games room with a Wif-Waf table and when you hit the ball it never falls to the floor but floats for ever in the air instead. And there is a dining salon where they serve foods from all over the Solar System and the views as you rise up from our world are said to be spectacular.'

'Like this, then, you would imagine?'

Alice found herself now to be sitting on a comfortable chair cushioned with rich blue velvet. Beside her was something resembling a ship's porthole, ringed by solid brass with many rivets.

Alice peeped through the porthole and saw the most wonderful sight. A sweeping arc of blue bisected the blackest of skies. This night-time sky was strewn with stars as Alice had never seen them before, each one a diamond or other rare jewel set in a black velvet heaven. The arc of blue she knew to be Earth, clouds lightly sprinkled above an ocean of turquoise.

The beauty brought tears to Alice's eyes. But she wept too for she knew it was all an illusion.

'The constable has caught me out. It is of course an illusion.'

Charles Babbage raised his left hand and spoke into his sleeve. 'I meant no offence,' said his voice, issuing from the brazen head. 'I confess that I feel considerable guilt when I deceive poor Lord Andrew Ditchfield with it. He believes that he possesses the only genuine *thinking machine* in the British Empire. Anywhere, in fact. I just cannot bring myself to shatter *his* illusion. I should have known better than to have tried it on with a sharp-eyed officer of the law, though.'

Constable Williams wore a smirk.

Commander Case did grindings of the teeth.

'So it is all stuff and nonsense,' said the commander.

'On the contrary, this machine literally manages the entire theatre. It lights the stage and shifts the scenery, it controls the temperature and quality of the air and a hundred other things besides. One day every great theatre will have a Harmonising Arithmetical Logisticator.'

'It has a somewhat unwieldy title,' observed Constable Williams. 'Perhaps you should shorten it.'

'I already have,' said Charles Babbage. 'Considerably.'

'You could use its initials,' the constable suggested. 'H. A. L. You could call it *Hal*.'

Charles Babbage thought about this. 'No,' he said. 'I think that would be silly.'

'This is all very wonderful,' said Alice, 'but all of course rather silly. I will never fly through the aether in a spaceship. I would like to return to my kiwis now.'

'There is something I need to say to you first, something you need to know.'

'Please tell me this,' said Alice. 'Am I dreaming? Or am I having some kind of magical experience, a vision or such-like? Or is this actually real, but in another reality that most people can never visit?'

'I cannot answer those questions,' said the kiwi. 'I was sent to give you a message. I thought I would make it enjoyable for you while I deliver it. As it is a rather gloomy message.'

'Who sent you?' asked Alice.

'It would surprise you very much if I told you. And frighten you just a little, too. So let me tell you what I must tell you and then you can return to your world and feed your kiwi birds.'

'All right, then tell me,' said Alice.

The kiwi nested himself onto the seat next to hers. 'It's about the magic,' he said. 'It has been brought to Earth. It should not have been. It was not supposed to have been. But an evil being took it and he brought it here. And it must be taken back before it does any more damage. And you must be the one to take it back. You have been chosen to be the one to take it back.'

Alice nodded her beautiful head. 'Whatever are you talking about?' she asked.

'I do not have time to waste, talking about nonsense names and party tricks.' Commander Case stamped his foot, which quite put the wind up the constable. 'Two men have died in balls of flame. Possibly three, counting the infamous Mr Crowley. But if there is any justice at all, God sent down a thunderbolt to deal with *that* individual. But the culprit, if one exists, must be brought to book.'

'If one exists?' queried Mr Babbage. 'I read your words well enough – you still have some utterly unfounded suspicions regarding—'

'*Hal*,' said Constable Williams.

'Be quiet,' said Commander Case. 'The answer to what happened will be found somewhere within this theatre. And I will find it, no matter how long it takes.'

'Have you rounded up all the Frenchmen in London?' asked Charles Babbage. 'That would be a start, at any rate.'

'Babbage?' said Commander Case. 'That is a French name, is it not?'

'Case derives from the Old French *cas*, meaning "a happening",' said Constable Williams, helpfully. 'Williams is Welsh, of course. And the Welsh *are* the true British.'

Commander Case struck down the British constable and stormed away to search for clues elsewhere.

'Magic comes from elsewhere.' The kiwi pointed with its beak towards the porthole. 'It does not originate upon Earth. There are planets where magic is part of everyday life.'

'Venus,' said Alice Lovell. 'I am told that Venusians use magic to make their spaceships work.'

'Yes, indeed, Venus,' said the kiwi. 'But not here upon the Earth.'

'But I have known magic,' said Alice. 'And I think I am experiencing it now.'

'I cannot explain everything to you now, but I will visit you again.' The kiwi tapped at Alice with its beak. 'The magical thing that has been brought to Earth must be returned to where it came from. You will play a part in this.' *Tap-tap-tap* went the kiwi's beak.

'Please don't do that,' said Alice.

'You will go on a very long journey.'

Tap-tap-tap-tap-tap.

'That really hurts,' said Alice. 'Please will you stop doing that.'

'A lot of horrid things will happen—'

Tap-tap-tap-tap-tap.

'But there will be a happy ending.'

Tap-tap-tap-tap-tap—

'Please stop doing *that!*' cried Alice.

And she awoke to find herself in the bedroom that she had settled into the night before, wearing the nightdress she had put on the night before and being peck-peck-pecked and tap-tap-tapped by several kiwi birds.

From downstairs came the sounds of breaking porcelain. The kiwi birds had somehow escaped from the outhouse and were wreaking havoc on the home of Cameron Bell.

23

arwin and the colonel lunched at The Spaceman's Club.

Darwin had some qualms about the menu.

Colonel Katterfelto tucked into a starter of

*Hummingbird Crème Fraiche
with purple basil*

A main course of

*Grilled Elephant Liver in a cinnamon gravy
Lightly fried White Tiger Steak with Marmot Ragout
Gorilla Goulash with chipped potatoes*

And a dessert of

Roly-poly pudding & treacle sponge bastard*

Darwin kept his head down and munched upon bananas. But joined the colonel in the brandy and cigars without

---

* *As populaised in the ever-green Music Hall song 'Treacle Sponge Bastard for Me, Please'.*

which no gentleman's meal could ever be successfully concluded.

Mark Rowland Ferris, the Fifth Earl of Hove, joined them at the table for a chat.

'I have no objection whatever,' he said to Colonel Katterfelto, 'to you representing this ape here as your nephew—'

The colonel all but choked upon his brandy.

'Steady on there,' said the Fifth Earl. 'I said I had no objection. If you have trained this little fellow to play Snap—'

He reached to tousle the little fellow's head.

The little fellow bared his pointy teeth.

'I have no objection at all. As long as you restrict your play to Jovians. I cannot have you out-Snapping any of the British members.'

'Would not think of such a thing.' The colonel puffed upon his cigar. 'Hardly sporting, *that*.'

'Quite so, then we understand one another. I do have to say that your *nephew* looks particularly well turned out today.'

And indeed Darwin did. He had earlier insisted that the colonel accompany him to a certain London tailoring establishment that Darwin had patronised during his more prosperous days. For he knew that they must still hold several suits of clothes he had ordered before his disastrous visit to the gaming tables of Monte Carlo.

Darwin now wore an elegant morning suit of black worsted wool, grey and white striped trousers with fitted tail-snood, black silk tie and matching socks, Oxford brogues and a shirt of Irish linen. He cut a considerable dash and to the first glance of most would have passed for a well-dressed midget. Albeit one sorely in need of a shave.

Indeed the clerk behind the desk at Coutts Bank,

Darwin's second port of call, hardly turned a brilliantined hair when the simian opened an account.

Darwin sucked upon his cigar. He did not like Mark Rowland Ferris. And he was happy enough when the Fifth Earl of Hove departed in the company of his three French bulldogs Ninja, Yoda and Groucho. Today these three French bulldogs all wore kilts.

The man and the monkey moved on to the Snap salon.

They were greeted jovially by the Jovians. Darwin ordered further brandy from a passing waiter and settled down to play.

The colonel took himself off to a wicker-bound steamer chair upon the terrace, sat himself upon it and continued with his cigar.

The vista was, as ever, one to inspire wonder. The capital of the Empire spreading in all directions. The historic buildings of mellow granite, stone and brick, crisply rendered by the sunlight. The crowded avenues and thoroughfares. The horse-drawn carriages, the new electric wheelers. The Tesla towers, the flying craft, the beauty of it all.

Colonel Katterfelto made a very thoughtful face. He was torn by certain contradictions. He loved London, and he loved the monarchy and the British Empire. He was loyal and he was true. And he wished no harm to come to anything he loved. Which left him where, exactly, regarding the construction of the Mechanical Messiah? This, the ultimate Marvel of the Modern Age, when imbued with life, would do *what*, exactly? The colonel wondered whether perhaps he had not thought all of this through properly. Would the Mechanical Messiah precipitate Armageddon and the coming of the Apocalypse? As the arrival of the Lamb of God was prophesied to do in the Book of Revelation? Colonel Katterfelto hoped not! That was *not* what he had in mind at all.

What he had in mind was that the Mechanical Messiah would put the world to right. That He would be recognised as *Heaven's Last and Best Gift to Mankind*. That a modern Utopia would be created. A Heaven upon Earth.

The colonel felt satisfied with this. *More* than satisfied. Mankind would certainly thank him for his tireless efforts. He might even receive a knighthood.

A Messiah, Utopia *and* a knighthood.

It did not get better than that.

The colonel's reverie was interrupted by the arrival of a particularly girthsome Jovian, whose presence on the terrace was not to be ignored.

The Jovian nodded towards the colonel.

'Joy be with thou,' he said, this being the traditional Jovian greeting.

'And more unto thee,' replied the colonel, who knew the traditional response.

A part of the Jovians' charm for the colonel lay in the way they spoke. Very much in the manner of Old Testament prophets. It had come as no surprise to those who spoke the Queen's English to discover that the Queen's English was the Universal Tongue, adopted by beings from all worlds so far discovered. Such was only to be expected, really. The Queen's English and 'civilisation' being hand in glove, as it were.

Certainly some spoke it with an accent so thick as to be hardly distinguishable, the Martians, for instance. And Venusians had a private language, *The Spiritual Tongue*, which they spoke only to each other. But Jovians carried on like Noah or Moses, whilst espousing no religion whatsoever. Although it did have to be said that there were subtle differences in nuance and syntax and things of that nature that marked them out from those holy fathers of old. Perhaps there was a hint of 'Yorkshire' to it.

'Wouldst thou mind if I park me bum on the sitter next to thou?' enquired the girthsome off-worlder.

The colonel expressed no preference one way or the other.

The Jovian lowered himself onto the adjacent seat. The wickerwork shrieked as if under torture. The Jovian settled with care.

'Art thou Katterfelto?' asked the Jovian.

'*Colonel* Katterfelto,' said the colonel.

'Doest thou pardon me.' The Jovian leaned over, to the accompaniment of much groaning wickerwork, and extended his big hand towards the colonel. 'Mingus Larkspur,' he said. 'Nowt but a lowly corporal in the Third Mounted Nunbuck.* Thou doest outrank me somewhat.'

'No ranks here,' said Colonel Katterfelto, shaking the outstretched hand. 'All brother travellers of the void. How d'ya know m'name, by the by?'

'Earl Ferris recommended thou to me.'

'Recommended?' The colonel tapped ash from his cigar into the fitted ash bowl of his seat. 'Recommended for *what*, might I ask?'

'As one that hast led a hunt.'

'*Big-game* hunt, d'you mean?' The colonel smiled and nodded as he did so.

'Big-game hunt 'pon Mars,' said Corporal Larkspur.

'Led more than a few,' quoth the colonel. 'Minimal fatalities generally.'

'Wouldst thou consider leading another?'

'Another?' Colonel Katterfelto thoughtfully stroked at his mustachios. There was certainly a thrill to a big-game hunt

* *Nunbuck – a six-legged Jovian horse of irascible disposition.*

180

that was to be found in no other sporting activity. But he was not as young as he had been and sometimes one had to move with speed to avoid a ferocious onrushing *something* that one has upset with an ill-aimed ray-gun burst.

'Interesting proposition,' puffed the colonel. 'Haven't been to Mars for some years now.'

Corporal Larkspur glanced around and about the terrace. Assured that he and the colonel were otherwise alone, he whispered, 'Not Mars, but Venus.'

'*Venus?*' Colonel Katterfelto added huffing to his puff. Then continued in hoarse whispers, saying, 'Can't hunt on Venus, old sport. Not permitted. Interplanetary treaty agreed with Her Majesty forbids it. Venusians take a very dim view of that kind of caper.'

'They forbid it,' agreed the Jovian. 'But may I showest thee something?' And from an ample pocket he produced a folded map. Which he unfolded. And displayed to Colonel Katterfelto.

'Map of Venus?' asked the colonel. 'Not seen one of those before.'

'Acquired as thou must imagine at a goodly price and after a right old struggle.'

'Quite so.' The colonel viewed the map with interest. 'Seems to be mostly forest and plain,' said he.

'Jungle,' whispered Corporal Larkspur. 'But here liest the thing. They knowest their world as Magonia.'

Colonel Katterfelto knew this.

'Their capital city is Rimmer.'

The colonel did not know *that*.

'There art five other cities. Enormous art they. But vastly doth the jungle cover the lands of Magonia. And sacred unto the people is it, such as they dare not enter, for such is sacrilege unto them. More power to our elbow, thusly.'

The colonel gave his mustachios a further thoughtful stroke. 'There was an expedition,' said he, 'some years back. Big-game hunt led by an old chum of mine. Major Thadeus Tinker. Lost in jungle? Murdered by Venusians? Never came back to tell.'

'I knowest.' The Jovian refolded his map. 'Such a venture requirest great bottle and wouldst be rewarded by great wonga.'

Bottle and wonga? queried the colonel. But he gathered the gist.

'Expensive expedition to mount,' he said. 'How many in the hunting party?'

'Twelve,' replied the Jovian. 'Thou, I, ten hunters that payest handsomely.'

'And I would lead the party? Be in charge?'

'As thou wisheth it,' replied the Jovian.

'And the remuneration?'

'Ten thousand English pounds,' the corporal suggested.

'*Ten thousand pounds?*' Colonel Katterfelto grew breathless at the thought of such a fortune.

Corporal Larkspur, misinterpreting this breathlessness, said, 'Let us say twenty thousand then, if thou wilt.'

The colonel all but swallowed his cigar.

'Guineas then,' said the Jovian. 'Thou art a gentleman, of course. And dealest only in guineas.'

The colonel coughed and spat out his cigar. Which sailed over the terrace and down to the capital below. Where it would fall upon a lady in a straw hat, who having read the papers regarding the HYDE PARK CORNER MAS-SACRE would take it to be an aerial attack by the unwholesome Johnny Frenchman and get into an affray with a seller of horsehair biscuit that would lead to her subsequent arrest.

The Jovian patted the colonel's back.

The colonel shook the Jovian by the hand.

'I will lead the hunting party,' said the colonel. 'The expedition will take considerable time to organise. Need copious provisions. Appropriate firearms. All and sundry et cetera.'

'We leavest in two days' time,' said the Jovian.

The colonel all but exploded. 'Can't be done, my dear fellow,' he croaked. 'Take months of planning.'

'The ship is provisioned. For verily thus and so have I laboured these many months upon this expedition.'

'Humph,' humphed Colonel Katterfelto. 'But left it to the very last minute to employ the services of one who would lead the hunting party.'

'Not quite thusly so.'

'Ah,' said the colonel. 'I get the picture. Pulled out at the eleventh hour, did he? Turned from fox to rabbit? Not a military man, I'll wager.'

'A Venusian,' said the Jovian.

'Well, local knowledge will always be a big plus. Got cold feet in the end, though, did he?'

'There was an accident. And sadly did he goeth on to his death.'

'London roads can be treacherous,' said the colonel. 'Have to know your left hand from your right.'

'An electrical accident,' said the corporal.

'Wet fingers,' said the colonel. 'Must not touch the socket with wet fingers.'

'He exploded,' said the corporal. 'For verily had he retired as a huntsman, due unto an injury that felleth onto his hand. And lo he had taken unto himself a new profession here upon Earth. Disguised as an Englishman. Which art no small feat for a Venusian, but 'appen he did pulleth it off.'

'What was the name of this cove?' asked the colonel.

'Harry "Hurty-Finger" Hamilton,' said the Jovian corporal.

24

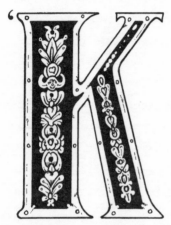'iwis are cantankerous birds,' said Alice as she chased the fleet-footed vandals around the house. 'Wilful creatures, too,' she continued, as one dashed between her legs and upset a jardinière stand, causing an aspidistra pot to shatter on the marble floor of the hall.

'Oh please,' cried Alice. 'Return to the outhouse or we shall be forced to sleep upon the street.'

Amidst much cajoling and the employment of the stout stick that Cameron Bell kept in his umbrella stand for the purpose of belabouring Jehovah's Witnesses, the boisterous birds were returned at length to the outhouse, and the door bolted firmly upon them.

'And no breakfast for you today, bad birds,' said Alice.

The damage was considerable. Alice did her best to tidy up, but tidying up was not really something that she excelled at. It was not something that she had practised with rigour. She found a broom and pushed it around a bit and then discovered a news journal on the hall table and felt the need to improve herself by sitting down to study it.

She read a bit about cake-making and this recalled to her

that she had taken no meals as yet this day and was in fact most hungry.

Alice took herself to the kitchen. And here she achieved both coffee and toast and, pleased with these achievements, sat herself at the kitchen table to eat and read the rest of the journal.

The cries of horror that came from the hall were an irksome interruption.

'My home.' The raised voice was that of Cameron Bell. 'Those damnable birds have wrecked my home. Destroyed my priceless heirlooms.'

Alice rose from the table and put her head around the kitchen door. 'Welcome home, Cameron,' she called.

Cameron's mouth made goldfish impersonations. 'It is four in the afternoon. My house is destroyed. You are not dressed. And you are—' Cameron sniffed at the air. 'Dining on coffee and toast.'

'I think you must have forgotten to bolt the outhouse door,' said Alice. 'But they are in now and all bolted safely. A few things did get a little knocked about, I am sorry.'

'*Sorry?*' Cameron's face had now become purple. He flung down his hat and, quite beyond reason, jumped up and down upon it. 'You . . . you . . . you . . .' he went, utterly lost for words.

Now Alice's mother had taught her as a child, as all mothers teach their daughters, that when they are grown up and faced with a situation that might reflect poorly upon them, two options existed.

The first was to 'blame others'.

Alice had, in her fashion, just taken up that option, without success, it would appear.

The second of the two and by far the more effective was to 'look helpless and whimper'.

Alice made a helpless face and burst into a mighty flood of tears.

'Oh dear lady, please.' Mr Bell ceased stamping on his hat. He pulled out a fresh pocket handkerchief and stepped towards the poor distressed young thing. 'I did not mean to make you cry,' he continued, offering her the hankie to sniff upon. 'A few trifling antiques. A few irreplaceable family heirlooms. But at least no harm came to you.'

Alice sobbed and sniffed into the hankie.

'Come,' said Cameron. 'Back into the kitchen. Sit yourself down, I will pour you another cup of coffee.'

'Could you boil me an egg, please, to go with my toast?' asked Alice.

'I've something to ask you, dear fellow,' said Colonel Katterfelto.

He and Darwin were back in the bar of The Spaceman's Club.

Darwin had enjoyed a most successful afternoon's Snapping, but had been forced to retire from the table due to the overconsumption of brandy, which had somewhat slowed his technique. He was sobering up now upon champagne and a bowl of exotic fruit.

'Opportunity's come up,' said the colonel, lighting another cigar. 'Financial opportunity. Not to be sniffed at. Question is whether you're up for it.'

Darwin hiccupped and almost got a grape into his mouth.

'Big-game hunt,' whispered the colonel. 'Some Jovian cove willing to fork out twenty thousand guineas if I lead a hunting party. All live happily on that kind of wonga, what d'you think?'

'Wonga?' queried Darwin. Then, '*Twenty thousand*

guineas?' went the ape. The sum having something of a sobering effect.

'Take years here to earn that sort of loot,' the colonel continued. 'But the choice is yours. We can dissolve our partnership now. You take today's winnings and carry on as you will. Or accompany me on the hunt and take ten thousand guineas. Deal's a deal. Hands shaken and all that kind of business. Officer and gentleman, me, you know the drill. Regrettably be forced to break my contract with the Electric Alhambra. Not too regrettably, though, eh? What with the thrown fruit and all. So what d'you say then, Darwin?'

Ten thousand guineas? Many thoughts went through the monkey's head. A sum like that would set him up for life. But a big-game hunt? The lunchtime menu had been a fearful enough thing in itself. But to witness fellow wild-life being blasted down by hunters? That was above and beyond just viewing some meat on a plate. But, ten thousand guineas . . .

'Take your time,' said the colonel. 'Big decision. Best to think it through.'

'Will we be travelling by airship?' asked Darwin, who did not relish the thought of another overseas flight. His experiences aboard the ill-fated *Empress of Mars* still reasonably fresh in his mind.

'Spaceship,' whispered the colonel. 'Big-game hunt upon Venus.'

Darwin made a smiling face. 'A trip on a spaceship,' said he.

'Once-in-a-lifetime experience,' said the colonel. 'Or not, as in my case. But not something most folk get a crack at. Province of the wealthy and things of that nature generally.'

'I accept,' said Darwin and he put out his hand for a shake.

The colonel shook it warmly. 'Glad you're coming,' he said. 'Grown rather fond of you, must confess. Never had children of my own. Lonely life, really.'

The monkey looked up at the man. 'I would ask a favour,' he said.

'Anything, my dear fellow. Name it and it is yours.'

'I want to pilot the spaceship, please,' said Darwin.

'I wish to hire the Crystal Palace, please.' Lord Andrew Ditchfield spoke into a complicated contraption composed of valves and items that resembled brass ear-trumpets. It was a device designed to communicate words across a distance of miles without the need for cables. The wireless transmission of words, as it were. A marvel of the modern age designed by Lord Nikola Tesla.

Words accompanied by a fair degree of electrical hissings and poppings were returned to Lord Andrew through the medium of an identical device housed at the Crystal Palace. Words to the effect that this mighty edifice would be at his disposal as of the following evening. Monies were spoken of, a verbal agreement was made. Lord Andrew bade his fare-wells, flicked switches and smiled as the room returned to its silence.

He had not, from the very first, been entirely honest with Mr Cameron Bell. It was a matter of pride, really. Of ego. He liked it to be known that he owned the Electric Alhambra – in fact he lied about this to all and sundry on a daily basis. But he did *not* own the Electric Alhambra. The state-of-the-present-art Music Hall, with its luxurious auditorium and wonderfully vocal Harmonising Arithmetical Logisticator, was in fact the property of a millionaire indus-trialist who chose not to have his name associated with the

Music Hall, no matter how glorious its interior, or miraculous its Logisticator. The name of the millionaire industrialist was Mark Rowland Ferris and he was the Fifth Earl of Hove. He was also, as it happened, the owner of the Crystal Palace. The former owner having gambled it away at the Snap table of The Spaceman's Club. There had been no monkey involvement upon that occasion, but it *was* the Fifth Earl who dealt out the cards.

'Perhaps I should take this as an omen,' said Lord Andrew to himself. 'The Crystal Palace seats ten thousand. To manage the Crystal Palace, with its classical concerts and gala affairs, would have considerably more cache than managing the Electric Alhambra, no matter how swank its interior. Although folk do think I own it. Perhaps they might be persuaded to believe I own the Crystal Palace.'

Lord Andrew smiled as he thought about all the glamorous opera-singing ladies who appeared at the Crystal Palace. He glanced over to the item of furniture across the room which he referred to as the Casting Chaise. Things would work out for the best, he felt sure. But one thing he most sorely needed now was a brand-new bill-topper for tomorrow night's show.

This *did* create a problem.

The untimely and unpleasant deaths of the last two bill-toppers were not going to inspire confidence from other bill-toppers of the capital. The likelihood of getting one at such short notice was problematic enough, and with artistes being so superstitious, who would care to step up and risk being unlucky number three?

No one I can think of, thought Lord Andrew. Little Tich, George Robey and the like would not agree. Even for large money and a chance to play at the Crystal Palace. There was only one thing for it really and that was to promote one of the performers on the existing playbill. Elevate them to the number-one slot.

Lord Andrew brought a playbill from his desk drawer and perused it. Colonel Katterfelto? No, not him, he would remain at the bottom of the bill to dodge the fruit and veg. Who then? The Travelling Formbys? Too many of them, they would all demand top pay. The jugglers? No. Peter Pinkerton? There was something about Peter Pinkerton that annoyed Lord Andrew, although he did not know what. So who then? Who was left?

'Ah,' said Lord Andrew Ditchfield and his gaze strayed once again towards the Casting Chaise. 'A little someone who has yet to entertain me fully. I will contact the printers at once and have them run up posters and playbills for tomorrow night. In fact I will rename the entire show, I can see it now.'

And Lord Andrew could. The playbill read –

Lord Andrew Ditchfield presents:

THE GENTLEMEN'S FAVOURITE

ALICE
at the
PALACE

Starring Alice Lovell and her
Acrobatic Kiwi Birds

190

Unaware of neither her impending elevation to stardom nor indeed the threat of an assault upon her virtue, Alice sat in Cameron's kitchen, enjoying not only boiled eggs upon toast, but tasty fried bacon and sausage as well.

'You are such a kind gentleman,' she said, between vigorous munchings. 'Such a kind friend, Cameron.'

Cameron Bell was engaged in mental calculations as to just how large the financial depletions of this estate had become with the loss of so many treasured articles.

'I will be sorry to see you go,' he said. And he meant this, too, for he was in love with Alice Lovell.

'Go?' asked Alice, chewing as she did so. 'Where would I be going to?'

'The Electric Alhambra is to be closed indefinitely, as you know, but Lord Andrew has hired a new venue for the show.'

'Most if not all are within a cab ride from here.'

'Not this one,' said Cameron Bell. '*I* suggested it to Lord Andrew, actually.' Sometimes Mr Bell hated himself for the words of untruth that he spoke. But he just could not help it. They just came out. 'You will be playing at the Crystal Palace,' he said.

'*The Crystal Palace?*' Alice spat her afternoon breakfast all over Cameron Bell. 'Oh, I am *so* sorry. But the Crystal Palace? Did you really say the Crystal Palace?'

'I really *did*,' said Cameron Bell. 'But perhaps you could remain lodged here. Take the train each day to Sydenham. Your kiwi birds could take lodgings in the grounds of the palace. They would enjoy it there.'

Alice thought about this proposition. And smiled sweetly as she did so.

Then, 'No,' she said. 'I will take diggings in Sydenham.

This is the most wonderful day of my life and I have *you* to thank for it.'

'It was *nothing*,' said Cameron Bell, blushing somewhat.

'What can I do to thank you?'

'Nothing, dear lady.' Cameron smiled.

'Nothing,' said Alice, smiling too. 'Well, that is *something* indeed. Because there is literally nothing that I would not have done to play at the Crystal Palace.'

Cameron Bell bit hard upon his lip.

Alice danced off to get dressed.

25

ife can, it seems, at times become so very complicated. Colonel Katterfelto would, in a way, have preferred to simply tick along at the Electric Alhambra. Spend afternoons at The Spaceman's Club watching Darwin Snap. And occupy his mornings in the construction of the Mechanical Messiah, within the abandoned chapel that he now rented.

This big-game hunting trip had put the tiger in amongst the chickens and no mistake. Less than two days to get ready for *that* and what of the Great Quest in the meanwhile?

After all, he might be away upon the hunting trip for weeks, months even. He really should have discussed that with Corporal Mingus Larkspur. He had, however, got an advance from the adventurous Jovian. And this the colonel sought to spend wisely.

Upon the Great Quest.

Upon the creation of . . .

The Mechanical Messiah.

So, yes, life could at times become very complicated, but there were some days, some *very* special days, when things fell so perfectly into place that anyone could be forgiven for believing that a Divine Purpose lay at the heart of it all. For Colonel Katterfelto, *this* would be one of those days.

He bathed and dressed, eschewed a breakfast, and made off from his diggings. Eight-thirty of the morning clock found him in the back of an electric wheeler and on the road to Alperton.

'Don't drive out to Alperton too often,' called the driver back to him.

The colonel considered this a statement that did not require an answer.

'Had an aunt once in Park Royal,' called the driver. 'Don't know whose aunt she was, though, but I had her all the same.'

'Are you a married man?' asked the colonel.

Words of explanation followed and thereafter the journey to Alperton continued in silence. But for the purring of cogwheels and sounds of late larks singing in the trees.

Alperton was a pleasant enough little village. Although the engineering works tended to dominate the skyline. Throwing much of Alperton into shadow during the afternoon. The villagers did not complain about this, for they were all employed by the engineering works. The words

FERRIS ENGINEERING

were picked out imaginatively in electrical vacuum bulbs upon high. Which must have brought comfort to the villagers at night. Above the double-gated entrance ran a legend in scrolled ironwork to the effect that work would make you free.

The electric wheeler stopped outside the double-gated entrance.

'Do you want me to wait for you, guv'nor?' asked the driver.

The colonel nodded. 'I think that would be for the best.'

'I'll want paying now for the journey here and five bob waiting time, in advance, in case you change your mind.'

'I will not change my mind.' The colonel paid for the outgoing fare and grudgingly parted with a further five shillings.

The driver of the electric wheeler waited patiently while the colonel passed through the gateway. Then put his vehicle into gear and drove straight back to London.

Colonel Katterfelto had words with the gatekeeper and was directed to the sales office.

The sales office was a triumph of decorative metalwork. Panels depicting the dignity of labour were elaborately crafted in various metals. Gilded steel columns supported a ceiling on which a fresco, dedicated to commerce, was colourfully featured. At the very centre of this, the smiling face of Mark Rowland Ferris, Fifth Earl of Hove, beamed down blessings upon all and sundry. Behind a desk of trellised copper sat a gentleman wearing a brass top hat with fitted goggle attachments. He bowed with his head and gestured with an artificial arm towards a vacant aluminium chair.

The colonel sat down upon it.

'The Ferris Engineering Works of Alperton welcomes you,' said the gentleman in the brass top hat. 'And what might we do to add pleasure to your day?'

'I wish to place an order for something,' said the colonel. 'It is a private project and must be handled with discretion.'

'Absolutely no problem at all, sir.' The brass top-hatter spoke in a confidential tone. 'It is a fate that awaits us all when we reach a certain age.'

'Excuse me?' said the colonel.

'Down below.' The brass-hatter gestured with his artificial arm to an area just below his waist. 'We can fit you out with a pneumatic prosthesis so lifelike in appearance that your lady wife won't know the difference.'

'How *dare* you!' cried the colonel. 'And I have no lady wife.'

'Ah.' The brass-hatter now added a lewd wink to go with his artificial arm gesturings. 'All is in complete confidentiality here, sir. Should Mr Oscar Wilde himself come in for a fitting, we would not turn him away.'

Colonel Katterfelto reached towards his ray gun. 'I'll shoot you dead, you scoundrel,' he declared.

'But not in the heart, I'll wager, sir.' The sitter at the desk opened his shirt to reveal a large metal plate apparently bolted into the flesh of his chest. 'Lost both heart and arm in the Martian campaign,' said he.

'You were in the service of Her Majesty?' asked the colonel. Slightly less furious now.

'Queen's Own Electric Fusiliers,' said the fellow with the artificial parts. 'And you a colonel in the same by your uniform.' He saluted with his ersatz limb, nearly putting his eye out.

'At ease,' said the colonel. 'And enough of this nonsense. Don't need any private parts refurbishing. Need a piece of construction work done. A metal figure. Clockwork minstrel kind of jobbie.'

'Well, certainly, sir. We specialise in that sort of thing. Stage magicians' illusions. Clockwork marionettes.'

'Know you do,' said the colonel. 'That's why I'm here. Need a job doing and doing well. Know you're the chaps to do it.'

'Do you have the plans with you, sir?'

'Certainly do.' The colonel drew Herr Döktor's book from a jacket pocket. Hesitated a moment. 'Complete confidentiality?' he said.

'Absolutely, sir. Discretion our watchword. Customer satisfaction our rule of law.'

'There then, take the thing. Don't have time to mess about having a bit made here and a bit made there. Need you to make the lot. Plans in the back. Think you're up to the job?'

The brass-hatted fellow took the book from the colonel. It was all but falling to pieces now, but the plans for the construction of the Mechanical Messiah were still clear enough.

'Ah,' said the brass-hatted sales manager. 'We haven't had an order for one of these in a while.'

'What?' puffed the colonel. 'What?'

'I understand they were quite the rage when the book first came out. Before my time, though. Back in the days when old Mr Ferris the Fourth Earl ran the company. Sort of went out of fashion, you know. Used to come with a companion piece. The Automated Mary, that was the more popular model.'

'Wellington's boots!' went the colonel. 'So I'm not the first at this?'

'Heavens no, sir. If you want a Mechanical Messiah making, you come to us.' The fellow now affected a smirk. 'You will never guess what,' he said. 'I had word, on the old engineering jungle drums, as it were, that not so long ago a chap in America had one run up. Employed various engineering works in Wormcast, Arizona. They made a right pig's ear out of it and the fellow concerned was run out of town. Makes you wonder what it's all about, doesn't it?'

The colonel ground his teeth together. 'It certainly *does*,' said he.

'But anyway. Absolutely no problem at all. We can have this all assembled for you in a couple of weeks.'

'All assembled?' The colonel gave a thoughtful nod. 'Thought I would have to do the assembling.'

'We provide a *complete* service, sir.'

'And the cost?' asked the colonel. 'What about the cost?'

'Seven hundred and fifty pounds, sir. Which would include packing and delivery. Within the London area, of course.'

'Of course,' agreed the colonel. 'And I have the money with me.'

And he *did* because he *had* got the advance from Corporal Mingus Larkspur.

'I will give you the address it is to be delivered to and the key to the premises. I will be away for a while. I will pick the key up from you when I return.'

'Absolutely splendid,' said the man in the brass top hat. 'But there is one thing that we must get altogether straight. Because it is our policy to please the customer. And we would not have you get all disappointed later and demand your money back.'

'Make yourself clear,' said the colonel.

'Well, sir must understand that the Mechanical Messiah will not actually work. It is a purely decorative item. An inspirational item. It cannot be imbued with life. It will not do anything at all.'

'Well,' said the colonel. But he said no more.

'You see,' the sales manager tapped his artificial fingers onto his metallic desktop, creating a kind of xylophone effect, 'and please do not think that I am an expert in such matters. It is only that I heard all about it from my predecessor, when the Mechanical Messiahs were all the rage. But folk tried to energise them and when they could not, they came here demanding their money back.'

'I won't be doing *that*,' said the colonel.

'Splendid, splendid. You could say it's a basic design flaw really, but without the missing component the Mechanical Messiah could never be energised.'

'Missing component?' The colonel was intrigued.

'Again, don't quote me on this, sir, but it is something to do with magic and magic not functioning upon this world. That Earthly metals cannot carry magic. You will note that the plans for the Messiah figure show an empty compartment in the chest.'

The colonel nodded at this. He was aware of the empty compartment. Although up until now he had not discussed it with anyone.

'The component has to go into the empty compartment, sir.' The artificial hand tapped at the artificial heart.

'A mechanism, do you mean?' asked Colonel Katterfelto.

'No, merely a piece of metal, or more rightly a piece of mineral matter. To carry the magic, as it were.'

'And can you supply *that*?' asked the colonel.

'Oh no dear no, sir.' Laughter was now to be heard. 'We deal here in purely Earthly metals. The component is not of this world. It carried magic because where it is to be found, magic would appear to be commonplace. The mineral in question is called *Magoniam*. But as no human being has ever seen a piece, let alone touched a piece, it is neither here nor there.'

The colonel's face now suddenly shone. As if he had just received Enlightenment, which in fact he *had*.

'So I will have to ask you to sign a disclaimer,' said the

sales manager, 'stating that you are aware that the item we will construct for you will be absolutely non-functional.'

The colonel rose as one who had reached apotheosis. This was all fate. It had to be. Him coming here and hearing this. It had to be the very Will of God. A Divine Purpose lay at the very heart of it. There could be no other explanation. 'This mineral,' he said in a still, small voice. 'This energising agent, as it were, that will carry magic—'

'*Magoniam*, yes?' said the chap in the brass top hat. 'I understand, but again do not quote me, that it literally lies all over the ground, there for the picking up, as it were. Not that any human being ever will pick it up.' And he laughed again. 'Not unless they fly to Venus. And that's not very likely, is it, now?'

26

eautifully reconstructed, from the ground up, after its complete destruction during Worlds War Two, the Crystal Palace did what it was good at and dazzled in the English summer sun.

Proud atop Sydenham Hill, it gazed down upon the rolling lawns, ornamental fountains, floral clocks and flower gardens that led a leisurely way towards the spaceport.

The Royal London Spaceport.

The spaceport of the British Empire, the only spaceport on Earth. Here craft from Venus and Jupiter rested. Bloated Jupiterian packets with swollen hulls and bulbous parts lolled upon the cobbled landing strip. Whilst fey Venusian aether ships, rising like ghostly galleons, seemed tethered, as though a gentle breeze might waft them all away.

And then there were the flagships of the Empire. Some restored, remodelled Martian craft, put to service for the Crown. Their hulls made colourful with painted Union Jacks. Others new, the pleasure vessels of wealthy folk. Manufactured, under licence and using the technology of Mars, by entrepreneurs who knew where the future lay.

In the colonisation of distant worlds. And in their exploitation, too.

These pleasure craft were marvellous affairs. Part Crystal Palace, part airship, part grand hotel. Sleek and silver, tattooed with the flag of Empire. Her Majesty's Ships of Space.

The largest of these, and indeed the most luxuriously appointed, was HMSS *Enterprise*. The very first spaceship built upon Earth, the one against which all future spacecraft would be judged.

A triumph of British engineering, it truly was a marvel of the modern age.

It was *not*, however, the craft that Corporal Mingus Larkspur had chartered for the space-treaty-breaking journey to the planet Venus.

This was a slightly more basic affair, lacking the dining halls, ballrooms and Wif-Waf courts of HMSS *Enterprise*. This was one of the original Martian ships of war. Back-engineered by Lord Nikola Tesla and Sir Charles Babbage and then employed in the top-secret transportation of terminally ill victims of disease. Dispatched to Mars, under the authority of Mr Winston Churchill, to infect the population of the Red Planet and ensure that no more attacks would be made upon Earth. A shameful episode (although, it might be argued, a shrewd one) that would never be recorded in any annals of the British Empire.

The ship had subsequently been fumigated and then served for a while as a military vehicle, transporting battalions of the Queen's Own Electric Fusiliers to Mars. These stalwarts were sent to engage in 'mopping-up operations', but as they found the Martians dead to a Martian-man, they spent their time behaving badly and laying waste to indigenous wildlife. And thus the big-game hunt on Mars was born. And thus was the history of this particular craft, from that day to this. A sturdy basic model with no frills for roughty-toughty fellows of a sporting disposition who sought exotic trophies for their study walls.

And so the Crystal Palace glittered in the sun, the trim lawns twinkled, sweet flowers bloomed, fountains tossed rainbows to the sky and spacecraft sprawled upon the landing strips. Another summer's day in Sydenham.

The horse broke wind and Cameron Bell was forced to cover his nose for the umpteenth time. Alice Lovell tittered behind him; her kiwi birds in their travelling cage made rebellious sounds.

Cameron Bell was not a natural driver of a horse and he knew full well he should never have allowed himself to be talked into hiring the horse and trap to take Alice Lovell on a day trip to Sydenham to become acquainted with the environs and acquire suitable lodgings for herself and her avian charges. It was afternoon now, and although they had enjoyed a charming lunch at the Crystal Palace, at Cameron's expense, and a later tea in a Sydenham tea room, also, of course, at his expense, and done an awful lot of walking about and looking at flowers, no theatrical diggings of a suitable nature had presented themselves.

Cameron Bell was not *too* saddened by this, as it meant that the lovely Alice Lovell might well end up staying a few more days at his house. On the proviso, naturally, that her outrageous birds would *not*.

But for Cameron Bell, the private detective, the day had been utterly wasted. There were numerous lines of inquiry he wished to follow up. And certain theories were forming in his marvellous mind.

Cameron Bell smiled painfully back at Alice Lovell.

'I do not think you should have fed this horse that choc-olate at lunchtime,' he said.

Alice giggled prettily and Cameron, gazing at her, looked with love.

But just what was he to make of Alice? She had been in his company long enough for him to draw many con-clusions, not all of them complimentary, but none that drastically affected his feelings for her. He had looked long and hard upon her shoes and apparel and drawn from these the better part of her life's history. Where she had been brought up and schooled and with whom she had lived. There were curious depths, too, that the detective could not fathom. Missing areas of time, when it might have appeared that Alice had simply vanished from this world to enter some other. Cameron Bell could divine this from the lace cuffs of her childhood nightdress.

'What are you dreaming about?' asked Alice.

'Only you,' the smitten man replied. And then, gathering himself, he said, 'I have an idea. I suggest we return to the village.'

Alice twirled her parasol. 'Whatever you say, kind sir,' said she.

The village of Sydenham owned to a single hotel. The Adequate. And upon arrival there, Cameron was hardly surprised to see a number of theatrical artistes checking in. The Travelling Formbys. Peter Pinkerton. Colonel Katter-felto and his monkey. Word had been passed by messenger from Lord Andrew that the artistes must take themselves immediately to Sydenham for tonight's first night at the Crystal Palace.

The logistics of moving an entire Music Hall troupe, complete with scenery and props, to a new location all in a single day, might to an outsider, one not of the theatrical persuasion, have seemed an impossibility. But the theatre owed much to its predecessor, the travelling show or circus. And up-sticking and moving on at the hurry-up was simply something it did. When needs must and the Devil drove and all that kind of business.

Cameron Bell spied out the colonel and recalled that he meant to have words with this gentleman regarding the mysterious crystal that Mr Bell had recovered from the body of the enigmatic creature he had shot. Before it, in turn, was recovered by the gentlemen in black.

'You will take a room here,' the private detective told Alice.

'But we already came here,' replied the lovely girl, 'and they made it more than plain that they would not take my kiwi birds.'

'Your kiwi birds will take lodgings elsewhere.'

'At your house?'

'*Not* at my house, but across the street.' Mr Bell pointed and Alice followed the direction of this pointing.

'It is a pet shop,' she said. 'I have no wish to sell my kiwi birds.' And this was *mostly* true, although Alice was beginning to find caring for the kiwi birds a trying experience. Not that she did not love them. But . . .

'I am not suggesting that you sell them,' said Cameron Bell. 'Merely that you offer them to the proprietor to exhibit in his front window during the day.' And here Cameron Bell was suddenly struck by a thought. 'Are not kiwi birds nocturnal?' he asked. 'Yours seem to keep the most un-natural hours.'

'Time is twelve hours different in New Zealand,' said Alice, and that was all the explanation Cameron Bell was getting. And so he continued:

'You will inform the pet shop proprietor that these birds

are the star turn at the Crystal Palace.' Cameron Bell ground his teeth somewhat at this. He and Alice had arrived in Sydenham to find the posters advertising ALICE AT THE PALACE already up. And whilst Alice herself had engaged in some kind of female convulsive expression of joy at this, Cameron Bell had seen in his mind's eye a dire headline which read

ANOTHER MUSIC HALL HORROR
ALICE LOVELL
THIRD IN HIDEOUS DEATH TOLL

Cameron Bell continued, 'You will tell the proprietor that you are willing to *rent* the birds to him during the day on the condition that he looks after them during the night.'

'How very clever of you,' said Alice, folding her parasol. 'What a very clever man you are, dear Cameron.'

Not as clever in matters of love as I truly wish I was, thought the love-struck Mr Bell. 'Go now,' he said to Alice, 'whilst I arrange a room for you at the Adequate.

'A room with a view,' said Colonel Katterfelto to the clerk at the reception of the Adequate. It was a reception not without interest, although not one of *particular* interests. The furnishings were *sufficient*. Things looked as if they would do. For now. 'Best you have in the building,' the colonel continued. 'And only for the one night. Off tomorrow into space. Ship sails at midnight and all that cosmic caper.'

The clerk looked suspiciously down at Darwin. 'Regrettably,' he said, 'as I informed a lady earlier, we do not take pets.'

'*Pets?*' roared the colonel, making motions towards his ray-gun holster. 'That's me hairy nephew, Humphrey.

P'haps a tad fuzzy in the facial featurings. But *pet*? How dare you, sir!'

'Humphrey?' went the clerk. 'Humphrey the nephew is it, sir?'

'It is,' said the colonel. 'It is.'

'And very well dressed, too, is Humphrey.'

'Somewhat better dressed than you are,' said the colonel.

The clerk now affected a very smug face indeed. 'Well,' he said, 'if Humphrey is indeed your nephew, and *not* a pet *monkey*—' he laid great emphasis upon *that* word '—he will have no objection to signing his own name on the register.'

And looking now smugger than one might have thought humanly possible, the clerk handed his dip-pen to the colonel.

Colonel Katterfelto *observed* the clerk's smug smile and raised one of his own.

'Take the dip-pen, Humphrey,' he said to Darwin, 'and sign your name for the nice gentleman.'

Darwin leapt up onto the desk and signed the name

Humphrey Banana

Cameron Bell watched this scene with amusement and wondered just what he was actually seeing. He cast a professional eye over the shoes and suitings of both man and monkey and drew a surprising and accurate conclusion.

'Excuse me, Colonel,' said Cameron Bell, when the old soldier, chuckling softly, had concluded his own signing of the register, 'but might I trouble you for a word or two?'

'Ah, detective fellow,' said the colonel. '*Balls*, isn't it?'

'*Bell*,' said the detective fellow. 'Cameron Bell.'

'Yes, that would be it. What do you want?'

'I just need a word or two in private, if you will. I wish to draw upon your experiences as a space traveller.'

'Small world,' said the colonel. 'Going up again tomorrow night.'

'Then I am lucky to have caught you. Over there perhaps?' Cameron Bell indicated a sofa that was neither grand nor down at heel, but somewhere in between.

'Darwin,' said the colonel. 'I mean, *Humphrey*, dear boy. Would you engage the services of a porter and have our belongings taken up to our room? I will meet you shortly in the bar.'

Humphrey Banana snapped his fingers at a porter.

The colonel stifled further mirth and joined the detective on the sofa.

'Interesting fellow, your nephew,' said Mr Bell. 'One of a kind, I am thinking.'

The colonel puffed as the colonel did. 'What's on your mind?' he asked.

'I am continuing my investigations into the deaths at the Electric Alhambra,' said Cameron Bell.

'Well well well,' said the colonel, beaming mightily. 'Come to the right fellow, you did. Gleaned a bit of info on the cases myself, one of them at least.'

'Go on please,' said Cameron Bell.

The colonel now spoke in whispered tones. 'That Harry Hamilton,' he whispered. 'Turns out, not a real fellow at all. Impostor. Damned Venusian. Cleverly disguised to look like one of us.'

'I knew it,' said Cameron Bell. 'But how did you learn of *this*?'

'Met one of his chums, so to speak. Let the pussycat out of the bag, as it were. Hamilton used to lead hunting parties on Mars. Retired after an injury to his hand. Disguised himself as an Englishman. Became a sensation. Was to lead a hunt tomorrow, but someone zapped him. Pop! With a ray gun, as I told you before.'

'And more likely it is looking by the minute,' said Cameron Bell. 'I am very grateful for this information. I think I have these cases all but put to bed.'

'You wanted to ask me something,' said the colonel. 'What is it, then?'

'I came into the possession of an object.' Cameron Bell's voice became soft and conspiratorial. 'It is in safe keeping now but I am at a loss to know what it is. It is *not*, how shall I put this, of this Earth.'

'Alien trinket then,' gruffed the colonel. 'What of it?'

'I was hoping you might know what it is. It is about this long,' Cameron indicated the length, 'this wide and composed of a diamond-hard material. It resembles a crystal from a chandelier but at its centre—'

Colonel Katterfelto raised a finger. 'Something moves,' he said, in a quavery voice.

The private detective took off his hat and nodded his baldy head. 'Something moves indeed,' he said. 'And *you* know what it is. You have seen such a thing before.'

'I have,' said the colonel. 'I certainly have. Though I truly wish to God that I had not.'

27

'enomorph,' the colonel said. 'As dangerous as they come.'

'From Venus?' asked Cameron Bell.

'From Mars,' said Colonel Katterfelto. 'Used to have a pop at them on the big-game hunts I led there. But the hunters were never keen to shoot 'em. Look too much like children from a distance.'

Cameron Bell could understand *that*. 'And dangerous, you said?' he asked.

'Ferocious, come at you like a mad dog. Lost a few Jovian hunters. Went up to pet the blighters. Damn near got torn all to pieces.'

'And the crystals are their eggs?'

'They self-reproduce. Always carry their young with them. But listen, if you got to see an egg, how so? Did you bag one of the blighters yourself?'

'Actually yes,' said Cameron Bell.

'Then bravo, old chap. But *here*? You shot the blighter here?'

'In London, yes.'

'And where is the egg?'

'At the London Hospital. Sir Frederick Treves is examining it.'

'Queen's physician, eh?' The colonel did fiddlings with his mustachios. 'Then you had best tell him to toss it in the furnace. Damned impossible to break open with a hammer or whatnot. Xenocryst is a kind of crystal, d'you see? Your Xenomorph is protected pretty damn well. Until it's time to hatch. Then – snap-snap-snap. Horrible mess. Give 'em the business end of a ray gun. That puts a stop to the devils.'

The colonel had quite exhausted himself with so much conversation. And as Humphrey Banana had returned from the best room in the hotel, which was not as good as others, but better than some at a pinch, the colonel excused himself from the company of Cameron Bell and took himself off to the bar.

Alice Lovell appeared in the company of her luggage. But happily, in the opinion of Cameron Bell, *not* in the company of her kiwi birds.

'The gentleman at the pet shop is prepared to pay five shillings a day to exhibit the kiwi birds in his front window. And he will look after them at night into the bargain.'

'What excellent news,' the detective said. 'You could, if you so wish, cancel your reservation here and return to the guest bedroom at my humble abode.'

'Dear Cameron,' smiled Alice. 'You are *too* kind. But I would not trouble you further.'

'It would be absolutely *no* trouble, I assure you.'

'No, I would not hear of it.' Alice Lovell smiled a smile. Cameron Bell did not.

'Well, thus and so,' he said at length. 'I have certain matters to attend to. But I will return this evening to watch you take your much-deserved place at the top of the bill.'

'I will wave if I see you,' said Alice. 'And if I do not. Then

211

thank you once more for your kindness and I am sorry that my naughty birds made a mess in your house.'

More than just a mess, thought Cameron grimly. But he beamed at Alice, bowed politely to her, told her to 'break a leg' as one must to superstitious artistes and promised that he would see her later.

And with that he left the Adequate, with thoughts of Alice in his head and heart.

Before returning home to bathe and change for the evening's performance, Cameron steered the flatulent horse back into the grounds of the Crystal Palace. Here, at the box office, he purchased a ticket for the very best seat in the house. And from the florist's shop in the great glazed entranceway, a dozen red roses to be delivered with a hand-written note to the dressing room of Miss Alice Lovell. ALICE AT THE PALACE as was.

Satisfied with this, he returned to the trap, whipped up the horse, covered his nose and returned at a pace to London.

At the London Hospital he spoke with Sir Frederick Treves.

'You again, Bell,' said that man, heaving out a kidney from a well-carved cadaver. 'I have nothing new, I am afraid.'

'I do,' said Cameron. 'Two things, in fact. The hurty-finger is indeed that of a Venusian.'

Sir Frederick Treves took to weighing the kidney. 'You'd get three square meals out of this,' he said distractedly.

'Pardon?' asked the detective.

'Nothing at all. But Venusian, you say. I will write up a full report. Definitely more plant than mammal. Interesting species.'

'And the crystal—' Cameron Bell began.

212

'Yes, what larks,' said the surgeon, surreptitiously licking his fingers.

'Larks?' queried Cameron Bell.

The surgeon nodded and smiled. 'I told Merrick I would give him a bag of humbugs if he could get it open. What a carry on, I confess that I wet myself watching him try.'

'Oh my dear dead mother,' cried Cameron Bell. 'It is the egg of something called a Xenomorph. A very nasty, vicious creature. It must be destroyed.'

'Oh joy of joys,' crowed the Queen's physician. 'I will bet there will be some howling from Merrick should he break it open.'

And, as if upon cue, there came such a howling.

'Arm yourself!' cried Cameron, drawing out his pistol.

Sir Frederick Treves took up the big bone saw.

The Elephant Man came staggering into the morgue, then collapsed in a heap on the cold tile floor.

Cameron Bell leapt forwards, pistol cocked. 'Where does it have you?' he yelled. 'Is it fastened upon your innards? Where?'

Mr Merrick peered up in some puzzlement.

'Where?' shouted Cameron Bell. 'And be prepared with a scalpel, Sir Frederick, we may have to cut it out.'

'Stop now,' said Joseph Merrick. 'This is not funny. You are frightening me.'

'Better we cut it out of you than let it eat you alive.'

'Please stop, I must insist.' The Elephant Man dragged himself to his misshapen feet. Or misshapen *foot*. As the right one was a perfect size eight. 'Stop pointing your pistol at me, it is not polite.'

'But the Xenomorph—' said Cameron Bell.

'*This?*' replied Mr Merrick, displaying the unfractured crystal egg.

'But you howled,' said Sir Frederick Treves.

'And you would too,' Mr Merrick complained. 'I pricked myself on the pointy end. I've got a really hurty-finger.'

Cameron Bell looked to Frederick Treves.

Who said, 'Go on then.'

Cameron Bell smiled at Mr Merrick.

Then knocked him unconscious with his pistol.

'Hurty-finger!' said he.

'The hurty-finger fellow and the smelly fellow, too,' said Commander Case, as he received Mr Cameron Bell into his office at Scotland Yard. It was *not* one of the better offices, blessed with tall casement windows, a carpet and a fine oak desk. It was little more than a cupboard really. Cameron Bell had quite some trouble even squeezing in.

'Decorating,' the commander explained. 'I have a very big office, you know. I am having it specially refurbished. Japanese silk wallpaper, Afghan carpet. Desk inlaid with ivory, they are sending one over from the V and A.'

Cameron Bell studied the room, the carpet. The desk and the occupant who sat behind it. As his shoes were visible beneath, the private detective studied these, too.

The conclusions drawn from observations of these separate sources produced a sum total within the mind of Cameron Bell. Commander Case had inhabited this cupboard for three years, five months and four days.

The exact period of time that had elapsed since the commander accidentally released the prime suspect in a string of copy-cat Jack the Ripper murders. A suspect who was later brought to justice by Mr Cameron Bell.

'I felt I should report to you what I know,' said Cameron Bell. 'Should you wish to use the information I pass on to you, it might, how shall I put this, speed up the decoration of your office.'

As his arms were somewhat jammed beneath his desk, Commander Case just nodded his head and said, 'I made it quite clear to you that you were no longer on this case.'

'All right,' said Cameron, attempting to shrug, but finding it somewhat difficult. 'I am sure you must have it all under control. Hundreds of constables scouring the stalls of the Electric Alhambra for clues.'

'Just the four,' said the commander. 'But we'll get there in the end.'

'I am sure that you will. But it behoves me to tell you what I know, in the hope that it will avert further deaths. It would not sit easily with me if more folk were to die, when a word from me to yourself could have saved them.'

'Tell me what you have, then,' said Commander Case.

'Harry "Hurty-Finger" Hamilton was a Venusian,' said Cameron Bell. 'A Venusian criminal, on the run from whatever law enforcement agency exists upon that far planet. He had stolen something from one of their High Magicians. A ring, referred to as the Ring of Moses. The whereabouts of this ring are presently unknown. I had it in my possession, but it was stolen from me by Aleister Crowley. Crowley came to a fitting end. Did the ring survive? I do not know the answer.

'A third party also seeks this ring. A sinister figure responsible for the murder of at least one young woman in the East End, and the abductions of several more. He to my opinion is also Venusian, but he is the one that you must focus your attention on. Forget about Harry Hamilton and also Charlie Belly. The big prize for you is the sinister figure. He means to commit atrocious acts upon the people of this world. He is probably the most evil creature that has ever walked abroad upon the streets of London.'

Cameron Bell paused after this.

Commander Case nodded his head.

'And that is what you have?' he said at length.

'I believe my own life to be in danger,' said Cameron Bell. 'I believe this sinister figure will draw the conclusion that *I* have the Ring of Moses. He stole the possessions of Harry Hamilton believing the ring to be amongst them. It did not occur to him that Harry would carry the ring on his person.'

'Splendid,' said Commander Case. 'Absolutely splendid. What sterling work you have done, Mr Bell. Murdered prossies in the East End.'

'Not prossies. Virgins. Required for a magical ritual.'

'Oh yes. Let us not forget the magic. A magic ring, is it not? And assassins from Venus out to off a Music Hall star who isn't a man at all but a Venusian in disguise? Well, it has the lot really, does it not? A penny dreadful if ever there was one. Or one of that Johnny Frenchman Verne's flights of fancy.'

'Perhaps I am not making myself clear,' said Cameron Bell. 'I require police protection. And if this evil creature is not brought to book, it is my belief that he will destroy us all.'

'No no no.' The commander did violent shakings of the head. 'It is full of holes. What, for instance, of Smelly Charlie Belly? Why was he killed? Another Venusian, was he? Are all our Music Hall performers off-worlders in disguise?'

'I have some loose ends to tie up,' said Cameron Bell.

'Out!' the commander ordered. 'Out of my office and out of Scotland Yard. I have theories of my own. Far less fanciful than yours. Dogged police work will pay off this time, you mark my words.'

'A single constable,' pleaded Cameron Bell, 'to stand guard outside my home. It only occurred to me on the way over here as to just how much danger I am in. I am not a man to beg, but alone I am not a match for this evil one.'

'*Evil one*, even better,' crowed Commander Case. 'The very Devil himself, I have no doubt. Find yourself a priest who makes house calls, Bell, and waste no more of my time.'

And with that said, Mr Bell was ushered from both the office and the building and stood by his hired horse feeling very glum.

The horse let free with a sound like tearing rags, but this time it elicited no comment or interest from the detective, who climbed aboard the trap and drove the foetid creature back to its owner.

It was nearly seven o'clock now and Cameron knew that he would have to make considerable haste if he wanted to reach the Crystal Palace in time to watch Alice Lovell perform. It did not matter to him about the other acts and he felt that, as he knew what he knew to be basically correct, he did not believe that she was in any danger. Although there did seem to be a lot of possible alternatives. And there were times, and this was one of them, where Cameron Bell found cause to doubt his logic and intuition. But for now he only thought of Alice. He would bathe and dress and hail a cab and probably be there by nine.

Cameron reached his door and took out his key and then felt once more that sickening feeling deep in the pit of his stomach. The front door was open and he had not left it so.

Cameron Bell drew his pistol, checked it and pushed open the front door. Devastation awaited. The hall, its fixtures, fittings, furnishings and whatnots had been torn into shreds. Thoroughly destroyed.

Cameron edged forwards, gun at the ready. He had never seen such absolute destruction. Treasured items were scarcely recognisable. Paper was ripped from the walls.

His study—

Cameron pushed open the door. Saw the horror within. Then gasped as something took him, spun him around. He was aware of a dark, brooding figure, a noxious hideous odour breathed upon him, a hand gripped his throat and then he knew no more.

28

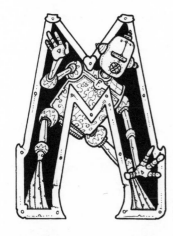r Bell awoke to utter darkness. He clutched his throat and vomited, his eyes rolled in his head. Struggling to his feet, he lurched about. Finding a wall before him, he leaned his weight upon it. Cameron patted about at himself for his case of lucifers. He could feel that his pockets had been torn from his jacket, but his watch chain remained dangling from a waistcoat buttonhole and on it his watch and silver match case. A feeling of dread all but consuming him now, he edged along the wall. Found a gas mantle, turned it up, fumbled with the match case and struck a lucifer.

And revealed a world gone mad.

His beautiful study had been completely destroyed. Books and treasures brought to devastation. Down, it seemed, to the smallest item, ravaged, decimated, torn asunder.

Cameron Bell sank back against the wall, now clutching at his heart. It was gone. All gone. Everything that mattered to him. That brought memories. His childhood bits and bobs and those of his father before him. Items gathered by his forebears upon the Grand Tour. Irreplaceable photographs in silk-bound albums. Glass that his mother had loved. And that he had loved, too.

An evil force, with no qualms, no conscience, no love, had taken everything away from him. Everything gone.

Just gone.

But the monster that had taken his world had also sought to take Cameron's life. It had breathed upon him that deadly gas that had swelled the lungs of the female corpse on Mr Treve's dissecting table. And it would surely have killed him, too, had he not had the foresight to breathe *out* rather than *in* when the murderous vapour came upon him. This quickest of thinkings had saved his life, as it had upon more than one occasion.

But saved his life for what?

That he should experience *this*? The violation of all he held precious? To have to see and feel all *this*?

Cameron dragged himself from his study, slammed shut the door. A door that itself was scoured by scratch marks. He slumped down upon the lowermost stair and buried his face in his hands and wept.

There was no purpose now, no reason to continue.

Cameron gazed up between his fingers towards the floor above. He would not go up there to see what horrors awaited him.

He would never climb those stairs again.

Cameron Bell took steadying breaths, but he shook from his head to his feet.

All that was precious was gone.

All that was precious was gone.

A mantra of gloom and desperation repeating itself again and again in his head.

All that was precious—

But no.

There was something precious that had not been destroyed. Some*one* precious. Someone that he loved most dearly. It was an unrequited love, certainly, and one that might remain so. But it was a love. And—

Cameron Bell examined his dangling pocket watch. Somehow *it* had survived. And it was still ticking, too. He sought his pince-nez, but they were gone. He squinted at the watch.

'Eight-thirty,' said Cameron Bell. 'I might still reach the Crystal Palace in time. If she is in danger, I must be there to protect her.'

But *was* she in danger? Was there any reason why she should be in danger? The creature certainly sought the Ring of Moses and not finding it here—

But how did it find my house? wondered Cameron. *If it can find* me, *then it can find her.*

Cameron Bell arose from the stair, straightened his ruined clothes as best he could, drew a deep breath and took a long, thoughtful look around. He must leave this house now and he knew that he would never, *could* never return. All was gone and all that mattered now was Alice.

Cameron took himself along the hall, turning on the gas mantles as he did so. As the dreadful smell of coal gas seeped into the air, Cameron plucked up a broken candle that had been torn from an antique candlestick. Then he took out his lucifers, lit the candle and placed it upon the floor.

'Farewell, home of my childhood and my life,' said Cameron Bell, and he left the house and closed the door behind him.

The driver of the hansom cab that picked up Cameron Bell upon the corner enquired as to whether his fare would like to reach his destination at a leisurely stroll, or in the fashion of a batsman out of 'ell.

Cameron requested the latter and named the Crystal Palace.

'It's *you*, guv'nor,' said the cabby. 'You as 'ad me chasin' around 'yde Park Corner after that Johnny Frenchman with the gun. Did you ever catch the blighter, guv'nor?'

Cameron Bell sank low in seat. 'No,' said he. 'But when I do, he will know a terrible end.'

There was something so cold and deadly in the manner in which his fare spoke those words that the driver of the cab closed the little hatchway and applied himself to his trade with no further wish for small talk.

A loud, dull thump rattled the windows of the cab. The private detective turned a deaf ear to the explosion that brought down the house he had lived in for all of his life.

Cameron Bell patted himself. What remained? Did he have money? Did he have his pistol? He found sufficient coinage in his trouser pocket to pay the driver of the hansom. But his pistol was gone. And so too was his wallet, which contained, of course, the ticket for tonight's performance.

Oh, be there, prayed Cameron Bell. *Be there in my seat. For surely I will strangle you slowly with my own bare hands.*

It was a pleasant summer's evening, and as the hansom reached the suburbs, the trees gave off their sleeping scents and nightjars sang in slumbering cottage gardens.

But Mr Bell could find no beauty here. He sought to protect the woman he loved and he sought a most terrible vengeance on the creature that had wrought such evil upon him.

As they approached the Crystal Palace, the driver flipped open the little hatchway and chirped, 'This'll cheer you up, guv'nor. A nice night out with ALICE AT THE PALACE. I'll be going there myself tomorrow. I always 'as Saturdays off.'

'It is Friday tomorrow,' Cameron wearily corrected the errant driver of the cab. Not that he really had the energy to do so.

'No, guv'nor.' The driver was not to be shaken. '*Today* is Friday. First night of ALICE AT THE PALACE – I should know, this is my second journey up here tonight.'

'Yes,' insisted Cameron. '*First* night. *Tonight is Thursday night.*'

'No, guv'nor, hate to correct you there. The show *was* scheduled to open yesterday night, *Thursday* night, but it had to be cancelled because they couldn't get the scenery out of the Electric Alhambra. All the automatic gubbins shut down and they 'ad to spend all last night, *Thursday night*, and 'alf of today taking it down manually. This new-fangled elect-ri-ma-trickly ain't what it's cracked up to be at times, is it?'

'Tonight is Friday?' said Cameron Bell. 'Friday? Tonight?'

'That's what I'm telling you, yes.'

A terrible chill enshrouded Cameron Bell. He had not been unconscious for a couple of hours, but for an evening, a night and a day. More than twenty-four hours he had lain on the floor of his study.

'Make haste!' cried Cameron Bell. 'Make haste to the door now, please.'

The Crystal Palace diamond-hung upon the hill at Sydenham. Lit to a dazzling brilliance by one hundred thousand neon tubes. The wireless transmission of electricity making the impossible possible.

The driver drew up before the gorgeous building. Cameron Bell climbed down from the hansom and took

223

himself around to the cab side that faced the rolling lawns. Took out his money and paid off his fare.

'Do you still have your blunderbuss?' enquired Mr Cameron Bell.

'No, guv, proved to be a tad unwieldy in a skirmish. Bought meself one of these little blighters.' The driver produced a bulbous object of brass and purple glass. 'Pocket ray gun,' he said. 'It's called the Educator – puts folk right when they's wrong.'

'I wish to buy it from you,' said Mr Bell. 'But I have no money, only this antique gold watch.' He handed this last cherished item to the driver.

A covetous expression passed over the driver's face. 'Well,' said he, 'I'm taking the poor end of the bargain, but lookin' at the state of yous, you're 'aving a right rough time. 'Ere, take the little blighter, and if you see Johnny Frenchman you can shoot 'im up the backside, eh?'

Cameron Bell took the ray gun. 'I am so sorry,' said he.

'Nothing to apologise for, guv'nor.' The driver pocketed Cameron's watch, grinning as he did so.

'I regret that there is.' Cameron Bell turned the ray gun on the driver. 'This is a highway robbery,' he said. 'Please hand over your money and return to me my watch.'

After the sulking driver had driven away at speed, Cameron Bell approached the palace of glass. He was aware of how rough he must look, his clothes as bespoiled as a beggar's. But he was also aware that *this* was the Music Hall, where *all* were welcome, as long as they could furnish the price of admission.

The grand entrance hall, a beautiful gallery, was made even more gorgeous by the pleasing arrangement of elegant naked statuary. Each carved from silica mined from Earth's moon. The moon now named Victoria. Sounds of singing echoed from the great auditorium beyond. Of the Travelling Formbys crooning the plaintive feline ballad 'Your Pussy Still Reminds Me of My Grandma's Ginger Beard'.

The box office, a glittering booth modelled after the style of the Taj Mahal, was manned by a swarthy son of the Empire, mightily bearded and sporting a jewel-speckled turban.

'The best seat you have in the house,' said Cameron Bell.

The gentleman of swarthiness viewed the potential purchaser of the best seat in the house as he might a pigeon poo that had fallen onto his diamond-spattered headwear.

'Most amusing,' said he.

'Judge me not upon these rags,' said Cameron Bell. 'I am a man of substance. I was attacked and brutalised.'

'You have the voice of a gentleman,' said the swarthily complexioned seller of tickets, shaking his turbaned head. 'But regrettably, at the Crystal Palace we enforce a strict code of dress in the exclusive boxes. Sir has no hat, no tie, no gloves, no tailcoat – no—' And then, 'No!' he said, much louder.

Cameron pointed the ray gun at the turbaned head. He flung all the money he had taken from the driver across the ticket counter.

'I am a desperate man,' he said. 'Hand me the ticket and keep the change, or I will shoot you dead.'

The son of Empire stared at Cameron Bell. 'Sir has given me sufficient money not only to purchase the best seat in the house, but also to rent the appropriate apparel. Take your ticket and *this*—' he displayed a special voucher to Cameron Bell, '—to the booth yonder and you will be fitted out at no further expense.'

'Thank you,' said Cameron Bell, taking both ticket and

voucher. 'And I apologise for *this*,' and he returned his ray gun to his trouser pocket.

It was the work of moments. The measurings up, the selection of clothes. Discarding the old and slipping on the new. 'Burn those,' said Cameron Bell to the fitter as he transferred his pocket watch, the last remaining symbol of his former life, to the silver-fabricked waistcoat of the smart dress suit.

'You must return the suit at the end of the performance,' said the fitter.

Cameron toyed with his ray gun.

'I will close up the booth and depart for home now,' said the fitter. 'I do hope that sir enjoys the performance. I am told that Alice Lovell—' And he made a lewd expression.

Mr Bell raised high the ray gun and struck the fitter down.

The best seat in the house – the best *remaining* seat – was on the second tier above the one reserved for royalty. Cameron Bell squinted at his ticket, but he knew the way well enough. He had attended concerts here before, classical concerts. He had seen Mrs Norman Nerruda, the greatest violinist of the day, perform Paganini.

Cameron crossed to the ornate staircase that led to the boxes, gained the first landing and then the second. Edged along the corridor alone with brooding thoughts. Applause reached him. He drew out his watch, squinted once more at the dial. It was well after eleven, the show was running late. But he had not missed Alice. She would be on next. The very top of the bill.

Cameron was approaching the door to his box when he heard the laughter. Not the laughter of the crowd, but of a single fellow, a high and horrible laughter, this. It brought Mr Bell to a halt. The private detective leaned towards the door of a box and pressed his ear against it. Further laughter and other sounds reached him. Curious sounds that he could not identify. But that laughter—

Cameron Bell drew out his ray gun once more. Held it high in his right hand and with his left gently turned the handle of the door. It clicked, the door opened slightly, Cameron put his shoulder to it and pushed.

The curtains were drawn upon the box, shielding it from the gaze of those filling the auditorium. The lights were dim but of what was to be seen there could be no doubt at all.

The eyes of Cameron Bell fell upon a naked man, engaged in filthy congress with what looked to be two Limehouse prostitutes and a plucked but lively chicken. The naked fellow looked up from his dirty doings. 'Why, Bell,' he said. 'Would you care to join in? There is always room for one more.'

Cameron Bell entered the box, closing the door behind him. 'Well,' he said, displaying his ray gun. 'We meet again, Mr Crowley.'

29

'ery nice,' said Aleister Crowley, viewing Cameron's ray gun. 'Is that one of those new surgical appliances whose healthy vibrations alleviate female hysteria?'

'A little ray gun called the Educator,' said Mr Bell. 'It has educated several this evening. It will now teach you its cruellest lesson, I am thinking.'

'Hold hard.' Mr Crowley rolled aside an enormous East end slosh pot. 'No need for any violence. I merely took what you promised me. A little early, perhaps, but I damaged none of your precious things. You do write the most personal accounts in your diary, do you not?'

Cameron Bell ignored this unpleasant remark. 'My world is in ruination,' he said. 'Everything that I held dear is gone. And *you* are partially to blame for this. Had you not stolen the ring, the creature that destroyed my house searching for it might have spared at least some of my belongings.'

'This is all very sad,' said Mr Crowley, pulling up his long johns as he did so. 'Your library and your curiosa, too?'

'All gone,' said Mr Bell. 'My house as well, destroyed by fire.'

'You may lodge with me,' said the Great Beast, beaming hugely. 'I inhabit superior rooms at the Savoy now. 'Tis the balance of equipoise, I suppose. My fortunes have risen, as yours have fallen.'

'Return the ring to me,' said Cameron Bell.

'That I regret I cannot do,' said Mr Aleister Crowley.

'Then before I shoot you dead and take it from your cold and lifeless finger, tell me this. If it was not *you* consumed by fire in your lodgings, then who?'

'Just a whore,' said the Logos of the Aeon. 'She had the gall to doubt my powers as a magician. I wore the Ring of Moses. She warmed to my skills most colourfully.' Crowley's voice took on a sinister and insinuating tone, his eyes fixed once again upon a spot to the rear of Cameron's head. 'But my dear Bell,' said he, 'you believed *me* to be dead. How touching. Or not, as the case may be. For I saw no notification of my death in the obituary column of *The Times* newspaper. No words of regret, penned by yourself, for the loss of England's greatest poet and holy guru. No eulogy, no—'

'Cease,' said Cameron Bell. 'The ring, or I shoot you where you stand. And the whores, too, for an encore. Found dead in your underpants in such unexalted company. I will be happy to write *that* up for *The Times*. Does the chicken have a name?'

'My dear Bell—'

'The ring and now.'

'But you do not understand its power. Or how to wield its power.' The Beast of the Apocalypse raised his left hand and displayed the Ring of Moses on his finger. 'By the power—' he began.

But, 'No!' cried Mr Bell and he shot Mr Crowley in the foot.

The ray gun made no sound at all and nor indeed did Mr

Crowley. With his mouth wide open and eyes somewhat crossed, he fainted and fell in a heap. The slosh pots opened *their* mouths to scream, but the detective waggled a cautionary finger.

'Ladies, leave,' he said. 'And do take the chicken with you.'

And making haste and donning clothes, the ladies took their leave. In company of fowl.

Mr Bell approached the fallen mystic, knelt, removed the Ring of Moses from his hand, slipped it onto his own finger. The holy guru stirred and mumbled. Cameron Bell put the ray gun to his temple—

'Ladies and gentle*men*,' came the voice of Tony Spaloney (the King of the Old Baloney). 'Tonight for your delirious delectation—' the crowd made cheerings '—the lovely lady whose feathered frolics gain a *standing ovation* from all the gentlemen. She's *here*, she's *dear* and her birds are rather *queer*. The beautiful Alice Lovell and her Acrobatic Kiwis.'

Aleister Crowley made groaning sounds.

Cameron Bell clunked him hard upon the head.

Then eased the curtains open a crack and peered into the splendid auditorium.

It was a sight that had hitherto never failed to inspire Mr Cameron Bell. Seating for ten thousand folk beneath a spreading canopy of glass. To either side the tiers of exclusive boxes rose, enclosed by cast-iron trelliswork, a confusion of intricate scrollings and traceries. Everywhere lit to perfection by modern electric.

The stage itself resembled the exposed interior of some grossly magnified Bedouin tent. Precious linens, cloths of gold framed it to a nicety. Above, the masks of Comedy and Tragedy were picked out in silver upon an enamelled entablature, richly smothered all about by luscious velvets that tumbled above and below.

There upon that stage stood Alice Lovell. And she had never looked more lovely in her life. She wore tonight a ringmaster's coat in silver brocade and a tiny matching top hat. A brass corset with copper filigree and mock rose-petal-work clenched her slender waist. Bright blue bloomers, sleek white stockings and high-heeled patent button-boots completed the prettiest of pictures.

The crowd erupted into near-frantic cheerings; gentlemen cast their hats into the air. The clockwork orchestra whirred and clicked and cranked out that ever popular Music Hall standard:

TREACLE SPONGE BASTARD FOR ME

And as Alice put the kiwis through their acrobatic routines, the crowd sang along with the orchestra, as would a mighty choir.

And this is what they sang:

> *Oh, treacle sponge bastard for me, please.*
> *I'll have a bite of that now.*
> *I don't want carrots and cheese, please,*
> *I don't want slices of cow.*
>
> *I don't want doughnuts or doorsteps of bread.*
> *I don't want cabbages, big as my head.*
> *I don't want mushrooms you grew in your shed.*
> *I want treacle sponge bastard for me—*

and so on—

Cameron Bell looked longingly at Alice. The most beautiful creature that he ever had seen. He rooted in the clothing of the Beast, located Aleister Crowley's paisley purse and took out a threepenny piece. This he dropped into a slot, activating the mechanism that released a pair of opera glasses. Cameron Bell raised these to his eyes, adjusted them and gazed awhile at Alice.

Her kiwis formed pyramids and played at leapfrog. Then cricket.

The private detective turned his opera glasses towards the exclusive boxes on the other side of the stage. Espied Mr Oscar Wilde in the company of Max Beerbohm and Aubrey Beardsley. A group of Venusians, their golden eyes trained upon the stage. Members of the aristocracy, sporting false moustaches. Here a foreign potentate. There a manufacturer of brass goggles to the gentrified classes. There—

Cameron Bell caught air in his throat. Refocused his opera glasses. There, almost directly opposite him, in the box below the Venusians, sat a single figure. Lean, gaunt-featured, all in black. The monster in human form.

Cameron Bell raised his ray gun, gripped it in a trembling hand. It would surely be but the work of a moment. A well-aimed charge of deadly energy. From between the scarcely open curtains. No one would even see him. He could slip away quietly once the deed was done. It was murder, of course. But then was it murder if what you killed was not a man? Interplanetary agreements decreed that within the boundaries of the British Empire, all men, be they of Earth, or Venus, or Jupiter, were equal in the eyes of the law. And entitled to the protection of the law. But was this fiend Venusian? Or was he something other?

Cameron Bell would dearly have liked to interview the being at some length. Whilst employing certain techniques beloved of medieval torturers. But an opportunity such as this might never present itself again.

Cameron aimed the pistol. His finger tightened upon the

ivory trigger. Then relaxed. He could not do it. He was a gentleman, of sorts. But an Englishman certainly. And this was *not* the English way of doing things. You had to give a fellow a sporting chance, no matter how unsporting he himself might be. And even though he hated this mannish thing with every fibre of his being and knew instinctively that it meant no good to the human race as a whole, he could not do it.

The sing-song came to an end. The crowd ceased their clamour and there was a moment of silence as Alice steered a kiwi dressed as Blondin along a slim raised tightrope.

Cameron Bell rose to his full height, flung aside the curtains and cried in the loudest of voices.

'Hey, villain,' cried he. 'I have the Ring of Moses. And I have this for you.'

The vast crowd, shaken to surprise by this sudden shouting, glanced towards its source and then took to ducking as a beam of red raw energy cleaved the air above.

The beam did not come from Cameron's side of the stage.

The detective fired back on the instant. Raising mixed emotions from the crowd. Some took at once to loud screamings and clamourings for escape. Others, and amongst these must be numbered many steadfast cockneys who, travelling from the relative civilisation of the East End to what they considered the very wilds of the country in Sydenham, had brought their weapons in case they encountered highwaymen or untamed savage beasts. These hearty fellows took at once to unholstering their weaponry.

Upon the stage stood Alice Lovell, by equal parts bewildered, afeared and appalled. Bewildered, because she recognised the shouting voice of Cameron Bell. Afeared, as anyone might be, by an ever-growing firefight. And appalled, nay, *utterly* appalled, that the attention of nearly ten thousand people was no longer all upon *her*.

Alice Lovell stamped a buttoned boot and called for calm. But in din and growing chaos all her words were lost.

Then a bolt of energy sliced down onto the stage.

'No!' bawled Cameron Bell. 'I am the one you want. Do not shoot at *her*.' But his voice too was lost in the swelling cacophony.

Cockney fellows aimed their guns towards exclusive boxes. Those who inhabited these and had weapons of their own brought them out and rained down fire upon the crowd below.

More beams swept across the stage. The scenery took fire.

Alice Lovell fled, her kiwi birds upon her fleeing heels. The object of Cameron Bell's hatred was suddenly no longer in his box. He was moving down the iron trelliswork, at speed and in a manner far from human. He moved like some great four-legged spider from tier to tier and onto the stage, amidst the smoke and flame.

Cameron Bell fired down upon him, missed, and rushed from his box. The corridor was no longer empty. Folk were running, screaming, falling. Cameron returned to the box, stepped over Aleister Crowley, climbed up onto the elbow rail and flung himself towards the burning stage. But Mr Bell was no athlete. He managed to grab at a curtain with his free hand, tearing it down and tumbling with it to the stage floor beneath. Flames were leaping higher now and, climbing painfully to his feet, Cameron struck at them with the curtain. But to no avail.

'Alice!' shouted Cameron Bell. 'Alice, where are you, Alice?' The backstage was in darkness and all about him now the fire rose. Cameron stumbled forwards, ray gun at the ready, shouting the name of Alice.

Into the blackness beyond.

But then to be met by light.

A curious light, though, this. A violet light, as of some will-o'-the-wisp or of St Elmo's fire. The source of this light, the evil creature, dressed though all in black.

Hissing sounds issued from its mouth and it raised its head to fix the detective with the most terrible eyes. They were ugly, reptilian and glowed a ghastly yellow.

And as it had been when the thing looked down upon him from the flying platform, it was as if Cameron Bell was alone with this creature, somehow removed from the world he knew and flung into one of terror.

The sounds of chaos and fiery destruction seemed to cease, to be drawn away, and he inhabited now a vacuum of silence. A place of dread cold fear.

But then another sound came to his ears. It was the scream of a woman. It was the scream of Alice Lovell. The monster hauled her into view, held her in front of him, held her by the throat.

Her terrified eyes stared at Cameron Bell. Her mouth pleaded soundlessly for help.

Cameron Bell held his ray gun now in both hands, aimed it unshakingly at the head of the monster he hated. Prepared to pull the trigger without any qualms at all.

'Hold hard.' The voice was as a snake might use had it been granted speech. 'So easily might you harm this woman who means so much to you.'

Perspiration dripped into Cameron's eyes. His body shook but his aim remained steady.

'You will hand me the Ring of Moses,' hissed the evil creature, 'or I will breathe death into this woman before I take it from you.'

Cameron Bell stared eye to eye with the monster.

The monster's fingers tightened around Alice's throat.

30

‘ou have no cause to harm an in- nocent woman.' Cameron Bell edged forwards, ray gun firmly gripped. 'Release her now and I will let you live.' It was bravado, of course, but Cameron Bell did *not* wish to show any fear if he could possibly avoid it.

'Let *me* live?' The creature's voice pressed hard upon the ears of the private detective. 'You dare to speak to *me* in such fashion? Down upon your knees.'

Cameron's heart was beating far too fast, but his hands remained steady, the nozzle of the ray gun aimed at the creature's head. He continued standing and glared at his mortal enemy.

'The ring,' the creature demanded. 'Hand me the ring and *I* will choose who lives. Pray you well that I choose kindly. Hand me the ring at once.' His cruel hand tightened further around Alice's throat. Alice's eyes were wide with fear and pain.

'All right,' cried Cameron Bell. 'You shall have the ring. But first let go your hold upon the woman.'

'Cast aside your weapon, then.'

Mr Bell clung tightly to his weapon. 'That thing I will never do,' said he.

'And so the woman dies.'

Alice's eyes were popping now, her face was going purple.

Cameron Bell slowly lowered his weapon, but he did not cast it aside. 'You shall have the ring,' he said, softly. 'But tell me, why all this? Who are you and what do you want on this planet?'

'*I* do not answer to *you*.'

Cameron Bell took a careful step forwards. His eyes swept over the being before him. Dressed as a man yet emanating the curious violet glow. The detective viewed the costume and the shoes, seeking to gain some vital information. But he could draw nothing. Perhaps the clothes and shoes were not what they appeared at all. Perhaps they were part of the creature itself. Some cunning form of anatomical camou-flage. As of the chameleon.

'You would know so much,' said the creature, and a terrible smile appeared on the terrible face. 'And you have come closer to discovering me than any other of your sorry race. Do you wish that I should tell you my name?'

Cameron Bell nodded slowly. Perspiration ran into his eyes.

The creature spoke and his words brought dreadful fear to Cameron Bell.

'*I am become Death*,' the creature spoke. 'Death, the *Destroyer of Worlds*.'

Cameron Bell still firmly held his ground. But it was not proving easy. He was doing his level best to retain the stiff upper lip of the English gentleman. But it was becoming increasingly difficult by the minute. And his fears for the life of Alice overwhelmed him.

'You are not of this world,' whispered the private detective. 'Why have you travelled here?'

'To destroy you. To erase you and your filthy race.'

'Harsh words,' said Mr Cameron Bell, whose teeth were starting to chatter.

'Your evil Empire must be brought to an end.'

'Evil Empire? Steady on.' The ray gun was trembling now in his hands.

'The British Empire.' The creature fairly spat out the words. 'Your British Empire has extended to your moon and to Mars. It must spread no further. If you are not stopped now you will rampage amongst the planets, spreading your pestilence. And then the stars will be your destination.'

'We would come in peace,' said Cameron Bell.

'You know only war,' declared the creature. 'War and the acquisition of all that is not yours. Your foul corruption must go no further. I am here to put an end to you.'

Cameron Bell fought hard to retain some semblance of control. 'You alone cannot defeat an entire race,' said he.

'Incorrect. For I possess something no man of Earth possesses.'

Enlightenment dawned upon Cameron Bell. 'You are a Venusian,' said he. 'And the thing you possess is magic.'

'Correct.' The creature's terrible smile exposed terrible pointed teeth. 'The ecclesiastics of Venus, those effete, aloof beings that visit here, take the vow as soon as they can speak – that they will never practise magic anywhere other than upon their home world. They fear that should they do so they would break the spell of protection that surrounds their planet and lose all powers they have.'

'Then to use magic here you will harm and possibly destroy your own kind.'

'I am not as they. I am the last of my kind. They destroy

my kind upon birth. But my mother hid me. And I shall wreak revenge upon them, as I bring justice to all worlds by your destruction.'

Cameron Bell concluded that this being certainly had a number of unresolved psychological issues that would be of interest to young Dr Freud. Now, however, was not the time to suggest a consultation. But as Cameron Bell stared in the creature's direction he became suddenly aware of something that brought a wry smile to his face. Something he felt might slightly tip the scales of the present power struggle in his favour.

'Right, then,' said Cameron Bell, forcing as much fearlessness into his voice as he could muster. 'I think you have told me all I need to hear. Unhand the woman and take your leave and don't let me catch you behaving so badly again.'

'*What?*' The creature was brought to a pure fury. Its eyes flashed unbridled hatred. It rose upon its toes, dragging Alice from her feet. '*The ring*,' it hissed. 'Hand the ring to *me*.'

Cameron Bell displayed the magical object on his finger. 'I think I will keep this as a souvenir of our encounter,' he said. 'It is a garish gewgaw of no intrinsic value. But it amuses me.'

'*And so die, puny Earthling!*'

The creature loosed its hold upon Alice, who sank to the floor in a faint. Then made to leap and then destroy Mr Bell.

But did not.

Because of a sudden the creature vanished. Vanished and went down in a great blur of fluttering feathers and pecking beaks. For the something that had brought the wry smile to the face of Mr Bell had been the stealthy arrival of Alice's kiwi birds, creeping up to attack the thing that dared to menace their mistress.

Cameron aimed his ray gun, but could not shoot for fear

of harming the loyal birds. So instead he pocketed his pistol, threw himself forward and hastened to the rescue of Alice. The slender girl felt all but weightless as he scooped her up in his arms and took himself at speed to seek an exit.

Sounds rushed back to fill the vacuum of otherwise silence. Sounds of fire-fighting appliances and police vehicles wildly ringing their bells. Sounds of crackling flames and the screamings of men and of women. The Crystal Palace was now mightily ablaze, panels of glass exploding from its great arched roof. The auditorium had become a raging inferno.

Cameron Bell emerged from the rear of the stricken building to comparative sanity. Bearing Alice in his arms and caring now only for her safety, he ran towards the carriage park. Here to encounter very much confusion.

Wealthy patrons sought escape from the grounds in their carriages. Carriages that were now somewhat all jammed up together. An appropriate word to describe this jamming-up arose unbidden in the mind of Cameron Bell. The word was 'gridlock'.

'Out of my way!' he shouted, fighting his way through the toffs who had managed to get themselves all wedged in amongst the carriages. 'Out of my way. Injured woman in need of medical attention.'

He elbowed here and elbowed there and presently winkled his way to the single cause of the gridlock: a parked hansom cab that blocked the way of all, besieged by toffs who each sought to claim it as their own.

Through a somewhat complicated piece of girl-juggling, Cameron Bell managed to draw out his ray gun without dropping Alice to the ground. Still unconscious, Alice did not see what followed.

Cameron Bell shot at the driver's hat. Reducing it to

ashes. 'Down from there,' he shouted. 'I am commandeering this cab.'

'Lord save me!' cried the driver, clutching at his hair which smouldered somewhat. 'It's 'im. 'Im as robbed me before.'

Some toffs took to backing away at this. Cameron brandished his ray gun at them. The circle widened further.

'I've called the bobbies on you,' quoth the driver. 'And not just me, it seems. That Johnny Foreigner in the ticket office called 'em, too. And the fitter of clothes. You are a wanted man, Mr Pickwick.'

'Down!' shouted Cameron Bell. 'Or I add murder to the charges against me. Take the woman from me, place her in the cab, sit beside her and see that she comes to no harm.'

'Now see here—' said a toff.

Cameron clunked him with the ray gun.

The driver descended and did as he was bid. Cameron climbed up to take his place at the reins.

'Out of the way,' he shouted at the toffs. The toffs got out of the way.

Cameron Bell took up the whip, cracked it in the air. 'Gee-up, Shergar,' he shouted to the horse. 'Fly like a batsman out of Hell.'

It certainly eased the gridlock.

But it did not please the thousands fleeing down the hill upon foot.

'Out of the way!' shouted Mr Bell once more, whipping away at Shergar.

Patrons of the Music Hall dodged to either side as best they could as Cameron steered the hansom cab forward. And then above the awful sounds of fiery destruction, the screams of fear and cries of anger as Cameron drove over fellows' feet, came other sounds that Mr Bell did not find any too pleasing.

These were the sounds of police whistles blowing. And of policemen shouting. 'There he is, driving that hansom,' came one such shout. 'It's Mr Pickwick all right,' came another. Further shouts identified this Mr Pickwick to be a robber, a fanatic, an assassin and an arsonist.

From his perch upon high Cameron could see the bobbies climbing into the cockpits of their new electric Marias. He also noted, without satisfaction, that they were armed with ray guns far bigger than his own.

'Faster, Shergar,' Cameron shouted. 'Out of the way there, *please*.'

Down the sweeping drive from the Crystal Palace ploughed the hansom. Flames roared within the mighty building, flared out through the fractured roof. Electric Marias purred after Cameron Bell. Phrases such as 'dead or alive' were being bandied about. Thousands fled in terror and Mr Bell whipped Shergar into a frenzy.

Down the hill and gathering pace towards the Royal Spaceport.

Upon the departure strip of the Royal London Spaceport stood a single ship of space preparing to depart. It was a somewhat battered old hulk, although serviceable, and Colonel Katterfelto, arriving half an hour before, had identified it to be none other than—

'The good old *Marie Lloyd*, Darwin. Flown in this old spacebird before, damn me. Very small world at times, doncha think?' he asked.

Darwin had agreed that yes, he considered that it really was a *very* small world at times. Perhaps at certain times to a degree where such an abundance of coincidences surely argued for the existence of a higher force, orchestrating such coincidences for a purpose presently beyond all Earthly comprehension.

'Possibly so,' the colonel had said. 'Now give us a hand with me bags.'

The bags were now aboard the *Marie Lloyd*. The Jovians too were all aboard and they were all strapped in. Their luggage and their weapons stowed, their space-sickness tablets taken. Corporal Larkspur was demonstrating how to use the oxygen masks, if they were needed, and where the emergency exits were.

Colonel Katterfelto took a last look at the Earth through the open doorway. 'Van Allen's Belt and braces,' puffed the colonel. 'The bally Crystal Palace is ablaze. Folk in their thousands running down the hill.'

Exactly why the sounds of all this had failed to reach the spacecraft before now was open to conjecture. Some form of acoustic anomaly, perhaps, or the direction of the prevailing wind. Or a careless oversight, who could possibly say?

Darwin the monkey bounced up and down. Fire was fun, *at a distance*.

'Best offer assistance,' puffed the colonel. 'Put the launch on hold for now. Women and children first.'

'Canst not be done,' declared the corporal, buckling up his safety belt. 'The automatic pilot hath been engaged. And verily the ship will rise into the heavens in but seconds now.'

Colonel Katterfelto, not a man to dither, dithered.

Then cried, 'Bless my soul.'

For approaching at considerable speed and apparently pursued by most of the Metropolitan Police Force was a single hansom cab.

Colonel Katterfelto squinted. 'It's that Balls chap,' said he.

Darwin the monkey gibbered and pointed.

'Yes, my dear fellow, I see her, too. It's young Alice in the cab. Unconscious, by the looks.'

'Closeth the door,' demanded the corporal, growing somewhat frantic. 'If thou dost not close it, yea we shall be suckéd through it upon take-off.'

Colonel Katterfelto put his hands to the door, but did not swing it shut.

'Stop, hold hard,' cried Cameron Bell, drawing the hansom to a halt.

'Sorry, old chap,' called the colonel. 'We have to be off, I'm afraid.'

Darwin bit the colonel on the leg. Darwin the monkey still had a thing about Alice.

'Yes, you're right, my dear fellow. Go on, hurry, help him.'

Darwin skittered down the gangway and helped Cameron Bell in lifting Alice down from the hansom cab.

The driver took to cowering. As bobbies in range took to blasting away with their ray guns.

Up the gangway went Cameron Bell, with Alice over one shoulder.

Darwin did what Darwin did: dropped his trousers, produced and flung dung towards the advancing policemen.

'Inside, quickly now,' called the colonel.

Cameron Bell, carrying Alice, entered the spaceship, and Darwin, too. The colonel slammed shut the door.

Ray-gun fire without disintegrated the gangway.

Within the spaceship came a shuddering.

Followed by a great roar of engines.

The *Marie Lloyd* rose up from the spaceport.

And made off into the sky.

31

ut into space went the *Marie Lloyd*, leaving the Earth behind.

Darwin clung to the colonel's leg. The colonel peeped out through a porthole.

'Always a stirring sight,' said he. 'Forgotten how much I love this kind of business.'

Corporal Larkspur was out of his seat now. 'What hast thou done?' he asked.

'Done?' said the colonel. 'Done? Helped a fellow in distress. A lady too, doncha know.'

The fellow in distress lay upon the floor in a somewhat sweaty heap. The lady had been safety-belted into the colonel's seat.

Darwin the monkey said, 'I should be flying this ship.'

'Thy nephew canst *not* fly the ship,' Corporal larkspur told the colonel. 'It is automatically set, it needeth no pilot whatever.'

Darwin considered biting the corporal; his 'uncle' sensing that this might just be the case, advised against it. 'Bit early in the hunt for that kind of stuff,' he said. 'Best all pull together as a team.'

The Jovian hunting party snored in their seats. They had downed soporifics and nodded off just prior to take-off. They would be out for hours. Not so, however, a certain private detective.

Cameron Bell made a groaning ascent into the vertical plane. He was now severely space-sick. He needed the toilet.

'That way,' directed the colonel. 'And if you are going to chuck-up, follow the instructions carefully. Gravity be shutting off in a moment. Could get rather nasty in there.'

Cameron Bell made off in haste towards the bathroom.

There was not much in Mr Bell's stomach, but what little there was he hurled into the Thomas Crapper. Flushed and washed his hands and face, then found himself wonderfully floating. It was unlike anything he had ever experienced before, except within the world of his dreams. And he was not dreaming now.

Alice awoke with a sudden start and glanced around fearfully. She gazed towards a porthole and saw what lay beyond.

'Oh not again,' said Alice. 'I am once more away with the fairies.'

Colonel Katterfelto smiled down upon her. His feet were not touching the spaceship's floor.

'I want to go home at once,' said Alice. 'I want my kiwi birds.'

But then the memories of what had gone before came rushing into her head. 'That monster,' she cried. 'That monster.'

'You are quite safe now,' said the colonel, floating over her head. 'That Balls chap brought you aboard the spaceship.'

'Aboard the spaceship?' Alice stiffened. 'Am I really here?'

'Really here, my dear. Like to drop you off. But not

possible, I'm afraid. Automatic pilot and all that kind of gubbinry.'

Cameron Bell returned from the bathroom. Somewhat pale of face, but not without a certain chipperness. He bobbed along the ceiling, propelling himself with breast-stroke motions. 'What larks,' he cried, and, 'Alice, are you well?'

Alice Lovell felt at her throat. 'Did you save my life?' she asked.

'Well,' said Cameron, thinking of the kiwi birds, 'you might say that—'

'Thank you,' said Alice. 'You are a wonderful man.'

'Only doing what any gentleman would.' Cameron Bell performed an aerial head-over-heels and said, 'You really should join me up here, Alice. If you do not feel unwell.'

'Thou must come down,' said Corporal Larkspur. 'We must discusseth the matter of your fares. Thou hast pushed thyself aboard a most exclusive big-game hunting trip. Thou canst not travel for nowt.'

Cameron Bell steered himself down. Steered himself into the corporal's seat and strapped himself in with the safety belt.

'Perhaps you might drop us off in Africa,' said he. 'I certainly cannot return to London for the moment. Neither would it be safe for Alice to do so. Her life would be in jeopardy.'

'Would it?' said Alice. 'What have I done?'

'The creature cannot let you live,' said Cameron Bell. 'I am so sorry that you became involved in this.'

Alice glanced wistfully once more out of the porthole. 'It was preordained,' said she. 'I have visions, you see.'

'Ah,' said Cameron. 'Visions? I thought it might be something of the kind.'

'I had a vision of being on a spaceship. And here I am.'

'Indeed. So, would Africa be all right for you? Or would you prefer Australia?'

'Thou talkest the toot,' said the Jovian corporal. 'The controls are preset. We continueth upon our voyage. Thou canst not be returned unto the Earth.'

'Well well well,' said Cameron Bell, and then he smiled most hugely. 'That suits me rather well, as it happens. There would be far too much explaining to do to Commander Case. And what with the danger to Alice and all, a week or two of big-game hunting on Mars would be a most bracing and refreshing experience.'

Corporal Larkspur mumbled and grumbled.

'Not *Mars*,' the colonel piped up. 'Venus, actually.'

'Venus?' said Cameron Bell. 'You have acquired special visas to land upon Venus?'

'Not as such,' puffed the colonel. 'Not as such, old chap.'

'Well now,' said the private detective. 'Not so much a hunting party, more a gang of poachers.'

'A most *exclusive* big-game hunting trip.' Corporal Larkspur, secured to the floor by magnetised boots, stalked heavily away upon these towards his cabin.

'Word of advice,' said the colonel to the private detective. 'Word to the wise and all that. Never get a chap's dander up on a hunting trip. One can get *accidentally* shot up the bum parts. Catch my drift?' He tapped away at his nose.

'Point well taken,' said Cameron Bell. 'My thanks. But tell me, who is the brains behind this most illegal hunting trip?'

'Jovian chap you just spoke with,' said the colonel.

But Cameron Bell shook his head. 'My observations of that gentleman inform me that he is merely a link in the chain, as it were. The man behind this trip is a resident of Earth. He is not aboard this ship.'

'No idea how you reasoned *that* out,' said the colonel. 'But you know your own business best. Larkspur fellow paying me. That is all I know.'

'Interesting,' said the private detective.

'Would someone please pay some attention to me?' said Alice. 'I would like a cup of tea. Or better, a gin and tonic.'

The *Marie Lloyd* pressed on through the aether of space. An unappealing hulk of riveted metal, the product of a Martian armaments factory built solely for service with little aesthetics attached. Five thousand miles out from Earth an automated system kicked in and it began to revolve slowly, creating its own artificial gravity. At length the Jovian hunters awoke, surprised to discover Alice and Cameron amongst them. Found themselves amused by their presence, then suggested they all repair to the bar. Corporal Larkspur, now dressed as a barman, served with a practised ease.

Alice Lovell sipped her gin and tonic. She sat at a table with Colonel Katterfelto, Darwin and Cameron Bell. The Jovians engaged in drinking games that involved laughter and falling over. Corporal Larkspur moped behind the bar.

The ship flew on through space.

'This is a very big adventure,' said Alice. 'I wonder what excitements there will be?'

'You'd best be advised to remain on board, once we get there.' Colonel Katterfelto downed Jovian rum. 'Door locked. Blinds down. Better safe than sorry.'

'Cameron will protect me,' said Alice, and she fluttered her eyelashes at the private detective.

Cameron Bell, somewhat drained by recent experiences, felt a frisson of excitement himself. Was that amorous eyelash fluttering? he wondered. Did this beautiful woman have *feelings* for him?'

Overwhelmed by the very thought, Cameron too sank Jovian rum and sought some other subject for discussion.

Darwin ate noisily from a bag of salted peanuts. Colonel Katterfelto tousled his hairy head.

'Herr Doktör,' said Cameron Bell of a sudden. 'But of course.'

Colonel Katterfelto was startled by this. 'You have read the book?' he asked the detective. 'You know about the Great Quest?'

'I am referring to your "nephew",' said Cameron Bell. 'I recall now reading of a certain Herr Doktör who claims that it is possible to teach apes to read and write and speak also. In order that they may take the necessary evolutionary step forward, which might otherwise go untrodden for another million years.'

Darwin the monkey continued with his peanuts. He had nothing to say.

'Remarkable,' said Cameron Bell. 'And I would gather that his vocabulary is quite extensive.'

'Why not ask him yourself?' said the colonel.

Alice looked intrigued.

'It is an honour to meet you.' Cameron Bell put out his hand towards Darwin. The ape regarded him with a quizzical expression and then shook the detective's hand.

'It is an honour to meet *you*, Mr Bell,' said he. 'We have met before, of course, but never been formally introduced.'

'Most splendid,' said Mr Cameron Bell. 'Have you been taught to play chess?'

Darwin shook his hairy head.

'Would you care to have me teach you?'

Darwin nodded his hairy head.

'Then splendid once again. I spied a travellers' chess set on the bar counter. I will fetch it and teach you how to play.'

Alice Lovell made a face. She recalled certain experiences regarding chess pieces that she had been put through beyond the looking glass.

'Will someone please pay *me* attention,' she said.

Time passed and routines were established. There were cabins available to all and no one had to share. Corporal Larkspur cooked and cleaned and served behind the bar.

Darwin learned chess and soon proved a worthy opponent.

Alice Lovell sulked for much of the time, whilst staring through a porthole.

Cameron Bell, severely tongue-tied now in her presence, mostly said and did the wrong things and hated himself for so doing.

On the fourth day out they sighted Venus.

And on the fifth day they fell into orbit around her.

32

ueer as it might seem now, there was a time when astronomers and scientists of Earth actually believed that the planet Venus was an inhospitable horror of a place. Heated to intolerable temperatures, scorched by rains of sulphuric acid and with an atmosphere so poisonous as to spell death in every language or dialect thereof that existed.

In this modern age of progress and of knowledge such nonsenses are easily put aside. Although it did have to be said that very few members of the human race had ever set foot upon Venus. A British Embassy had been set up there, but the British ambassador was forbidden to leave the compound. Certain explorers had made illegal landings, notably Major Thadeus Tinker the famous big-game hunter, but none had ever been seen again. Though how they came to their ends, if they did, remained so far uncertain.

As the *Marie Lloyd* swung around upon its orbit, each porthole on the starboard side had a face peeping out from it. A green and splendid planet turned below. An emerald world that looked so much as paradise must look. The Jovian hunters cheered and chuckled, clinking their glasses together. The folk of Earth looked out in awe, each alone with their thoughts.

Colonel Katterfelto thought about the Mechanical Messiah. Soon the *Marie Lloyd* would set down upon the beautiful planet and he would be able to avail himself of some *Magoniam*. The missing component. The special something that would enable him to imbue the mechanical marvel with life.

But then what?

As Cameron Bell viewed the gorgeous planet, his thoughts returned to the horrible doings at the Crystal Palace. The destruction of that wonderful building had been *partially* his fault. Although it *was* in a good cause. But what of the creature? What of *I am become Death, the Destroyer of Worlds*? Dead and gone, concluded Mr Bell. As a child, he had read many books of travel and adventure and he recalled one about New Zealand and the Maori people. These savage tribesmen had many cruel habits, but the cruellest of all was the one they meted out to captured enemy chieftains. *Death by Kiwi Bird*. As a child, Master Bell had shuddered at the details and well he remembered them now. Hopefully the creature had literally been consumed by Alice's avian avengers. Certainly one or two of the birds would have perished in the conflict. But such are the casualties of war. So the baddy was gone and Cameron had time to think. His personal world had been brought to ruination. He was now a wanted man. Things had not gone as he might have hoped that they would.

And he was also about to join an illegal landing party and add the breaking of interplanetary law to the charge sheet awaiting him upon Earth. He did not look forward to going back, but he knew that sometime he must.

But then what?

Alice Lovell had been thinking of her kiwi birds. She had

not been worrying about them, however. Because she had no need to. Because had not that kind Cameron told her, when questioned as to the details of what had occurred after she fainted at the Crystal Palace, that the kiwi birds had all been safely rounded up and returned to the Sydenham pet shop to await her return? Such a thoughtful man, that Cameron Bell. But just what lay ahead? She was about to embark on a very great adventure, but it was not one that would add to her fame as it would have to remain a secret. She had topped the bill at the Crystal Palace. But only for moments. Would she ever be given a second chance? And what of the danger she was in from that monster which had attacked her? Cameron's replies to her questions regarding this had all become a bit contradictory and confusing. But whatever happened on Venus, as long as she survived, she would eventually return to Earth.

But then what?

Darwin, the very first monkey in space, had enjoyed the voyage to Venus. He had enjoyed the learning and playing of chess and he greatly enjoyed the company of Mr Cameron Bell. The big question in Darwin's mind, as he peered through a porthole towards the planet beneath, was, *Do they have bananas upon Venus?*

Corporal Larkspur cast the briefest of glances towards the planet below. He was busily engaged in checking provisions and weaponry and tropical kit. Ticking away at a clipboard and whistling to himself, his thoughts were focused upon the success of the venture. Although his definition of the word *success* differed considerably from that of the Jovian hunters on board.

At midday Earth time he called a meeting in the mess hall that all should attend. Dressed now in full tropical kit with pith helmet and jungle goggles, he addressed his fellow space travellers.

'Gentlemen and lady,' he began, strutting as best a Jovian could, given the girth of his thighs. 'Thou hast arrived safely unto the orbit of Venus. The journey hath been without incident. Although I hopéd that whoever blockéd the saloon bar toilet might have hadst the grace to unblocketh it.'

There was much laughter at this from the Jovian hunters, but as they were always given to much laughter, it did not necessarily signal that it was in any way actually funny.

'We shalt be landing,' the corporal continued, 'in an area of subtropical Venus knownst as Elfland.'

'Elfland?' queried Alice. 'As in Fairyland?'

'The region hast many such names,' the corporal went on. 'Goblin Creek, the Bog of the Trolls. We shalt land in Elfland for lo it is the farthest region from any Venusian habitation.'

'No fairies, then?' said Alice.

'*No* fairies. But—' And now he read from a dog-eared pamphlet. ' "An area of outstanding natural beauty with many walks and picturesque vistas. Marvellous rock formations and mineral beds. Docile wildlife makes for an outstanding hunt. Many photo opportunities." '

'What are you reading from?' asked Mr Cameron Bell.

'*The Rough Guide to Venus*,' replied Corporal Larkspur. 'A banned publication. I hast one of the few remaining copies.'

Cameron Bell said, 'Very well done.'

'Well prepared is best prepared.' The corporal continued, 'I shalt bring the ship in to landeth beneath the giant Nabana trees.'

'Banana trees?' asked Darwin.

Corporal Larkspur made an exasperated face. '*Nabana* trees,' he shouted. Darwin bared his teeth. 'Nabana trees,' the corporal said more softly. 'Their trunks riseth to nearly one thousand feet before the foliage spreadeth. Once the ship is beneath these trees it will be hidden from the death patrols.'

'Ahem,' went Colonel Katterfelto. 'Hate to interrupt you there, old chap, but did you say *death patrols*?'

'*Death patrols!*' shouted the corporal. 'I meanest *yes*. The valleys, mountains, forests and all are sacred. Venusian aether ships drift across the skies. Shouldst they sight an idolater violating their holy lands, they dealeth the harshest of punishments.'

The Jovian hunters did not make laughter at this. Although one of them chuckled somewhat at a joke he had heard earlier.

'Which is why,' said Corporal Larkspur, 'thou leadest this hunting party, Colonel. Thou hast experience in both war and on the hunt.'

'Damned right,' puffed the colonel. 'You fellows will fare well enough if you follow my instructions. Stealthily does it and all that kind of how's-your-father-hiding-up-the-chimney. If you know what I mean.'

The Jovian hunters laughed as if they did.

'We shalt remain in Elfland for one week's hunting.'

'Earth week or Venusian week?' asked Darwin.

Corporal Larkspur made fists with his ham-hock hands.

'Nephew's got a good point,' said Colonel Katterfelto. 'Did all this stuff in basic training. One Venusian day equals two hundred and forty-three Earth days, doncha know? Lovely sunsets if you can be bothered to wait, so I'm told.'

Corporal Larkspur did deep-breathing exercises to steady himself. They succeeded only in making him breathless and he had to have a good sit down.

Eventually he rose again to finish what he had to say.

'Please waiteth until the conclusion of my talk before thou askest questions,' he began.

Then he began. To continue.

'The equivalent of one Earth week,' he continued. 'Venturing out each Earth dawn, returningest to the ship each Earth evening. We will synchronise watches. Under the colonel's leadership thou canst bag as much game as thou wishest. The patent Ferris Refridgetorium hath sufficient room to store and preserve trophies. I knowest a taxidermist upon Earth who asketh no questions.'

Much applause was offered up by the jovial Jovian hunters.

'After one Earth week, we moveth on. Once the Refridgetorium is full, we returneth to Earth.' He smiled upon all and sundry. 'And questions *now*?' he asked.

'Can I steer the ship down?' asked Darwin.

Darwin did not steer the ship down. But neither did he bite Corporal Larkspur, as the colonel advised strongly against it for fear that Darwin might unexpectedly end up in the patent Ferris Refridgetorium. The hunters kitted themselves out in safari suits, big boots and camouflaged pith helmets. Checked their weaponry and took to a form of behaviour that Mr Cameron Bell found himself coining a new term for: *macho posturing*. Although they did it overall with good heart.

The colonel, who lived in his dress uniform, took off his medals and hid them in his cabin. And gave his ray gun an extra charge up from the shaving socket* in the bathroom.

Darwin, with several changes of clothes in his luggage,

* *The patent Ferris Electrical Dewhiskerisor being a must-have for any gentleman's travelling case.*

chose to sport a colonial-style white linen suit with panama hat.

Alice discarded her ringmaster's jacket and, availing herself of the ship's stores, affected a rather fetching mosquito-net face-veil. In her brass corset, bloomers, white stockings and buttoned black boots she was not exactly dressed for a big-game hunt. But what gentleman with blood in his veins could have refused her company?

'Please strappest thou in for landing,' came the voice of Corporal Larkspur from the cockpit. And a sign that read SEAT BELTS ON and advised that cigars should be extinguished started to flash on and off.

Darwin made a grumpy face as the colonel adjusted his seat belt for him.

'If thou hast prayers,' continued the voice of Corporal Larkspur, in a manner that would never catch on with future commercial flights, 'now wouldst be the time to speaketh them.'

A mighty rumbling shook the ship as the corporal steered it downwards.

There followed a period of considerable drama, the *Marie Lloyd* shaking fearfully. The friction of atmosphere scorching the hull. The forces of gravity acting this way and that. Alice, seated next to Cameron, clung on tight to his arm. Cameron, finding joy in this, sat with his eyes firmly shut. Darwin held the colonel's hand, which the old campaigner found to be somewhat moving.

The Jovians cheered and some broke wind. What with the excitement of it all.

Down and down went the *Marie Lloyd*, then took to a swerving course. The corporal levelled out the ship of space, brought it in towards an achingly beautiful valley and then grounded it in a forest of mighty trees. There was a hideous tooth-grinding *gromching* of metal on rock and on soil and on shrub.

The *Marie Lloyd* came shuddering to a halt.

'All safe and sound, I trusteth,' came the voice of the pilot.

'I could have done better than that,' came the voice of Darwin.

There *had* been no injuries and the Jovian hunters cheered once more and waited for the seat-belt sign to go off.

Alice leaned towards the nearest porthole and peeped out.

Beyond the ship lay an Arcadian scene, a veritable Garden of Eden.

Alice's breath caught in her throat.

'It is Wonderland,' said Alice.

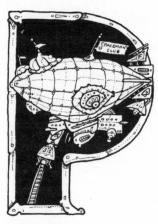

33

atent pressurising equilibriators fussed noisily in the engine compartment of the *Marie Lloyd*. Air from the planet Venus hissed through grilles, bringing with it fragrances as yet unsniffed by any aboard the spaceship.

'Oh,' sighed Alice. 'How beautiful.' And she longed to leave the craft and explore.

'Synchronise thy watches,' said Corporal Larkspur, adjusting his goggles to compensate for any unwished-for glare. 'Two p.m. of the afternoon clock. Returneth by six, if you will. Dinner at eight. Five courses, formal attire, please, gentlemen.'

Thus saying this, he sprang the bolts and opened the door to Venus.

Alice took a swift step back, so too Cameron Bell, the colonel and Darwin the space-travelling monkey, as the Jovian hunters fought to be first through the doorway.

'Gentlemen, *please*,' called Corporal Larkspur from the place of safety that he had wisely chosen. 'And please tryeth to remain beneath the cover of the trees. Forgeteth not the death patrols. Please.'

'Come to order!' shouted Colonel Katterfelto. '*Atten-shun!*'

Which halted the doorway strugglings and brought a modicum of order.

'Ladies first?' suggested Alice.

'I would rather you stayed inside for now, my dear,' the colonel told her.

'Cameron?' asked Alice, fluttering her eyelashes with renewed vigour at the smitten detective.

'The colonel is in charge,' said Cameron Bell. 'I will wait here with you, if you wish.'

Alice Lovell folded her arms and made a grumpy face.

Colonel Katterfelto led the hunters from the craft. He would dearly have loved to gather *Magonium*, as that was his number-one personal priority. But the colonel was an honourable man and he knew it was his duty to offer what protection he could to the Jovian hunters. The *Magonium* would have to wait for now.

The valley was as pleasant a place as could possibly be imagined. The high canopy of the Nabana trees shaded all, yet shafts of light, crystal-rainbow hued, fell between these trees, painting pastel colours onto flowers and shrubs, at once exotic, yet somehow familiar.

Darwin gazed up at the towering trees, thinking them good for a climb. Yet he strayed not from the colonel's side as his little sniffing nose scented creatures unknown and, in all possibility, dangerous.

Colonel Katterfelto drew out an ACME Thunderer and blew upon it. This had the desired effect of halting the Jovian hunters who were about to plunge off in all directions, guns held high, to blast at anything that moved.

'Certain small matters,' the colonel puffed. 'Led hunting parties before. Let me tell you this. Chaps who rush off on their own rarely return to say what ate them. Make myself clear?'

The Jovians nodded. One of them said, 'Yes, sir.'

'Excellent stuff,' said the colonel. 'Put your faith in me and you won't go wrong. Professional fellow. Experience in these matters.'

The Jovians nodded once more.

The colonel reached for his ray gun and then recalled that he had left it extra-charging in the bathroom.

'Just a mo,' he said. 'Won't be a minute.'

And he was less than a minute.

But he returned with his ray gun in his hand to find only Darwin waiting.

'Silly damn fools,' said the colonel. 'Let's see if we can find 'em.'

Within the *Marie Lloyd*, on a bar stool at the bar sat Alice Lovell. Corporal Larkspur had been busy doing something else and she had been forced to serve herself, which had made her even more grumpy.

'You can't make me stay here,' she told Mr Cameron Bell, who sipped away at Jovian rum and felt most deeply embarrassed. 'You are not my father. I can do what I like.'

'You are very brave,' said Cameron Bell. Knowing she was nothing of the kind. 'The creature that attacked you at the Crystal Palace was Venusian. I expect there must be others of his kind lurking about out there, ready to prey upon a pretty young lady like yourself.'

'You have a gun, don't you?' said Alice.

Cameron Bell sighed deeply. 'Yes, I do.'

'And the colonel is not in charge of *you*.'

'True enough,' said Cameron Bell. *Oh dear, oh dear*, he thought.

'A little stroll wouldn't hurt,' said Alice. 'We could keep the spaceship in sight.'

'Things might lie in wait,' said Cameron Bell.

'You are not afraid, *are you*?' Alice turned those big blue eyes upon him.

'I would not want any harm to come to you,' said Mr Bell, in all honesty. 'Perhaps we could just put our heads outside.'

'You are a darling.' Alice jumped off the stool and kissed him on the cheek. 'Come on,' she called, already making for the door.

The two stepped out onto the planet's surface. A carpet of purple lichen strewn with queer blooms that opened and shut as if breathing the air.

Alice looked up at the marvellous trees. Swept her blue eyes over the wonderful sights.

'We should not be here,' she whispered. 'This truly is a sacred place.'

'Do you wish to return inside?' asked Cameron Bell.

'No,' said Alice, tossing her head, then readjusting her mosquito-net veil. 'We are here now, let us just enjoy it.'

From the near distance came sounds of a whistle being blown and shouts of, 'Come back here, you fools.'

'I saw some deckchairs on board,' said Cameron Bell. 'Should I bring out a couple and also our drinks?'

'That would be lovely,' said Alice.

Cameron Bell returned to the spaceship and brought forth deckchairs and drinks.

Alice Lovell, however, had wandered away.

She heard the desperate cries of her name, but she ignored Mr Bell. She would not wander far, and she certainly was *not* brave by nature. But there was something so beautiful, so innocent about the sylvan paradise that she felt it could not possibly harbour any predatory beasts that would carry her off and eat her up for their dinner. This was certainly Elfland. And there might well be elves.

Alice wandered on a while, scuffing her feet in the lichen at intervals. Marking the way she had come.

Alice wondered, as she wandered, whether this magical land was as the Earth had been before the dawning of Mankind. She had always supposed herself to be a Christian, as this was the religion of her upbringing. She had learned much of the Old Testament at Sunday School and had assumed that the words of Genesis must be basically sound. That God *did* create Heaven and Earth and that he did create Adam and Eve to dwell in the Garden of Eden.

True, as the years had passed, she had experienced the occasional doubt and Mr Darwin's theory of evolution was enjoying a degree of acceptance and popularity. And true, her experiences within the rabbit hole and beyond the looking glass were mystical to say the least, but the actual existence of God was not something that, in all truth, she had ever given very much thought to.

A young lady of this modern age had so many other *modern* things to think about.

But here . . . Alice paused and breathed once more the scented air. Here there was magic. Here there was . . . holiness. If the existence of God was to be doubted and debated over in London, it could not be so upon this lovely world. The presence of God was here, shining down in rainbow rays though the tall and noble trees.

Alice sat down and had a little weep.

It was all too wonderful for words.

★

The wonder of it all was not for a moment lost upon Colonel Katterfelto. But he was a man of duty and of honour and he had taken on the responsibility of leading this hunting party. And to do so he must now track down the errant hunters. This was not an altogether difficult business. The amply proportioned Jovians left a notable spoor. Their footprints were most well dug in. And none of them, it seemed, had travelled far.

He came upon the first of them in a clearing, sitting on the ground and clutching at his leg.

'I have a hurty-ankle,' said the Jovian.

The colonel sighed. 'Limp slowly after me,' he said.

The second had tripped over a rock and suffered a hurty-wrist. The third had a hurty-knee. And so on.

Colonel Katterfelto gave them all a sound telling off.

'Stay behind me,' he ordered, 'and I'll find you something to shoot at.'

Darwin looked up at his martial companion. Darwin was not keen. Were there monkeys here, he wondered, distant cousins, somewhat like himself? Would the hunters shoot them dead and mount their hairy heads on plaques to hang upon their walls?

Darwin sniffed once more at the air. He could smell *something* and it was coming closer.

Whether the colonel smelled this too, Darwin did not know, but the old soldier suddenly raised his hand and counselled the keeping of absolute silence. 'The game is afoot,' said he.

Cameron Bell sat down on a rock and clutched at a wounded foot. He was not a man who travelled well through unpaved areas. His natural habitat was London. He knew the capital well. On more than one occasion he had won a bet that he could be blindfolded, taken to any area of the great metropolis and by merely sniffing the air correctly identify its location. It was not really down to the sniffing, though, for once again Mr Bell had not been altogether honest. It was that, given the location he began at, and his knowledge of the streets of London, he could work out, even blindfolded, merely by the twists and turnings of the hansom cab precisely where he was at any time.

But here was not London.

And Cameron Bell was lost.

He was on the trail of Alice, this he knew. Tracking a suspect was a necessary skill in his profession. But Alice's wanderings were many and various, and her trail criss-crossed itself, went around in circles, meandered here, meandered there, meandered all over the place.

'At least there is plenty of daylight,' said Cameron Bell, making scuffings of his own in the hope of not following the same trail once again. 'And still several hours before dinner, I'm thinking.' He took out his watch and squinted at it. Sadly the watch had stopped. He had done the synchronising back at the spaceship, but he had forgotten to wind it.

'No matter,' said Cameron Bell. 'I will find her shortly and I will *not* let her out of my sight again.'

'Down, men.' The colonel gestured downwards with his ray gun. 'On your knees and follow. Come on. Pacey, pacey.'

Lumbering Jovians sagged onto their knees and much to Darwin's amusement waddled after the colonel like so many slightly undersized young elephants. Mumbling about their hurty bits and bobs, but generally chuckling with good nature.

They approached long grasses, tall and pink, that rose to spires of crimson curlicues.

266

'Fan out,' whispered the colonel, gesturing to the left and the right. With big bottoms high, the Jovians fanned out.

As silently as could be, the hunters eased forward, ray-gun rifles cocked and ready, eager for a kill.

Ahead something moved. A white fur-covered head was to be glimpsed. Something non-human, non-Jupiterian, something about to be killed as game.

The hunters now all but surrounded a dreamy glade, kissed by wavering rainbow shafts of sunlight. The muzzles of their ray guns nosed from the long grass, trained upon the creature. The colonel, his own vision somewhat limited by an inconveniently placed − if delightfully beautiful − bush, raised his hand and counted down from three upon his fingers.

'Three,' he counted silently.

'And two − and—'

At the centre of a glade stood Alice.

Chatting with a tall white rabbit.

'One,' the colonel counted down.

Then all the Jovians fired.

34

'think I hear people shouting somewhat,' said Alice.

The white rabbit cocked an ear to the not-too-far-distant cacophony. 'Hunters,' said he, and he sniffed at the air. 'In a nearby glade. I do believe that they might have shot one another.'

'Serves them jolly well right, I think,' said Alice.

Colonel Katterfelto did a body count. 'Just the two dead,' said he. 'Not bad for a first day out.'

'Might I have a word or two in private, please?' said Darwin.

'Certainly, my dear fellow,' replied the colonel, accompanying the monkey a little way off, where they might speak in private uninterrupted by the howls of pain emanating from a number of Jovians who had only been wounded, rather than killed. 'What can I do for you?'

'I understood,' said Darwin, 'in fact, you gave us all to understand that you have led big-game hunts before.'

'Certainly have,' said the colonel, lighting up a cigar. 'Certainly have.'

'Did many of the hunters actually survive?' enquired Darwin.

'Ah,' said the colonel, puffing smoke. 'See where you're going with this. *Did* say that I've led hunts before—'

Darwin nodded thoughtfully.

'*Didn't* say that I was any damn good at it.'

'Ah,' said Darwin, whose thoughtful noddings were now joined by a facial expression indicative of enlightenment.

'Pay's rather good, though, you must agree.'

Darwin nodded with vigour.

'Anything else on your mind?' asked the colonel.

Darwin now shook his head.

The white rabbit was now shaking *his* head. 'Foolish hunters,' he said. 'They cannot shoot anything here but each other.'

'I think they will certainly try,' said Alice.

'And then they will certainly fail.'

Alice shrugged, but did not ask why. Instead she said, 'Fancy meeting you again and *here*.'

'Where else would you expect to meet me other than here?' asked the white rabbit. 'If I wasn't here and you weren't here, then neither of us could meet each other, could we?'

'No,' said Alice. 'I suppose we could not. But I did not expect to meet you again here on this planet.'

'It is where you met me before,' said the white rabbit.

'I met you before in Tunbridge Wells,' said Alice. 'I followed you down a rabbit hole.'

'It might have looked to be that way,' said the white rabbit, preening at his whiskers, 'but just because a thing looks to be a certain way, that does not mean that it *is* a certain way.'

Alice agreed that this might be the case.

'It *is* the case,' said the rabbit. 'I met you here, because it was to here that you were brought.'

'To Venus?' said Alice.

'To Venus. Your uncle unwittingly put magic mushrooms in your soap.'

'Oh,' said Alice. 'I was drugged, so none of it really happened.'

'Are you drugged now?' asked the rabbit.

'I do not think so,' said Alice.

'Then do not interrupt when I am talking.'

'Sorry,' said Alice. Who wasn't really sorry.

'You were kidnapped,' said the white rabbit, 'whilst in an altered state of mind. You were brought here to Venus upon two occasions.'

'By whom?' asked Alice. 'And why?'

The white rabbit twitched his nose and said, 'You ask too many questions.'

'Was I brought here in a spaceship?' Alice asked.

'There you are, doing it again. But I will tell you this. Not because I need to, but because I wish to. The ecclesiastics of Venus have been kidnapping people from Earth for many years. They bring them here and try to teach them things. Special things. Spiritual things that cannot be learned upon Earth. Only here in a world that is still filled with magic. They wish to convert all the peoples of the solar system to their way of thinking. To enlighten them, that they might share the wonder.'

Alice gazed about at the beautiful glade. A four-winged butterfly settled upon a flower that was easily the size of a dinner plate. 'It is very wonderful here,' said Alice.

'It is certainly better than where I come from,' said the white rabbit.

'So you were kidnapped, too?'

'Where I come from we do not call it kidnapping,' said the white rabbit. 'Where I come from we call it *abduction. Alien Abduction.*'

'Curiouser and curiouser,' said Alice.

Cameron Bell was curious to know what all the shouting and howling was about. But intuition correctly informed him that it was *not* about Alice.

Mr Bell, who had not donned tropical kit, took off his dinner jacket and fanned at himself. He was growing rather hot. All this walking, he supposed. Exercise was all well and good, but if he was to be having a bit of a holiday here upon Venus, he really would have preferred it to be mostly a sitting down in deckchairs and drinking gin and tonics sort of holiday. *Not* a tracking a wilful woman through uncertain terrain sort of holiday. Oh no, not that *at all.*

Cameron Bell ran his fingers over his naked scalp. He really should have worn a hat. He was prone to over-perspiration. Hatbands absorbed perspiration. That was one of the major points of hatbands.

Cameron Bell suddenly said, 'Now now now.' His mind was sorely wandering, as was the wilful woman. He glanced at his hand and viewed the Ring of Moses. Now what *was* he to make of *that*? A magic ring? A ring that could *carry* magic? The *real* Ring of Moses? Moses the Venusian? 'My mind wanders,' said Cameron Bell to himself. 'Because I do *not* believe that this case is truly ended. The Death character might well have been pecked to oblivion by the kiwi birds, but there is more to the case than him. I do not believe that he killed the Music Hall bill-toppers. I do have a theory regarding that, but it is a theory that must be put to the test. I suspect the involvement of another. A powerful individual who seeks even more power. But here I am upon Venus chasing after a foolish female.'

The private detective sighed. He had no control over the situation. He had no idea precisely how long he would be here. He had no idea precisely how much trouble he would be in when he returned to Earth. He had no idea about so many things.

But at least he *was* dressed for dinner.

And although it is never really wise, if you are all by yourself in a potentially dangerous environment, to draw attention to your location by shouting, Cameron Bell considered that shouting might draw greater returns than aimless wandering.

'Alice,' called Cameron Bell, most loudly. 'Alice, where are you?'

'Someone is calling your name,' said the white rabbit. 'I suppose that you had better go.'

'It is Cameron,' said Alice. 'He will be worrying about me.'

'You are lucky, then,' said the white rabbit. 'No one ever worries about me.'

'Your mother must have worried,' said Alice.

'My mother was a *rabbit*,' said the rabbit. 'Mother rabbits just make more rabbits. More and more rabbits. That's what they do. If they were to worry about each rabbit they gave birth to, they would certainly worry themselves into an early grave.'

'I suppose they would,' agreed Alice.

'So I will say goodbye for now.'

'You do not have to,' said Alice. 'You could come back to the spaceship with me if you want to.'

'I am far too shy,' said the white rabbit. 'And your hunter friends would surely try to shoot me.'

'You said that they would not be able to shoot anything other than each other.'

'Well, at least you were listening. But I will say goodbye to you and see you again soon.'

And with that the white rabbit vanished.

Just like *that*.

'Don't put on a tourniquet like *that*,' said Colonel Katterfelto. 'Around a chap's arm, perhaps. But never around his throat.'

The surviving Jovians, who had not been wounded, were making poor work of applying the field dressings from the colonel's first-aid kit (which, with uncanny forethought, the colonel had brought along with him).

'Let me do it,' said this gentleman. 'And Darwin, stop swigging from my hip flask. Victims only, doncha know.'

Darwin offered the hip flask to a Jovian with a hurty-stump.

'Not a banana in sight,' said the monkey. 'I think that we should all go back for tea.'

'Dear Cameron,' said Alice. 'I thought you were bringing out a deckchair and a gin and tonic for me.'

Cameron Bell shook his head most sadly. 'We had better go back now,' he said.

'I heard shouting,' said Alice, who was not making any particular motions towards joining the private detective in a stroll back to the spaceship. 'I do believe that some of the hunters might have injured themselves, or others.'

'Happily,' said Cameron Bell, 'that is *not* my responsibility.'

'Am *I* your responsibility, then?' asked Alice.

'Would you care to be?' Cameron Bell surprised even *himself* with this question.

'A lady likes to have a gallant protector,' said Alice. 'Come on, I'll race you back to the spaceship.'

'It is not in *that* direction.'

But Alice was off once again.

The big-game hunt had not got off to a particularly good start, all things considered. No big game had actually been bagged, two Jovians were dead and three more quite badly injured. Colonel Katterfelto had created a triage system to judge the seriousness of what had occurred.

Number One, which was to say the highest category, was, of course, *death*.

Number Two, an injury serious enough to soon elevate the injured party to the Number One category.

Number Three, the loss of some body part previously considered vital, but whose loss did not in fact lead to death.

Number Four, anything else.

So far there were two *Number Ones*, one *Number Two* and two *Number Threes*. Which the colonel still considered not bad for the first day out. As he and the remaining hunters limped back towards the spaceship, hauling makeshift stretchers, he thought he would get a bit of a community sing on the go as a morale booster. He chose that evergreen popular Music Hall standard: the 'Two-by-One' song.

An anthem in praise of planed timber, approximately two inches by one inch, but sawn to any length you might require.

As the verses were quite long and complicated, he stuck to the chorus, which went:

The two-by-one,
The two-by-one —
That's the stuff for you, old son.
You'll have laughter,
You'll have fun
When working with the two-by-one.
It's a marvel of the age,
The greatest of them all.
The four-by-two is much too large
And the one-by-one's too small.

It certainly had the desired effect and soon all the *Number Four* survivors were laughing once again.

The colonel, Darwin, the walking wounded and the rest met up with Alice and soon after with Cameron Bell.

All were somewhat surprised and a tad disheartened when they returned to the landing site and found that the *Marie Lloyd* was missing.

35

'one,' said Colonel Katterfelto. 'The spaceship has upped and gone.'

Darwin the monkey gibbered mournfully. Alice thought it most queer. No laughter came from the Jovian hunters. Most looked rather downcast.

Cameron Bell sat down on a rock and viewed the landing site. He viewed the lichen, the trunks of the trees, the foliage high above.

Alice sat down beside Mr Bell and gave his arm a squeeze.

'Do you think we will be marooned here for ever?' she asked him. 'Do you suppose that I will have to become Eve to all you gentleman Adams?'

Cameron Bell was made speechless by this.

'I want to go home,' said Alice.

'And I too, sweet lady,' said the private detective. 'When *I* choose to do so. It is all a most curious business.'

'Curiouser and curiouser?' said Alice.

'Decidedly so. Because although the spaceship is not here, it cannot have left.'

'Why not?' asked Alice.

'Because I have *this*.' Cameron Bell exhibited a large brass key. 'Call me a suspicious fellow,' he said, 'but as the space-ship represents our only means of transport back to planet Earth, I had no wish for it to leave without me.'

'Why would that happen?' asked Alice.

'I can think of a number of reasons. Which is why, when I returned to the spaceship to gather deckchairs and drinks, which you will notice are also missing, I availed myself of this key. I believe the technical term for it is the *ignition key*. The spaceship will not fly without it.'

'But clearly it has,' said Alice.

Cameron Bell shook his head. 'Let us suppose that an-other ignition key exists – and I do not believe that one does – how would you explain the marks left upon the lichen by the weight of the spaceship when it rested there?'

Alice stared. 'There are no marks,' said she.

'Precisely. Which is why I say to you that the spaceship never left.'

Others were gathering now about Mr Bell, either in-trigued or annoyed by his conversation.

'What *exactly* are you saying?' asked the colonel.

'I am saying that the spaceship never left.'

'Hate to contradict you,' said the old soldier, 'but as you can see – or as you *cannot* – there is no spaceship. It's gone.'

'I perceive by the lower buttons of your jacket that you are a gambling man,' said Cameron Bell, and the colonel grunted in assent to this. 'Then I will wager you one hun-dred pounds that you cannot walk from here directly to those trees over there.'

'To beyond where the spaceship stood?' asked the colonel.

Cameron Bell brought out a handkerchief and dabbed at the head he was nodding.

'One hundred pounds?' The colonel glanced at Darwin.

Darwin shrugged his shoulders.

'Just to walk from here to there?'

'In a straight line, yes.'

'Then you have a wager, sir.' The colonel extended his tanned and wrinkly hand. Cameron Bell gave this hand a good shaking.

'In your own time, then,' said the private detective.

'Man's a damn fool,' said the colonel.

'Hold hard, if thou pleaseth,' said a Jovian hunter, who had this very afternoon acquired the new nickname of Stumpy. 'Canst anyone take this bet?'

'Certainly,' said Cameron Bell. Giving Stumpy's stump a little shake.

Colonel Katterfelto and three chuckling Jovians set out to earn themselves an easy one hundred pounds each at the expense of a private detective who had clearly been out in the shafts of sunlight for a little too long.

Darwin eyed the private detective. This man was no sun-struck fool, he felt sure.

'Excuse me, please,' said the monkey of space.

'How might I help you, Darwin?' asked Mr Cameron Bell.

'My feelings are,' said Darwin, 'that you are about to win the bets. But please assure me that in doing so no harm will come to the colonel. He may lack for certain necessary skills as the leader of a big-game hunt, but I do consider him to be my closest friend.'

'If I am correct,' said Cameron Bell, 'he will experience nothing more than a headache. If I am incorrect, however, I have no idea how I will pay him his winnings.'

The detective and the monkey looked on.

And one at least was surprised by what happened next.

There came a sound as of a wooden ball striking a coconut after a well-thrown hurl at a fairground shy.

'Damn and blast!' cried Colonel Katterfelto, staggering backwards and falling down in a heap.

'Blasteth also,' came further cries, to the accompaniment of further such horrible coconut-striking sounds.

'Quite as I suspected,' said Mr Cameron Bell, making the very smuggest of faces. 'But as to how it is done, I do not have the foggiest idea.'

'They hit their heads upon nothing,' said Alice. 'Oh no – I understand you now. Not upon *nothing*, but upon something that we can no longer see.'

'Precisely,' said Cameron Bell. 'The spaceship is there, but somehow quite invisible.'

'It is the glamour,' said Alice, with wonder in her voice. 'The glamour of Fairyland. It can be nothing else.'

Darwin's face wore a helpless look.

Alice tried to explain. 'It is magic,' she told the monkey. 'Upon this magical planet, magic really works. On Earth many people, perhaps myself included, believe in the fairy folk. They are said to have magical powers, one of which is called the glamour. They can make things appear to be other things. Or not appear to be there at all. I find it rather wonderful. But it also makes me afraid.'

'I wonder,' said Cameron Bell, 'whether the spaceship is invisible on the *inside*. Come, Darwin, I shall collect my winnings and then we shall both find out.'

The *Marie Lloyd* was *not* invisible on the inside. And once Cameron Bell had explained to the losers of the bet that someone or some*thing* had placed a cloak of invisibility about the spaceship, the spell appeared to be broken and the exterior of the ship in wavering rainbow patterns came once more to be seen.

Which Alice for one considered to be something of a shame. Because it was, after all, a rather ugly spaceship and it *did* spoil the view of the valley.

'Which I suspect might well be the point,' said Cameron Bell, over dinner. 'I am coming to the conclusion that magic thrives upon Venus. Perhaps the very planet itself is magical. And this, believe me, is radical thinking upon my part. I am a man of Earthly logic and although scientists of Earth in their arrogant bravado would seek to explain the universe and its origins, I am of no such ilk. I am of the opinion that this planet does not want us upon it. I am of the opinion that it would be in all of our interests to depart this world as speedily as we might.'

Corporal Larkspur, who was serving the evening's repast – rather splendid lamb shanks in gravy with two veg and Treacle Sponge Bastard for pudding – overheard these words and was moved to contribute some of his own.

'The hunters hath paid a great deal of money to cometh on this trip,' he told Mr Bell. 'Once we hath sufficient trophies to fill the Refridgetorium, we shalt depart for Earth.'

'Might not be as simple as that,' said the colonel, splashing red wine into glasses about the table. 'Big white furry thing in the glade this afternoon. All took aim. All missed. Chaps shot each other. Big white furry thing should have been caught in the crossfire. But no trace. Nothing. Odd planet, this. At least on Mars, if you shot something with a ray gun, it had the decency to die. Here things come and go as they please.'

'Dost thou wish then to resign from thy post?' asked Corporal Larkspur. 'Thou wouldst forfeit thy fee, of course.'

'Not saying *that*,' puffed the colonel. 'But agree with the Balls chap here. Queer planet, this. Need to step carefully is all.'

'Cream or custard with your Treacle Sponge Bastard?' asked Corporal Larkspur.

'Both,' said Colonel Katterfelto.

Dinner was brought to a satisfactory conclusion and the Jovian hunters prepared to engage in drinking games and songs around the piano. Colonel Katterfelto put a slight dampener upon this, however, by suggesting that they should do the decent thing and bury their dead before the local wildlife tucked in. Grumbling somewhat, the *Number Four* Jovians were issued with spades and garden forks from the ship's stores and set out to accomplish this grim task.

'Game of chess, Darwin?' asked Cameron Bell.

'That would be nice,' said Darwin.

Alice opened her mouth rather wide. But upon this occasion it was not to complain that she was not being shown sufficient attention, but instead to admit the entrance of a large slice of Treacle Sponge Bastard, with custard.

The evening passed and although it was still daylight outside and would be for at least another ninety Earth days, midnight came to pocket watches, and all and sundry turned in.

Most had enjoyed their first day on Venus. Most were now eager for sleep.

Cameron Bell said his goodnights and took himself off to his cabin. But he did not find sleep. His driven mind was rarely ever at peace and to be here upon Venus and seemingly in the presence of genuine magic gave the private detective a lot to think about.

He lay upon his bunk for a considerable while, but as it

was impossible to sleep he eventually left his cabin, poured himself a brandy at the bar and took himself outside the spaceship for a smoke.

The two deckchairs he had brought out for himself and Alice had de-glamorised along with the *Marie Lloyd* and Cameron Bell seated himself upon one of them, placed his brandy glass upon the lichen floor of the valley and sought a cigar to smoke.

But had none.

He was about to return to the ship's bar, where a selection of cigars were displayed in a glass-fronted case, when he heard footsteps behind him.

It was certainly an instinctive thing with Cameron Bell. Rather than rise and say hello to whoever was stepping from the *Marie Lloyd*, Mr Bell chose instead to sink slightly lower in his deckchair and hope that he was not observed.

He was not.

Corporal Larkspur passed him by. The corporal carried some tools and a bulky piece of electrical apparatus.

Cameron watched him creep, for creep indeed he did, off into the distance. Then the detective followed.

He did not have far to follow.

Once out of sight of the spaceship, Corporal Larkspur put down his tools, placed his piece of electrical apparatus upon the ground and began to tinker with it, making adjustments here and there and extending a sectioned metal rod.

He then donned a pair of modernistic ear accoutrements and spoke into the electrical apparatus.

Cameron Bell crept near to hear what he was saying.

'Agent Larkspur calleth Ground Base One,' said Corporal Larkspur. 'Agent Larkspur calleth Ground Base One.'

Words were evidently returned to his ears, but Cameron Bell could not hear these.

'All goeth precisely unto plan,' said Corporal Larkspur.

Further words. Then—

'Two dead so far,' he replied. 'No great loss unto the universe in general, thinketh I.'

Further words were spoken into his ears.

'O yea and verily,' said Corporal Larkspur. 'He cameth aboard with the woman at the spaceport. I trusteth him not.'

The corporal listened intently as further words came to him through the aether of space.

'Yes, sir,' said he. 'I shalt acquireth the necessary samples of *Magoniam* tonight. And dealeth with Mr Bell as and when it suiteth me to do it.'

Further words presumably followed.

'Killeth him when convenient,' said Corporal Larkspur. 'And the woman?'

A pause for further words and then—

'Returneth her to Earth for blood sacrifice. I understandeth. Over and out.'

36

tealthily Cameron Bell returned to the spaceship. Sensing a golden opportunity, he eschewed returning to his cabin and chose instead to search the private quarters of *Agent* Larkspur.

With nothing more than a dining fork, he picked the cabin door lock, then slipped inside and had a good look around. Sunlight streamed in colourfully through the porthole, lighting upon a room of chronic untidiness. Cameron Bell found himself wading amongst soiled socks and cast-aside long johns. A musky odour brought no joy to the private detective's nostrils. Not a room to be in when the contents all became weightless in space, he concluded.

Beneath the bunk was a steamer trunk and Cameron eased this out. Applying his fork to the locks, he sprang them open. The trunk contained one of those brand-new silver-coloured atmospheric suits in which a space traveller could breathe and enjoy a degree of comfort in conditions of extremity when there was a lack of air. It resembled a deep-sea diver's costume, with large brass helmet and boots with magnetised soles. Upon a cylindrical air tank was a brazen boss engraved with the maker's name.

M. R. FERRIS & Co.
Alperton, England.

'I wonder if anyone else has been issued with one of *these*?' whispered Cameron Bell, surreptitiously making one or two minor adjustments to the valve-settings on the air cylinder.

Pleased with his handiwork, he closed the steamer trunk, relocked it and pushed it back beneath the bed, rearranging the floor litter around it into an unpleasing composition.

Cameron then continued his searchings. Uncovering a number of books about mineralogy authored by a certain Herr Döktor. A wallet containing a quantity of calling cards, one of which Mr Bell slipped into his waistcoat pocket. Personal items and private possessions, all of which he perused then carefully returned to their places.

Nodding his bald head in some satisfaction, he left the private quarters of Corporal Mingus Larkspur and returned to his own. There he bolted the door and wedged a chair beneath the handle. Then he prepared for sleep.

Darwin the space monkey woke to a clamour of bells. He could have had a cabin to himself, as there were more than sufficient to go around, but he chose instead to remain in the company of his friend and business partner.

Colonel Katterfelto floundered about, discovered the noisily ringing alarm clock and flung it to the cabin floor, where it gave up its ghost and lay silent.

'Seemed like a good idea at the time,' said the colonel. 'But then always been an early riser myself. Sorry to stir you from your slumberings, my dear fellow.'

Darwin the monkey yawned and stretched. He wore a gingham nightshirt with matching nightcap, and looked very *dear* indeed.

Colonel Katterfelto broke morning wind. 'Sorry pardon,' said he.

As the porthole did not open, Darwin left the cabin.

A buffet breakfast had been laid out in the dining room and Darwin helped himself to cornflakes.

Several Jovians, already in their safari suits, were munching fried sausages and toast. One of them, catching Darwin's eye, made gun-fingers with his big right hand and mimed a-firing at the hairy fellow.

Darwin the monkey returned in haste to his cabin.

The colonel was lathering up for a shave. 'Speedy breakfast,' said he.

'A Jovian pretended to shoot me,' said the monkey. 'Although Venus is a pretty place and the financial remuneration considerable, I confess that I would rather be back at the Snap tables of The Spaceman's Club.'

'Have no fear for your safety,' said the colonel, spitting shaving soap in numerous directions. 'I'll look after you. And you'll come out of this rich as a monkey can be.'

'Are you leading them out on another safari today?'

'Thought I'd make 'em leave their guns behind. Rope the blighters together. See if we can get through a morning without any further loss of life.'

'I might just stay in the cabin and read a book,' said the ape of space.

At a little after ten of the London morning clock, those Jovians within whom the spark of life still flickered assembled outside the *Marie Lloyd*. Eight now remained out of the original ten and this eight seemed more inclined to heed the words of Colonel Katterfelto than they had upon the previous afternoon. All had been issued with spades. All were now roped together about their ample waists.

'No shooting today,' said the colonel, swagger stick lodged beneath one arm, boots both highly polished.

'Awwwwwww,' went the Jovians, most harmoniously.

'Appalling mess yesterday,' said the colonel, ignoring this *awwwwing*. 'Can't have any more of that. Need to get organised. Need to get disciplined. Understand me?'

Jovians dismally nodded their heads. One said, 'Canst we go fishing instead?'

'Probably end up drowning yourselves,' said the colonel. 'No, what we're going to do is have a little competition. You all have your spades?'

The Jovians displayed these without enthusiasm.

'Any of you fellows heard of *Magoniam*?' the colonel asked.

A single Jovian raised a single hand.

'Ah,' said the colonel. 'Stumpy. Heard of the stuff, then, have you? Know what it looks like?'

'Gold,' said Stumpy.

'Gold-coloured, eh?'

'Just gold,' said Stumpy.

'Looks a bit like gold, is that what you're saying?'

'*Is* gold,' said Stumpy. 'Or as we knowest it upon Jupiter, *Jovite*. On Earth thou callest it gold. Upon Venus, *Magoniam*. Surely thou knowest *that*?'

'Hm,' puffed the colonel. 'Only testing. Glad to see you were paying attention. So, treasure hunt this morning. Prize for whoever brings back the most *Magoniam*.'

The Jovian hunters now sought to make off in different directions, but as they were firmly roped together, this resulted in considerable confusion and much comedic falling over.

'Still not all batting from the same end,' said the colonel, 'but we'll have you chaps licked into shape by lunchtime.'

Darwin took a late breakfast then returned to his cabin to read. Cameron Bell took his breakfast with Alice and now the two sat out in deckchairs.

'I really hope they don't kill anything,' said Alice. 'It would be so wrong to kill anything here.'

'I regret that it *is* what they have come for.' Cameron Bell lit up a recently acquired cigar. 'But as to how many of them will actually return to Jupiter with their trophies, who can say?'

'Would you kill something here and take it home?' asked Alice.

'I do not have a home any more, I'm afraid.'

'You have a beautiful home,' said Alice, 'full of beautiful things.'

'All destroyed,' said Cameron Bell. 'The house blown up. All gone.'

'That is awful.' Alice gave his arm a little squeeze. 'Was it that horrible man in black who attacked me at the Crystal Palace?'

Cameron nodded and said that it was. 'But it does not matter now.'

'But all your books and family photographs?'

'What is done is done,' said Cameron Bell, 'and cannot be undone. And strange as it might sound, I no longer feel any loss. I feel now somehow liberated. As if my own past in the shape of those objects somehow held me captive.'

'I know exactly what you mean,' said Alice. And she considered telling Cameron all about her queer experiences and identifying herself as the Alice of the popular storybooks. She might even mention her meeting yesterday with the white rabbit.

But she did not.

Because he would think me quite mad, thought Alice, and so she changed the subject.

'I wonder if my kiwi birds are missing me,' she said.

'How about a nice cup of tea?' asked Cameron Bell.

Colonel Katterfelto had tea in a vacuum flask and whilst the Jovians, looking now to be for all of the world an over-weight chain gang, toiled away in search of *Magoniam*, he unscrewed the lid and poured himself some and smiled a little bit.

Vacuum flasks always made the colonel smile. Ever since he had attempted to explain their workings to Darwin.

'You put in something hot and it stays hot,' Colonel Katterfelto told the monkey, 'and something cold and it stays cold.'

'But how does it know?' asked Darwin. Which had sounded funny at the time.

So for now the colonel sipped at his tea and watched the Jovians dig. They went at it with a will and with good grace and with their usual humour. The colonel determined that he would do his level best to see that as many as possible survived to the end of the big-game hunt.

'*Magoniam!*' cried one of the Jovian diggers.

'Put it on your own pile,' said Colonel Katterfelto, observing with some delight the growing heaps of Venusian gold. This planet was a, well, a veritable gold mine, so it seemed. The old soldier sipped some more at his tea and smiled a bit more also. The Jovians could surely come to no harm by simply digging and he had already crammed more than enough *Magoniam* into every pocket of his uniform to overfill the empty compartment of the Mechanical Messiah, which was probably even now being manufactured for him.

'It does not get better than this,' puffed the colonel. 'Does not get better than this.'

Cameron Bell would certainly have agreed with the colonel. The private detective had brewed tea in the galley and brought out a pot, with cups for two and a nice plate of biscuits beside. He settled himself down in the deckchair next to Alice, poured her a cup and placed one sugar in it.

'It really is paradise here,' said Alice, taking two biscuits from the nice plate she was offered. 'I do miss my kiwi birds. But I would not have missed this for all of the world.'

The biscuit plate now being empty, Cameron went without. But he smiled at Alice and agreed that being here was very special indeed.

'I think that I have never known such peace,' he said.

Rainbow shafts fell here and there onto the valley floor. A gentle breeze turned the occasional fallen leaf and butterflies danced in the crystal air. Something furry bobbed in the distance, and Cameron Bell sighed softly.

Then stiffened as he heard the sudden shouting.

'Whatever is *that*?' asked Alice. 'What is that terrible noise?'

Cameron Bell cupped a hand to an ear. 'The Jovian hunters,' he said.

'They have not shot each other again, surely?' Alice set aside her tea and biscuits and rose from her deckchair to peer into the distance.

Cameron Bell was rising too as the sounds of shouting grew louder.

'I think we had better return to the spaceship,' he told Alice.

'If someone is in trouble, perhaps *you* should help them,' said Alice. 'While *I* wait safely in the spaceship.'

'Yes,' said Cameron Bell, who was having his doubts. What with the increasing volume and frantic nature of the shouting.

'Oh dear,' he continued as he sighted Colonel Katterfelto.

The old gentleman was running full pelt towards the *Marie Lloyd*, flapping his hands as he ran and shouting, 'Get inside, damn it! Get inside.'

'Let us get inside *now*,' said Cameron Bell.

Behind the colonel ran the hunters, still roped together but making extraordinary progress. For big and bulbous beings they were putting on an impressive display of speed.

But not without good cause, for now both Cameron and Alice beheld the reason for all this running and shouting.

'Oh my goodness,' said Cameron Bell.

'That is a dragon,' said Alice.

oologically speaking,' said Colonel Katterfelto, as he caught at his breath and peeped out through a porthole of the *Marie Lloyd*, 'dragons are improbable at best.'

Cameron Bell was intrigued by the beast and as all of the hunting party, the colonel, Alice and himself were now relatively secure within the spaceship and the door firmly bolted upon the magical world beyond, he took a little quiet time to contemplate the dragon.

His skill to draw conclusions through intense observation had been put to the test upon animals of Earthly origin. He recalled a time whilst seeking a criminal mastermind in New York City when the direction of the hairs on a wiener dog's tail had led him to the conclusion that its owner was not the humble person he claimed to be, but rather the notorious Lord of Misrule, Eskimo Jim McNaulty. Cameron also remembered how his own mother had taught him to accurately predict thunderstorms by 'reading' the lay of a spaniel's ears. But then the divination of future events through the study of spaniel ears dated back to Pythagoras and Pliny.

Dragons were untrodden territory for Mr Bell. And so

when Alice asked him whether the dragon would eat them all, he had little he could tell her in reply.

'Arm up, chaps,' called Colonel Katterfelto. 'If you're up to shooting something, now would be the time.'

Alice peeped out at the dragon. It really was a most exquisite creature and looked to her exactly how a dragon really should. Fifty feet from tail to snout. Green and scaly all about. Tiny wings upon its back and smoke coming out of its nostrils. It paced up and down outside the spaceship upon four stubby legs, occasionally flicking its barbed tail and snorting fearfully. It made Alice feel most terribly afraid, but also strangely excited.

The Jovian hunters, now unroped, were cocking their ray-gun rifles.

'Rank up facing the door,' said Colonel Katterfelto. 'Two ranks, one kneeling, other standing behind, that's the stuff. Now imagine you're potting the Zulus at Rorke's Drift. Or, if that means nothing to you, just do as I say. When I unbolt the door, front rank fire, then we'll take it from there.'

Colonel Katterfelto approached the door. Darwin the monkey shook his head.

'Ah,' said the colonel. 'Understand your doubts. Might get cut down when they all fire together.'

Darwin the monkey nodded.

'You must not shoot it,' said Alice.

'Madam,' said the colonel, 'I have no wish to be ungallant, but I will leave the training of kiwis to you and you must leave the slaying of dragons to me.'

'Saint George had a lance,' said Alice. 'Ray guns are not very sporting.'

'Sure Saint George would have *liked* a ray gun,' muttered the colonel, positioning himself to the rear of the hunters' ranks. 'Open the door, please, Stumpy, then we'll have a pop at the beast.'

Corporal Larkspur came bustling up from somewhere.

'Thou shalt not discharge any weapon aboard this spaceship,' said he, in no uncertain manner. 'One misplaced bolt might breacheth the hull. A hole spelleth doom in space.'

'Fellow's right,' agreed the colonel. 'Stumpy, open up the door. Others march outside and form new ranks.'

None of the Jovians seemed too keen to comply.

'Imagine that head on your study wall,' said the colonel. But even this incentive failed to move the hunters.

'I shalt turn the cannon upon it,' said Corporal Larkspur. 'And lo the beast shall grievous fall beneath its mighty prang.'

'Cannon?' queried the colonel. 'Prang?' he queried also.

'Mark Five Patent Prang Cannon,' explained the corporal. 'Latest thing, thou knowest. It employeth the trans-substantiation of pseudo-kharmic antipasti.'

'Think you have that in a bit of a twist,' said the colonel, who did his best to keep abreast of all the latest innovations in death-ray technology. 'But catch the drift. Give the beast both barrels and see if the job gets jobbed.'

'Cameron, stop this, please,' said Alice.

'Perhaps if we all stay very quiet it will lose interest and go elsewhere,' Cameron Bell suggested to Corporal Larkspur.

The corporal eyed the private detective in a manner far from friendly. 'Perhaps thou wouldst care to stepeth outside and shooeth it away,' he suggested.

The dragon now struck the side of the spaceship, shaking the occupants all about and causing considerable alarm.

'Breeched hull will meaneth all die-eth,' said the corporal.

'Man the prang cannon,' said the colonel.

The existence of the prang cannon came as something of a surprise to Cameron Bell. This was, after all, a commercial vehicle of space, *not* an armed man-o'-war. A spaceship such as this, one that might be chartered by whomever could afford such a luxury, would not normally be expected to carry inbuilt weaponry. True it had originally been a Martian invasion craft. But these did not have cannons mounted upon them.

There was clearly much much more to this venture beyond an illegal hunt.

Darwin the monkey tugged at the colonel's trousers.

'What is it, my dear fellow?' asked the oldster.

'I want to fire the prang cannon,' said Darwin.

But this he was denied.

In fact no one upon this particular midday of the London clock got to fire the prang cannon. There was a manual containing many pages of complicated instructions that had to be read and thoroughly absorbed before this technological terror weapon was even switched on. And the firing seat had thirty-two different position settings and the prang cannon could not be charged up ready for firing without the brass ignition key to the spaceship being inserted into its dashboard.

And the brass ignition key had unaccountably gone missing.

Which caused considerable distress to Corporal Larkspur.

'I am sure it will turn up,' said Cameron Bell, smiling somewhat as he said it.

Another great buffet upon the hull informed all and sundry that the dragon's intentions, whatever they proved ultimately to be, included gaining access to the *Marie Lloyd*.

'Back to Plan A,' said the colonel. 'Open the door, Stumpy.'

'No,' cried Alice. 'Please don't shoot the dragon.'

'Balls,' said Colonel Katterfelto, 'take the young lady to her cabin, if you will.'

The dragon struck the hull once more and everyone fell over.

'Right,' said the colonel, struggling up to his feet. 'Nothing for it. I will deal with this.' And drawing his ray gun from its holster he ordered Stumpy to unbolt the door.

'Perhaps we might reconsider our options,' Darwin suggested. 'I have no doubts as to your bravery, but many for your prospects of survival.'

'Duty,' said the colonel. 'My responsibility. Safety of all up to me.'

'Perhaps it *might* just go away,' said Darwin.

The dragon struck the *Marie Lloyd* once more.

Stumpy drew the bolts with some difficulty, then kicked open the door. Colonel Katterfelto charged out through it, ray gun raised on high.

Stumpy hastily drew the door shut and nudged the bolts back into place.

'Brave fellow,' said Cameron Bell. 'I will miss him.'

Darwin's face was one of horror. 'Someone help him,' he cried.

But none showed any enthusiasm. All just peered through the portholes.

Beyond the portholes stood the colonel, squaring up to the dragon. The thing of myth and wonder towered above, smoke issuing from its nostrils, up on its stocky hind legs, scaly and fearsome to behold.

Colonel Katterfelto aimed his ray gun at its head. 'Now see here,' he told it. 'Have to ask you to take your leave. Or be forced to shoot you dead. Understand? Don't speak dragon language, but I'm sure you catch my drift.'

The dragon glared down on the figure below. Flames licked at its lips and its jaws went *snap-snap-snap*.

'Cut along now,' ordered the colonel. 'Nothing for you here. Back to your nest, or whatever.'

Flames roared down from the dragon above.

The colonel stepped nimbly aside.

'Final warning,' said he. 'Make off now, or in future folk will know me as Colonel Katterfelto, the chap with the dragon-skin luggage.'

'And hero of the Martian Campaign.'

'Napoleon's pickled nads,' said the colonel, employing an expression indicative of extreme surprise. 'Talking dragon, is it, be damned?'

'Same old Katterfelto.'

'Didn't see your lips move,' said the colonel.

'If you look over here, then you might.'

'Know that voice,' said the colonel. 'Recall it from somewhere.'

'Of course you do, you fearless fool. And please don't shoot me pet.'

The old soldier stared and then he said, 'Damn me, Tinker, it's you.'

A ragged figure stood beside the dragon. He wore the ruins of a military uniform and sported a vast mop of snow-white hair with massive matching beard.

'Major Thadeus Tinker, Queen's Own Electric Fusiliers,' said this war-torn apparition. 'Permission to come aboard the *Marie Lloyd*?'

'Permission granted.' The colonel saluted. 'But leave your pet outside.'

38

'tay here, Colin, and don't cause any fuss,' Major Thadeus Tinker told the dragon.

'*Colin?*' queried Colonel Katterfelto.

'Seemed as good a name as any.'

The colonel ordered the opening up of the spaceship's door and he accompanied his old friend aboard the *Marie Lloyd*. And then made introductions all around.

'Bar, I think,' said the colonel. 'I'm sure you can remember where it is.'

Off to the bar went the reunited friends, followed by everyone else. Seats were taken, champagne poured and the major told his tale.

'As some of you will know,' he began, 'after the defeat of the Martians, Katters here took to leading big-game hunts on the red planet. Terrible business, very sad—'

The colonel raised an eyebrow.

'Quite so,' continued the major. 'I myself had always had adventure in me veins. So, got a licence from the Ministry of Serendipity in London to explore and chart Mars. Then thought I'd take off and have a look around hereabouts.

Things, however, went the shape of a pear and found meself marooned. Chummed up with Colin for company, as it were. Waited for rescue. Pleased that you came so quickly, really.' The major, evidently of the opinion that his tale was now told, got stuck into the champagne proper and sought to help himself to biscuits.

'Not quite following you there, old bean,' said Colonel Katterfelto, drawing the biscuit plate beyond the major's reach. 'We all thought that you were long dead, doncha know.'

'*Long dead?*' said the major. 'In a *week*?'

'Not quite following you there, either.' The colonel helped himself to a biscuit and dunked it in his champagne. 'You have been missing for seven years. *Not* seven days.'

'Hardly sporting to pull a chap's plonker with a lady present,' replied Major Thadeus Tinker. 'The first day dragged a bit, I recall. The other six went speedily.'

'Oh my,' said Alice. 'I understand.'

'*I* certainly don't,' said the colonel.

'This is a magical world,' said Alice. 'Time is different here. As it is said to be in Fairyland. When I was a child, my uncle told me stories of children in past times who wandered into fairy mounds, met with the secret folk, danced with them and ate their food. These children returned to their own world after what they thought to be a few hours to find that one hundred years had passed.'

'Tish, tosh and old wet fish,' said the colonel. 'Never heard such folderol.'

Darwin the monkey nudged at the colonel's elbow. 'Let us not forget the matter of the invisible spaceship and the dragon outside,' he whispered.

'Quite so,' puffed the colonel. 'But tell me this, Major, old mucker me lad. If you are convinced that you've only been here seven days, explain the face furniture and the long snowy locks on your bonce.'

'Thought it something to do with the atmosphere.' The major reached out and drew the biscuit plate to him. 'Felt a lot fitter since I've been here.'

'As a matter of interest,' said Cameron Bell, 'my eyesight has improved considerably since we landed here. Always needed my pince-nez before, but I seem to have perfect vision once again.'

As evidently this was *not* considered a matter of interest amongst the general assembly, Cameron Bell said no more. He sought to get a biscuit, but there were none to be had.

'Tell us about the dragon, please,' said Alice.

'Colin?' said Major Tinker. 'Harmless enough beast in his way. But apparently dragons guard gold. That's their role in life. Other than for getting up to unspeakable carryings-on with virgins—' Alice blushed at this. The dragon *had* stirred certain feelings within her, this was true. '—and being bothered by knights in armour. They guard gold. Like griffins do. And other beasties, too, I understand. My fellow explorers got a bit carried away when they discovered just how much gold there was on this world. I was away when Colin came upon them. There was considerable unpleasantness. Not much left to bury, if you follow what I'm saying.'

Heads nodded gravely. Jovians glowered at Colonel Katterfelto.

'Come now,' huffed and puffed the colonel. 'How was I supposed to know *that*?' He straightened his uniform, which bulged with its hoard of Venusian gold.

'Kept dogs all my life,' the major continued. 'Spaniels mostly, just to know the weather in advance. But there's not much difference between a spaniel and a dragon. But for the

300

size, and the scalyness, and the wings, and the fiery breath, and the—'

'But similar to train,' said the colonel.

'Not really,' said the major. 'But for the sake of argument, let's say yes.'

'Why did you not fly back to Earth in your spaceship?' Alice asked.

'Yes,' agreed the colonel. 'Good question. Was going to ask that myself. Yes indeed. Most certainly.'

'It vanished,' said Major Thadeus Tinker.

'Ah,' said the colonel. 'Let me put you straight, my good fellow. Turned invisible is what it did. Ours did likewise, too.'

'I know it turned invisible,' said the major. 'I'm not a dammed loony, you know. Came back to find Colin charcoal-grilling my fellow explorers and the ship no longer where it should be. But no dents in the ground where it stood. Suspected some kind of trickery involved. Did bang my head the first time, though.'

'So your spaceship is still where you left it,' said Alice.

'No, dear lady, no. It reappeared, but then went away for good two days later. Vanished a bit at a time. First the tail fins, then the stores, then the whole damn shebang. By the fourth day the ship had gone completely. I should have taken off when I still had the chance. But you know how it is. If you've never had a dragon for a pet before, you get carried away. But the spaceship, poof, gone, pity really, but there you are.'

Darwin looked at the colonel. The Jovians looked at one another. Corporal Larkspur looked at all and sundry.

'Given the temporal differences,' he said, 'and the strong possibility that this spaceship will inevitably become subject to a supernatural disassociation with our reality, it is my considered belief that we should not remain upon this planet any longer than another twelve Earth hours.'

Corporal Larkspur blinked. All eyes were suddenly upon him. 'Why do you look at me so?' he asked. 'Surely I am voicing a consensus opinion. We do not wish to become marooned upon Venus, do we? *What?*'

'Your accent,' said Darwin, saying what all others thought. 'You are suddenly speaking like an English gentleman rather than a Jovian. What of this?'

Corporal Larkspur looked from one to the other. And from one to the other and back again. 'I tookest a language course,' said he. 'I readeth a pronunciation book by Herr Döktor. Learneth to speaketh the Queen's English. It ith my ambition to gaineth the job of Society columnist on *The Times* newspaper. Yea, verily, thus and so and things of that nature generaleth.'

'Well, that's all right then,' said the colonel. 'Thought for one moment that something suspicious was going on.'

Corporal Larkspur shook his head vigorously. 'Noteth one bit of it,' said he.

The Jovians began to laugh, which eased away much of the tension.

Cameron Bell quietly ground his teeth and felt shamed to his very core. Corporal Larkspur was clearly *not* a real Jovian. But somehow, even after searching his private quarters, this had slipped by Cameron Bell.

'Are you all right, Cameron?' asked Alice. 'You seem to have turned a most unpleasing tone of grey.'

'Iffy biscuit, perhaps,' said the private detective. 'Might I ask the major a question?'

'You certainly might,' said himself.

'During your stay here have you had any contact with the Venusians?'

'Happily not.' The major drained champagne from his glass. 'They adopt the methods of our American cousins when dealing with Red Indians: shoot first and ask questions later. I have seen their aether ships many times, drifting overhead like fairy castles in the sky. It's a queer world here, right enough. Ray guns don't work on the animals. Make them damned angry, though.'

The Jovians were once more done with laughter and took again to making grumpy faces.

Stumpy said, 'I think I shalt require my money back.'

Corporal Larkspur made an uneasy expression. 'The colonel shalt organise something,' he said. 'Shouldest he wish to pocketeth his fee.'

'Bows and arrows, perhaps,' said the colonel. 'Catapults at a push.'

'I think our major concern,' said Cameron Bell, 'should be for the time differences, naturally not forgetting that the spaceship might start to vanish for good. If a day here represents a year upon Earth—' But then he paused and smiled. The passing of a year upon Earth actually suited him rather well. Things would have quietened down considerably in a year. The Crystal Palace would probably have been rebuilt and Commander Case, having failed to solve the cases of the incinerated bill-toppers, would be very grateful indeed to become reacquainted with Mr Cameron Bell.

'Another twelve Earth hours on our watches,' said Cameron Bell. 'Then we should depart, no matter what.'

'How proposeth thou to pay for thy return flight?' asked Corporal Larkspur. But Cameron Bell did not reply to *this*.

'Damned fine to see you again, though, Tinker,' said the colonel. 'Let's pop another bottle of bubbly. Talk the toot like the old days. Get all rat-faced and maudlin. How does that suit you?'

'Very well,' said the major. 'And damn fine to see you, too. It will be absolutely splendid to get back to London once more. We might have a night out at the Music Hall. What do you say to that?'

'We might,' said the colonel. 'We might.'

'Of course we might, we can chuck old fruit and veg at the useless bugger who bottoms the bill and eye up the dolly-mop girls of easy virtue who parade about onstage training their birdies. What do you say to *that*?'

The colonel glanced at Alice, who made a certain face.

'Perhaps a game of Snap at my club instead,' suggested the colonel.

'Game of Snap, splendid.' The major beckoned the colonel close and whispered into his ear. 'I have a bag of uncut diamonds in my pocket. Worth a fortune back home. Don't mind cutting you in for a guinea or two if you get me back to Blighty aboard the good old *Marie Lloyd*.'

'More champagne,' the colonel called. 'And set another place at my table for dinner.'

'It is only lunchtime now,' grumbled Corporal Larkspur. 'And I shalt have to asketh the major to cleareth up after his dragon. For verily it hath poopeth outside the door.'

Colonel Katterfelto laughed somewhat at this.

Alice whispered to him, 'Are you intending to take the Jovians out on another hunt?' she asked.

'They will want *something* for their money,' said the colonel. 'And I have to earn mine. Sorry and all that. No help for it.'

'And you intend to arm them with bows and arrows?'

'Stones to throw?' the colonel suggested. 'Small stones. Pointy sticks, perhaps.'

'Well,' said Alice, and she peeped once more through the nearest porthole. 'You had better make haste, then, for the sun is going down.'

'What? What? What?' went the colonel. 'Sundown isn't due for ninety Earth days yet.'

But be that the case, or be it not, the sun *was* going down.

'Ah,' said the major. 'I should have mentioned this. Horrid things happen in the night.'

39

enus could certainly boast a splendid sunset.

The Earth folk and the Jovians oohed and ahhhed at it.

Alice cried out in delight as the descending solar disc bloated into lemons, greens and purples.

Cameron Bell, who stood beside her, considered Alice to be the most enchanting creature that ever there was and wished very hard that some miracle should occur that would maroon just her and he upon this world for ever. It was a mad wish, of course, and the private detective knew it. But he ached to slip his hand about her delicate shoulders and draw her close to him.

'We must cherish this moment,' said Alice, precisely reflecting Cameron's thoughts. 'We will probably never again see such a sight as this.'

'I feel honoured to see it,' said Cameron Bell.

'Honoured,' said Alice. 'That is a good way to feel.' Alice suddenly glanced all around. 'Where did Colin the dragon go?' she asked.

Major Thadeus Tinker, port glass in one hand and cigar in the other, said, 'He pops off at night.'

Alice shrugged.

The major continued, 'You never actually see him go, but go he does until morning.'

'It is growing rather dark now and somewhat chilly, too,' said Alice.

'And we had better go inside,' said the major, 'because things come that really aren't very nice.'

Dinner was not the jolly affair that it had been on previous occasions. All dressed formally, of course. Because, after all, dinner is dinner no matter where it might be taken, and standards must never drop. But the Jovians sat sullenly, exchanging little but surly mutterings.

Alice, Cameron, Colonel Katterfelto, Darwin and Major Thadeus Tinker occupied a table to themselves and suddenly felt somewhat isolated. Somewhat vulnerable.

'Don't think badly of me for saying this,' said the colonel, in a hushed yet puffing fashion, 'but the natives are restless, as it were. Jungle drums beating. That kind of dangerous business.'

'What is he saying?' Alice asked Cameron.

'He is saying that he fears the Jovians might do something, how can I put this, mutinous. They have paid a lot of money to come here and shoot things. They might choose to shoot things that are other than Venusian.'

Alice's eyes opened wide. 'They might shoot *us*?' she said.

'Word to the wise,' said Major Tinker. 'Chummed up with a Jovian once. Hired him as a forward scout on Mars. Used to send him out first thing to check for danger.'

Alice raised a quizzical eyebrow.

'Yes yes yes,' said Major Tinker. 'I could have sent an Earth fellow, I know, but you know how it is.'

Alice thought that she probably did.

'Thing was,' the major went on, 'he showed me some photographs of his home. Very pretty things, full colour, not the usual sepia. One was of what he called his "Recreation Room", had all his hunting trophies up on the wall. I'm not sure he meant to show me that one. The one with three mounted human heads upon wooden shields hung over his desk.'

'How perfectly frightful,' said Alice.

'That's not the worst of it,' said the major. 'He had a woman, too, stuffed and posed giving a—'

'That is quite enough of *that*,' said Cameron Bell. 'I would suggest that when dinner is concluded we all go directly to our cabins and lock ourselves in most securely.'

Darwin the monkey picked at his salad and whimpered to the colonel, 'That Jovian who made the gun-fingers at me keeps grinning in my direction,' he said.

'I'll protect you. Have no fear, my dear fellow.'

'I found the best way,' said Major Thadeus Tinker, 'is to pull a pillow over your head and assume the foetal position.'

'This is not the time for *that* kind of talk,' said the colonel.

'When they come,' said the major.

'Stop it, Tinker, you saucy fellow, it's not appropriate here.'

'I mean when the ghosties come in the night,' said Major Tinker, and his hard and horny hands shook as he said it. 'If you can't see them and you can't hear them, then it's almost as if they are not there at all.'

Alice said, 'This is all too awful. I am afraid of ghosts.'

'Ghosts can't hurt you,' said the colonel. 'Bother you, yes. But hurt you, no. Saw one on Mars once. Strangest business. Sleepin' peacefully in me tent when I heard a kind of whooshing sound. Woke me up, you see. Went outside and damndest thing. Sort of metal box on legs, big thing, mind you, like a little house. Spaceship of some sort.'

'That isn't really a ghost, is it?' said Darwin, who having had no personal experience of ghosties in general sought to have none in particular. 'A spaceship is a spaceship, not a ghost.'

'You'd think,' said the colonel. 'But think on this. The spaceship – if such it was – had the letters USA on the side. United States of America, that stands for.'

'I think he is making this up,' said Cameron Bell. 'America is never likely to send a man into space. Americans cannot even speak the Queen's English, for goodness' sake.'

There was some laughter at this. But it was a bit forced.

'Saw the ghost of the spaceman,' the colonel continued. 'He wore one of the new atmospheric suits. But he was a ghost. His suit was white instead of the proper silver. Had his name on the breast. NASA. Odd name for a fellow, Nasa. Don't know what to make of it at all.'

Silence fell upon the table. No one knew just what to make of *that*. And when the Treacle Sponge Bastard was served, no one, it seemed, was in the mood to enjoy it.

Brandies were drunk, cigars were smoked, then all turned in for the night.

It would be a night to remember that nobody wished to remember.

A small child came to Cameron Bell. A small child that he knew.

'Mother does not love you,' said this small child. 'Mother loves *me* the best.'

Cameron Bell gaped from his bunk. 'My twin brother, Peter,' he said.

'You killed me, Cameron,' said Peter. 'You held my head

309

under the water of the ornamental fountain. You killed me because Mother loved me the most.'

'It was not *me*,' said Cameron Bell. 'It was Uncle Johnny. I proved it in court. It was my first case. The stains on his shirt cuffs proved it.'

'He tried to pull me out and save me. But you sent *him* to the gallows.'

'No,' said Cameron. 'You have it all wrong. It was not me, I swear.'

The troops just marched past the colonel. More and more of them, but each a soldier that he knew. Each a soldier who had served under him, who had lost their life upon one campaign or another. And Jovians too marched with them. Jovian hunters were these and as each one passed they pointed a finger, coldly, at the colonel.

Darwin hid beneath his pillow trembling terribly. He could not see the ghostly troops, but he could sense they were there.

The white rabbit came once more to Alice.

'You are not a ghost, you are a rabbit,' said Alice.

'You will never be free of Venus,' said the white rabbit. 'The ecclesiastics will call you to them again and again for ever.'

'I should be very afraid if that were to happen,' said Alice. 'Please tell me what I must do to make it stop.'

'You must do *this*,' said the rabbit and he whispered at Alice's ear.

'Oh!' said Alice. 'I don't think I could do *that*.'

Major Thadeus Tinker hid his head beneath his pillow. He had been through this for the last seven nights and had not enjoyed a single moment of it. Ghosties swirled about him in a fervour. The major kept his head down.

The ghosties fairly tormented the Jovian hunters. They chased them all over the spaceship making them howl with fear.

Ray guns would certainly have been discharged in every direction had not Colonel Katterfelto displayed another moment of foresight and had them all locked away in the gun cabinet.

The ghosties did not bother Corporal Larkspur. He sat cross-legged upon the floor of his private quarters, surrounded by a ring of *Magoniam* pieces. He chanted words that were neither of Earthly nor Jovian origin and swayed backwards and forwards as he did so. Ghosties that sought to enter his cabin dissolved as dreams in sunlight.

When the light of the sun returned to the *Marie Lloyd*, it poked its glistening fingers through the portholes of the starboard side and touched upon the cowering folk whose cabins faced that way.

There was no joy to be found at all in breakfast.

'I leaveth the choice up to thee and thine,' announced Corporal Larkspur, the only inhabitant of the spaceship to look as if he had enjoyed a sound night's sleep. 'We can leaveth at once, assuming of course that the ignition key returneth.' He offered a penetrating gaze to Cameron Bell, who smiled in return. 'Or thou canst go out, armed with sticks and stones, and seek to bringeth down what game presenteth itself.'

'Or perhapseth just take the refund,' Stumpy suggested.

'I consulteth the contracts during the night,' said Corporal Larkspur most convincingly. 'No refunds canst be made.'

The Jovians now made the surliest faces. Major Tinker had a mental image of heads upon walls. His own next to Colonel Katterfelto's. Just below that of Corporal Larkspur.

'There is one thing,' said the major, 'which might relieve a sticky situation.' He drew from his pocket his pouch of uncut diamonds. 'These fellows seem to be lying around all over the place. And Colin only guards the gold. This one alone—' he displayed a rough gem '—would go for approximately ten thousand pounds at Hatton Garden.'

And then the major stepped nimbly aside as the Jovians made for the door.

'Be back by midday of the London clock,' Corporal Larkspur called after them.

Colonel Katterfelto shrugged. 'I think I'll just leave them to it this time,' he said.

Darwin wondered whether a few hours of diamond prospecting might prove *extremely* profitable. But, as Colin came suddenly lumbering by, the monkey of space decided to err on the side of caution and remain aboard the spaceship.

'Would you care for a last little walk?' Mr Cameron Bell asked Alice.

'I would,' said Alice. 'Very much indeed.'

They left the ship and Alice linked her arm with his. Cameron Bell sighed inwardly as he and the woman that he loved so much strolled through the sylvan glades, admiring the wonderful blooms, the colourful four-winged butterflies, the towering trees and all that lay around them.

'It is very Heaven,' said Alice. 'I am glad you chose to walk with me, rather than loot this magical world of its diamonds.'

Cameron Bell said nothing. His thoughts were all his own.

Alice turned her face up to his. 'What will you do when we return to Earth?' she asked.

'That very much depends upon how much time has passed there,' Cameron said.

'I hope not *too* long,' said Alice. 'Do you think I will top the bill at the Electric Alhambra?'

'I will personally see to it that you do,' said Mr Bell.

Time passed on in its magical way. The two walked on together.

'You look after me so wonderfully,' said Alice, a little later.

'Well,' said Cameron Bell, 'it is the wish of most men to look after someone they l—'

'What is *that*?' asked Alice. Pointing as she did so.

'I see trees and I see flowers,' said Cameron. 'And I lo—'

'Out there,' said Alice. 'Beyond those trees, but coming this way rather fast.'

Cameron stared, then said, 'Oh no. A Venusian death patrol.'

40

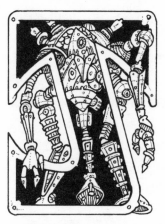ovian hunters were lumbering back to the spaceship. Some burdened, it appeared, by considerable mineral wealth, loaded into each pocket of their big safari suits. Some carried pith helmets stuffed with emeralds. All were once more making very good speed.

Major Tinker called to them to hurry as best they could.

'They'll scoop you up,' the major called, 'and that will be that for you.'

The Venusian death patrol craft was not without interest. It somewhat resembled a fanciful castle with towers and dwindling spires, but was composed, it so appeared, of gossamer, soap-bubbles, thistledown and things of a fairyish nature. With no obvious means of propulsion, it drifted on a steady course, one bound for the *Marie Lloyd*. As dreamy and fey as this sky castle was, those aboard it dealt death.

The wonderful structure was suddenly overhead, lost amongst the leafy canopies of the towering Nabana trees. But then down in a manner silent but deadly came slender silver rods. Scarcely the width of a broom handle but terminating with a single eye-part, within a thrice-pronged claw.

Cameron Bell had steered Alice back into the spaceship. Major Tinker entered too, still calling to the Jovians to hurry as best they could. A slender silver rod, writhing snakelike, snatched at the Jovian last in the scurrying party. The three-pronged claw caught him hard by a leg, hauled him from his feet. As his companions rushed on towards the possible safety of the *Marie Lloyd*, he was swept up into the sky, to meet, all supposed, a very terrible end. Further rods came flashing down. Two more Jovians, calling for mercy, found them-selves dragged skywards.

Only five of the original hunters now remained alive. And these five, once inside the spaceship, demanded the use of their ray guns to make a fight of it.

'Too dangerous,' cried Corporal Larkspur. 'Breaching the hull with gunfire could spell doom. Bolt the door and take your seats, we depart this planet with alacrity.'

'He's making very good progress with his Queen's English lessons,' Darwin observed as the colonel fastened the seat belt around the monkey's waist. 'I really have not taken to Venus. I don't think I'll come back.'

An awful scratching, raking sound now put many teeth upon edge. Major Tinker, strapping himself in next to the colonel, said, 'If they can get a purchase on the old *Marie Lloyd*, they'll drag her back to one of their cities. Things won't go well for us.'

'We'll make a damned good fight of it,' quoth Colonel Katterfelto. 'Corporal—'

Corporal Larkspur was heading for the cockpit. 'I don't have time to talk,' he said.

'And I don't have time to die. Give me the key to this prang cannon jobbie. I'll make short work of the blighters.'

'Ah,' went Corporal Larkspur. 'About the ignition key.'

'As chance would have it,' said Cameron Bell, 'I just found it on the floor. Perhaps you dropped it, Corporal.'

'Perhaps.' The corporal made a face of hatred. The spaceship shuddered as claws raked over its hull.

'Come to think of it,' said Colonel Katterfelto, 'don't quite see how this works. Need ignition key to get spaceship engine going, yes?'

'Yes,' went the corporal, looking most exasperated.

'But need same key to work prang cannon. Or do you have two?'

The corporal examined the single key that he now held in his hand. Words of profanity rose from his lips, in perfectly formed Queen's English.

'I can pick the lock,' said Cameron Bell. 'Corporal, get us into space. Colonel, accompany me to the prang cannon.'

'Which is *where*?' asked Colonel Katterfelto.

'Down that way. First on the right and up the stairs,' shouted the corporal, now rather red in the face.

Darwin was starting to shiver with fear. Alice moved from her seat into that vacated by the colonel.

'Might I sit here?' she asked the monkey. 'And perhaps hold your hand? I am rather afraid, you see.'

Darwin looked up at Alice and smiled. And put out his small hairy hand.

There were now a hundred snaking silver rods curling over the *Marie Lloyd*, touching, sweeping, probing with evil caresses. The Martian hulk was once more rocking as, snapping like serpents, these sinister agents of doom sought to penetrate the hull.

Corporal Larkspur dropped into the pilot's seat and keyed

the ignition. The engines gave a kind of strangled cough, then went very silent indeed.

'No,' said Corporal Larkspur. 'That is most unsatisfactory.' He let the key spring back into place then turned it once again. A lesser cough issued and then a greater silence.

'Oh no!' cried Corporal Larkspur. 'The battery's flat. But it should have been good for weeks.' A sudden thought entered the corporal's mind. 'It's the magical time here,' he said. 'The magical time is to blame.'

There is sometimes comfort to be found in explanation.

This was not one of those sometimes.

'We are doomed!' cried Corporal Larkspur. 'Doomed!'

Things were not going as well as they might have been in the armoured gun port that housed the prang cannon.

'This one makes the seat go up, I think,' went the major, harnessed into the firing seat and pushing a button to no response whatever.

' "Thank you for choosing the
MARK FIVE PATENT PRANG CANNON." '

Cameron Bell was reading aloud from the instruction manual.

' "The Mark Five supersedes the Mark Four,
lessening the danger of severe radiation
damage to the operator. Incidences of fatal
static discharge to the operator are minimised by almost
three per cent. Rubber boots and a hardy disposition
are, however, recommended.

' "Sterility may be avoided through the
simple expedient of shielding the operator's
private regions by wearing the
MARK FIVE LEAD-LINED LONG JOHNS.

' "Thank you for choosing the
MARK FIVE LEAD-LINED LONG JOHNS.
The Mark Fives supersede—

'This might take a little time,' said Cameron Bell.
But time, however, was *not* upon his side.

A horrible groaning sound accompanied by a sudden forward movement informed all aboard the *Marie Lloyd* that the
ship was taking off. Not, though, by the power of its very
own engines. The snaking silver rods had woven themselves
into a kind of web about the hull and were dragging the
helpless hulk into the sky.

'Oooooh!' went all who were not firmly strapped in.
Cameron Bell amongst them.

'Start, you ★★★★★!' went Corporal Larkspur, frantically
twisting the key.

In a great swinging arc, which avoided any damage at all
to the mighty Nabana trees, the *Marie Lloyd* was drawn from
its hiding place into the naked heavens.

Within there was madness and mayhem as, but for most of
the passengers, absolutely nothing had been secured prior to
this unscheduled take-off. Food and furniture, beer bottles,
brandy balloons, shoes and safari suits, servings of Treacle
Sponge Bastard, each of these and so much more were all
flung about within the spaceship.

Cameron Bell found himself catapulted from the

armoured gun port and bounced down the central aisle between the ranks of passenger seats.

'Come back, Balls,' bawled the colonel. 'Must I do everything myself?'

The *Marie Lloyd* was now some three thousand feet up in the bright blue sky. A beautiful cloudless sky today, had anyone sought to enjoy it. But within this captured spaceship most were consumed by terror. The engines clearly were not on the go and should the Venusians choose simply to release their captive from the silver cables that netted the ship, all aboard would surely die when it struck the valley floor.

That the Venusians had no such intentions might have been speculated upon. To them an object of blasphemy had been removed from the sacred valley of Elfland. It and all it contained would be destroyed in the great furnace at Rimmer, which had been specially constructed for such purposes.

A letter of stern protest would be penned to the British ambassador. And the delivery of those little round chocolate sweets that he loved so much would be curtailed for a month, in punishment.

Darwin held tightly to Alice's hand and wondered what dying was like. Since he had learned to speak the Queen's English and to read and write also, Darwin had read many books. Amongst these the Bible. He had been greatly taken with the Old Testament. Especially all the animals going into Noah's ark, two by two by two. But there had been a question nagging away at him and that was regarding souls. Men had souls, the Bible made clear, but what about the monkeys?

The swinging about of the spaceship made for upset stomachs, but there was a queer calm silence all around.

'Alice,' said Darwin, 'might I ask you a question?'

'Certainly,' said Alice, who was shaking very much.

'When we die in a minute,' said Darwin, 'will you take me to Heaven with you?'

Alice looked at the monkey and tears welled in her eyes.

Cameron Bell had tears in his eyes. But these were not from emotion. These tears were from a cheesecake that had struck him in the face. He was back on his feet now and at the cockpit door. Forcing his way in, he frowned at Corporal Larkspur.

'Why have you not switched on the engines?' he demanded to be told.

'The battery is flat. Because of the difference in time. It would have been good for weeks under normal circumstances.'

'Don't you carry a spare?'

Corporal Larkspur glared at the private detective. 'No,' said he. 'I do not.'

'Then improvise, man. Don't you realise what peril we are in?'

'Peril?' said Corporal Larkspur, bitterly. 'Oh, I thought we were all just going for a jolly joyride. You stupid ★★★★★!'

The two men looked hard at each other. Cameron Bell knew instinctively that only one of them would return to Earth alive.

The private detective drew out his ray gun.

'Ah!' cried Corporal Larkspur. 'So now you show your hand.'

'Out of the seat,' shouted Cameron Bell, 'and let me deal with this.'

'You cannot pilot the ship,' said Corporal Larkspur. 'In

fact no one can but I. If you wish to return in safety to Earth you would do well to offer me your protection.'

'I only mean to get the engines started.'

The city of Rimmer, capital of the magical world of Magonia, sparkled on the horizon like the Emerald City of Oz. Romantic, beautiful, unearthly. This city was ancient, built before Mankind had first set foot upon the Earth. Here the mighty ones of old, whose epic adventures were now the myths of other worlds, had done their deeds and lived their lives of magic.

Sailing towards it in gossamer glory, the aether ship of the death patrol dragged the *Marie Lloyd*.

The great furnaces were stoked, awaiting heretics to burn.

'You don't know what you are doing,' complained Corporal Larkspur. 'What *are* you doing, by the way?'

'Connecting the charging cable from my ray gun to the ignition panel,' explained Cameron Bell. 'I pull it out from the stock, see? Then plug it into here, see?'

'It is a *charging cable*,' said Corporal Larkspur, 'for charging the ray gun. Not the other way round.'

'Ah,' said Cameron Bell. 'But here is the beauty of it. If I make a small adjustment here to my ray gun—'

'Yes?' went the puzzled Corporal Larkspur.

'And reverse the neutron flow—' said Cameron Bell.

But then he looked up at the corporal.

'Is it getting hot in here?' he asked him.

Mighty furnace doors were opening below.

Above the *Marie Lloyd*, Venusians slipped the silver cables.

41

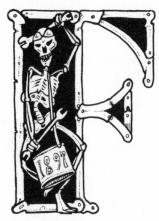alling like a stone towards the furnace, the *Marie Lloyd* went down and down and down.

Darwin clung to Alice and Alice clung to Darwin. The Jovians said prayers their mothers had taught them. Cameron Bell discovered God and wondered whether the Almighty really did offer his eternal blessings to those who made eleventh-hour conversions to His faith.

The flames roared up, the ship dropped down.

Down into the furnace and was gone.

Then up again in a roar of engines. Up into the sky.

Corporal Larkspur clung to the joystick, red of face, with eyes all popping out. Cameron had a fine sweat on and offered his thanks to God.

The Jovians cheered, Alice cried and Darwin the monkey fainted.

'Out into space,' cried Cameron Bell. 'Back to the Earth at the double.'

'I know what I'm doing,' Corporal Larkspur said with bitterness. 'You might thank me for saving your life.'

'I think you will find that it was I who started the engines,' said Cameron Bell.

'But I who flew us from the jaws of death.'

'But you who let the batteries run flat.'

'But you who stole the ignition key.'

'But—'

'Gentlemen,' said Colonel Katterfelto, 'best cease congratulating each other. Aether ship on our tail, doncha know? Best get a move on, eh?'

'Is the prang cannon operational?' Cameron asked the colonel.

'Depends how you define *operational*, old chap. Have the firing seat working now. Come to borrow the ignition key.' The colonel reached towards it.

'Best not,' said Cameron Bell. 'I will pick the lock on the cannon.'

It was certainly to be hoped that things would all work out right in the end. As Cameron and Colonel Katterfelto scuttled off towards the armoured gun port, the pursuing Venusian craft trained cannons of its own upon the speeding *Marie Lloyd*.

Scholars of cosmology and those who write wordy treatises upon the life of the inhabited worlds have long found wordless gaps in their work when they write of the planet Venus. How exactly a race so polite, charming, godly, peaceful and cooperative had for so long managed to stymie all attempts at anthropological study by other races was, if nothing else, a triumph of interworld diplomacy.

Attempts had been made, some of these most valiant. *The Rough Guide to Venus*, briefly published before the threat of war had it removed from the shelves of W. H. Smith, included maps, a history of Venus and a *Good Food Guide* to Rimmer. Authored, very possibly, by the enigmatic Herr Döktor and now more highly prized than an original copy of *The Necronomicon*, this small tome represented *all* that was known of the planet Venus and her people.

In the section entitled MAGICAL WEAPONRY, these words were to be found:

> As with the Venusian ships of space,
> which are referred to as Holier–than–Air
> craft and move through the aether
> by the power of faith alone, the weapons
> of this magical world do not function by
> mechanical means. An ecclesiastic, trained
> in the aiming of the 'Weapon of Wrath',
> concentrates his thoughts through a
> meditative process into a 'will to punish',
> then mentally propels them through the
> nozzle of the gun. This nozzle is fashioned
> from the sacred metal *Magoniam*, a subtle
> form of gold capable of carrying the
> power of magic. It is said that no minerals
> on any other planets possess this property.

White stripes of destructive force issued from the aether ship. The death patrol was now in hot pursuit.

Corporal Larkspur glanced into a wing mirror then made what he considered to be an evasive manoeuvre. Cameron Bell found himself plastered to the ceiling of the armoured gun port.

The colonel, once more harnessed to the firing seat, said, 'Don't be a silly arse, Balls. We've serious business here.'

The *Marie Lloyd* did loopings of the loop then swept towards the blackness of space. The equivalent of Earth's gravitational pull increased by a factor of three and had Cameron now pasted to the floor and the colonel's mustachios meeting at the back of his neck. But at least these loopings of the loop brought artificial gravity to the *Marie Lloyd*.

'Tally-ho!' cried the old soldier, when he was able. 'Damn good fun, eh, Balls?'

Cameron scraped himself into the vertical plane.

A white stripe of concentrated malice cleaved a tail fin from the *Marie Lloyd*, sending the craft into a corkscrew trajectory that was most unpleasing to the spaceship's occupants.

Jovians brought up their breakfast.

Darwin fainted again.

Cameron Bell tinkered at the prang cannon's dashboard with his fork. The colonel spun stopcocks and gave valves professional flickings.

'Fast as you can now, please,' was his advice.

Cameron tinkered, then threw up his arms, drew out his ray gun and pointed it at the dashboard.

'Ah,' said the colonel. 'Good idea. Use the retractable charge cable in the ray gun's stock. Reverse the neutron flow. Job done.'

Cameron took aim and shot the dashboard.

Bulbs sprang into vivid life along the cannon's length. A whining, as of dangerous power, rose to an eardrum-splitting pitch. Cameron Bell pocketed his ray gun. 'Aim it and fire it!' he cried, clamping his hands over his ears. 'Fire it before it overloads.'

'Speak up!' shouted the colonel. 'A lot of noise in here.'

'*Fire it!*' shouted Cameron.

'Fire it? Jolly good.'

The *Marie Lloyd* lost another tail fin, which at least stopped all the spiralling. Jovians peered pale-faced through their portholes as the Venusian aether ship began to draw alongside.

'Hold hard a moment,' shouted Cameron Bell. The din of the prang cannon overcharging itself had risen to a pitch beyond that of human register. On Venus the dogs all started to howl. Which meant they have dogs upon Venus.

'What are you saying?' shouted the colonel, for everything else in the armoured port was still rattling noisily about. 'Can't hear what you're saying.'

'They don't know we are armed,' bawled Cameron Bell. 'Don't shoot until they are right alongside. Then give them everything that we have.'

'Just like we did to Johnny Martian, eh?' The colonel made the thumbs-up.

Alice now peeped through her porthole. She saw the beautiful craft. So close it was that she could see that it more resembled a galleon than a flying castle. There were Venusians upon the decks, laughing and pointing. Some appeared to be drinking cocktails. One was aiming a very big gun indeed.

Alice saw a Venusian in an extravagantly decorated uniform approach the being that manned the very big gun. He raised his hand then brought it down and there was a terrible bang.

The explosion tore the ship apart, dissolved it into atoms, made it simply cease to be.

A single craft now moved through the silence of space.

'Alexander's greatcoat!' said the colonel. 'That was a prang if ever there was one. Damn fine job there, Balls.'

After a great deal of watch-checking and heated debate, it was finally agreed that the time was nearing one of the lunchtime clock. Earth time.

'And the sun is bound to be over the yardarm,' said the colonel. 'Drinks all round, my treat.'

Major Thadeus Tinker patted the old campaigner on his bowing back. 'This fellow's a hero,' said he. 'Best give him a round of applause.'

'Balls did most of the work,' puffed the colonel. 'I just pressed the firing button. Let's have three big cheers for Mr Balls.'

'Let us not bother,' said Cameron Bell. 'And please stop calling me Balls.'

There had been drinking before on the *Marie Lloyd*. Heroic drinking by men of the Queen's Own Electric Fusiliers. On the way back from the Martian Campaign, with crates of Martian gin. And the colonel had enjoyed a particularly memorable booze-up with the survivors of a previous big-game hunt. Two of them had died from alcohol poisoning, the colonel recalled. But this was somehow a special party. A special party indeed.

To Colonel Katterfelto's enormous surprise, Corporal Larkspur paid him the balance of his wage, in cash, without any fuss.

Darwin stuck out a hairy hand and the colonel gave him half.

'We have triumphed,' quoth the colonel, ordering all the champagne on board to be uncorked and offered around. 'Those of us who have survived will be wealthy men when we reach Earth.' He raised his glass to the Jovians. 'You fellows, already wealthy,' he said. 'But with the diamonds, even wealthier now, eh?'

The Jovians laughed and cheered the colonel, then all drank champagne.

'Think we'll be going home with our heads on our

bodies,' Colonel Katterfelto whispered to Darwin. 'So all is well as ends well, I suppose.'

Darwin was already enjoying a slight degree of simian insobriety.

'You are my bestest friend,' he told the colonel.

'And you mine, my dear fellow, you mine.'

The two clinked glasses. Darwin poured some champagne into his ear.

Major Thadeus Tinker appeared with a smile on his face. It was a visible smile now as he had shaved away his great white beard and given himself a haircut.

'You missed a bit under your ear there, Tinker,' said Colonel Katterfelto. 'But damn me if you don't look ten years younger.'

'I am very grateful to you, Katters.' The major put his arm about his old friend's shoulders. Darwin made a face and turned away. 'I will be very glad to get back to Blighty. And we must take that night out at the Music Hall. What do you say?'

'Well, about that—' huffed the colonel. But Alice started to sing.

It was that much-loved Music Hall standard, a poignant Irish ballad of a mother's love for a boy with very big ears. Who leaves his mother all alone to bring up five children when he joins the British Army and marches off to fight the enemies of the Crown. So sad a song was this as to be capable of raising a tear from the eye of a tiger.

Me Big-Eared Boy Has Gone To The War And Broken His Mammy's Heart

The Jovians who knew it sang along; the others, who did not, simply wept.

The verse that most remembered went as follows:

> The big-eared boy has gone away
> To fight a foreign war,
> No more to hear the children play
> But only cannons roar.
> His mother now has lost her joy.
> She walks a lonely road
> Where he marched away as a soldier boy –
> Ungrateful little toad!

Amidst the cheering, Cameron Bell took out his hankie and noisily blew at his nose.

As the champagne was danced around again and again others rose to perform their party pieces.

The colonel performed a high-stepping dance that he'd learned in Afghanistan.

Darwin recited the Twenty-Third Psalm, and this made Alice cry again.

Major Tinker dropped his trousers and prepared to perform a trick he'd seen done in the officers' mess at Sandhurst.

Cameron Bell put his hands over Alice's eyes.

The private detective later impressed all lovers of river craft with his impersonation of a tugboat.

The *Marie Lloyd* moved on towards Earth and all grew drunker and drunker.

42

enus now lay far astern; the *Marie Lloyd* flew on. Most of the champagne now was gone, and the Jovians had moved on to the creation of imaginative cocktails conjured from what remained behind the bar counter. Colonel Katterfelto had discovered some rum and this he shared with Mr Cameron Bell. Darwin was asleep with his head on the colonel's lap.

'You did a man's job in the gun turret, Bell,' said the colonel, patting Cameron hard upon the back. 'Conducted yourself as a gentleman should, bravo.'

'It is my hope that I can always rise to the occasion when required,' said Mr Bell, wistfully looking towards Alice Lovell and wondering whether there might possibly be any way for him to continue his acquaintanceship with her once they had returned to Earth.

'Thoughtful look in your eye there, Bell.' The colonel refilled the detective's glass. 'Setting your cap at a Music Hall gal. Not too wise a proposition.'

'She is pure enough,' said Cameron Bell. 'But speaking of the Music Hall, I observed you receiving your wages from the charming Mingus Larkspur. I imagine that you will not be continuing with your career upon the boards.'

'You imagine correctly.' The colonel, now far gone with drink, beckoned Cameron closer. 'Can you keep a secret?' he asked.

'Keeping a secret is my middle name,' said Mr Bell, equally far gone with drink.

'Good man. Then between one prang-gunner and another, have a bit of a project on the go. Secret project. Word to the wise.' The colonel tapped at his nose and almost missed.

'The project you have sought to pursue for all of your adult life?' said Cameron Bell.

'How the Devil did you know *that*?' The colonel sat back, appalled.

'Colonel,' said Cameron Bell, 'ever since we first met, you have worn that uniform. Day in and day out.' Cameron Bell made hiccups. 'Pardon me.' He continued, 'I draw inferences from observation. Most of your life is written for me upon your uniform.' Cameron Bell drained further rum. 'Did any of that make any sense?' he asked.

'S'pose so,' said the colonel. 'And true as true. Single project. Obsessed me all me life, you might say. Have the means to bring it to fruition. Cheers to *that*, says I.'

The two drained glasses, the colonel refilled them both.

They both said, 'Cheers,' and both drank once again.

'You said it was a secret,' said Cameron Bell. 'But you did not tell me what it was.'

'Cos it's a secret,' said the colonel.

'But you *were* going to tell me.'

'Ah yes. So I was. Read this book, you see—'

'The one you carry in your left-hand inside jacket pocket, over your heart?'

'Stop it now, Bell, or I'll have you burned for a witch.'

The two men laughed, and the colonel carried on.

'Chap called Herr Döktor,' he said. 'You mentioned him, with regard to how Darwin learned his skills. Read the book I carry with me when I was a child, all about—' The colonel drew the private detective very very near. 'All about the Mechanical Messiah.'

'Oh,' said Mr Cameron Bell. 'Well, I was not expecting *that*.'

'Built one in America,' the colonel continued. 'Unfortunate business. Villagers with flaming torches. Had to make a break for it. You know the drill.'

Cameron nodded. 'Not really,' he said.

'But having it built in London. Right now. Well, with time differences, months ago. Should be ready and waiting when we get home.' The colonel clinked his glass against Cameron Bell's.

Cameron Bell asked, 'Just what will it *do*?'

'Do?' asked the colonel. '*What* will *what* do?'

'The Mechanical Messiah. I assume the intention is to somehow bring it to some form of sentience. But when that is done, what will it actually do? Will it be—' Cameron started to titter foolishly '—like a monkey butler?'

'*Monkey butler?*' cried the colonel.

'What?' went Darwin. 'What?'

'Not you, my dear fellow, go back to sleep.'

Darwin went back to sleep.

'Sorry,' said Mr Cameron Bell. 'But I assume this mechanical being is some form of automaton.'

'*Some* form, yes,' agreed the colonel. 'But imbued with spiritual forces, literally possessed by the divine. It will bring peace on Earth to all men.'

'I will drink to *that*,' said Mr Bell. And he did. 'But please bear with me for a little longer,' he also said. 'The one you built in America, did you bring that one to life?'

'Couldn't,' puffed the colonel. 'Missing part. Didn't know about that until later.'

'Hope you asked for your money back,' said Cameron Bell, who was beginning to grin rather foolishly.

'Couldn't get the part on Earth.' The colonel dug into a pocket and produced a lump of *Magoniam*. 'Only exists on Venus. Magical rock. Special compartment in the chest where the heart should be. In it goes and job jobbed.'

'Really?' said Mr Bell, trying to focus. 'So you are confident that you will bring your Mechanical Messiah to life by placing a piece of Venusian gold inside its—'

There was a pause. The colonel puffed. Cameron Bell was asleep.

'Wake up!' shouted the colonel.

Darwin woke up. 'What?' he asked.

'Sorry,' said the colonel.

Cameron Bell awoke.

'Conversation is getting too damned complicated.' The colonel drank more rum.

Cameron Bell could now see *two* Colonel Katterfeltos. 'We need cigars,' he announced. 'Cigars will sober us up.'

'Bet you can't make it to the bar and back without falling on your arse,' said the colonel.

'Bet I can,' said Cameron Bell.

But he could not.

Corporal Larkspur stood behind the bar. He was fiercely sober.

'Can I help you, sir?' he asked.

'All the cigars you have,' said Cameron Bell.

The corporal grinned at the drunken detective. It was an

evil grin. 'And the condemned man requested a final cigar,' he said beneath his breath.

'Pardon me?' asked Cameron Bell.

'The gentleman requests cigars,' said the evil grinner. 'And cigars he will have.'

Corporal Mingus Larkspur opened the glass-fronted case and tipped its entire contents onto the bar counter.

'Shall I put all these on your bill?' he asked.

'The colonel is paying,' said Cameron, trying without success to stuff cigars into the top pocket of his now most thoroughly soiled suit jacket. He staggered somewhat and barely caught the bar in time to avoid a further tumble.

'Sir seems in a bit of a state,' said the grinning Mingus. 'Would sir care for me to escort sir to his cabin?'

'Sir would *not!*' said Cameron Bell. 'You are a scoundrel, *sir*. And I will have satisfaction. Would you care to step outside and settle it man to man?'

'Outside the spaceship?' asked the corporal.

'Damned right,' said the drunken detective. And he did that thing that gentlemen do with their gloves when they are challenging a rival to a duel: go smack–smack–smack in the other fellow's face with them.

As Cameron Bell possessed no gloves, he smack–smack–smacked the corporal's face with several large cigars.

'Ray guns at dawn?' the corporal suggested.

'Ray guns at dawn,' said Cameron Bell.

'Having a chat with that Larkspur cove, I see,' said Colonel Katterfelto, when Cameron Bell, by a weaving route, re-turned at length to the table. 'Something of the rotter about that chap.'

The detective slumped once more into his chair and

offered the colonel a broken cigar. 'I have challenged him to a duel,' he said.

'*Duel?*' said the colonel. 'Chaps don't fight duels any more. Duke of Wellington one of the last chaps to fight a duel, doncha know. Lucky to stay out of prison.'

'The laws of the Empire do not apply in space.' Cameron Bell put the broken end of a cigar into his mouth and then spat it out again. 'Ray guns at dawn. I can't go back on it now.'

'Hmph!' the colonel grunted. 'Seems to me that you're three sheets to the wind, my dear fellow. When you sober up in the morning you'd best apologise. Can't have chaps shooting each other for no good reason. Only a few of us left, damn me.'

Cameron Bell was now asleep.

A cigar was stuck up his nose.

The drinking had gone on for a very long time and when by Earth time it was dawn folk did not feel too well.

The colonel had made attempts to intercede on Mr Bell's behalf with Mingus Larkspur, explaining that there was no reason at all for a duel and that Mr Bell was drunk and that he, the colonel, was prepared to apologise on his behalf, if it would help.

Corporal Larkspur explained that it would *not*. His dignity had been affronted. He had been called a scoundrel and struck across the face by cigars. An offence punishable by death on Jupiter, he further explained. There was nothing for it but for him and Mr Bell to leave the confines of the ship and settle this matter man to man as proper gentlemen should.

The colonel had shrugged at this and given up and gone to bed, carrying Darwin on his shoulder.

The colonel was up at the cracking of the dawn, hoping to dissuade Mr Bell.

It might well have been assumed by those who observed Mr Bell's decline into alcoholic oblivion the previous evening that he would be in no fit state even to rise from his bed upon this Earthly dawn, let alone conduct himself with sufficient sensibility to engage in a deadly duel.

But Cameron was whistling while he washed. He hummed a little whilst he shaved and sang whilst he went to the toilet. After he had dressed and laced up his shoes, he did a tiny tap dance, too.

It was not the way of Cameron Bell to suffer 'the morning after the night before'. He was quite immune to that kind of thing. His doctor had told him time and again that he drank too much, but Mr Bell dismissed these words, although he knew them to be true.

He would not, of course, be letting on to Corporal Mingus Larkspur as to quite how chipper he felt. Although his acting skills stretched to little more than the impersonation of tugboats, the private detective felt confident that he could create the impression of a man with a blinding headache without the need to be coached by Sir Henry Irving.

But, thought Mr Bell. Had it been a rash move upon his part, challenging the corporal to a duel? No, he considered, it had *not*. Certain details of the corporal's person, observed by Cameron Bell, had informed the private detective that Mingus Larkspur was neither brave, nor a crack shot. Cunning, yes. But brave, or a crack shot, no. And Cameron's intuition had told him that Corporal Larkspur surely planned his murder. As after all he had overheard Larkspur's conversation on the transmitting device on Venus, that

Cameron would be killed and Alice returned to London for a blood sacrifice. Better then a fairish fight than to keep looking over his shoulder.

Alice Lovell knew nothing of this. She had tired of men-talk relatively early and gone off to bed in a huff. Now she slept on soundly and dreamed of tall dark men.

A tall man with a greying head knocked upon Cameron's door.

Bolts were drawn, the door opened. 'Good morning, Colonel,' said Cameron Bell.

'Impressive constitution,' said the colonel, viewing the vigorous figure before him through somewhat bleary eyes. 'You still intending to proceed with this dangerous farce?'

'There is no other way for it.' Cameron Bell viewed the rather tatty atmospheric suit the colonel was carrying. 'Is that my size?' he asked.

'One size fits all,' said the colonel. 'Found this one in the ship's stores. Best of a bad bunch. Seams are good enough. Tank's three-quarters full of air. Gives you half an hour outside. Wish you'd reconsider, though.'

'As a matter of interest,' said Cameron Bell, taking the suit from the colonel, 'what odds are the Jovians offering on who will win this duel?'

'Well—' puffed the colonel. 'Well—'

'Not good odds on me, then?'

'Not as such, my dear fellow, no.'

Cameron Bell struggled with the atmospheric suit. He was having trouble just getting his legs in. 'As a betting man yourself,' he said to the colonel, 'who, might I ask, have you laid a bet upon?'

'Well . . . my dear fellow,' the colonel puffed.

'I see,' said Cameron Bell. 'And upon what grounds, *precisely*, have the odds become so stacked against me?'

Colonel Katterfelto shrugged.

'Tell me,' said Cameron Bell.

'Well. You know,' the colonel blustered. 'One thing and another. Chaps chat. Seems Larkspur has a bit of a reputation for this kind of thing.'

'He does?' said Cameron Bell.

'Bit of a master of deception apparently. How should I put this? Gives off the wrong impressions, you might say.'

'He does?' said Cameron Bell once more. In a slightly higher-pitched voice.

'Apparently so. Stumpy was telling me that Larkspur is noted for his bravery in such situations. Him being such a crack shot and all.'

43

retting somewhat, Cameron Bell
was helped into the atmospheric
suit. Colonel Katterfelto screwed on
the helmet.

'I'll open up the little visor door
so you can breathe the ship's air for
now,' he said. 'And I'll link up the
air bottle on your back. You can't
actually adjust the controls once
it's on, so I'll wait until the last
moment to switch the valve. Give you as long as possible
with an air supply, eh? Not that you will be needing all of
it.'

'What was that last bit *again*?' asked Cameron Bell.

'Nothing. Nothing. Now, do you have your ray gun?'

'Trouser pocket,' said Cameron, peeping out through the
opening in the front of his space helmet. 'The trousers I
wore last night are on the floor, I'm afraid. I did consume a
tad too much rum.'

'Wouldn't be in this fix if you hadn't.' The colonel rooted
about in the rumpled-up trousers and produced the ray gun.
'Really wish you'd reconsider,' he said. And he looked
the duellist up and down. 'Not much room in there, eh?
Somewhat tight beneath the armpits.'

'Somewhat tight all over,' said Cameron Bell, uncomfortably.

'Well, best get it over with. Take your gun.'

Cameron took his gun.

'And follow me,' said Colonel Katterfelto.

Corporal Larkspur looked rather splendid in his brand-new atmospheric suit. Rather dashing, quite a romantic figure. Cameron Bell had not been fully aware before as to just how tall and imposing Corporal Larkspur actually was. He had always slouched around with his head hung down in a subservient manner. He was certainly skilled in creating the *wrong* impression.

The corporal squared up before the private detective, looked down upon him and toyed with a ray gun so much bigger than Mr Cameron Bell's.

'Cargo area,' he said, his voice muffled within his sealed space helmet.

Cameron Bell turned to Colonel Katterfelto.

'Two of you wait in the cargo area,' said the old soldier. 'I'll leave, close the airtight door to the rest of the ship. Once done you can open the outer door and step outside. I've roped you both up to this bulkhead so you won't drift off into space. And this—' he displayed a cable with a plug upon each end '—this goes here and here—' He plugged one end into Cameron's spacesuit and the other into that of Corporal Larkspur. 'Now you can talk to one another outside. You won't be able to hear me. Nor me you. So—' he shook each man by the spacesuit-gloved hand '—may the best man win and all that how's-your-father-up-in-Heaven kind of caper. Farewell.'

The colonel saluted and left the cargo hold, closing and locking the inner door securely behind him. He went off to join the Jovians who were thronged along the portholes of the ship's starboard side awaiting the opening of the cargo bay's outer door and for all the fun to begin.

In the cargo hold there stood two men who did not care for each other. Two men who would leave the ship in a moment or two, knowing that only one of them would return alive.

Within his snugly fitting atmospheric suit, Cameron Bell was perspiring freely. His fingers felt numb and his heart was beating much too fast. Corporal Larkspur applied himself to the outer door, spun the turn-screw, let it fall open. The air from the cargo hold rushed into space. And Cameron stared after it into the star-strewn nothingness.

'After you.' The voice of Corporal Larkspur boomed in Cameron's ear. 'Let us have this over and done. I have other things to be getting on with.'

Cameron Bell spoke softly. 'Quietly now, I have a terrible hangover,' he lied. 'But at least no further pretence upon your part as to being a Jovian.'

'Jovian?' The corporal's laugh banged about in Cameron's helmet. 'Buffoons to a man of them. Cannon fodder, they are, and nothing more.'

'You are not wholly human,' said Cameron Bell. 'How shall I put this?' He was trying most hard to stop his voice quavering. 'Are you perhaps of *mixed race*? An English mother of – how shall I put this? – loose morals—'

Cameron heard the rush of air as the corporal drew in breath. 'Outside,' he shouted. 'I'll deal with you—'

'You first,' said Mr Bell. 'I would hate for there to be an accident. Your ray gun accidentally discharging into my back, for instance.'

'No need for that.' Corporal Larkspur lunged at Cameron

Bell, sought to fling the private detective into space. Mr Bell, however, had seen that coming. He stepped nimbly aside, tripped the corporal and sent him blundering forwards, through the open outer door, out into the universe beyond.

Cameron Bell watched him floundering weightlessly. He could of course just slam the outer door shut and leave the corporal hanging there. Slamming the outer door shut might well sever the rope that tethered him to the ship. That would be that.

Cameron Bell shook his head and followed the corporal into space. They were still linked together by the communication cable, although secured to the ship by separate ropes. Cameron Bell said, 'Sorry, I tripped, far too much rum last night.'

Corporal Larkspur had steadied himself. 'Your next drink will be with the Devil,' was what he had to say.

'I am quietly confident,' said Cameron Bell, in a way that sounded as if he must truly have meant it. 'But before we perform the duel, might I ask you a question or two?'

Laughter rang in the detective's ear. 'Oh, please do, Mr Bell.'

'Who employs you?' asked Cameron Bell. 'And what was your real reason for coming to Venus?'

Corporal Larkspur seemingly hovered before Mr Bell. And although the *Marie Lloyd* rushed on towards Earth, there was no sense of motion. Just two men floating in a blackness that appeared almost liquid. It was one of the most curious experiences Cameron Bell had ever had. If it were not for the prospect of imminent death it would also have been one of the most pleasurable.

'I work for a great man,' said Corporal Larkspur. 'The greatest of this or any age. Soon his name will be known on all the inhabited worlds of the Solar System. Because he will rule them all.'

'I feel the Governments of Earth, Jupiter and Venus might have something to say about that,' said Mr Bell, who could see Mars quite clearly from where he drifted and very nice it looked, too.

'All will soon be his.'

'But you would not care to tell me how?'

'No,' said the corporal. 'I would not. But I will tell you this. The reason for the journey to Venus was so that I could acquire a certain mineral.'

'*Magoniam*,' said Cameron Bell.

'Correct. The Jovian hunters were just a means to an end. If there was any trouble with the natives they could shoot it out, like those cowboy fellows in America, whilst I absconded with the mineral prize.'

'And the colonel?'

'Expendable along with the rest. A brave man, I knew he would defend his employer. He actually thinks I will allow him to leave the ship alive with all that money.'

'You intend to kill everyone on board, then?'

'I have a rather splendid Treacle Sponge Bastard prepared. Laced with poison. I will be serving it tonight. Then I return to Earth alone.'

'That is assuming that you are lucky enough to win this duel.'

'Lucky enough?' The laughter now hurt Cameron's ear. 'I do not think that luck will play any part in this.'

'Events do not always go precisely as one might wish,' said Cameron Bell. 'One side believes that he has the advantage, when in fact it was the other side all along.'

'On this occasion you will find that *I* have the advantage.'

'How so?' asked Cameron Bell.

'Well, let me see.' Within his helmet, Corporal Larkspur's face took on a thoughtful expression. 'I am younger, fitter, stronger, braver and more skilful with a ray gun than yourself.'

'I am not as old as you might think,' said Cameron Bell. 'I suffered premature baldness. It runs in my family.'

'It will run no longer, Mr Bell.'

'And as to skills with a ray gun – I will have you know that I am a member of the Hurlingham Shooting Club. I won a gold cup two years ago for bagging eighteen pair of grouse on a single day at Lord Hartington's estate in Sheen.'

Laughter fairly rattled Cameron's head.

'Perhaps you should have brought your shotgun along,' the corporal suggested.

'I have the trusty Educator.' Cameron waggled his ray gun about.

'Oh yes. Your dear little ray gun. The one you used to start the spaceship.'

'That very one,' said Cameron Bell.

'The one on which you reversed the neutron flow to charge the battery of the ship's engine.'

'Saved all our lives,' said Cameron, proudly. 'And you never acknowledged *that*.'

'No. You are right. I should.' Corporal Larkspur could hardly speak at all now, he was laughing so hard. 'So you are going to shoot *me* with *that*?' he managed to say.

'That *is* my intention,' said Cameron Bell.

'But just tell me how, if you will?' Corporal Larkspur was shaking now from head to floating foot.

'I thought I might just point it at you and squeeze the trigger,' the detective suggested.

'Oh do. Please do.'

'Do you not want us to count up to ten?' asked Cameron Bell.

'No.' Corporal Larkspur was literally sobbing with laughter. 'Just aim and pull the trigger. Go on, do.'

'Splendid,' said Cameron Bell and without further words on his part he aimed the ray gun at Corporal Larkspur and pulled the trigger.

Cameron Bell pulled the trigger again and again.

But nothing happened. Not a thing. Not one little thing.

Cameron squinted through his helmet glass at the Educator. There was a little red light showing on the side. A little red light that meant the battery was flat.

'In all the excitement,' Corporal Larkspur laughed as he spoke, 'you forgot to charge it again. I could see the red battery light as you floated out into space.'

'Oh,' said Cameron Bell. 'This is most inconvenient.'

'Yes, it is.' The corporal roared with laughter.

'Perhaps if you were to wait here I might pop inside and borrow a gun with a full charge in it.'

'You might.' Corporal Larkspur clutched at his belly. 'But I'll just bet that I will not let you do it.'

'Oh,' said Cameron Bell once more.

Corporal Larkspur now displayed *his* ray gun. Held it before him in both hands. Made as if to kiss it through his helmet. 'This is a Mark Nine Ferris Firestorm. This pretty thing could reduce an elephant to a pile of ashes from a distance of two hundred yards. Once switched on, the electricity leaps between these two terminals atop the Mark Nine and through a system, which I am reliably informed does *not* involve the transperambulation of pseudo-cosmic anti-matter, then a big bad beam comes out of the snout and fries Mr Cameron Bell.'

'Hm,' went the unarmed detective. 'Yours *is* charged up, I suppose.'

'Why don't we find out?' Still shaking mirthfully, Corporal Larkspur aimed the Mark Nine Ferris Firestorm at the head of Cameron Bell, switched it on and squeezed upon the trigger.

There was a very horrid explosion.

And that was the end of the duel.

44

hastly bits and bobs of flesh bespattered Cameron Bell. The defaced detective gave the visor of his helmet a wipe with a space-gloved hand. The hull of the ship was likewise besmirched by all that now remained of Corporal Larkspur.

Cameron Bell did feelings at himself. His suit, it seemed, remained airtight, and matters had adjusted themselves to his satisfaction. He hauled upon the rope that moored him and returned to the *Marie Lloyd*.

Having closed the outer door, he waited patiently while Colonel Katterfelto turned a stopcock that allowed air to re-enter the cargo hold, before opening the inner door and re-entering himself.

'Damnedest duel I've ever seen,' said the old soldier, carefully unscrewing Cameron's gory helmet. 'You fire at him and your gun doesn't work. He fires at you and blows himself up.'

Unzippings were done and Cameron Bell, unscathed and victorious, if somewhat sweaty, stepped from the atmospheric suit.

'I would like to take a bath,' he said. 'And then I will join you in the saloon bar.'

The Jovians did *not* look pleased to see Mr Cameron Bell. They applauded half-heartedly, but did not laugh at all.

Mr Bell sat himself down at the colonel's table and accepted the glass of rum that was offered to him.

'A bit early in the day for this,' he said, 'but I could certainly do with it.'

Darwin the monkey was grinning away. The colonel told him to stop it.

'Ah,' said Mr Bell, observing the smiling simian. 'I get the picture. You took the Jovians' bets and had a little one with them, upon me.'

'He had a *big* bet with them,' said the colonel. 'Half of his wages. *That* big.'

Darwin could not stop grinning. Cameron shook his hand.

'Bravo, Darwin,' he said to the monkey. 'At least *you* had faith in me.'

Colonel Katterfelto tasted rum. 'Some jiggery-pokery went on outside,' he said. 'Care to let us in on the secret stuff?'

Cameron Bell found his glass now empty. Colonel Katterfelto refilled it.

'I forgot to recharge my ray gun,' he told the colonel. 'I genuinely forgot. If it hadn't been for the fact that I had taken certain precautionary measures, I would surely be dead.'

'Certain precautionary measures?' The colonel mulled *that* over.

'On our first day on Venus,' Mr Bell explained, 'Corporal Larkspur was behaving suspiciously. I followed him into the valley. He had some kind of transmitting apparatus. Called himself *Agent* Larkspur. Spoke to his superior. It was Larkspur's intention to kill us all on the journey home. Do *not* under any circumstances eat any more Treacle Sponge Bastard. Best hide the lot away from the Jovians.'

'The absolute rotter,' said the colonel. 'Go on, if you will.'

'I took the opportunity to search his cabin and uncovered a number of interesting items. His calling card. His atmospheric suit. When I found *that*, an idea entered my head. Rather than passively await my doom at his hands, I would call him out for a duel. I confess that I made certain adjustments to his air tank. I altered the "mix" of air, shall we say, and wedged open the overflow pipe so that once he turned on his air, he would be leaking oxygen.'

'But he exploded,' said the colonel. 'He didn't suffocate.'

'He had a Mark Nine Ferris Firestorm, like all the Jovian hunters. Electricity darts across the terminals prior to firing. He was leaking pure oxygen, the spark set it off, led it back to his air tank like a fuse to a stick of dynamite.'

'Hmph,' went the colonel. 'I'll not mention the matter again.'

'One or two matters do give me some cause for concern,' said Cameron Bell. 'The spaceship is returning to Earth steered by its automated pilot device. But someone who is conversant with the controls will have to land it.'

Darwin the monkey put up his hand. 'I will pilot the ship.'

'*I* can do *that*,' said Colonel Katterfelto. 'Flown this lady more than once—'

'With no loss of life?'

'None at all. Ah, here's Tinker. Tinker, did I or did I not fly this ship with no loss of life whatsoever?'

'Well,' said Major Thadeus Tinker. 'No loss of life amongst those onboard. But we had knocked a few back, I recall. And you did set the ship down upon that lady in a straw hat.'

'Ah. Forgot about that. But no loss of life amongst those on board. And that is the main thing.'

'My mind is at rest upon that, then.' Cameron Bell now drew the colonel close. 'You might, however, suggest to Darwin that he "lose" some of the Jovians' money back to them somehow. They have no trophies. They witnessed an Earth man somehow killing a supposed Jovian in rather suspicious circumstances. We need our heads on our bodies.' Cameron Bell tapped at his nose.

'Word to the wise,' said the colonel.

There was *some* unpleasantness. Corporal Larkspur had played so many roles upon board. Pilot. Barkeeper. Cook. The Jovians grumbled about who would be feeding them. Stumpy complained that if someone did not put a slim dark chocolate upon his pillow each night there was a likelihood of trouble.

'Darwin and I will take care of the cooking,' said the colonel.

'What?' went Darwin. 'But I am rich.'

'Needs must when the Devil drives, my dear fellow.'

'I will gladly take on the role of barkeeper,' volunteered Major Tinker. 'I have skills regarding the creation of cocktails. I will keep these fellows jolly enough.'

'Which leaves me,' said Cameron Bell, 'to clean, wash dishes, make beds and all the rest of it.'

'Then that's agreed,' said the colonel.

Alice appeared wearing a delightful pale blue dress with big white puffed shoulders, white knee socks and buckled shoes. 'I found these in the ship's stores,' she said. 'And they fit. Where is Corporal Larkspur? I want my breakfast. I need new sheets on my bed and my cabin sink is blocked.'

The colonel and Darwin prepared a splendid breakfast.

Cameron Bell and Alice sat together.

'You look a little sad, Cameron,' said Alice. 'Are you not looking forward to going back to Earth?'

'I do not know quite what awaits me there. The burning down of the Crystal Palace *was* blamed upon me, you know.'

'I will speak up for you.'

'Ah,' said Cameron Bell. 'Actually, *that* might help.'

'Once I have been reunited with my darling kiwi birds.'

'Ah,' said Cameron Bell.

The colonel had a chef's hat on. Darwin the monkey was brewing up coffee and quite enjoying himself.

Colonel Katterfelto spread lard over the eggs that he was frying. 'Be home in a few days now,' he told his hirsute companion. 'What is the first thing you would like to do when we return to London?'

'Eat a banana,' said Darwin.

'And the second?'

'Another banana?' said Darwin.

'And after you are completely full of bananas?'

'I might have a poo,' said Darwin. 'And a little sleep.'

'Yes and right. But in the long term? You are an ape of means, you know. What are your long-term plans?'

'I shall arrange a consultation meeting with the manager at Coutts. Have him recommend investment opportunities. Employ someone with knowledge of the stock market. I will buy property, of course. Sloane Square is coming up, I have heard. I might purchase a little pied-à-terre there.'

Darwin glanced at the colonel.

The colonel simply smiled.

'And you?' enquired the monkey. 'You will energise your Mechanical Messiah, I suppose.'

'That is my intention.' The colonel's eyes fairly shone, for he was utterly entranced at the prospect. 'I have the *Magoniam*,' he said, 'to draw the divine energies into Heaven's last and best gift to Mankind.'

'I wish you luck,' said Darwin. 'It will not affect property prices, I trust.'

'Darwin, it will affect everything. The world will be put to rights, my little friend. Utopian vision. All men equal. Monkeys, too. Peace and love abounding. Things of a sublime nature generally.'

'Man and monkey equal?' mused Darwin.

'The Jehovah's Witness chaps believe it,' said the colonel, with joy in his voice. 'A new Heaven and a new Earth. As in the Book of Revelation.'

'I liked the lamb in that,' said Darwin. 'Not too keen on that beast, though.'

'Picture it, my friend.' The colonel put his arm about the monkey's shoulders. 'No more wars, picture *that*. The lion will lie down with the lamb.'

Might the monkey lie down with the Music Hall girl? wondered Darwin.

'It is a *very* ambitious project,' he said to his friend the colonel. 'Certainly not something that could be achieved overnight. I hope that *something* happens, though. I hope that you are *not* disappointed.'

'And we will remain companions,' said Colonel Katterfelto. 'Keep in touch, eh? Have dinner once in a while? At my club. Grown very fond of you, my dear fellow. In a manly father-and-son kind of fashion. Wouldn't want us to go our separate ways for ever. Wouldn't like that one bit.'

Darwin looked up at the colonel and thought to discern a tear in his eye. The colonel wiped this away.

'We will always be friends,' said Darwin, wiping away a little tear of his own.

And so it continued and days passed by. The planet Venus became a silver dot in the sky of forever night and a blue world expanded before the ship. A blue world called Planet Earth.

The drink was gone and so too the food when the *Marie Lloyd* finally fell into orbit.

'All you fellows strap in,' Colonel Katterfelto told the Jovians. 'You might experience some slight discomfort during our decent. Bit of rattling. Shaking about. All that kind of palaver.'

The Jovians took to strapping in. Most were laughing once more. Alice sat with Major Tinker, who was admiring her legs.

Darwin stepped down the middle aisle between the ranks of passenger seats. He was carrying an empty food platter.

'Colonel,' said Darwin. 'Excuse me, please.'

'No time to chat now,' said the colonel. 'Have to pilot the spaceship down.'

'Yes,' said Darwin. 'But this platter.'

'Nice platter,' said the colonel. 'Suppose you can have it if I you want it.'

'I don't want it,' said Darwin.

'Then put it back. Alice will help you with your safety belt.'

'This platter is empty,' said Darwin the monkey.

'Yes. See that. Must pilot the ship now. Sorry.'

'It's the Treacle Sponge Bastard platter,' said Darwin. 'I left it in the Refridgetorium. *The* Treacle Sponge Bastard platter.'

'Ah,' said the colonel. '*That* Treacle Sponge Bastard platter. But it's empty.'

Darwin the monkey shook his head. Most sorrowfully he shook it.

'Oh dear,' said the colonel. And then he addressed the Jovians. 'As a matter of interest,' he said, 'and no recriminations or suchlike – did any of *you* eat the Treacle Sponge Bastard?'

The Jovians looked guilty. Stumpy raised his stump.

'We all did,' he confessed. 'There was no more food. We were hungry.'

'Oh dear,' said the colonel. 'Then any minute now.'

There was a kind of collective gasp. And the last folk alive on the *Marie Lloyd* were those born on Planet Earth.

'Shame to see them go like that,' said Colonel Katterfelto to Mr Cameron Bell, who was acting as co-pilot. The two sat in the cockpit. Cameron Bell looked glum.

'Still,' said the colonel, 'accidents *will* happen, I suppose.'

'I suppose,' the detective agreed.

'You all strapped in?' the colonel asked.

'All strapped in,' said Mr Bell.

'Then I will take us down.'

'Just one thing,' said Cameron Bell. 'It has occurred to me that the Royal London Spaceport might not be now the best place to land. What with the captain of the ship missing and all those dead Jovians in the passenger compartment.

Questions might be asked. Questions that might be difficult to answer.'

'Take your point,' said the colonel. 'Where do you fancy, then? Isle of Wight's rather nice.'

'Perhaps a little far south. How about Ealing Common?'

'Splendid,' said the colonel. 'We'll set down there and go our separate ways. Plenty of public transport thereabouts.'

'That will be fine, then.' Cameron Bell settled back in his seat. 'What does the co-pilot do?' he enquired.

'Haven't the foggiest,' said the colonel. 'Hold on tight now. I am taking us down.'

Colonel Katterfelto pressed the joystick forwards. The *Marie Lloyd* dived into the atmosphere of Earth at a reckless speed.

'Isn't that a bit fast?' asked Cameron Bell.

'Sensitive controls,' said the colonel. 'Just need to straighten her up a little.'

Flames suddenly appeared before the cockpit. There was a definite feeling of *heat*.

'Slow down,' cried Cameron Bell.

'Trying to,' cried the colonel in reply. 'Controls not responding. Not doing anything at all.'

Cameron Bell now recalled what Corporal Larkspur had said to him. About Corporal Larkspur being the only one who could pilot the ship successfully.

'Oh my dear dead mother,' said Cameron Bell. 'Larkspur altered the controls. We are—'

'Doomed?' asked the colonel as the ship plunged down.

'Doomed!' the detective agreed.

45

arth became bigger and bigger. The colonel clung on to the joystick and Cameron Bell threw what levers he could, but nothing seemed to help. The heat in the cockpit was becoming intolerable. Cameron shielded his face.

'No good,' gruffed the colonel. 'Ship's out of control.'

'It was a pleasure to know you.' Cameron Bell clasped his hands in prayer and recommended himself to the Almighty. The ship was now shaking fearfully and the cockpit windscreen was surely starting to melt.

Down and down went the *Marie Lloyd*, heading to her doom. 'Bail out somewhere,' shouted the colonel. 'Too hot in here, by golly.'

Ghastly groaning, crackling sounds announced the departure of riveted hull plates. The falling spaceship was also falling apart.

'Best tell that Alice girl you love her,' bawled the colonel above the growing din. 'Go on, Bell, I'll still do what I can.'

Cameron Bell made to leave the cockpit as Darwin was suddenly entering it.

'Let me at the controls,' cried the ape of space. 'I can steer the ship.'

Cameron Bell blundered past him. Darwin jumped up onto the colonel's lap.

The superheated windscreen glass bulged dangerously inwards.

'Let me take the controls,' cried Darwin. 'I know what I'm doing.'

'Nothing works,' the colonel shouted. 'This is the end, my only friend. The end.'

'I know these controls,' insisted Darwin. 'It was me they were altered for.'

'Damn me, *what?*'

The monkey took hold of the joystick. His little hands pressed buttons unseen to the colonel. The engines were flung into reverse, ailerons extended. Darwin tugged on the handbrake.

Shaking, groaning, grumbling and all but falling apart, the *Marie Lloyd* levelled out, slowed in speed and drifted over an ocean.

'Good God!' cried the colonel. 'Well done, that man. Bravo and things of that nature.'

That man? thought Darwin. 'Thank you,' he said.

'But how?' the colonel asked.

'Because this used to be *my* spaceship,' Darwin explained. '*Very* briefly, when I still had Lord Brentford's inheritance money. I had the controls altered to make it easier for me to fly it. Sadly, though, I never got the chance. Lost all my money at the gaming tables of Monte Carlo shortly afterwards. Bet the spaceship too and that was that.'

'Well, well, well,' went the colonel. 'What a fortunate coincidence *that* turned out to be.'

'Some *might* call it *that*,' said Darwin.

Cameron Bell was back at the cockpit door.

And Alice was with him.

Colonel Katterfelto winked at Cameron Bell. 'Well?' he said. 'Did you tell her?'

'Tell me *what*?' asked Alice.

'Nothing important.' Cameron Bell sighed, mopping sweat from his brow. 'But how—' he indicated all around and about '—how did you save the day?'

'Darwin did,' said the colonel. 'Long story. Somewhat unlikely one, too. But let's not labour the point. Thing is we're all still alive. That's what matters, eh?'

'That's what matters,' said Cameron Bell, gazing fondly at Alice.

'From what I know of the topography,' said Colonel Katterfelto, rum glass in hand, sitting in the co-pilot's seat, 'we are flying over the South China Sea. Take a good few hours to get back to Blighty.'

Alice sat in the pilot's seat. Darwin sat upon Alice.

'Well, I'm staying right *here*,' said Alice. 'I don't want to go back into the passenger compartment and sit with all those dead bodies.'

'Understandable,' said the colonel. 'Where's Tinker?'

'Having a sleep,' said Cameron Bell. 'But we must discuss just where we are going to land.'

'I must go back to the Crystal Palace,' said Alice, 'and collect my darling kiwi birds.'

'If we land at the spaceport we will surely be arrested,' said Mr Bell, helping himself to some of the colonel's rum. 'Where do you keep finding these bottles of drink?' he asked the old campaigner. 'I thought we were all out of alcohol.'

The colonel mumbled. But offered no explanation.

Alice said, 'I've done nothing illegal.'

'There would be so much explaining to do,' said Cameron. 'I suggest we put the ship down somewhere quiet, and I know just the place.'

Horsell Common, near Woking in Surrey, was the landing place of the first craft of the Martian invasion fleet, more than a decade before in eighteen eighty-five. Being the very small world that it was proving to be, the *Marie Lloyd* had been the very first Martian spaceship to land upon Earth, in the middle of Horsell Common.

'Horsell Common,' said Colonel Katterfelto. 'Has a certain humour to it, I suppose.'

'Lost on me,' said Darwin. 'But you show me where to land this spaceship and I will land it for you. Do you suppose—' And here he paused.

'Suppose what, my dear fellow?'

'Well . . .' The monkey gave thought to his words. 'After I have safely landed the ship, we could leave it, then return to it later, as if discovering it there, and then claim salvage rights, as one would for a sailing ship that had been brought ashore in a storm with all hands lost.'

The colonel glanced at Cameron Bell.

'An ingenious plan,' said the private detective. 'But please let me be far away before you put it into action.'

'You can come with me,' said Alice. Which brought a smile to the face of Cameron Bell.

'And we will pick up my kiwi birds together.'

Which did *not*.

'So, all agreed upon Horsell Common?' asked Colonel Katterfelto.

And all agreed they were all agreed and the *Marie Lloyd* flew on.

Making rather unhealthy sounds, but flying nonetheless.

Hours passed and the colonel needed the toilet. He left the cockpit and took himself down the central aisle between the passenger seats. And here he encountered Major Tinker.

'What are you doing there, Tinker?' asked the colonel.

'Looting,' the major replied. 'Dead men need no diamonds. I'm sure you agree.'

'Actually do.' The colonel did. 'And the fewer the traces left on this ship that she's been to Venus the better.'

'My thoughts entirely,' said Major Tinker. 'And the thought of what I might buy with the countless wealth from all these diamonds.'

'Quite so,' said the colonel. 'Just popping off to the loo.'

Seas and lands passed far beneath and some time later Europe came and went.

The survivors of the voyage to Venus were all crammed into the cockpit. Which although not the safest way to travel was at least away from the corpses. Corpses that no one personally wanted the job of shifting.

'Aha,' said the colonel, pointing ahead. 'Behold the white cliffs of Dover.'

Alice hugged at Cameron's arm, raising hope within the private detective that some chance might exist for him.

In truth, Cameron Bell was a man of most troubled mind. What *exactly* was he returning to? He had no home. He had no employment. He was certain that Lord Andrew Ditchfield, manager of the Electric Alhambra, would have given up on paying his expenses many months ago. There would probably be several warrants out for his arrest and worst of all, in his personal opinion, he would eventually have to confess to Alice that in all likelihood her kiwi birds had been consumed in the great fire at the Crystal Palace. Those whose necks had not previously been wrung during the pecking to death of the dark and sinister being.

If not for his love of Alice, Cameron could find absolutely no reason whatsoever for returning to London.

The detective peered through the heat-scarred windscreen towards the white cliffs of Dover. These cliffs shone in fine bright sunshine. Cameron Bell's watch told him that it might possibly be about three in the afternoon. But as to which month, or even which *year*, that was anyone's guess.

'You know, we should really wait until nightfall before we land,' said Mr Bell. 'Sneak in, unseen, as it were.'

Darwin the pilot shook his hairy head.

'No?' asked Cameron Bell. 'Why not?'

Darwin pointed towards the fuel gauge. The needle pointed to a red segment labelled EMPTY.

'Oh my dear dead mother,' said Cameron Bell.

'We will have to land as soon as we're there,' said Darwin. 'Colonel, point the way.'

'Quite so,' said the colonel. 'Head in that direction towards Brighton, then we'll follow the A23.'

Nasty coughing sounds were now to be heard. The strangled gasps of engines becoming starved of fuel.

'Couldn't we stop somewhere and take some fuel aboard?' Alice asked. 'What sort of fuel makes the engines run, by the way?'

But no one was listening to Alice. So she folded her arms and grumped somewhat and tried to ignore the bad noises.

'We will have to land,' said Darwin. 'Choose a field, Colonel. One without sheep in it would be nice.'

'Quite right, my dear fellow, let me see.'

Even though all but gone with the fuel, the *Marie Lloyd* was still cracking along at a goodly pace. They had reached the outskirts of Croydon now. And all agreed, without the need for words, that they had no wish to set down there.

Darwin made adjustments to the controls. 'Well now,' he said. 'There is a thing.'

'A *good* thing?' asked Cameron Bell.

'Not as such,' said the monkey. 'Do you recall when we left Venus? How we were chased by the aether ship?'

Heads went nodding all around.

'And how it shot at us?'

Heads went nodding once again.

'And how it shot off two of the tail fins?'

Heads stopped nodding. But all remembered *that*.

'The thing,' said Darwin. 'Is. That lacking those two tail fins, the landing of the ship might prove problematic.'

'Problematic?' asked Cameron Bell. 'As in difficult? Or impossible?'

Darwin made a so-so gesture.

'Oh my dear dead mother,' said Cameron Bell.

The *Marie Lloyd* passed over the Crystal Palace.

'How splendid,' said Cameron. 'It has been rebuilt. But look at the spaceport, odd.'

The survivors peered towards the spaceport.

'Where are all the spaceships?' asked the colonel. 'Damn place is deserted. Nose up, Darwin, if you will.'

Darwin struggled to bring up the nose of the *Marie Lloyd*, but at least one of the engines had now given up the ghost.

'We're heading towards the centre of London now,' the colonel huffed and puffed. 'Might be an idea to veer off towards the outskirts.'

'It might be,' said Darwin. 'But sorry to say . . .' And he cupped a hairy hand to his ear.

And all listened and all heard . . . nothing at all but silence.

'We are out of fuel,' said Darwin. 'Please say prayers for me.'

The *Marie Lloyd* dropped towards London. Its undercarriage struck one of the tall Tesla towers, dislodging the great steel ball from the top in a bright cascade of sparks. Causing chaos and destruction far below.

As all aboard stared white-faced and praying through the blurred windscreen, the spaceship smashed into the roof of Buckingham Palace, cleaving away a vast section of the front façade, struck the Mall with a hideous rending of metal, ploughed along its length then bounced over the archway and plunged with a devastating swerving crash into Trafalgar Square.

Bringing down Nelson's Column and burying its nose deep into the front of the National Gallery.

46

 state of National Emergency was brought into being. A regiment of the Household Calvary rode out from their barracks at the rear of the stricken palace. Electric tanks growled onto the streets of the great metropolis. Black Marias, some bearing the distinctive crest of the Metropolitan Police Force, others not, clattered towards Trafalgar Square. Chaos had come to the Empire's heart, and many were fleeing in terror. A platoon of the Queen's Own Electric Fusiliers circled the sky above the ruination aboard a sleek silver airship. In the wheelhouse stood young Mr Winston Churchill, cigar in mouth, examining a map of London.

An hour had passed since the *Marie Lloyd* crashed and already newsboys were hawking broadsheets which announced in letters bold and black that

**MARTIANS ATTACK LONDON
AGAIN!
1000s ALREADY DEAD**

In fact, miraculously, there had been no loss of life, although a lady in a straw hat had been elevated to a state of hysteria by a close encounter with a falling statue of Nelson.

The *Marie Lloyd* lay crumpled and broken, smoke rising gently from battered bits and bobs.

No Martian storm troopers had so far emerged from the wreck to lay further waste to London.

At a little after five of the Greenwich Meridian clock, Mr Winston Churchill ordered an assault to be made upon the invaders and joined one hundred fusiliers as they abseiled down to the square.

These noble warriors of the British Empire met with no resistance as they charged the crumpled craft. Onboard they found the bodies of the dead Jovians dressed in their safari suits.

But no one else at all.

Colonel Katterfelto, Major Tinker, Cameron Bell, Alice and Darwin the monkey had quietly slipped away from the wreck of the *Marie Lloyd* long before the cordoning off of central London and the arrival of assorted troops. They had mingled with those fleeing the National Gallery and Trafalgar Square. They had, miraculously once more, remained uninjured by the crash.

They now sat in the Ritz taking afternoon tea.

There had been some unpleasantness, though.

The gentlemen of the party had *not* been wearing ties and the Ritz enforces a strict dress code for afternoon tea.

The maître d' had supplied them with ties. And a striped cravat for Darwin.

'Well,' huffed, puffed and gruffed the colonel, lifting his teacup and taking a sip. 'I've said it once. I've said it twice. Very close thing, was that.'

Cameron Bell had his face buried deep in his hands. 'Buckingham Palace,' he was heard to mumble. 'The Mall. Nelson's Column. The National Gallery. Dear oh dear oh dear.'

'Could have been worse,' said Major Tinker. 'Could have hit the Electric Alhambra. Anyone fancy joining me in a box there tonight?'

No one seemed particularly keen.

Darwin the monkey said, 'I don't see bananas on the menu.'

'If we are to go our separate ways,' said Cameron Bell, 'which I would personally recommend as our departure from the *Marie Lloyd* might well have been observed and our descriptions circulated, might I ask where I can find you all should the need arise?'

'Here,' said Darwin. 'I will be engaging a suite of rooms right here.'

'And you, Colonel?' asked Cameron Bell.

'Have to go to Alperton. Pick up the key to the chapel I rented. The you-know-what should already have been delivered there, ready to be energised.'

Alice did not know what the you-know-what was, but neither did she care.

'Then I'll probably take a room here, too,' continued the colonel.

'Me also,' said Major Tinker. 'Handy for the Halls and all that.'

'It is not really *going our separate ways*, is it?' said Cameron Bell. 'Alice, what of you?'

'I am going with *you*,' said Alice.

'Oh,' said Cameron Bell.

'To the pet shop in Sydenham to collect my kiwi birds. We can then take rooms at the Adequate.'

'Yes,' said Mr Bell, between gritted teeth. He had quite forgotten about the Adequate. The kiwi birds, however, were being constantly brought to mind.

'Unless you wish simply to abandon me,' said Alice.

Cameron Bell shook his head.

Major Thadeus Tinker asked, 'Is there Treacle Sponge Bastard on the menu?'

The drive out to Sydenham in the hansom cab was quite without incident. The driver did not ask Cameron whether he wished to travel like a batsman out of Hell. Nor did he throw up his hands in horror, recalling how Cameron had robbed him at ray-gun-point at the Crystal Palace.

Because he was not *that* hansom cabbie.

That sometimes it was *not* a small world brought some small degree of cheer to Mr Cameron Bell.

The fact that the pet shop was still open on their arrival at Sydenham did *not*, however.

Alice paid for the hansom cab, as Cameron Bell did not have a single penny to his name.

'It is *you*,' cried the pet-shop owner. Which rattled the private detective.

'ALICE AT THE PALACE!' he continued.

Cameron mouthed a silent prayer of thanks. The pet-shop owner went on, 'We all thought that you were dead,' he went on. 'There was a lovely obituary in *The Times* newspaper. Did you know,' he said to Cameron, 'that this young woman is the Alice in Wonderland of the books?'

'No,' said Cameron. 'I did not.' And he hated himself for not knowing.

'I do not like to talk about that,' said Alice. 'But where are my kiwi birds? I hope you did not sell them when you thought that I was dead.'

'I wish that I had,' said the pet-shop owner.

'That is a strange thing to say,' said Alice.

'We live in very strange times.' The pet-shop owner turned his full gaze upon Mr Cameron Bell. 'Now you, sir, look very familiar,' he said. 'I know your face from somewhere.'

'People are always saying that,' replied Mr Bell.

'And what about these Martians?' the pet-shop owner asked. 'Attacking London *again*. You would have thought they'd have learned their lesson when we completely wiped out their race, wouldn't you?'

Cameron agreed that this was so.

'Stop changing the subject,' said Alice. 'Where are my kiwi birds?'

'If you stay around here you'll know soon enough. Be inside before dark if you value your life.'

'What of *this*?' asked Cameron Bell.

'What of this *indeed*?' demanded Alice.

'It all began a year ago on the night of the terrible fire,' the pet-shop owner began. 'But then you would know that, because you were there. People were fleeing down the hill from the burning palace. But up there—' the pet-shop owner pointed with a trembling finger '—up there amidst the conflagration the kiwi birds got their first taste of human flesh.'

'Oh dear, oh dear,' said Cameron Bell.

'Be quiet *please*,' said Alice.

'A toff, they say,' continued the storyteller. 'They brought him out all pecked into pieces. Though they say that he still lives.'

'Oh dear,' said Cameron.

Alice glared at him.

'The birds, having feasted upon this innocent toff, escaped into the grounds of the Crystal Palace. And despite all attempts to capture them, there they remain. Breeding.' The pet-shop owner's voice took on a sinister tone. 'And now there are dozens of them. All hungry for man meat. And being nocturnal by nature, they hunt their prey at night.'

Alice's eyes were very wide indeed.

Cameron Bell chewed on his bottom lip.

'Where did they take the *innocent gentleman* who was attacked?' he asked.

'That doesn't matter!' shouted Alice. 'My poor kiwi birds, living out in the cold. Being hunted down. This is terrible.'

'Terrible,' agreed the pet-shop owner. 'As are their terrible feastings. They eat—' He drew his visitors closer with an ever-more-trembling finger. 'They feast upon virgins. Five have gone missing at night from the village. Not a trace of them ever found.'

Cameron prepared to mouth another, *Oh no.*

Alice offered him a bitter look. 'This is all *your* fault,' she said.

'*My fault?*' said Cameron Bell. 'By what stretch of the imagination can it be *my* fault?'

'Hold on there,' said the pet-shop owner. 'I *do* recognise you now. Hold on—' And he rooted about beneath his counter and brought to light a crumpled WANTED poster.

Beneath an illustration of Mr Pickwick, by Boz, were printed the words:

REWARD OF £1000

FOR INFORMATION LEADING TO THE ARREST
OF THIS DANGEROUS MAN
CAMERON JAMES BELL

———

To answer charges of
The instigation of the Hyde Park Massacre
The Arson Attack upon the Crystal Palace
The murders of Harry 'Hurty-Finger' Hamilton
and Smelly Charlie Belly
The malicious wounding of Mr Aleister Crowley and the
theft of his grandfather Moses Crowley's golden ring
And divers other charges, including the
horrible incendiary attack upon

MASTER MAKEPIECE SCRIBBENS
THE BRENTFORD SNAIL BOY.

'The Brentford Snail Boy?' said Cameron Bell.

'Raised by snails,' said the pet-shop owner. 'He topped the bill at the Electric Alhambra when it finally reopened after the tragic death of Smelly Charlie Belly. Sang his famous song –

> *Don't take the shell off your racing snail*
> *it will only make him sluggish.*

Cameron Bell shrugged helplessly.

'He went on as top of the bill,' said the pet-shop owner. 'Sang his famous song, then went up in a burst of flame like the other two. But his shell protected him. He was lucky. Got off with ninety per cent burns and total paralysis.'

'I should be so lucky,' mused Cameron Bell.

'But what am I telling *you* for?' asked the pet-shop owner. 'You are Cameron James Bell and I am making a citizen's arrest.' And he now drew out from beneath his counter a most impressive ray gun. 'This is the Mark Five Ferris Firestorm,' the pet-shop owner informed the wanted criminal.

'Put that away and don't be so silly,' said Alice. 'This man is my close friend and I can vouch for him completely.'

Cameron nodded his head at this. A head that was sweating somewhat.

'You put me in a very difficult position,' said the pet-shop owner. 'You are a lady and as such must be treated respectfully by a gentleman.'

Alice nodded. 'What are you trying to say?' she asked.

'I am saying – and please do not take offence at this, I am one of your biggest followers, I saw all your performances at the Electric Alhambra – but the law is the law. What can I say?'

'You can say you are sorry to Cameron,' said Alice. 'And then you can help me search for my kiwi birds.'

'Not *that*.' The pet-shop owner shivered. 'This shop will be bolted and barred before nightfall. But I am not alluding to this madman.'

'Pardon *me*?' said Cameron Bell.

'Rumour has it that he is a French spy,' said the pet-shop owner. 'But it is *you* I am talking about.'

With his free hand he brought out yet another poster of the WANTED persuasion.

Alice's image was upon it.

EVIL KIWI GIRL

Alice read:

> Formerly believed to have succumbed
> in the great fire at the Crystal Palace,
> recent information suggests that
> she is living in a feral state
> and leading a flock of
> ferocious kiwi birds
> on nefarious nocturnal escapades
> of a murderous nature.

'It says, "WANTED DEAD OR ALIVE",' said the pet-shop owner. 'Somewhat extreme, I grant you, but the way things are at present, hardly surprising, I suppose. The poster only arrived this very morning, and *you* arrive this very afternoon. What a small world it is.' He cocked the Mark Five Ferris Firestorm, sending that deadly crackle of electrical energy between the polished terminals. 'I think it probably for the best if I just shoot you both now, to avoid any complications.'

He aimed his weapon at Alice.

'Ladies first,' said he.

47

ameron Bell surprised even himself with the speed of the actions he took. He threw himself across the counter, tore the ray gun from the pet-shop owner's grasp and used the stock to batter him rather brutally in the face.

Somewhat begored about the snout, the pet-shop owner sank beneath his counter.

'My hero,' cried Alice, flinging her arms about Cameron Bell.

'Thank you, Alice,' said Cameron, savouring the moment. 'Now, if you might find some rope, I think it would be for the best if we tied up the pet-shop owner.'

The receptionist at the Adequate had seen some sights in his time. Eccentric visitors to the Crystal Palace. Weird folk of the Music Hall – even, once, a boy who'd been raised by snails. He had never, however, seen such a queer pair of people as entered upon this evening.

The reception area of the Adequate was lit in a manner which could have been better, but could have been so much worse. The reception desk would do for now and the carpet served as best it could. The receptionist was dressed sufficiently well as to just about pass muster. He stared in awe at the two folk who were approaching.

A man and a woman, it so appeared, of some strange foreign extraction. The man was broad and bulky, with a dark brown complexion. He wore on his head a mighty turban that matched his ample flowing robes. The woman looked particularly exotic, with similarly tanned skin, a caste mark upon her forehead and a sari of red–purple velvet.

A thought flickered momentarily into the mind of the receptionist that the sari of the exotic woman was a perfect match for the curtains in the pet shop just across the road.

'Good evening,' said the turbaned traveller. The receptionist noted now that this extraordinary being bore across his shoulders a Mark Five Ferris Firestorm. And also that he spoke in that sing-song fashion that tends to identify a man as hailing either from India or Wales.

'Good evening, sir,' said the receptionist, in a manner that was neither impolite, nor otherwise. 'And how might I help you upon this fine summer's evening?'

'Two rooms,' said the turbaned fellow, who seemed at close quarters to exude an unusual fragrance, that of animals and bootblack. The words HIGSON'S HAMSTER FOOD could be seen in the folds of his headwear.

'My wife and I require two rooms. I am Prince Rhia Rhama Rhoos, fearless kiwi hunter.'

'Oh,' went the receptionist, in a manner indicative of surprise, but not too much of it. 'You are certainly welcome. We have a number of rooms available that measure up at least to the minimum requirements. A great number, in fact.' And he sighed. Most sadly did he sigh.

Then he pushed an open hotel register across the counter.

The turbaned prince examined it. 'Is no one else staying here at all?' he asked.

'In truth,' said the receptionist, 'you are the first guests in months. The kiwis, you see. Business should pick up to a moderate level once again when they are all bagged and it is safe to step out in the hours of darkness.'

The swarthy princess made a very grumpy face. But did not speak a word.

'The two best rooms in the hotel,' said the prince. 'Our baggage is being sent on. Kindly lead the way.'

In a bedroom just sufficient for its purpose, Alice Lovell sat and sulked and rubbed somewhat at her face. 'This boot-black will ruin my skin,' she said.

'Better that than death at the hands of some self-styled bounty hunter,' said Mr Cameron Bell. 'It rather suits you, too.'

'Does it?' said Alice. 'But surely we cannot expect to actually get away with such a deception?'

'The receptionist is grateful for customers,' said Cameron Bell. 'Especially when they are fearless kiwi hunters.'

'If you harm just one feather of my kiwi birds.' Alice shook a delicate fist. And then she burst into tears. 'This is all too much,' she said between weepings. 'My life is in ruins. What am I going to do?'

'Tomorrow we will return to London.' Cameron longed to put his arm about Alice's shoulders and comfort her in a physical manner. 'I will sort everything out.'

'You promise?' said Alice, turning her big moist eyes towards him.

'I *absolutely* promise,' said Cameron Bell. 'Now I suggest that you go to your room and get some sleep. It has been a very long day and you must be quite exhausted.'

Alice glanced about the room. It was perhaps a modicum more adequate than hers.

'You go to the other one,' she said. 'I am staying here.'

There were fireworks that night at the Crystal Palace. But few folk had turned out to watch them and when their carriages rolled away there was silence and darkness in the little village of Sydenham.

Alice had washed the bootblack from her face. She sat before the window, gazing out into the night. Above, stars twinkled in a cloudless sky. Planets, too. One of them was Venus, but Alice did not know which one it was.

She yawned and stretched and let her curtain sari fall to the rugless floor. She still wore her pale blue dress with the white puffed shoulders. But it was rather grubby now and she really needed a bath. Alice reached out to draw the curtains closed.

But then she saw him.

He stood in the darkened doorway of the pet shop. A lone figure, tall, and staring up at her.

'Oh my goodness,' said Alice. 'The giant kiwi bird.'

It was the same giant kiwi bird that Alice had encountered in her dream. A dream of twelve months past. The kiwi bird that had accompanied her on the imaginary trip to Venus.

The hotel's front door was not particularly well locked, and Alice slipped quietly into the darkened street.

The kiwi bird beckoned with its beak. Then spoke.

'About time, too,' it said. 'Where have you been for so long?'

'On a voyage to Venus and back,' said Alice. 'As you told me that I would.'

'And I wonder, did you bring back any magic?' said the kiwi bird.

'I did not bring back anything other than myself.'

'Then you *did* bring back the magic.' The kiwi bird smiled with his beak. 'You passed the test and the magic is now inside you.'

'I do not understand,' said Alice. 'You are confusing me.'

'You went on a journey to the most magical planet in the Solar System. Others went with you, but you were the only one who did not steal something away from that world called Magonia. You passed the test. The magic is now in you.'

'I do not feel very magical,' said Alice. 'Very tired and rather hungry, though. They do not serve an evening meal at the Adequate.'

'Horrid things have happened while you have been away,' said the kiwi bird, bobbing its head in time to its words. 'A horrid beast stalks the streets. Your kiwis are blamed for its horrors.'

'Where are my birds?' asked Alice.

'I will bring them to you presently. But you must listen to me. Even now the horrid beast gains terrible power. You will play your part in defeating him. The ecclesiastics of Venus have schooled you for this, although you do not remember.'

'You frighten me,' said Alice. 'I want my kiwi birds back and I want nothing to do with any horrid beast.'

The horrid beast did not look particularly horrid upon this warm summer's night. But then there was not much of him to be seen. He wore his long black cloak and his tall black hat and sported a black silk veil. He had indeed taken particularly horrid woundings at the beaks of Alice's kiwi birds on the night of the Crystal Palace fire, and beneath the black silk veil were terrible scars. He sat alone in the rear of an electrically powered Black Maria. One that lacked for crests upon its night-dark flanks.

The electric Maria purred between the guard posts that had been set up at the head of the Strand and passed into Trafalgar Square. Tall neon tubes, powered by the wireless transmission of electricity, had been set up all over the square to light the wrecked spaceship. Soldiers stood on watch, mostly chatting and sharing cigarettes.

They stiffened to attention as the electric Maria drew up and the figure in black stepped from it.

'Where is your commanding officer?' The voice hissed like a serpent's and quite put the wind up the soldier boys.

'I'll fetch him, sir,' said one, saluting as he made off in the direction of the mashed-up *Marie Lloyd*.

Mr Winston Churchill emerged from the broken craft. Cigar in hand. The look upon his baby face was not one of joy at the figure in black's arrival.

'What do *you* want?' asked the young Mr Churchill.

'You will show me the politeness that my position in the Government merits,' hissed the figure in black.

'What do you want, *sir*?' asked Mr Churchill, taking a mighty suck upon his cigar.

'You have never cared for me, have you, Churchill?' asked the figure in black.

Mr Churchill shook his head. 'You are the Chancellor of the Exchequer,' said he. 'Exactly how you gained this exalted position, no one seems to know. Or should I say that those who *do* know do not dare to say?'

'Strong words,' hissed the figure. 'You would do well to modify your behaviour and your manners if you wish to retain *your* exalted position.'

Mr Churchill made a frowning face. Then sucked once more on his cigar.

'What do you want, *sir*?' he repeated through the smoke.

'The case of minerals aboard the ship. The minerals that Corporal Mingus Larkspur collected for me. In a bound box with the initials M. L. upon the top.'

'We did find such a box of gold in one of the cabins,' said Mr Churchill.

'It is so much more than gold, my friend.'

'No friend, I,' said Mr Churchill, chugging at his cigar.

'Fetch me the box and *now*,' said the figure in black and he poked at Mr Churchill with a blackly gloved finger.

Poke-poke-poke, it went.

Poke-poke-poke and peck-peck-peck as well.

Alice Lovell awoke in a bed that offered moderate comfort. She awoke to sun shining in at the window and poke-poke-poke-and-peck.

Alice blinked her eyes and said, 'Oh my.'

For bumbling all around and about a-poking and a-pecking too were dozens and dozens of kiwi birds.

'Oh mercy me,' said Alice.

48

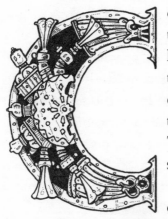

olonel Katterfelto slept rather longer than usual and finally awoke to find himself in circumstances very much to his liking. He and Darwin had engaged a double suite of rooms at the Ritz the previous afternoon. The double suite was luxurious to say the very least.

Done to a perfection in the style of the legendary Enrico Dalberty, the walls were clothed in sumptuous silks that glowed in the early sunlight. Lacquered tables and burnished brass vases created the ambience of an Aladdin's cave, where treasures twinkled in every corner and there were wonders galore.

The colonel bathed in a circular bath hewn from a single piece of speckled basalt and fed with heated water by golden taps in the shape of diving dolphins. Lemongrass bath oil offered a heady fragrance. The colonel's uniform hung on a peg, thoroughly laundered by lackeys who laboured at night.

As he bobbed about and tasted a morning snifter of champagne, the old soldier thought back to the doings of the previous day. In particular to the latter doings. When he had revisited the engineering works at Alperton to collect his key to the rented chapel, wherein awaited the Mechanical Messiah.

He had experienced extraordinary difficulty even entering the engineering works. The colonel had hired one of the new electrically powered flying hansoms, but when this put down before FERRIS ENGINEERING, armed guards immediately surrounded it.

'What goes on here?' the colonel demanded to be told.

But he was hauled immediately from the hansom and marched away to a gatepost. Where his name, rank and number were taken.

Huffing and puffing in the manner of a small steam train, the colonel was forced to await the arrival of a slight officious fellow with a polished iron beard and a black uniform that bore insignia quite unknown to the old campaigner.

Within a tiny room that lacked for windows and charm, a curious interview followed.

'Please be seated.' The slight officious fellow indicated a stool. Then sat himself down on a taller chair.

'Prefer to stand,' said the colonel. 'Prefer more to get what I came for and go.'

'This is now a restricted area where weapons are designed and manufactured. FERRIS ENGINEERING leads the world in such marvels of the modern age,' said the slight officious fellow with the polished iron beard. 'You cannot simply turn up here without the correct clearance documentation. A state of National Emergency exists.'

'Ah,' puffed the colonel. 'You mean that business with the spaceship in Trafalgar Square. Rum do that, to be sure.'

'Have you been abroad?' asked the iron-bearder, making certain notes upon paper attached to a clipboard with a pen of advanced design that whistled when he used it. 'In France, perhaps?'

'Could say I've been abroad.' The colonel viewed this bothersome being with ill-concealed contempt. 'Hunting trip. Big-game hunt. Been away for a year, it seems.'

'Ah, the Dark Continent.' The iron-bearder made more notes with his whistling pen. 'Soon to become a much lighter continent.' He laughed as if this were quite a joke. The colonel was perplexed.

'The State of National Emergency has existed now for several months. Since the installation of the new administration, the National Executive has identified certain factions within our very midst. Subversive factions. Factions that must be brought under control.'

'Anarchists and the like?' said the colonel.

'Anarchists, Bolsheviks, foreigners, off-worlders, Jews. To name but a few.'

'Pardon me?' said the colonel, his mouth dropping horribly open.

'The list grows longer every day. They say Her Majesty never leaves her sitting room at Windsor now. Gentlemen of the National Executive Special Operations Unit maintain a constant vigil. And a good thing too, you will agree, after what happened yesterday. A suicide mission in a stolen spaceship set to destroy the Royal Family.'

The colonel made coughing sounds deep in his throat. 'Suicide mission?' he ventured.

'Exactly what the National Executive has been predicting. As soon as the nation that launched this outrage has been identified, war will be declared upon them.'

'Don't think *that's* really necessary,' mumbled the colonel. Then, viewing the very hard stare he received, he said, 'But you chaps know your own job best, I suppose.'

'You will receive your recall papers shortly,' said he of the iron beard.

'My *what*?' went Colonel Katterfelto.

'Your records are on the way from London. Once I have checked through them I will assign you a rank.'

'I am a *colonel*, be damned!' boomed the colonel. 'And now an angry one, too.'

'Some vacancies exist in the catering corps,' said the man upon the high chair, showing not a hint of concern. 'A chap of your advanced years should at least be able to cook up some beans without getting himself into trouble.' The iron-bearder smiled upon the colonel.

There had been some unpleasantness.

Burly guards had been forced to restrain the colonel.

They had not treated him kindly at all.

It was many hours later and after a very great deal of further interviewing from a chap who, unlike his predecessor, had not had his iron beard forcibly rammed into a private place, that Colonel Katterfelto left FERRIS ENGINEERING, carrying the key to his rented chapel.

The flying hansom had long departed, and the colonel had a long march back to London.

But that was yesterday and today was a new day and one filled with hope for the colonel. Today in fact might well be the very day when he would put all the world to right.

The day when he would energise *Heaven's Last and Best Gift to Mankind*. The Mechanical Messiah.

His ablutions completed, shaving done and other details too, Colonel Katterfelto donned his very-clean-but-now-quite-faded uniform, slipped the *Magoniam* that had spent the night beneath his pillow into its pockets and took himself downstairs for a bang-up breakfast.

He sat all alone in the magnificent dining room and was pleasantly surprised by the unexpected arrival of Darwin.

The monkey carried a rolled newspaper. He sat himself down opposite the colonel and ordered coffee, which rather startled the waitress.

'Probably prudent not to be *too* chatty,' said the colonel. 'Not everyone prepared to buy the idea that you're me weirdo nephew.'

Darwin spied a fruit bowl and helped himself to all the bananas in it. 'Have you read the news today?' said Darwin. 'Oh boy!'

'Trouble?' said the colonel. 'Trouble about the spaceship, I'll wager.'

'Trouble all over,' said Darwin. 'The Prime Minister is no longer in power, it appears. Some strange National Executive run by the Chancellor of the Exchequer controls the country now. Folk are being called up to prepare for a "Righteous War".'

'Had a bit of a set-to at Alperton yesterday.' The colonel feasted on cornflakes. 'Didn't want to bother you with it last night, you were asleep when I got back. World's gone mad since we've been away.'

'Are you visiting your rented chapel today?' asked Darwin.

The colonel nodded, munching as he did so.

Darwin peeled a banana and pushed it complete into his mouth.

'Mmmph grumpgh mm mmph,' he said.

'Rude to speak with your mouth full, old chap.'

Darwin swallowed. 'I said I will gladly come with you,' he said.

'Jolly good show,' said the colonel.

The waitress brought Darwin coffee. She was a pretty

waitress. Darwin thanked her and offered her a wink. The waitress all but fainted.

'The world needs us, Darwin,' said the colonel, pouring coffee for his friend. 'Today could be the most important day of your life. You and me together, eh? Get the job all jobbed, doncha know.'

'Yes,' said Darwin. 'Quite so. And then in return I would appreciate it if you accompanied me to Coutts. There you must endorse my role as your "weirdo nephew". The reaction of the waitress leads me to believe that folk are presently in a somewhat nervous state. I need you with me, Colonel.'

'Happy to help, my dear fellow. Happy to help, oh yes.'

There was a certain unease. Although the sun shone down upon the great heart of the British Empire, there was no joy to be found upon the streets. Darwin and the colonel noticed things that they had not upon the previous day. What with all the excitement and everything. There were posters everywhere, pasted upon walls and shop windows. Posters that offered dire predictions. Demanded vigilance. Warned of an 'enemy within' that was preparing to strike. Offered financial incentives for those loyal persons willing to inform against potential enemies of the nation. The word WAR figured big and everywhere.

And Londoners no longer walked along with heads held high. They scuttled almost insect-like with eyes turned to the pavement.

The colonel and the monkey viewed this from their horse-drawn hansom cab.

'Damned queer business, all this,' puffed Colonel Katter-felto. 'Not the British way of doing things at all.'

The hansom's driver peeped down through the little hatchway.

'Sorry to bother you, guv'nor,' he said, 'but you do 'ave a licence for that thing, don't you?'

'For that *thing*?' bawled the colonel.

'Well, it 'as to 'ave a licence. Prove it's your pet and that.'

'Have you gone completely mad?' asked Colonel Katterfelto.

'No, guv. But come on now. That little fellow could be taken for a Johnny Frenchman any old day of the week.'

'*He is a monkey!*' roared the colonel. 'A monkey, can't you see?'

'Whatever you say, guv'nor.' The hansom driver laughed. 'But if he starts talking, I'll know 'im for a Frenchie and put a bullet in 'is 'ead.'

Darwin opened his mouth to protest. The colonel covered it quickly with his hand.

'That might explain the waitress,' he whispered. 'New billet for us tonight, I'm thinking. Whole damn world's gone mad.'

Whitechapel seemed as ever it was, but such indeed was Whitechapel. The folk here were always poor and always ground down. A new direction in government meant very little to them. As long as they had sufficient pennies in their ragged pockets to drink and fornicate and visit the Music Hall they were as happy as they would ever be in life. And as they had not suffered the unexplained loss of any virgins for the last year, this fashion apparently having shifted itself to Sydenham, the home of the new Chancellor of the Exchequer, the plain folk of Whitechapel all seemed happy enough.

Colonel Katterfelto paid off the driver of the hansom cab, offering him a two-fingered gesture of contempt upon his departure. He then applied his key to the chapel door and followed Darwin inside.

Long fingers of sunlight diddled about through the stained-glass windows and flickered over a large packing case that stood all alone in the middle of the floor.

'Oh yes,' said Colonel Katterfelto, drawing his ray gun. 'This is it now, Darwin.'

The monkey looked up at the colonel. 'Are you going to shoot it?' Darwin asked.

'Course not, my dear fellow. Just knock the case open. Don't have a crowbar. Shouldn't take a jiffy.'

The colonel crossed to the packing case, a full head higher than himself, and began to belabour it with the butt of his ray gun.

Darwin stood and watched him. And wondered what would unfold. Darwin looked up at the stained-glass windows, recognising many of the biblical scenes pictured upon them.

There was Balaam's talking donkey. And old father Noah, of course. Two monkeys on the roof of the ark. *My first parents?* wondered Darwin, scratching at his head.

'Aha!' cried Colonel Katterfelto. 'Absolutely splendid. Darwin, come and look.'

The monkey skipped across the chapel floor and joined the old soldier, who was tearing away at the wood shavings that were used as packing. The shavings gave off a delicious scent of pine. Darwin breathed it in.

'Oh yes,' cried Colonel Katterfelto. 'Yes.'

He tore away the last of the packing, then reached down and took Darwin by the hand.

And then the two stepped back to behold

The Mechanical Messiah

49

he prince and princess enjoyed a breakfast that was barely enjoyable. The princess paid for the rooms and breakfasts. The princess seemed rather grumpy.

'I will pay you back for everything,' Cameron assured Alice as they were driven towards London aboard a hired horse-drawn cart. This cart was towing a very large makeshift cage upon wheels. A cage that contained snoozing kiwi birds. 'I have one of the uncut diamonds from Venus. Major Thadeus Tinker gave it to me. I had hoped to have it made into a ring.' Cameron Bell sighed wistfully. An engagement ring for Alice was what he had hoped.

'I will sell it at Hatton Garden,' said Cameron. 'You can have all of the money.'

Alice thought back to what the kiwi bird had said to her last night. That she was the only one who had not returned to Earth with something stolen from Venus.

'I don't want the money,' said Alice. 'I am going to see Lord Andrew Ditchfield. Perhaps the Electric Alhambra has been opened again. Perhaps he will let me top the bill once more.'

'Oh no,' said Cameron Bell, shaking his head with vigour. 'Firstly, even if the Electric Alhambra has reopened, it would not be safe for you to top the bill. There have been three deaths amongst those who topped the bill.'

Alice made her sulky face.

'And secondly, you are a wanted woman – THE EVIL KIWI GIRL, if you recall. Hence our disguises.'

Alice made her angry face.

'You must let me sort it out,' said Cameron Bell. 'I will speak with Commander Case at Scotland Yard. And later with Sir Andrew Ditchfield, if he still manages the Electric Alhambra. I will sort this out for you. Please trust me.'

Back at the Adequate, the receptionist unrolled a poster that had arrived in the morning post.

DANGEROUS ASSASSIN

announced the poster.

TO BE SHOT UPON SIGHT

it continued.

Below this there was that illustration by Boz of Mr Pickwick and words to the effect that Cameron James Bell had now been positively identified, by no lesser a figure than the Chancellor of the Exchequer himself, to have been the would-be suicide pilot who had crashed a Martian spaceship into the heart of London. The reward for this criminal's carcass stood at two thousand pounds.

'Everything will be fine,' said Cameron to Alice. 'A few misunderstandings. Nothing more.'

★

The prince and the princess did not earn a warm welcome from the people of London. Usually such an unusual pair of seemingly exotic beings would have received little more than whistles and jovial cheers from the populace. But not today. Today, instead, people jeered. Someone threw a stone. Another cried, 'Down with Johnny Foreigner.'

'Outrageous,' declared Alice. 'And me a princess, too.'

'I shall return you to the Ritz,' said Cameron. 'Major Tinker will still be there having a lie-in. He can look after you until I return.'

Alice Lovell folded her arms, then dodged a Brussels sprout.

When Sir Arthur Conan Doyle modelled Sherlock Holmes upon Cameron Bell, it was only the private detective's mental capacity, his skills at drawing inference from observation, that he used. Doyle drew the looks of Holmes from his own brother Terry, a lanky fellow whom history would fail to record. Doyle's Holmes was a veritable master of disguise who fooled his biographer Watson on many occasions. Cameron Bell was *not* a master of disguise.

He and Alice found Major Tinker breakfasting at the Ritz. The major nearly made himself sick from laughing at their disguises. He agreed, however, to offer Alice sanctuary in his room. Agreed rather too eagerly in Cameron's opinion. And agreed also to allow Cameron to change his disguise there to something less foreign.

'I can't wait,' said Major Tinker.

They joined the major in a more than adequate breakfast and were just finishing up when the doorman of the Ritz approached Major Tinker. 'They are all up in your room now,' he said.

'All of whom?' asked the major.

'About two dozen kiwi birds,' said the doorman. 'It was a right old struggle, I'll tell you. But they're all up there now, just as the princess ordered. She said you'd cover any damage.'

Major Tinker made gagging sounds.

The princess smiled upon him.

At a little after ten of the London clock, a portly fellow in a slightly soiled dress suit, with extreme bandaging to his face and borrowed money in his pocket, left the Ritz and ordered a hansom to take him to Scotland Yard.

'Morning to you, guv'nor,' called the driver through the little hatch. ''Ow do you fancy travelling today? Should I dawdle along, or whip up me 'orse Shergar and 'ave 'im shift you like a batsman out of 'ell?'

Cameron Bell made groaning sounds.

'Badly wounded, eh, guv'nor?' called the cabby. 'Probably 'ad that spaceship fall on your 'ead. Never mind, you don't 'as to speak. We'll go by the park and I'll do me recitation of "The Daffodils".'

Cameron Bell groaned just a bit more, but settled back in his seat. He viewed what the colonel and Darwin had viewed. The posters. The mood of the people. Then suddenly he saw something more and called for the driver to bring the hansom to a halt.

'Right in the middle of me recitation,' the driver complained. 'I was wandering lonely as a clown and everything.'

'What is the meaning of *that*?' asked Cameron Bell.

They were parked before the Houses of Parliament. The driver having a route of his own that led to Scotland Yard.

'What *what* is *that*?' the driver asked.

'*That!*' Cameron Bell pointed.

'Ah,' said the driver. 'You are referring to the banner extending down the tower of Big Ben. Which I will 'ave you know is the name of the bell and not the mech-an-e-mism what makes the clock work. The banner is of the Chancellor of the Exchequer.'

'It is a black silhouette,' Mr Bell said through his bandages. 'A tall black hat, a long black cloak, but no facial features at all.'

'That's because no one's seen his facial phy-si-o-og-nomy. 'E's too modest, see. No one even knows 'is name. 'E came into power as if from 'Eaven. Runs the whole Government all by 'is self, they say. The Prime Minister's 'ad to go away for treatment for alco-mor-lism or some such thing. Troubled, 'e is, the papers say.'

Cameron Bell made a very large groan indeed.

'You sound sick, guv'nor. Should I take you instead to the London 'Ospital? Old Jo Merrick the Queen's physician will give you a looking over.'

Cameron Bell began to sweat beneath his bandages.

'Joseph Merrick?' he managed to mumble. 'The Queen's physician?'

'Poor old Mr Treves,' said the driver. ''E slipped on a banana skin in the morgue, fell 'eadfirst onto 'is big bone saw.'

Cameron Bell made further groanings.

Then looked on in some dismay as a number of gentle-men wearing all-black clothing and all-black pince-nez glasses issued from the Houses of Parliament and demanded that the hansom cab move on at once in the interests of National Security.

The driver gave Shergar a good geeing-up. 'Don't want to argue with the gentleman in black,' said he. 'No telling where you might end up in bits.'

At Scotland Yard Cameron paid off the driver.

'Cheers, guv'nor,' said the man. 'Do you know what? Even with those bandages on your bonce, you remind me of someone.' And then he shook his head and drove away.

Cameron thought back to his previous encounter with that driver at the Crystal Palace. The matter of the Educator ray gun and his precious gold watch. Cameron still had his precious gold watch. He now remembered that he had left the Mark Five Ferris Firestorm behind in his room at the Adequate.

Cameron sighed. There *had* been a time when his life had been uncomplicated. When he had his work and his house and his treasures. How had it all gone so terribly wrong? What had been the catalyst that had sparked his descent into chaos and complication?

Cameron Bell made the grimmest of faces beneath his bandages. It had been his visit to the Electric Alhambra to see Alice Lovell and her Acrobatic Kiwi Birds. If he had not been there upon that particular night—

Cameron Bell now entered Scotland Yard.

At the desk in the grand entrance hall sat a policeman. He was a young policeman and wore a uniform that Cameron Bell did not recognise. An all-black uniform with strange insignia. He looked up from the notes he was making and viewed the bandaged visitor.

'Yes?' he said in a manner somewhat surly.

'I would like to speak with Commander Case,' said Mr Cameron Bell.

'*Commander Case?*' The young man in the uniform of black tapped the keys of a lettered board beneath a complicated apparatus of brass.

'That looks rather splendid,' Cameron Bell observed.

'It's a crime engine,' the young man replied. 'Very latest thing. All the information required is in here. On punched pieces of paper.'

'How does it work?' asked Cameron.

The young policeman struck it with his fist. 'It mostly doesn't,' he said.

'I only want to speak with Commander Case.'

The young policeman struck the crime engine once again. 'Stupid thing,' he said. 'It was working a minute ago.'

Cameron looked down at the desk. The young police-man's name was printed on a little brass plaque.

'Constable Gates,' said Cameron Bell, 'I know my way to the commander's office. I will trouble you no more.'

'Ah, there,' said the constable. 'I have it now. No I don't. Yes I do. No I don't. Oh yes. We have no Commander Case.'

'Oh dear me,' said Cameron Bell.

'We have a *Sergeant* Case, though. Ah yes, I remember. He was in charge of the murder investigations at the Electric Alhambra. He closed the place for six months while he searched it. Then declared it safe. It reopened the very next night. Master Scribbens the Brentford Snail Boy topped the bill. Horrible business—'

'Quite so,' said Cameron Bell. 'If you would direct me to his office?'

'Oh, he doesn't have an office any more,' said Constable Gates. 'He has a hut.'

'A *hut*?' said Cameron Bell.

'Outside. He's in charge of the carriage park.'

The hut in the carriage park was not a thing of beauty. By comparison it made former Commander Case's former office seem a veritable luxury suite at the Ritz. The ex-commander had installed a paraffin stove for brewing tea. And he was not a man to be trifled with if you parked your carriage over one of the lines he had painted to mark out who parked where.

Cameron Bell wore a sympathetic face beneath his bandages.

The sergeant sitting in his hut looked up at his approach.

He looked up once. Then looked up once again. Then rose to his feet and made two very big fists.

'It is the assassin!' he cried aloud. 'The ruiner of my prospects! The thief! The arsonist! The murderer!' And now he tugged from his trouser pocket a ray gun. It was an Educator, and this he pointed at the bandaged detective.

'Cameron James Bell,' the sergeant declared. 'I am arresting you in the name of the law. You do not have to say anything, but anything you do say will be ignored anyway and I may just have to shoot you.'

Sergeant Case kicked over his paraffin stove. As an afterthought he then kicked over his hut.

'Hello, two thousand pounds,' said he. 'I am taking early retirement.'

50

t this very moment in an East End chapel, a man and a monkey beheld a wondrous thing. Before them stood a metallic creation of quite outstanding beauty. It was most unlike its American predecessor. That automaton, constructed in parts by various engineering works around and about Wormcast, Arizona, had about it the functional, workable quality of a machine and nothing more.

This, however, was something far superior. This was a man formed from brass and burnished as of gold. A man who bore the classic proportions of Michelangelo's *David*. A metal figure, fully articulated, precise in every muscle and sinew down to the finest detail.

Darwin took a smart step back. 'I am fearful,' he said to the colonel.

'Understand your feelings, my dear fellow.' The colonel stepped forwards, reached out to touch the chest of the golden figure. His fingers hovered and then retreated. 'Come,' said the colonel, 'help me knock off the rest of the packing case. Behold the rest of the wonder, as it were.'

Darwin was not keen, but he tugged away the pine

shavings as Colonel Katterfelto reduced the remains of the packing case to sections and stacked them against the wall beneath the stained-glass window. Sunlight now fell fully on the wonderful creation.

Sparkled on its shoulder plates and upon its noble brow. For the head and face of the Mechanical Messiah alone were sufficient to inspire awe. As Colonel Katterfelto peered up at the face with its classical features and fine aquiline nose, he was entranced to see that the eyelids were fully articulated and pure white ivory teeth showed between jointed lips, which had about them such a reality as if it was a living person turned by some Medusa's glance into a thing of metal.

'I now feel very fearful indeed,' said Darwin. 'This is a . . . a . . .'

'Please say it, my little friend,' said Colonel Katterfelto.

'This is . . . a holy thing,' said Darwin. 'And I do not know whether *I* should be in its presence.'

'Oh, you should, my dear fellow, for you are good and true.'

'But I may have no soul,' said Darwin, turning his eyes to the floor.

The colonel patted Darwin's head. 'You do have a soul,' he said. 'You couldn't have such feelings if you didn't.'

'Really?' Darwin looked up at the colonel. 'You really think that I do?'

'I do.' The colonel straightened his shoulders as best he could and fought against the tears. 'And you are here at this moment. We shall make history together. We shall mould the future. Make things right, eh, Darwin, my boy? Make the world go right?'

'How can it be so different?' Darwin whispered. 'From the one in America? So special? So holy?'

'British engineering,' said the colonel. 'Best in the world and always will be. Tell you what.' He looked down at the monkey. 'Before I pop in the *Magoniam*, I think that we should say a little prayer.'

'I don't know how to pray,' said Darwin.

'Well, you just follow me. I've said a few in me time. In moments of battle. Death staring me in the face. All that kind of horrible stuff and things of that nature generally.'

Darwin put his hands together and tightly closed his eyes.

Colonel Katterfelto cleared his throat. 'For what we are about the receive, may the Lord make us truly thankful.'

Darwin opened up an eye. 'That is grace,' he said.

'Just getting started,' said the colonel. And then he looked up at the marvellous figure standing there before them. 'Tell you what,' he said. 'A man of deeds rather than words, me. Have the magic here in me pocket.'

'The magic?' Darwin asked.

'The American version wouldn't work,' said the colonel, 'because it lacked a vital component. *Magoniam*. Only found on Venus. Have it here in me pocket.' He tugged out a piece of *Magoniam* and held it upon his palm. 'Pop it into the chest and off we go.'

Darwin the monkey was thoughtful. 'You are really to-tally sure that you are doing the right thing?' he said.

'Sure I'm sure,' said the colonel. 'Never been surer in my life.'

He looked down at the *Magoniam* that glittered in his hand.

'Gold,' said Sergeant Case, his ray gun pointed at Cameron Bell. 'Pure gold, you are. Thank you so much for surrender-ing to me.'

'I did not come here to surrender as such,' said Cameron

Bell, making calming gestures with his now raised hands. 'I came here to ask for your help. In return for which I will close the Electric Alhambra cases for you. Allowing *you* to take *all* the credit and regain your rank as commander.'

'I don't think so,' said Sergeant Case. 'Two thousand pounds will last me the rest of my life.'

'If I am not allowed to act unhindered,' said Cameron Bell, 'your life may be a short one.'

'You think to threaten me?' There was a touch of madness in the eyes of Sergeant Case. Cameron's observation of the ex-commander's left trouser cuff informed him that the man holding the ray gun was now a heavy drinker.

'I can give you back your rank,' said the private detective. 'You have to trust me. You know that I am not guilty of those crimes I am accused of.'

'Two thousand pounds,' said Sergeant Case. 'That is the price on your head.'

'You would sell me, even though you know me to be innocent?' Cameron Bell glanced all around and about the carriage park. So far no one had entered it but him. No one else had heard the sergeant's shouts, nor seen what was occurring.

'If it is money you want,' said Cameron Bell, 'then I will pay you more in return for my freedom. And I *will* solve the cases. And *you* will prosper for it.'

'Your house burned,' said Sergeant Case. 'You have no money. Unless you have added bank robbery to your extensive charge sheet.'

'I have this.' Cameron Bell reached slowly into his pocket. Drew out the uncut diamond, held it up.

'I have an extensive knowledge of gemstones,' said Mr Bell. 'This I know will fetch three thousand pounds at least on the open market.'

Sergeant Case eyed the gemstone greedily. 'Three thousand pounds?' he said.

'At the very least,' said Cameron Bell. 'Probably more.' The lies were easily back on his lips. The uncut diamond was worth no more than five hundred pounds at most.

Sergeant Case returned his ray gun to his pocket. 'Let us repair to the pub,' said he, 'and discuss these matters at length.'

In Whitechapel a length of time had passed.

The colonel held the *Magoniam*. The little door to the empty compartment in the chest of the Mechanical Messiah was open. Awaiting a golden heart to make it complete.

The colonel stood in silent prayer.

'Oh, please go on,' said Darwin. 'I cannot stand the suspense.'

Colonel Katterfelto bowed his head, did a sort of curtsey and then with great reverence placed the piece of glittering *Magoniam* into the empty compartment of the metal being's chest and closed the little door.

'Oh Lord,' said Colonel Katterfelto, 'have mercy upon us and please save this wretched world.'

'It *is* a wretched world,' said Sergeant Case, downing half a pint of porter at a single gulp. 'And you didn't help matters, Bell. I trusted you to solve those murders, and what do you do? You burn down the Crystal Palace and fly away in a spaceship.'

'It wasn't quite like that,' said Cameron Bell, although he knew that it was very much like that. 'There were complications. But I know who the guilty parties are and I will bring them to justice.'

'Take off those ridiculous bandages,' said Sergeant Case.

'I dare not, as you know full well.'

'Say I trust you,' said the sergeant, his fingers tightly gripping the uncut diamond. 'How do you propose to close the cases? By bumbling around like that? Looking like Mr Wells' Invisible Man?'

'Obviously not,' said Cameron Bell, downing whisky as he spoke. 'I cannot function efficiently with a price upon my head. This is why I came to you. I need you to arrest me.'

Sergeant Case threw up his hands, splashing porter about. 'That was what I intended to do in the carriage park,' said he. 'If that was your intention, why waste my time here?'

'I am paying for your time.' Cameron Bell indicated the uncut diamond. 'You will arrest me and incarcerate me in a cell at Scotland Yard. You will not, however, claim the reward money.'

'And why would I not do *that*?'

'Because you will not be able to. You will arrest me and incarcerate me and you will notify all of the newspapers. They will print my face upon their front pages and crow that the monster murderer and assassin has been caught and is awaiting trial. Then I will be free to close the cases.'

'How?' asked Sergeant Case.

'Because *you* will secretly release me from captivity so that I can go about my business without someone taking a pot-shot at me for the bounty.'

'I am utterly confused,' said Sergeant Case.

'It is simplicity itself. You arrest me. A blaze of publicity occurs. Your rank is restored. You take on exclusive charge of your notorious prisoner. No one enters my cell but you.'

'Ah,' said the sergeant, 'I see. But you will not be in the cell, you will be out solving the cases.'

'I have already solved them,' said Cameron Bell, 'but I must bring the criminals to justice in order to clear myself of the charges against me. Naturally, once I have proved myself innocent, the reward money for my capture will dissolve into nothingness. But you will have the uncut diamond. The credit for solving the cases. Your rank returned to you also. And I would demand a very large office if I were you, too.'

Sergeant Case did noddings of the head.

'And one thing more,' said Cameron Bell. 'If I am denied the freedom and opportunity to bring the guilty parties to justice—'

'Part*ies*?' said Sergeant Case. 'There is more than one?'

'Three,' said Cameron Bell. 'Although only two can actually be brought to justice. One of which is the most evil being that has ever walked upon the face of this Earth, and the other the greatest criminal mastermind in history.'

'And I will take credit for bringing both of *these* to justice?'

'Yes,' said Cameron Bell. 'And within twenty-four hours. That is all the time I need. Twenty-four hours and all will be done, I promise you. But if I am not allowed to go about my business freely, within a week from now the British Empire will be at war and thousands will be dead.'

'Truly?' asked the sergeant.

'Truly,' said the detective.

'Then the Lord save us all,' said Sergeant Case. 'The good Lord save us all.'

'Lord save us all,' said Colonel Katterfelto, falling to his knees upon the cold chapel floor. Darwin the monkey took several paces back and hid himself behind a pillar.

The sunlight shone through the stained-glass windows, playing rainbows over the silent figure's beautiful brazen body.

Colonel Katterfelto caught his breath.

There came a sound, as of a distant choir.
As of angelic voices raised in song.
As of a time, not now, but long ago.
And growing, did this sound appear
To fill the chapel, thrill the ear.
A chorus of Angelic Host,
Of Father, Son and Holy Ghost,
Of love and light, and light and breath
And being in a golden golden glow.

Colonel Katterfelto wrung his ageing hands.
Darwin the monkey trembled.
The Mechanical Messiah opened its eyes.

51

ameron Bell had not been entirely honest with Sergeant Case. It was not just the matter of Cameron's overvaluation of the uncut diamond. It was also the method by which the private detective meant to bring one of the criminals to justice. It was not a method that Sergeant Case would have approved of and so Cameron Bell had not mentioned it.

He had, however, agreed to officially give himself up to Sergeant Case at five o'clock this very evening. At Scotland Yard. This would give Cameron Bell time to make certain important preparations and Sergeant Case sufficient time to rally Fleet Street's finest journalists to Scotland Yard for a press conference at five fifteen. Which meant that the six o'clock evening papers could splash Cameron's capture all over their front pages.

If all goes well, thought Cameron Bell, *I really will be able to bring this entire dire business to an end before tomorrow morning. Assuming nothing untoward occurs to complicate matters.*

The doorman of the Ritz had a piece of paper in his gloved hand. He was discussing what was printed upon it with the driver of a hansom cab that stood waiting before the marvellous hotel.

'Says she's a princess,' said the doorman to the driver. 'And true as true she's all dressed up in velvet with the swarthy looks of a Joany Foreigner.'

The driver nodded. As yet, though, he had nothing to say.

'But it's all those kiwi birds,' continued the doorman. 'There must be two dozen of them. I had to herd them into the lift.'

The driver still had nothing to say.

'So what I'm thinking,' the doorman went on, 'is what if she isn't an Indian princess at all? What if she's the EVIL KIWI GIRL on this here poster?' He waggled the poster. 'In disguise, you see.'

The driver continued with his silence.

'There's only one way to be sure,' said the doorman. 'I am going to call Scotland Yard. Have them send down one of their sergeants. Then if she is the EVIL KIWI GIRL I will get the reward and give up door-keeping and retire to the Sussex Downs to keep bees instead. What do you think?'

The driver looked towards the doorman. 'Sorry,' he said. 'I wasn't listening. I was thinking about a fare what I just dropped at Scotland Yard. I know as 'ow 'e looked familiar and stone me if I don't now remember just who the blighter is.'

'Speak,' said Colonel Katterfelto, down upon his knees. 'Speak to us, O Lord. Let the world know who you are.'

The Mechanical Messiah stood motionless, but for a gentle blinking of its eyes. These eyes were of the palest blue, crafted from turquoise and glass. They slowly moved from side to side then focused on the kneeling figure of Colonel Katterfelto. The fingers of the brass hands twitched, closed upon the metal palms, unclosed. The shoulders flexed, the head moved on its stately neck. The mouth opened slightly exposing more of the pure white ivory teeth.

And then the being spoke.

The Book of Revelation speaks of angels with the voices of trumpets and so was this voice. Gently though the words were spoken, and pure the tone that came not out of any human throat. The trumpet horns of Heaven given speech.

'Who am I?' asked the being formed of brass. The Mechanical Messiah stared blankly into space.

Darwin crept from his hiding place and approached the brazen figure. Colonel Katterfelto was climbing to his feet.

'He doesn't know,' the colonel puffed, his knee joints clicking noisily. 'He doesn't know who He is.'

Darwin looked up at the beautiful creation. 'Perhaps you have to tell Him,' said the monkey.

'Tell Him, you think?' The colonel peered at the face, which shone as polished gold. The expression was completely blank.

'Who am I?' the figure asked once more.

The colonel looked down towards Darwin.

'You have to tell Him,' said the monkey. 'You have brought life to Him. The *Magoniam* has energised Him. But you must explain to Him *what* He is.'

'Hmph.' The colonel cleared his throat. 'Think I know what you're saying. I have brought Him life. But He must bring the spirit into Himself.'

'His soul,' said Darwin. 'His holy soul. And then He will truly be what He should be.'

The sunlight fell through the stained-glass windows onto the man-made God. A God of brass that shone as holy gold.

★

'My God!' cried Constable Gates, punching the crime engine. 'You useless heap of brass.'

A cleaning lady in a straw hat who was passing by asked, 'Have you tried turning it off and then on again?'

A bell began to ring.

'At least *that* is working,' said Constable Gates, tugging the brand-new nice brass Mark One Ferris Telephonicon towards him and bringing the handset to his ear.

'Scotland Yard,' he said.

Words were issued to him via the earpiece.

'The EVIL KIWI GIRL?' he continued. 'Are you sure?'

More words entered his ear.

Constable Gates was an ambitious young policeman and not one to turn a blind eye to a fast-track promotion when one was staring him right in the face. Or in this case, right in the ear. Thoughts now entered the constable's head, although where they entered *from*, even he could not say.

'Could you just hold on for a moment?' said Constable Gates. 'While I have a word with my superior officer.' And then he did what future generations would learn to do. He put his hand over the mouthpiece of the Telephonicon, and in this case counted up to fifty.

'Hello?' he said, removing his hand. 'My sergeant says that I am to deal with this personally. I will gather up a few constables and we will be over to the Ritz directly. Please keep a close watch upon the hotel room of the EVIL KIWI GIRL until I get there. Do you understand?'

'Do you understand what I am saying?' asked the colonel.

'I understand you,' said the figure of brass.

'But you do not know who you are?'

'I know not.'

'Darwin.' The colonel glanced down at his simian friend.

'Darwin, go and look for a Bible. This is a chapel, there must be one somewhere. Perhaps if I read that to Him.'

The bandaged detective read the sign.

FOR SALE

it said, in letters big and red.

Cameron Bell paid off the driver of *another* hansom cab and looked up at the façade of the Electric Alhambra. It did not sparkle quite as much as it used to. Pigeons roosted amongst the gold-plated letters above. The capital E had fallen from *Electric*.

'Oh dear, oh dear,' said Cameron Bell, trying one of the entrance doors and finding that it opened. The foyer was no longer lit by its thousands of vacuum bulbs. A few candles served to light upon a cleaning lady in a straw hat (this the sister of the cleaning lady at Scotland Yard, as it happened, proving once more the smallness of the world). This lady pushed a broom about with no particular interest, but smiled upon Mr Bell as he approached.

'Are you a buyer?' she asked.

'A buyer?' asked Cameron Bell.

'Come to buy the Alhambra, of course.'

'Well, actually, yes,' the detective lied. 'It has all gone a bit downhill.'

'After poor Makepiece Scribbens got all roasted in his shell, the owner decided to put it up for sale. He still holds his private meetings here, of course.'

'At midnight?' asked the private detective.

'So you know of them.'

'Shall we say I suspected something of the sort? Is Lord Andrew in his office?'

'Where else would he be?' asked the cleaning lady. 'He thought he was moving up in the world, that he would manage the Music Hall at the Crystal Palace. But on the opening night there it burned down and he got sent back here. Months went by while Commander Case mucked about, then the theatre reopened with Master Makepiece Scribbens topping the bill.'

'And the rest is history,' said Cameron Bell. 'But thank you for sharing *that* with me. Does the lift still work?'

The cleaning lady shook her hatted head.

'Then I will take the stairs.'

Cameron Bell had a fine sweat on by the time he tapped upon the door of Lord Andrew's lofty suite of rooms.

After some time the door swung partially open and a bleary-eyed face peered out at Cameron Bell.

'Who are you?' asked Lord Andrew Ditchfield.

'I am your salvation,' said Mr Cameron Bell.

The being who might be the world's salvation sat upon the stack of box bits under the stained-glass window. He stared into nothingness and His jaw moved up and down.

The colonel sat on the floor before Him and so did Darwin the monkey. Darwin was holding a battered Bible, which he passed to the colonel.

'Read to Him about Noah,' said Darwin. 'I *do* love all of those animals.'

'I think we will start with the New Testament,' said the colonel. 'And I am thinking the Book of Revelation.'

Cameron Bell could offer no revelations. He entered Lord Andrew's suite of rooms and was appalled by the mess. Empty bottles and discarded cartons littered the floor.

Cameron stopped and picked up one of the cartons. He peered at it and said, 'A pot of noodles.'

'What do you want?' asked Lord Andrew Ditchfield. 'And why are you all bandaged up like that? Another letter didn't fall off the front of the building and hit you on the head, did it?'

Cameron shook his bandaged head. And then took off the bandages.

'Oh no!' screamed Lord Andrew Ditchfield. 'It is you. The murderer. The assassin. The incendiary. Destroyer of my life.'

Cameron Bell turned a deaf ear to this.

Twice in one day was really too much.

'I am your salvation,' he said once again.

Lord Andrew Ditchfield had taken to flapping his hands and spinning around in small circles. Cameron Bell drew him smartly to a halt and gave him a smack on the face.

'You have come to murder me, too.' His lordship all but fainted away.

'I have come to save the day,' said Cameron Bell. 'Well, to save *tomorrow*, shall we say. How would you feel about reopening the Electric Alhambra tomorrow?'

'You are mad! Quite mad!' Lord Andrew took once more to spinning. Cameron slapped him again.

'And I'm not paying you,' said Lord Andrew, rubbing sulkily at his cheek. 'I'm not paying you a penny. If you've come here for money you won't get it. Oh, please don't kill me.' And then he burst into tears.

Cameron helped him onto the casting chaise, which had known no action for many months. 'Just listen to what I have to say,' he said, 'and if you let me do what I need to do, I promise you, you will reopen for business tomorrow night.'

Lord Andrew Ditchfield did little sobbings. 'As if that were possible,' he sniffed.

'It *is* possible,' said Cameron. 'It *will* happen.'

'But even if I could reopen – who would top the bill?'

Cameron Bell beamed hugely. 'Alice Lovell and her Acrobatic Kiwi Birds,' he said.

'She's still in there and I can hear the kiwi birds tearing things to pieces,' the doorman of the Ritz whispered to Constable Gates. They stood upon the second floor of the hotel, just along from Major Tinker's room.

The major had gone off to Hatton Garden.

Alice was all alone with her kiwi birds.

Constable Gates had a service revolver, as only senior ranks were issued with ray guns. He pulled this revolver from its holster and signalled his fellow constables, four in number, to gather behind him, with their pistols drawn also.

'You have a spare room key?' he whispered to the doorman.

The doorman nodded and waggled the key on a chain.

'Then you quietly open the door. And *we*—' he indicated himself and his fellow officers, '—will go in shooting.'

'She's a woman,' said the doorman. 'A pretty woman, too. Are you sure you want to shoot her?'

'She's a fiend in human form, half-woman, half-kiwi, I've heard. She and her evil flock prey upon the young women of Sydenham. Those kiwis will rip your throat out soon as look at you.'

The constables moved uncomfortably. All took to cocking their pistols.

'On the count of three,' whispered Constable Gates, as the doorman placed the key in the lock and with a trembling hand began to turn it.

'One.'

The constables pointed their pistols at the door and from beyond came sounds of bumbling kiwis.

'Two.'

The constables' fingers tightened on their triggers.

Alice's voice came to them saying,' Oh, you naughty birds.'

'Three!'

The doorman twisted key and handle and pushed the door open, ducking aside as the constables rushed forwards, firing their guns as they did so.

They fired and they fired and they fired and they fired.

The doorman burst into tears.

52

moke shrouded the hotel room and nothing remained alive there but for five young constables clicking upon the triggers of empty pistols.

Lord Andrew Ditchfield flicked at his teeth with the tip of his tongue. 'You are surely insane,' he said to Cameron Bell. 'THE EVIL KIWI GIRL? You think I would want *her* to top my bill?'

'She is innocent of all charges,' replied Mr Bell. 'And if all goes as I am planning tonight, this will be proved beyond doubt and the publicity will make her the most longed-to-see Music Hall act in the world.'

'In the world?' mused Lord Andrew Ditchfield.

'Undoubtedly,' the detective said. 'But I need you to do several things for me in order for me to bring this all about.'

'You expect me to trust you, after all that has happened?'

'You will prosper if you do so. And what in truth do you have to lose?'

'I could hand you in to the authorities and claim the reward,' said his lordship.

Cameron Bell squared up before the titled manager. He

could look quite menacing when he really wanted to. This was one of those occasions when he *really* wanted to.

'What do you want me to do?' asked Lord Andrew, getting a fine shake on.

'Three things,' said Cameron Bell. 'Firstly, I wish you to switch on the electrical system for the entire theatre.'

'Why?' asked Lord Andrew Ditchfield.

'Because I need to test a proposition. It is most important.'

'And secondly?' his lordship asked.

'Secondly, the actual testing. I need half an hour alone in the Electric Alhambra, with every door opened to me. Every door, do you understand?'

'Not really,' said Lord Andrew. 'And thirdly?'

'I need the loan of three hundred guineas.'

Lord Andrew Ditchfield sighed. 'I am a broken man,' sighed he. 'I had such great ambitions.'

'And they will be realised.' Cameron Bell became thoughtful. 'I too have ambitions,' he said, 'both professional and romantically inclined. If you put your trust in me I promise it will not be ill-founded. What do you say?'

The detective offered his hand to be shaken.

Lord Andrew Ditchfield paused.

'The most longed-for Music Hall star in the world and she will be all yours.'

Lord Andrew Ditchfield shook the hand of Mr Cameron Bell.

'Where is she?' a constable asked, fanning smoke from his face. 'Where did she go and where are the kiwi birds?'

Constable Gates flapped at the thinning smoke. 'We saw her,' he said. 'We heard her and her birds before we rushed in. And we saw her. *I* saw her. Sitting on the bed in a blue dress with white puffed shoulders.'

'I saw her *too*,' agreed a constable. 'And all the birds.'

The constables nodded their helmeted heads. They had *all* seen all of the birds.

'But when we fired . . .' Constable Gates' voice trailed off and there was a bit of a silence.

'She vanished,' said one of the constables. 'She and her birds just vanished away.'

'No no no.' Constable Gates was now shaking his head, and his helmet almost fell off. 'She cannot just have vanished. She must be hiding. And her birds. Guard the door, then, one of you and all the rest search with me.'

And so they searched.

And searched.

And searched a little more.

'She *has* gone,' said a nameless constable. 'She and her birds, they simply vanished away.'

The constables nodded once again.

'She vanished in front of our eyes,' they all agreed.

Constable Gates did further head shakings, but he in truth had seen her vanish, too. One moment she had been there and in the next just gone.

'It must be magic,' said Constable Gates, with wonder in his voice.

The colonel's reading voice lacked somewhat when trying to express the wonder of the Book of Revelation. He droned on a bit, did the colonel. He huffed and puffed, but he veritably droned.

'Let me help you,' said Darwin. 'I would be pleased to read.'

The glass and turquoise eyes of the Mechanical Messiah moved, focusing upon the man and then upon the monkey. 'Are you brothers?' he asked.

'Brothers?' asked the colonel, and looked down upon his friend.

Darwin looked up at the colonel.

'In a manner, *yes*,' said Colonel Katterfelto.

Darwin the monkey grinned.

'I'll pop out and get a glass of water,' said the colonel. 'You read some more Revelation.'

The colonel sought a tap and cup, and Darwin read from the Bible.

> '—*and they worshipped the beast,*
> *saying who is like unto the beast?*
> *Who is able to make war with him?*'

'But what does it mean?' asked the Mechanical Messiah.

'It is what *You* do,' said Darwin. 'You banish the beast.'

'*What* is the Beast?' asked the metal figure.

'I do not know,' said Darwin. 'Would You like me to read some more?'

'Read it all to me – Darwin, is it?'

'Darwin is my name,' said Darwin the monkey.

'Then please read it all to me and then perhaps we will both understand it.'

Darwin continued to read.

When Cameron Bell stood once more beneath the FOR SALE sign, he had several hundred pounds in his pocket and in his personal opinion, all the details of the various cases all completely wrapped up.

Cameron Bell knew exactly what had happened, how and why. He knew who was to blame for what and he had formulated a plan that he hoped would be foolproof and not become subject to further complications.

He now had to meet with certain dubious underworld figures of his acquaintance and purchase from them certain items that were far from legal for him to possess and then, he felt confident, he could put all the pieces of this complex jigsaw together and see just how perfectly they fitted.

'It will be my finest achievement. Crowned only by Alice Lovell's acceptance of my proposal of marriage to her,' said the private detective. 'I shall then live happily ever after.'

Cameron Bell thought about that uncut diamond. He would need to get that back from Sergeant Case. That was going to be turned into the gemstone of an engagement ring.

JOSHUA COHEN'S EMPORIUM

read the sign above the door. In the front window diamonds dazzled. Another sign, propped up amongst so many rings and ear studs, necklaces and bracelets, broaches and jewelled pocket watches, advertised that Mr Cohen was always willing to value gems and purchase at the very fairest of prices.

Major Tinker peered in at the window. Gazed upon the diamond hoard. Saw how tiny the diamonds looked in comparison to those he had bagged up in his pocket. And the prices? Major Tinker smiled most broadly, pushed upon the door and entered the shop.

The doorbell pinged and Mr Cohen looked up from his countertop doings. Mr Cohen would never be mistaken for an Irish butcher. Even upon a Tuesday when there was an R in the month.

Mr Cohen had one of those magnifying eyeglass affairs attached to his gold-rimmed spectacles, which he pushed to one side as he greeted his visitor.

'Hello to you,' said Mr Cohen. 'A very fine day, I trust you are well and how may I help you, sir?'

'I would like a valuation upon a diamond,' said Major Tinker, approaching the counter. 'A discreet valuation, if you understand what I mean.'

'I will ask you no questions and you will tell me no lies.'

'Something like that,' said the major. 'I acquired this on my travels. It is an uncut diamond. Perhaps it might interest you.'

He dug into his pocket, rooted about in his pouch and drew out the very largest uncut diamond. This he placed with almost reverence onto the countertop.

Mr Cohen stiffened slightly, but he was a professional. 'On your travels,' he said, thoughtfully.

'In distant lands,' said the major. 'Most distant.'

'Indeed. Indeed. May I touch?'

'You may touch and weigh and value and then buy,' said Major Tinker, smiling as he said these words.

'Indeed, indeed, indeed.' Mr Cohen took up the gem-stone. It was approximately the size of a golf ball. And a rather large golf ball at that. Mr Cohen lowered his magnifying eyeglass affair and peered awhile at the gemstone.

The major affected nonchalance, hummed a Music Hall tune.

When your grey hair turns to silver won't you change me half a quid?

Mr Cohen glanced up at the major then peered back at the gemstone. A bead of perspiration ran down Mr Cohen's forehead.

Major Tinker cut to the chase and said, 'what do you think it's worth?'

'Worth?' Mr Cohen placed the uncut diamond before him upon the countertop. '*Worth?*'

'To the nearest few thousand pounds.'

Mr Cohen said, 'A diamond of this size, somewhat larger

than the Koh-i-noor, would be about five thousand carats. I would value such a diamond, modestly, at perhaps ten million pounds.'

'Ten . . . million . . . pounds?' Major Tinker tried very hard to retain his composure. 'You did say ten million pounds?' he said. 'That really is what you said?'

'For a diamond this size, yes.'

'Oh joy,' cried Major Tinker. 'Oh such joy indeed.'

Mr Cohen eyed him thoughtfully. 'You, sir, are a schmuck,' he said. 'A thoroughly schmecking schmuck.'

'Excuse me?' said the major.

'You think that a funny joke?' Mr Cohen looked an angry fellow. 'You come in here thinking I am some kind of schmuck? You show me this. You show me *this*?'

He took the uncut diamond and held it before the major.

'I will take nine million pounds for it,' said he.

'Nine million? Nine million?' Mr Cohen closed his hand upon the uncut diamond. Squeezed it hard. There was a crumbling, crunching sound and glittering dust went tinkling to the counter.

'Sugar,' said Mr Cohen. 'You offer me a lump of sugar?'

'Sugar?' cried Major Tinker. 'You think to trick me, sir?' And with that said he tore the pouch from his pocket and emptied its contents onto the countertop. 'Sleight of hand,' he shouted. 'But you won't fool me.' He took up an uncut diamond and closed *his* hand upon it. Glittering crystals tumbled from his fingers.

'No,' cried Major Tinker. 'No. My diamonds. My fortune. No.'

Mr Cohen eyed him queerly. 'You really did not know?' he said to the major.

'They were real. I know that they were real.'

'And so it looked to me,' said Mr Cohen. 'And the more I wished to own it, the more it seemed to turn itself to sugar.'

'No!' cried Major Tinker. 'No, this cannot be.'

Mr Cohen shook his head. 'Only once have I heard of such a thing,' he said, 'when a man I am told of stole from the fairy kingdom. He thought that he had stolen emeralds. But he had not. His emeralds turned to clods of earth. It is called the Glamour.'

A broken man was Major Tinker as he left the shop of Mr Cohen.

On his way out he passed a fellow who was going in.

This fellow was whistling a popular Music Hall tune.

This fellow's name was Sergeant Case.

53

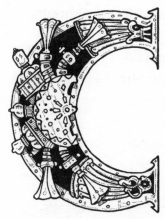ameron Bell continued with his business. He purchased two large carpet bags. He visited divers places and acquired numerous items. He journeyed to the post office in Marylebone Street and sent off a number of telegrams. He had meetings in darkened alleyways and spoke with dubious fellows. Money changed hands at these meetings, illegal things went into the carpet bags.

At fifteen minutes to five a carriage dropped him off at Scotland Yard. Cameron Bell paid the driver and removed the disguising bandages from his face.

'Well,' he said to himself. 'I am here.'

'Where am I?' asked Alice Lovell. 'What am I doing here?'

But she recognised just where she was. In Tunbridge Wells, beside the rabbit hole. Her kiwi birds flustered around her, even more confused than usual.

'Well,' Alice told them. 'There is nothing for it. You must all now follow me, into the rabbit hole.'

Down and down fell Alice, as she had done before. And after came her kiwi birds in a great big fluttering bundle going, 'Ki-wi, ki-wi, ki-wi,' for such is the cry of the kiwi bird when it is *very* confused.

At length, Alice found herself upon the floor of a small room. At slightly more length she found herself engulfed by tumbling kiwi birds. And at further length, when some semblance of order had been restored, confronting a very large kiwi bird, who sat in a rocking chair smoking a small cigar.

'Ah, there you are at last,' said the kiwi bird. And as Alice stared at him and his small cigar, he changed before her very eyes, first into the large white rabbit and then back again.

'It is you,' said Alice. 'And you are both.'

'And *you* have used up valuable magic.'

'I was in a room,' Alice said. 'And policemen attacked me with guns. I wished very hard that they would not shoot me—'

'Nor your kiwi birds,' said the kiwi-rabbit combination.

'No, of course I did not want them to shoot my kiwi birds.'

'And so you are here.' The kiwi beak went puff-puff-puff upon the small cigar. 'And you know how to use your magic.'

'I just wished,' said Alice.

'Magic is mostly just wishing,' said the kiwi/rabbit. 'Wishing and hoping, and believing, too.'

'I would like to take my kiwi birds back to New Zealand,' said Alice. 'London has become a horrid place and I do not want to be there any more.'

'You can of course go wherever you wish.' Puff-puff-puff went the small cigar.

Alice said, 'Will you please put out that cigar?'

'Why?' asked the kiwi that was the rabbit and likewise.

'Because I wish you to,' said Alice.

And then the cigar was gone.

'Oh,' said Alice and felt her heart flutter. 'Does that mean I can wish for *anything*?'

'Not *precisely*,' said the bird-bunny chimera. 'If that were so, I do believe you would reduce this world to chaos in less than half an hour.'

'Do not be so rude,' said Alice, making her sulky face. 'Or—' And then she paused.

'*Or* you might wish me *away*?'

'What *can* I wish for?' Alice asked.

'Perhaps for a happy ending. Although that sometimes comes at a price.'

'You confuse me once more,' said Alice. 'Why am I *here*? I did not wish to be *here*.'

The words, 'I am here,' had barely left the mouth of Cameron Bell before he found himself thoroughly engulfed. Not by kiwi birds, as had Alice, but by members of the capital's press, who, having sensed that something big might be on the go, had arrived early. They had been lying in wait all around and about, and now fell madly upon Mr Bell.

'Mr Bell,' cried one. 'Will you be destroying any more of the nation's monuments?'

'Mr Bell,' cried another. 'Have you committed any more outrageous atrocities that you'd care to talk about?'

'Mr Bell,' cried yet another. 'Why exactly have you chosen to give yourself up?'

'Ah,' said Cameron Bell, trying to force his way into the premises of Scotland Yard. 'I will answer that one. I am surrendering to Sergeant Case. London's greatest policeman. He tracked me down fair and square by the power of his remarkable intellect. By morning you will know absolutely everything. For now my only comment must be that I,

England's most wanted man, am surrendering myself to that exemplar of justice, Sergeant Case.'

Within Scotland Yard, beyond the main door that barred the way to members of the press, stood Sergeant Case.

Cameron Bell shook off a photographer who was imploring him to pose 'with your top off' and entered Scotland Yard.

'Mr Bell,' said Sergeant Case, smiling ever so sweetly. 'Mr Bell, how wonderful to see you. And right upon time, how splendid, how splendid indeed.'

Mr Bell smiled back at Sergeant Case. 'Everything prepared,' he said. Giving the heavy carpet bags a little shake by their handles. 'Now if you will be so kind as to lead me to my cell, everything will be just perfect.'

'Oh, indeed it will,' said Sergeant Case. 'Just perfect.' He leaned towards Mr Bell and whispered, 'Let's make this look *really* convincing, shall we?'

Cameron shrugged.

Sergeant Case blew his whistle. A number of constables leapt from their hiding places, truncheons in hand, and began to belabour the private detective.

'Ooh!' cried Cameron. 'Ooooh!' and, 'Ow!'

'Take him down to the cells, my bonny boys!' cried Sergeant Case. And with much jollity upon the part of the constables, several of whom had not truncheoned anybody since lunchtime, Cameron Bell was chivvied down to the cells.

The iron door of one of these was opened.

Cameron Bell, his bags and all, were hurled into the cell.

The private detective fell in a painful heap. The constables departed, all a-chuckling. As Mr Bell struggled up to his knees, Sergeant Case put his head around the door.

'Most convincing,' said he.

'A little too convincing for my liking,' replied Mr Bell, feeling at his many bruised places.

'Well, we had to make it look real.'

'I suppose you did,' said Cameron Bell.

'Because things are either real or they are not,' said Sergeant Case.

'In a manner of speaking,' said Mr Bell.

'Although,' Sergeant Case continued, 'things can appear to be real at first glance and then turn out not to be real at all.'

Cameron Bell was dusting about at himself. 'That is also the case,' said he, in a distracted fashion.

'Yes,' said Sergeant Case. 'A man might be given something that he is told – promised, in fact – to be of value. But that something turns out to be of no value whatsoever.'

Cameron Bell glanced up at Sergeant Case. 'Ah,' said Mr Cameron Bell. 'Well now indeed. I think I get the picture.'

'You tricked me, sir,' cried Sergeant Case.

'Hardly too much trickery,' said Cameron Bell. 'Five hundred pounds is a tidy sum.'

'That diamond was not worth five hundred pounds. Not one single pound, in fact.'

'What of this?' asked Cameron Bell.

'It turned to sugar in the shop.'

'Oh dear me,' said Mr Bell. 'Oh my dear dead mother.'

'And as such,' continued Sergeant Case, 'our agreement is null and void. Cancelled. Finished.'

'But, listen—' said Cameron Bell.

'Oh no.' The sergeant waggled his finger. 'I will listen no more to you. You have lied to me once too often. Your sins, Mr Bell, have found you out. I *shall* claim the reward for your capture. And *I* shall have a happy ever after. You, however, will do Jack Ketch's dance at the end of a rope.'

'But—' went Cameron Bell.

'*This* is the most secure cell in Scotland Yard,' said Sergeant Case. 'And *this* is the only key. Farewell, Mr Bell.'

And having said this he slammed shut the door and turned the key in the lock.

> '*And the key was turned*
> *and the seventh seal was*
> *opened and a star fell*
> *from Heaven onto the Earth.*'

Darwin the monkey ceased to read and drank from the cup of water that the colonel offered him.

The Mechanical Messiah was still staring into space while the big toe of His left foot described patterns in the floor dust. The fingers of His right hand were tapping on His knee.

'I hate to say it,' said Darwin, 'but I think we are wasting our time. I don't know what you have brought to life, Colonel, but I do not think it is *Heaven's Last and Best Gift to Mankind.*'

'Hmph,' hmphed the colonel. 'Terrible disappointment. Feel rather cheated. But we can't give up just yet.'

'We have been reading to Him for hours and hours,' said Darwin, 'and all He does is grin foolishly. When I read chapter fourteen, verse two – "*and I heard the voice of harpers harping with their harps*" – I thought He was going to wet Himself.'

The colonel hmphed once more.

'I am sorry,' said Darwin, 'but I regret that one is forced to apply the verity and cliché to our golden friend. He is very pretty, but He is not very bright.'

Colonel Katterfelto hung his head. 'This was my whole life's work,' he said. 'My very reason for being, as it were.'

'You have lived an extraordinary life,' said Darwin. 'Done extraordinary things. Brave things. Noble things.'

Colonel Katterfelto tousled Darwin's head. 'I have led a lonely life,' said he. 'And d'you know what? Meeting you has been one of the best things in it. Your friendship means the world to me.'

'As yours does to me,' said Darwin. 'Shall we leave this beautiful fellow here to fiddle in the dust and take some pie and porter at an alehouse?'

Colonel Katterfelto straightened up his shoulders. 'Come on, then,' he said to Darwin. 'Pie and porter it is.'

The Chancellor of the Exchequer eschewed pie and porter, dining rather upon venison haunch, broccoli spears, courgettes and sautéed potatoes. At periods he sipped red wine from a glass that had once touched the lips of Marie Antoinette. The wine had once been laid in Louis' cellar at Versailles.

The Chancellor of the Exchequer dined alone. In his private chambers in the Palace of Westminster. His personal valet and manservant coughed politely and announced the dessert.

The dessert was Treacle Sponge Bastard.

The Chancellor of the Exchequer beckoned this dish to his table with a languid though blackly gloved hand.

Outside Big Ben struck ten of the evening clock.

'Time is moving forward oh so fast,' hissed the Chancellor. His valet trembled as he served the Bastard.

But then—

'Sir, oh, sir.'

A menial entered the private chamber, waving a sheet of paper.

'I am *not* to be disturbed!' hissed the voice behind the black silk veil.

'But sir, it is the news you have been waiting for.'

'The news?'

'The evening's papers were delivered late.'

'Make sense, you fool,' the Chancellor hissed, 'or I will have your head.'

'The assassin,' said the menial, his knees now knocking together. 'The one you had the WANTED posters issued for. Cameron James Bell. He has been captured. He is under arrest. Held in a cell at Scotland Yard.'

The Chancellor in black rose to his feet, cast aside his chair and then his table. The crystal glass shattered, the vintage wine drained away into a priceless carpet.

'Then I have him,' he cried, his ghastly voice reducing those who heard it to their knees. 'And I will have *it*. The thing I seek. I shall kill him and take what is mine. Take the Ring of Moses.'

His menials quietly wet themselves.

The Chancellor stalked from the room.

54

ime is different in Fairyland, or in the world of dreams. Alice took tea with the white-rabbit-kiwi-bird, whilst her kiwis bumbled around and pecked at the crumbs she threw them.

'I am supposed to do something, aren't I?' said Alice. 'All this toing and froing of me into magical places – this has all been for a reason that you know about and I do not.'

The white-rabbit-kiwi-bird nodded its head. Its beak was in its cup and sipping tea.

'You must use the magic that you have been given to help others, Alice, and not to help yourself.'

'I am not selfish,' said Alice, growing somewhat grumpy as she said it.

'You must use your magic tonight when it is needed.'

'And how will I know when it is needed?'

'When it is needed you will know. And when you know you will walk through that door over there.'

The kiwi-rabbit combination pointed with its beak.

Alice glanced in that direction. There had been no door there formerly, but there was one there now.

The door was enamelled most prettily, with floral panels

and a central decoration depicting a country scene, with a big white rabbit right there in the middle.

Above the rabbit was a word, picked out in copper and gold. The word was

STALLS

They had little private stalls in Whitechapel public houses. So that gentlemen of high social standing might frequent the company of willing women with a degree of privacy.

Colonel Katterfelto inhabited one of these stalls. He and Darwin chewed at pies and sipped a bit at porter.

'Jolly poor show,' said Colonel Katterfelto. 'All that trouble and the fellow turns out to be a damned buffoon.'

'Harsh words,' said Darwin. 'He is perhaps a slow learner. But think, He is hardly born. Perhaps He is like an infant.'

'Perhaps,' puffed the colonel, 'perhaps. But *I* had hoped for such great things. Feel rather cheated. Let down, doncha know?'

'Perhaps it was just not meant to be,' Darwin said as he pushed a piece of pie into his mouth. Swallowing with effort, he asked, 'Are there bananas for pudding?'

'Just you and me, then, my dear fellow,' said the colonel, patting his hirsute companion.

'We can live very comfortably,' said Darwin. 'I can play the Snap tables again. We could buy a house in Mayfair. Life will be good. And as you grow older I will look after you. I am a professional monkey butler after all. We will live happily ever after, just you wait and see.'

'You are a good boy, Darwin,' said the colonel.

'A good boy?' said Darwin. 'A good *boy*, do you think?'

★

The man of metal sat alone within the rented chapel. Moon-light fell upon Him and the glow of gaslights, too. He nodded His beautiful head gently and diddled a tiny bit more with His toe upon the dusty chapel floor. Then He gave a little sigh, as of perhaps a cornet playing in the key of B flat.

His glass and turquoise eyes moved towards the Bible that lay where Darwin had left it. Leaning down, He picked it up and held it out before Him.

'Can *I* read?' He asked the empty chapel.

The Bible was open at the very last page.

The Mechanical Messiah read from it.

> '*I Jesus have sent mine angel to testify unto you these things in the churches. I am the root and off-spring of David and the bright and morning star.*'

The man of metal looked up towards the stained-glass window. Beyond and far distant shone Venus, the bright and morning star.

The unmarked Black Maria moved through the night-time streets. Its driver stared stiffly ahead, forbidden to engage in any cheery banter upon the pain of death. In the rear of this electrically powered marvel of the modern age sat the Chancellor of the Exchequer. His hands within their black leather gloves knotted themselves into fists again and again.

Words came from the mouth of the evil Chancellor. Words of a language quite unknown to Man. Of an ancient and forbidden tongue. Words that spelled no good at all for Mr Cameron Bell.

'Can you believe the nerve of that Bell?' asked Sergeant Case, or just plain Graham to his lovely wife.

His lovely wife was lathering sprouts as lovely wives will do.

'Your name is in all the papers, dear,' his lovely wife said as she lathered. 'You will be a commander again tomorrow.'

'I had better be.' Sergeant Graham Case did grindings with his teeth. 'That swine Bell had me over again. Can you believe the nerve of the fellow?'

'But you have him locked up nice and safe?'

'Oh yes.' Sergeant Graham rubbed his hands together before the tiny fire that burned in the tiny grate. For even though the time of year was summer, his kitchen was a cold and dismal place. 'I have him guarded by two dozen constables. He can sit there and stew without even a cup of tea to comfort him.'

'That will serve him right,' said Mrs Case. 'Would you look at the polish I have on this sprout?'

'Are sprouts in season at this time of year?' asked her husband.

His lovely wife responded with a shrug. 'The dog is in season,' she said to him. 'Would you like a nice cup of tea?'

There was much tea-drinking at Scotland Yard, with some teas sparked up somewhat by generous measures of Scotch.

Constable Gates sat once more at his desk. He had received a sound telling off for leaving it earlier in the day without permission. And there was an internal investigation ongoing regarding a report from the Ritz that he and several constables had entered one of the exclusive hotel rooms and discharged the contents of their weapons into the furniture.

Constable Gates was in disgrace and as punishment he would work an all-night shift.

His fellow officers were huddled around him in the entrance hall of Scotland Yard. It was far too nippy downstairs by the cells and rather depressing, too.

They had tired early of calling abuse to Cameron Bell through the little iron grille in the big iron door of his cell and had chosen instead some ground-floor camaraderie, with whisky-flavoured tea and a game of hunt the truncheon to pass the hours of night.

'Well,' said Colonel Katterfelto, full of belly and slightly taken with drink, 'we can't stay here all night. Back to the Ritz in a hansom for us, I'm thinking.'

Darwin wiped the residue of pudding from his chin and nodded his little hairy head. 'What about the man of brass?' he asked.

'Suppose He's my responsibility,' said the colonel, easing himself into the vertical plane. 'Let's go and fetch Him, Darwin, we'll take Him with us. What do you say to that?'

'I say yes,' said Darwin. 'And the pie and porter are on me. My treat.'

The colonel smiled. 'We will live happily ever after,' he said to his friend. 'And think, Darwin, maybe you won't have to be my monkey butler. Maybe we can have a big shiny brass butler to buttle away for us both.'

Darwin the monkey grinned and said, 'Can I have a piggyback?'

When they returned to the rented chapel it became readily apparent that things were not exactly as they had left them. Bright lights flashed from within the building and loud sounds were to be heard.

Darwin spoke at Colonel Katterfelto's ear. 'Please correct me if I am wrong,' he said, 'but that sounds very much to me to be the voices of harpers with their harps.'

The electric Maria was all but soundless. The fearful speakings had ceased in the back. The driver pulled on the handbrake.

'Scotland Yard,' he called over his shoulder. 'We are here now, sir.' And then he hastened to the rear of the vehicle and opened the door for the Chancellor of the Exchequer.

The tall, gaunt figure in black stepped down onto the cobbled street. Deserted but for a few newspaper reporters lounging about hoping for some kind of late-night scoop.

The Chancellor beckoned to them and they scuttled over. Faces displaying recognition, notepads open and pencils at the ready.

'Leave,' the Chancellor hissed at them in a dark and terrible tone.

Within the entrance hall the constables had got a bit of a party started. A constable with connections in low places had brought in a couple of willing women. Someone was playing a harmonica. Constable Gates was doing an Irish jig.

The unannounced arrival of the Chancellor of the Exchequer came as something of a body blow. Put a bit of a dampener on the festivities.

'Out!' hissed the figure all in black.

The constables took flight.

'You.' The Chancellor pointed at Constable Gates. 'Give me the key to the cell of Cameron Bell and give me precise instructions on how to reach it.'

Trembling as he did so, Constable Gates did both.

'And now *get out!*'

And willingly the constable did that also.

The Chancellor's shoes were soled with India rubber. They made no sound at all as the Chancellor walked.

He walked across the entrance hall. Down a flight of steps and along a dismal passageway that led between the ranks of very dismal cells.

Outside the one occupied by Cameron Bell, the Chancellor halted. He leaned forwards and peered through the little grille in the door.

The private detective sat with his back to this door. Shoulders hunched. Bald head shining by gaslight.

'Bell,' hissed the Chancellor of the Exchequer. 'Our paths cross once again.'

Mr Bell said nothing in reply. In fact he sat without moving. Apparently ignoring every word.

'Brave man, Bell,' the Chancellor hissed. 'For now it is all over for you. And I will treat you most cruelly. Or will I show you mercy? Perhaps. If the mood of generosity is upon me. Rise and hand the ring to me and I will let you live.'

Mr Bell said nothing once more. Nor did he move at all.

'Now!' cried the horrible figure in black. 'I will not be ignored. The ring and now or I enter the cell and tear you into pieces.'

But no sound came from Cameron Bell. He made no effort to rise.

'And so you die.' The Chancellor of the Exchequer put the key into the lock, turned it and kicked the door open before him.

'You will pay dearly for your ill manners,' hissed he.

In two long steps he crossed the cell and laid hands on the private detective.

He snatched at his shoulders and turned him around.

— And then took a single step back.

The figure before him was *not* Mr Cameron Bell.

It was a waxwork figure of Mr Pickwick.

The Chancellor of the Exchequer grabbed at this waxwork figure, hauled it up before him. It was unwontedly weighty for a waxwork. He tore the coat wide open.

To his horror now he saw the figure's interior.

Numerous sticks of dynamite attached to some kind of electrical device.

Outside in the carriage park hut, a ball of cotton wool in each of his ears, sat Mr Cameron Bell.

He pressed his thumb to an electrical switch.

Scotland Yard exploded noisily.

55

he front façade of Scotland Yard dated back to the time of Sir Christopher Wren. It was relatively undamaged, as Cameron hoped it would be. Within what had once been the building's interior a fire raged savagely. But *that* would presently die.

Mr Bell had reasoned, correctly enough, that once the Chancellor of the Exchequer learned of his capture, he would hasten to the detective's cell to acquire the Ring of Moses and dispose of Mr Bell. Cameron had also reasoned that he would probably wish to do this in private and so would dismiss all the police night staff from the building.

Cameron Bell emerged from the comparative safety of the carriage park hut, pulled the cotton wool from his ears and dusted away at himself. He wore an immaculate evening suit, black tailcoat, white tie, white gloves, silk top hat. And now, a black false moustache. He cut an impressive figure. An impressive *mustachioed* figure.

He gazed upon the ruination he had wrought and made so-so gestures with his gloved hands.

'Unfortunate about the building,' said he. 'But it had to be done. One down and one to go, methinks.'

He took himself to the street. The driver of the electrical Maria was patting dust from himself. He was also saying, 'Oh yes! Oh yes!' and occasionally punching at the sky.

Cameron Bell approached him.

The driver ceased his 'oh-yessings'.

'I am Lord Bell,' said Mr Cameron Bell. 'The Chancellor of the Exchequer has been assassinated. I am commandeering this vehicle. Take me at once to—'

'Ten Downing Street?' asked the driver.

'The Electric Alhambra,' said Cameron Bell, adjusting his moustache.

Colonel Katterfelto tugged upon his moustache.

'Is He having a party in there?' he asked.

Darwin climbed down from the colonel's back. 'It sounds like choirs, too,' said the awestruck monkey.

'Do you think . . . ?' The colonel looked down at his friend. 'Do you think He—' The colonel paused.

'Do I think that He now knows who He is?' Darwin the monkey nodded.

'Best go in then.' The colonel put his hand to the chapel door.

'I'll follow you,' said Darwin. 'For I am now *very* afraid.'

'I hope you will pardon me saying this,' said the driver of the electric Maria, 'but I for one was very afraid of the Chancellor of the Exchequer.'

'Myself also,' said Cameron Bell. 'In fact, I have never known such fear in my life.'

'Perhaps with him gone,' said the driver, 'and again no offence meant and pardon me for saying this, London might get back to normal.'

'That indeed is my hope.'

438

'And you just happened to be passing by, did you?' asked the driver.

'Just passing by,' said Cameron Bell.

'You were lucky to survive.'

'I trust that luck played no part in it.'

'But you *were* lucky.'

'If you insist,' said Cameron Bell.

'I do,' said the driver. 'After all, the blast did blow your moustache upside down.'

'To the Electric Alhambra,' said Cameron Bell. 'And drive, if you will, like a batsman out of Hell.'

Scenes of Heaven, scenes of Hell upon the stained-glass windows and a wonderful light of purest gold filling the rented chapel.

The colonel edged in cautiously, Darwin the monkey clutching the colonel's leg.

In the middle of the chapel floor there stood the Mechanical Messiah. The colonel blinked and focused his eyes as all about the golden figure in the golden light, a swirl of other figures moved. They looked all but transparent, the stuff of dreams or fairy enchantment. Sprites and elfin creatures, surely these were angels, too.

The colonel stood, transfixed, and as he viewed the beautiful metal man with the figures of myth and wonder and of holiness encircling Him and rising upwards and up- wards, the colonel realised that he had witnessed this scene before.

He had seen beings of wonder climbing one upon another upwards and upwards in the details of the auditorium walls of the Electric Alhambra.

Colonel Katterfelto fell to his knees.

Darwin the monkey did likewise and covered his head with his hands.

'Brothers,' said the Mechanical Messiah. 'Brothers, you have come unto me.'

Colonel Katterfelto bowed his head.

'And you have brought life unto me.'

The colonel made a silent puffing assent.

'And I must wage war upon the Beast.'

'The Beast is dead, but the case is far from over,' whispered Mr Cameron Bell as the electric Maria moved onwards.

Horse-drawn fire appliances, their bells ringing wildly, rushed towards Mr Bell, then passed him by on their way to Scotland Yard.

A fine crowd had gathered before the façade to view the fire beyond. Several members of London's underworld, whose criminal records had been lodged within, cheered wildly. One, whom history would only know by his nickname of 'Jack', smiled contentedly.

'That Case chap was on the verge of proving my guilt,' he said to one of Whitechapel's willing women.

'For what?' this lady of the night replied.

'Come to that dark alley over there,' said 'Jack', 'and we will discuss it.'

Ring-ring-ring went the fire-engine bells, bringing further joy to the assembled crowd.

But then a lady in a straw hat, who had been returning home after a bit of late-night cleaning that she would not be declaring for tax, pointed her finger towards what was left of the building and said, 'Now what is *that*?'

The crowd peered towards the flame-licked brickwork. For within the inferno beyond something dark was moving.

It seemed to rise and then move forwards. Stiff-legged, but alive. Alive within the flames.

'Someone lives,' cried the lady in the straw hat.

'A man,' cried someone else. 'A man walks from the flames.'

And a man indeed walked from the flames.

But only a man in semblance.

He wore a long black cloak and a high top hat. A black veil smothered his face. He stood in the door-gone entrance and flexed his narrow shoulders.

Although he had just emerged from fire, there was not a single mark upon him.

'It is a miracle,' someone cried.

'A miracle,' others agreed.

'A miracle,' said Colonel Katterfelto.

'I feel him,' said the man of burnished brass.

There were no sprites nor angels now. He stood upon the chapel floor with none but the man and the monkey.

'He has risen,' said the Mechanical Messiah.

Darwin the monkey looked up at the colonel.

The old soldier shrugged his shoulders.

'I feel him,' said the man-made God. 'Can you not feel him, too?'

'Can't,' said the colonel. 'Sorry.'

'He has brought great evil unto this world. You have brought *me* into this world.' The Mechanical Messiah spoke words of Revelation:

> '*And he laid hold on the dragon,*
> *that old serpent, which is the*
> *Devil and Satan and bound him*
> *a thousand years.*

'And cast him into the bottomless
pit and shut him up and set a
seal upon him that he should
deceive the nations no more.'

'He has done *what*?' Sergeant Case held in his hands a telegram. It had just been delivered to his door. The telegram had been sent much earlier in the day, but the post boy had been instructed to deliver it at a very particular time.

'Mr Bell gave clear instructions,' said the post boy. 'My timekeeping is impeccable. I am sure that you agree.'

Sergeant Case slammed shut the door upon the punctual post boy.

He tore open the telegram and viewed its contents.

HAD UNDERWORLD CONTACT CUT KEY FOR
CELL EARLIER IN DAY STOP ESCAPED
ONE HOUR AGO STOP REGRET THAT
IT WAS NECESSARY TO DESTROY
SCOTLAND YARD STOP WILL AWAIT
YOU AT ELECTRIC ALHAMBRA
WHEN ALL WILL BE EXPLAINED
STOP.

Sergeant Case made gagging sounds in his throat. His loving wife brought him a glass of water.

'Scotland Yard.' The sergeant's voice was quavery. 'He did for the Crystal Palace, Buckingham Palace, Nelson's Column and the National Gallery and now he's done for Scotland Yard. The man is systematically destroying London. And now—' He flapped his fingers at the telegram. 'Now he will do for the Electric Alhambra. Just you mark my words. But not on my watch, I tell you! He will *not* have the Electric Alhambra. I will have that Devil, you see if I don't.'

'Don't go out without your scarf, dear,' said his loving wife.

The driver of the electric Maria did not need a scarf. It was nice and warm inside the cockpit.

'We're here, your lordship,' he called to Mr Bell. 'The Electric Alhambra, sir.'

Cameron Bell stepped out into the empty street.

'Do you want me to wait?' asked the driver.

'No,' said the private detective. 'Go home to your loved ones. Tell them that you care.'

'Fair enough, your lordship.' The driver put the vehicle into gear. 'What a strange fellow, that Lord Bell,' he said to himself as he drove off home to his loved ones. 'And even with the moustache he does bear an uncanny resemblance to the evil criminal Cameron Bell. I wonder perhaps if they might be related.'

Alone in the street, Cameron Bell looked up at the Electric Alhambra. The most dangerous part of his mission was accomplished, he considered, with the destruction of the evil being. But there would be danger in the apprehension of the world's greatest criminal mastermind. He would not give himself up willingly. But Cameron Bell considered that as he, the private detective, *did* have certain tricks up his sleeve, so to speak, he *would* succeed in this criminal genius's capture.

'As long as there are no further complications,' said Mr Cameron Bell. And he entered the Electric Alhambra.

★

The Chancellor of the Exchequer hailed the single hansom that was moving down the road.

The Chancellor had removed himself from a fawning congregation of onlookers who had taken to the touching of his raiments when he walked unscathed from what should surely have been a fiery grave. He had taken himself along the road apiece.

Fire appliances passed him by and he had hailed the cab.

He flung himself into the hansom's seat.

The driver enquired as to his destination.

'I was on me way 'ome,' said the driver. 'You was lucky to catch me.'

'Lucky, yes,' said the Chancellor.

'So, where to?'

The figure in black took from his pocket something that glittered in the moonlight. Held it before his face. It was a piece of *Magoniam*.

'Lead me to the ring,' he hissed at this golden mineral. 'I asked you before but you have not aided me. But you have experienced the baptism of fire. We have experienced it together. Now aid me, I command you.'

The *Magoniam* shivered upon the leather-clad palm. Then rose in the air, swung several degrees and then halted.

The driver looked down aghast through his little hatchway.

'That way,' said the being in black. 'Towards, I believe, the Electric Alhambra.'

The driver stirred up Shergar and drove him like a batsman out of Hell.

56

he lighting in the great auditorium of the Electric Alhambra was, as Cameron Bell had set it earlier in the day, subdued. It was muted. Inspiring of a certain moodiness. Things of that ambient nature, generally.

There was silence in the great theatre as the private detective climbed the stairs, passed along a corridor and entered the Royal Box. Here he uncorked the champagne he had placed there, and although it was warm, the ice having melted, poured himself a glass.

And then he called, 'Hello there. Won't you step from the shadows?'

Cameron Bell gazed towards the stage. The curtains were open, but it was in darkness. 'Come,' he called, 'step into the light. There is no need to be shy.'

A scuffle of footsteps sounded upon the boards, but no one stepped forward to be seen. But then a voice called out to Mr Cameron Bell.

'Who are you?' called out this voice. 'Do I know you, sir?'

Cameron Bell leaned forwards in the box, cast away his false moustache and smiled.

'You,' said the voice. 'The assassin.'

'I am unarmed,' said Cameron Bell. One hand held high and empty. The other displaying his champagne glass.

'You are surely a dead man,' came the voice. 'The one I am to meet here will kill you in a most terrible fashion.'

'Ah, yes,' said Mr Bell and he sipped champagne. 'The Chancellor of the Exchequer. Pray step into the light.'

'I would prefer to retain my anonymity.'

'You are not anonymous to me,' said Mr Bell. 'Your name is Mark Rowland Ferris and you are the Fifth Earl of Hove.'

Mark Rowland Ferris stepped into the light. A handsome young man in top hat and tails.

'And I see you have brought your dogs,' said Mr Bell. 'Your three French bulldogs, Ninja, Yoda and Groucho.'

'How do you know me?' asked Mark Rowland Ferris. 'Our paths have never crossed.'

'No,' replied Cameron Bell. 'But I have seen your hand at work everywhere. You are the owner of this fine establishment and of The Spaceman's Club and of so many other enterprises. The manufacture of armaments. The commission of a spaceship that travelled to a forbidden place upon an illegal mission.'

'I do not answer to you,' said Mark Rowland Ferris. 'But you will answer to me.'

Cameron Bell reached slowly into his top pocket, withdrew from it a calling card, read from it aloud.

'MINGUS LARKSPUR
Special Representative of
The Ferris Engineering Works.'

'I vaguely recall that individual,' said the Fifth Earl of Hove. 'Although I do not know whatever became of him.'

'That fellow is literally all over the place,' said Mr Bell. 'His head orbits Venus, I think.'

'You are either a very brave man or a very stupid one,' said Mark Rowland Ferris.

'In truth I believe myself to be neither.' Cameron Bell sipped warm champagne. 'This is far better chilled,' said he, 'but would you care for a glass?'

'Enough,' said Mark Rowland Ferris. 'I will leave you to the untender mercies of the Chancellor. I will have him bring me *your* head in a bucket.'

'I regret to tell you,' said Cameron Bell, 'that the Chancellor will not be making an appearance here tonight. *I* sent you the telegram, requesting a confidential and discreet meeting here between him and yourself. Requesting that you came alone. You really will do anything he tells you.'

'He works for *me*,' said Mark Rowland Ferris.

'*Did*,' said Cameron. '*Did* work for you. But now, I regret to tell you, he is dead.'

'You think so, do you?' said Mark Rowland Ferris.

'I know so,' said Cameron Bell, 'for I killed him myself not half an hour ago.'

The three French bulldogs all began to howl.

Mark Rowland Ferris knelt and stroked their heads.

'Just tell me why?' asked Cameron Bell. 'You have so much. You have wealth beyond the dreams of most men. You hold an earldom. You are a young and handsome gentleman. Why involve yourself with such a monster? What did you ultimately hope to gain?'

Mark Rowland Ferris looked up at the Royal Box. 'I have read all about you, Bell,' said he. 'Of the cases you have solved. I have perfect recall and I know all about you.'

Cameron Bell nodded and toasted with his glass. 'And so?' he said.

'And so *you* answer those questions. You are supposedly the great detective who can discern a gentleman's sexual preferences from his hat brim. *You* tell *me*.'

Cameron Bell leaned forwards. 'My eyesight is beginning to fail me again,' said he, 'but I will tell you this. You dined tonight at your club. The Athenaeum. Fish dish for a main course. White wine, of course. And then you visited a lady and—'

The private detective paused. 'Oh no,' he continued. 'It was a gentleman. A *young* gentleman.'

Mark Rowland Ferris did pattings at himself. 'How could you know *that*?'

'You engaged in a practice known as "taking tea with the parson", which involved—'

'Stop,' cried Mark Rowland Ferris.

'It is nothing to me,' said Cameron Bell. 'Your private life is your own business. But as to what you planned for this world and why . . .' He peered and squinted, then he nodded his head. 'Simple greed,' said he. 'And a need for recognition. To be admired by all.'

'Then we share much in common, Mr Bell.'

'Ahem. But I do not wish millions dead. Nor think to employ a Venusian freak of nature. Did you really believe that you could control such a monster?'

'We had a certain arrangement.'

'He would have led the Empire to war.'

'A war that the Empire would have won with the weapons that *I* sold to the military. With *my* communications equipment. *My* electrically powered airships and submersibles.'

'And you would be a hero then, for your services to the Empire?'

Mark Rowland Ferris nodded.

'And then once all of this world was under the governorship of the British Empire, you would turn your gaze towards the stars.'

'My arrangement with the Chancellor ran to giving him full control over the surprise attack upon Venus. He has old scores to settle with the ecclesiastics. They persecuted his race to near extinction.'

'So I understand. And then Jupiter would be for the taking, I suppose?'

'Precisely. At which point a military coup would occur in Westminster. But a quiet one, unknown to the public. I would become Prime Minister. Lord Ferris, uncrowned King of the Solar System.'

'It does have a certain ring,' agreed Cameron Bell, decanting more champagne into his glass. 'And I thank you for filling in all the small details. They will flesh out the essential evil in your character when I write you up in my book.'

'I think not,' said Mark Rowland Ferris. 'For you will write no book.'

'I shall,' said Mr Bell. 'I toyed with the idea of a ghost-writer. But I think that is cheating, don't you?'

'The only way that you will write a book is if you prove capable of dictating it from beyond the grave.'

'Now you are just being silly,' said Cameron Bell.

'Silly?' said Mark Rowland Ferris. 'You are the fool here, Mr Bell. What are you expecting me to do? Surrender myself to you? Put my hands up and say, "Please arrest me, Mr Bell, I have been a very naughty boy"?'

'The alternative is unpleasant,' said Mr Bell. 'In fact, it would be a *fatal* mistake upon your part not to comply with my wishes.'

'You are unbelievable.' Mark Rowland Ferris now rocked with laughter. His three French bulldogs seemingly chuckled, too. 'You are aware of the power at my command. My wealth, my present position in society. Who would believe *your* word against mine?'

'I am counting on your reputation,' said Cameron Bell, 'as a technical innovator. Ferris Engineering is top of the tree when it comes to technical innovation.'

'Yes, it *is*,' said Mark Rowland Ferris. His three dogs nodded their heads.

'I have always been a traditionalist,' said Cameron Bell. 'Somewhat set in my ways. A tad reactionary, you might say. All these new marvels of the modern age. They are not really *me*, if you understand my meaning. But once in a while something does come along that really impresses me. Usually it is the product of Ferris Engineering.'

The man upon this stage was grinning broadly.

'I purchased *this* this afternoon,' said Mr Bell. 'From Harrods. I was assured that it is quite the latest thing.'

Cameron Bell lifted from the floor of the Royal Box a brass and copper contrivance, with glowing valves upon the top.

'Quite the latest thing,' said Cameron Bell. 'I switched it on when I sat down in this box.'

'That—' said Mark Rowland Ferris. '*That* is one of mine.'

'Certainly is. The *Microphone*, I believe it is called, is on the stage before you, connected by this cable to—' Cameron Bell read from the brass contrivance's name plate '—the Mark Seven Patent Ferris Audiophonicon. A remarkable contraption capable of capturing the human voice upon a wax cylinder. A startling piece of equipment. The recorded voice being so clear and recognisable. You will certainly make history, Earl Ferris. You will be the first man sent to the gallows upon the evidence of his own words, artificially recorded, as they have just been. Perhaps when they build the New Scotland Yard they will give this fine piece of Ferris Engineering pride of place in the black museum.'

'Oh yes?' cried Mark Rowland Ferris. 'Oh yes? You think you are so clever, do you?'

'From a detached viewpoint you must appreciate the symmetry,' said Mr Cameron Bell. 'Condemned by your own bravado and your own technology. Surely I deserve a small round of applause.'

'You will get what you deserve,' snarled the Fifth Earl of Hove.

'I do not think your dogs can jump high enough to get me,' said Cameron Bell. 'And I perfectly recall that in the telegram *I* sent you, it said to come here *unarmed*.'

Mark Rowland Ferris rocked upon his heels.

And then he began to laugh.

His three French bulldogs took up laughter and all became very merry up upon stage.

'Why, thank you,' said Cameron Bell. 'I am so pleased that the humour, although somewhat dark, has not slipped by you.'

'No indeed,' said Mark Rowland Ferris. 'It is all very funny indeed. And what a joy that we do not have to share the joke alone.'

'Sergeant Case, I presume?' said Cameron Bell, and he turned his head to gaze up the central aisle of the vast auditorium.

From the shadows beneath the tier of balconies a single figure stepped.

It was *not* Sergeant Case.

'You are a dead man, Cameron Bell,' this figure hissed.

57

 he evil Chancellor's left arm made a forward swinging motion, as if he was engaging in a game of bowls. The severed head of the hansom cab driver rolled down the central aisle of the auditorium and came to rest at the orchestra pit. The face stared blindly at Mark Rowland Ferris. The face wore a puzzled expression.

'How inconvenient,' said Cameron Bell, affecting bravado. 'Now I will have to drive myself back to my hotel.'

The being in black came striding down the aisle. 'The Ring of Moses,' he horribly hissed. 'The Ring of Moses, *now.*'

Cameron Bell concealed his hands. 'I gave that bauble away,' he lied.

The Chancellor threw back his head and breathed deeply through his veil. 'I smell your fear,' he hissed at Bell. 'And I smell too the magic of the ring.'

'Perhaps some agreement might be arrived at.'

'All that exists for you,' the serpent voice cried out to Cameron Bell, 'is a period of protracted torture, terminating eventually in a hideous death.'

The private detective weighed up his chances of survival. The scales came down rather heavily upon the none-whatsoever side.

The evil creature was now beneath the Royal Box. He angled up his head and Cameron Bell could palpably feel the eyes upon him, even though they remained hidden 'neath the veil.

The Chancellor of the Exchequer took his hat from his head and dropped it to the floor. Flung aside his cloak and let it fall. The veil, it seemed, dissolved, as did the clothes, and an unearthly being glared at Cameron Bell.

It resembled one of those medieval depictions of the Devil, as might be seen in old engravings, or upon the stained-glass windows of a church, or chapel, too.

Though in form it was a man, the skin was bloody red and scaled, as too the tail, which slim and barbed and snake-like whipped and curled. The hands were claws with taloned nails, the feet as of some lion. Upon the broad back two small bat's wings flapped and flapped and flapped.

But it was the face of the Beast that was more fearsome than any other part. More loathsome and inhuman, an atavistic horror, with serpent's eyes and cruel horns and jaws that snapped displaying awful teeth.

It was the very embodiment of evil. Of all evil compressed into a single form. The stench of brimstone filled the air, an air now chilled to freezing and below.

'You men,' hissed the evil one. 'You little men of this world. What are you to me? You are weak, you are nothing. Where is your God now?'

'Tell me, tell me, who you *really* are.' Cameron Bell was sweating, though his breath came steaming in the frigid air.

'You.' The Hellish creature swung around and pointed a dreadful claw at the Fifth Earl of Hove. The Fifth Earl's knees were knocking together, his three French bulldogs cowering behind him. '*You* who have so much to say. *You* who would tell our secrets to this meddler. *You* tell him all that I am.'

'Me, *sir?*' asked the shivering earl.

'You, *sir*, tell him.' The voice rang loud in the auditorium. Echoing from the domed ceiling, returning from the rear of the stage.

'Oh yes, *sir*, yes.' The Fifth Earl grinned most painfully. 'It is a biblical matter,' said he. 'A theological matter. It seems that when God created Heaven and Earth, he also created other inhabitable planets. He put life upon Mars and Venus and Jupiter, too. And each of these worlds was given an Adam and an Eve and placed in a Garden of Eden. God was sort of . . .' The Fifth Earl's teeth were chattering fearfully. 'Sort of hedging his bets. He thought he would try out four sets of Adam and Eves and see how it all worked out. There were four serpents, too, one for each garden. You have read the Bible, you know what happened to *our* Adam and Eve, how they were tempted by the serpent, ate of the Tree of Knowledge and were cast out of the garden.

'On Jupiter, however, the original Jovians did not eat from the Tree of Knowledge. They were too sated, having eaten nearly everything else in the garden. God threw them out for being so greedy, making such a mess of the place and not taking their roles as the father and mother of Jovian-kind seriously enough. But he did not visit his wrath upon them. God is rather fond of the Jupiterians.'

The Beast spat something resembling blood.

The Fifth Earl continued the tale. 'On Mars, things went rather differently. The Martians were just born bad, it seems. They shunned God from the start and worshipped the serpent. God turned their planet the colour of blood as a punishment. Evil things flourished on Mars.'

Cameron Bell recalled the evil thing he had shot in that bedroom now so long ago, which Colonel Katterfelto had identified as being a creature of Mars.

'On Venus, though,' continued the trembling earl, 'things were again different. When the serpent tempted the Venusian Adam and Eve, they did not heed it. In fact, the next time it visited, they killed it. They literally destroyed the evil of their world. Venus, I am told, is one big Garden of Eden.'

Cameron Bell gazed down at the monster, once more glaring up at him.

'And *you?*' he asked.

'Tell him,' roared the creature.

'God was so pleased with the Venusian Adam and Eve that he watched over them. Much of what we read in our Bible actually occurred on Venus, you know.'

Cameron Bell touched the Ring of Moses on his finger. He knew well enough.

'But God kept tempting his chosen people. He kept testing them. But they resisted temptation. Into each generation a serpent, as of the original tempter, would be born. The Venusians would kill this creature—'

'*Creature?*' roared the creature.

'This *being* that was not as they. And thus their world remained pure. The original magic of the Garden of Eden, the original magic given unto Moses, remained upon Venus. But in our time a Venusian mother gave birth to such a being, and she loved her baby and did not want it killed. She brought it here to Earth. This being stands before you now.'

The being growled, which rattled the chandeliers.

'Fascinating stuff,' said Cameron Bell, struggling with extreme difficulty to draw out his very last iota of bravado.

'I think I have all of that recorded. But I might have to change the wax cylinder.'

'Will you *please* kill this man?' Mark Rowland Ferris asked the terrible demon.

'Oh, be assured.' The being arose. Rose into the air. Its lion feet leaving the carpeted floor, its tiny back wings all a-flapping. Up that monster went.

And face to face it glared at Cameron Bell.

'You are a man of considerable ingenuity,' hissed the evil one. 'But I feel you have no more tricks to play.'

'Look out behind you,' suggested Cameron Bell and, pointing wildly, he continued, 'Zulus, thousands of them.'

And then the claw reached out and closed upon his throat and things went rather black for Cameron Bell.

The sky above and round about was black. And it was cold too in that sky. The colonel fairly shook.

He and Darwin had been carried aloft by the Mechanical Messiah. This now radiant being held the colonel under one arm and Darwin under the other and flew across the night-time London sky.

Below them, the tall Tesla Towers sparkled with electrical energy, St Paul's Cathedral swelled, gas-lit street lamps offered a crepuscular glow. In the distance many lights glistened upon The Spaceman's Club, that marvellous airship tethered to London below.

It was silent up in that sky and there was scarcely a breeze.

The colonel craned his head towards Darwin and whispered to his friend. 'There was nothing in the manual about flying,' he whispered.

'I think He made that up for Himself,' whispered Darwin. 'I would add that although I enjoy diddling about in the heights, as do any of my kind, this I find frankly alarming.'

'Soon be there,' said the Mechanical Messiah. 'We will soon arrive at our destination, where I must battle the Beast.'

'And You *will* win?' Darwin asked. 'As You do in the Book of Revelation?'

The Mechanical Messiah did not reply to this.

'Might I ask then *where* we are going?' enquired Darwin.

'To the Electric Alhambra, my little brother.'

Colonel Katterfelto groaned. 'Not fond of the place,' he declared, 'you're either dodging fruit or going up in flames. Lost its charm for me, I'll tell you that.'

'The evil one awaits,' said the man-made God. 'And he must be cast down.'

The evil one cast Cameron Bell down to the floor of the great auditorium. The private detective slumped in a painful heap. The creature dropped and stood astride its victim. Brimstone breath engulfed the fallen man.

'I shall skin you alive,' hissed the monster. 'But first I would have the Ring of Moses.'

The creature grabbed the hand of the semi-conscious Cameron, tore the ring from his finger. Placed it upon a claw-like digit, stepped back to admire the effect.

And then howled.

'No,' cried the Beast, 'it cannot be!' As smoke and flames engulfed his scaly claw.

Cameron Bell, his vision double, rose upon an elbow. 'It does look awfully like the Ring of Moses, doesn't it?' he said. 'I purchased it this afternoon. From a jeweller in Hatton Garden. Had it blessed against evil by the jeweller himself. A Cabbalist, you know.'

The Beast was staggering to and fro, fire leaping around it.

'You can never have *too* many tricks up your sleeve,' said

Mr Bell and he attempted to rise— 'Oh my dear dead mother,' he said. 'I think my leg is broken.'

'Get it off me! Get it off me!' The monster leapt the orchestra pit and came down upon the stage before Mark Rowland Ferris. 'Pull it from my hand. For I cannot.'

Mark Rowland Ferris stared hard at the Beast. Certain thoughts now entered the Fifth Earl's head.

'You would defy *me*?' The creature grasped the top of Earl Ferris's head with its non-flaming claw. Drew it back and rammed the fiery finger down his throat. He pushed down hard to make the earl's teeth grip. Then wrenched the finger from his mouth. Mark Rowland Ferris swallowed the ring and fainted dead away.

The cowering doggies started to howl.

The creature silenced them with a single stare.

And then examined his claw. 'That is better,' it said. 'And now I shall have the real Ring of Moses.'

The creature turned its terrible gaze towards Cameron Bell.

But the private detective was no longer where he had landed. He was crawling away as best he could up the central aisle to escape from the auditorium.

'Oh no you do *not*.' The Beast took flight. Soared with a single bound into the air. Came down between the damaged detective and the exit doors.

It hauled Mr Bell from his feet and held him aloft with its untoasted claw. Then slashed at his clothes with the other. 'Time to part you from your skin,' said the Beast.

Ripping away the shirt from the detective, it let out a cry of delight. About his neck on a silver chain there hung the Ring of Moses.

'Mine,' the evil monster said as its talons fixed upon the ring. 'Mine now the ancient power it commands. Mine to wreak revenge upon the Men of Venus. To wield its magic upon the men of all planets. They will know fear and they will know pain and then they will all know death.'

And with that said it tore the Ring of Moses from the neck of Cameron Bell and flung the detective once more to the floor.

58

nd lo, as it was predicted in the Book of Revelation, He came in glory from the clouds.

The centre of the great frescoed dome collapsed and down through the painted clouds came the Mechanical Messiah, a colonel under one arm, a monkey under the other.

To Cameron Bell, lying broken beneath, it was an entrance worthy of . . . well, a Messiah. The private detective shielded his face as lath and plaster and bits of the painted Queen Victoria descended upon him in dust and noise and quite a bit of hubbub generally.

'And what is *this*!' growled the Beastie, the Ring of Moses not yet on a second taloned claw.

The Mechanical Messiah crashed down onto a row of seats, reducing most to splintered ruination. Darwin scuttled to safety. The colonel fell hard upon his behind.

'Ouch,' was his comment on *that*.

The man of golden metal held His balance. The man-made God stared at His enemy.

'No?' The Beast cocked its head upon one side, twitched

its dreadful nostrils. 'I smell magic, powerful magic. But it cannot be, not *yet*.'

The Mechanical Messiah spread wide His arms. 'I am the Son of Man,' said He, 'and I have come to bind you for one thousand years.'

'I have read the Book,' the creature bellowed, 'and it is not *Your* time *yet*.'

'Deceiver of nations,' said the Son of Man. 'Father of Lies. Serpent of old.'

The creature paused and flexed its massive shoulders, shook its head from side to side, as might gentleman Jim Corbett, squaring up for a bare-knuckle fight, in a display of contempt for an unworthy opponent. The monster took the Ring of Moses in its right hand and sought to place it upon the claw of its left.

Only to have it snatched away by Mr Cameron Bell.

'Take it, Darwin, and run,' cried the private detective, flinging it towards the monkey. It was a brave enough try but the ring fell short. The creature swept Mr Bell from his feet and plunged forward to retrieve its treasure.

The Mechanical Messiah barred its way.

'Stand aside, *you*!' The creature swung a mighty fist, struck the metal chin, the sound rebounding about the auditorium like that of a great church bell.

The Mechanical Messiah staggered backwards, regained His composure, stroked at His chin then charged at the evil creature.

Cameron Bell ducked most nimbly aside for a man with a broken leg, as metal God and scaly Beast rolled over and over, shredding seats and wreaking mighty havoc.

Darwin was scrabbling about in search of the ring, which something instinctive told him was *very* important.

Colonel Katterfelto, up upon creaking knees, was reaching to his holster for his ray gun.

'Find the ring, Darwin,' he called to his friend. 'I'll take a potshot at the bastard.'

The bastard was clearly possessed of a most remarkable strength.

It leapt up and grabbed the Mechanical Messiah, lifted Him high above its head and flung Him with titanic force against a wall of the auditorium. The entire building seemed to shake at the impact. Sculpted figures tumbled, shattered on the floor. The metal God, though somewhat dented, threw Himself with force at His tormentor.

Cameron dragged his injured self to Colonel Katterfelto. 'Your ray gun is useless against the Beast,' he said, 'but without the ring it may still be vulnerable to your golden man. Good will triumph over evil, it is to be hoped.'

Darwin cried, 'I have it,' and held the ring aloft.

The creature turned its head at this.

The Mechanical Messiah caught its chin with a right uppercut.

'I will return to *you*,' growled the Beast and it hefted the man-made God of metal high and flung Him into the orchestra pit.

And then it advanced upon Darwin.

'Up the wall and out of the dome and run my friend,' called the colonel.

Darwin popped the ring into his mouth and took to scaling a wall. He leapt from one carved figure to another, from elf to demigod, from griffin to gremlin, from a fairy named Socks to an angel named Moroni. To the very dome climbed Darwin, swinging from one hairy handhold to the next.

'Hold hard!' The cry was loud in the monkey's ears

although it came from below. Darwin glanced down and terror gripped at his little heart.

The thing had Colonel Katterfelto and was holding him high by his ancient military jacket. The colonel, not a man to take such treatment lightly, discharged his ray gun into the monster's face. The thing of horror fell back, its face a tangle of spiralling tendrils, whirling fibres of flesh. These swung and twisted, returned to order, the ghastly face reassembled. The Beast dashed the ray gun from the colonel's hand. The old fellow punched it right in the eye.

'Take that, you scoundrel,' he shouted.

'Down,' cried the monster. 'Down, monkey, or I wring the neck of your friend.'

Darwin swung on a lofty perch. He looked down in fear to the colonel.

'Don't do it, my boy,' called this man. 'Escape with the ring, forget about me.'

Darwin the monkey paused.

'I shall break him,' growled the Beastie. 'Shall I snap off an arm to show you how it's done?'

Darwin the monkey didn't know what to do.

'Flee,' cried Colonel Katterfelto.

The Mechanical Messiah floundered in the orchestra pit. He had somehow become overly entangled with the clock-work orchestra.

The creature made a vicious move and snapped the colonel's arm.

The old man did not cry out. But bit upon his bottom lip until the red blood flowed.

'No,' called Darwin from on high. 'Do not hurt him further. He is my only friend.'

'No,' the colonel mumbled. 'Flee.' But the Beast put a clawed hand over his mouth and stifled the colonel's words.

Darwin climbed down hand over hand with tail brought into play.

He approached the creature that was hurting his friend. He took the ring from between his teeth and held it out before him.

'Give the Ring to me,' growled the Beast, tightening its hand across the old soldier's face. The colonel's eyes were popping, but they moved from side to side to signal Darwin *No!*

'Let him go,' said Darwin, approaching with the ring.

'Please,' cried Cameron Bell. 'You *must* run. Take the ring, throw it in the Thames. The Beast must not have it. It must not.'

'But the colonel is my friend.'

'It will not spare him,' Cameron said.

The Beast turned cold eyes upon the private detective. 'Give me the ring,' it said to the monkey, 'and you will save your friend.'

Darwin dithered, the ring in his outstretched hand.

'Don't do it,' shouted Cameron Bell. 'The ring is of *Magoniam*. It is the Ring of Moses, a sacred object of enormous power. The Beast must not have it.'

Darwin glanced towards the detective, then towards his friend. The colonel's face was purple and his eyes were bloodshot.

'Take the ring,' said Darwin. 'Hurt no more my friend.'

The monster snatched the Ring of Moses, loosened its grip on the colonel and then gave the old man's neck a twist.

Breaking it with a snap.

'No!' cried Darwin, as the creature let the broken soldier sink to the carpeted floor.

'Thank you,' said the monster and it tossed the ring into the air and caught it once again.

Darwin the monkey sprang to the fallen colonel. He cradled the head of his friend in his hands and howled and howled and howled.

Colonel Katterfelto's eyes flickered for a moment. A dying hand reached out to Darwin and tousled the monkey's head.

The colonel's mouth moved and his last words came from it.

'I love you, little brother,' he said.

And then the colonel died.

59

he Mechanical Messiah climbed from the orchestra pit. He viewed the broken body of the man who had brought Him life and his little brother weeping over it.

'No!' cried the man-made God of brass. 'Thou foul and filthy fiend.'

'It is all over for you now,' said the monster and it slipped the Ring of Moses onto its finger.

It was as if the air had turned to water and a mighty stone had been cast into it. Ripples, waves of power, spread from the terrible Beast. Cameron Bell, cowering beneath a row of seats, covered his head. Mark Rowland Ferris quivered in the foetal position up upon the stage. His dogs had their paws held over their heads, which can be cute with dogs.

But not cute now!

Darwin stroked at the colonel's head. His tears fell on his dead friend's face and dampened his moustache.

The monster knotted the fist with the ring, held it up towards the fractured dome. 'All will be mine,' it hissed and growled. 'Mine the triumph now.'

'Not while life remains within Me,' said the Mechanical Messiah.

'Then allow me to take it from You.' The monster threw itself upon the golden being. Struck Him a monstrous blow and then another and another. Held the dented figure by His elegant throat, tore open the little door in His chest, dragged out His *Magoniam* heart.

A perplexed expression flickered on the beautiful brazen face. The metal lips moved but no sound was heard. The head lolled and the shoulders sagged. The God of brass fell with a crash to the floor.

'Mine,' crowed the monster, admiring the ring. 'Mine the power and the glory.'

60

hen Alice was shown the door marked STALLS she had recognised it at once. She knew that it would lead her into the auditorium of the Electric Alhambra. But she did not know why, although she had hoped very much indeed that it might be so she could top the bill of a Music Hall show once again. And she with so many many kiwi birds.

She had *not* expected to see the horrors now laid out before her. The beautiful interior was gone to ruination. A ragged hole yawned in the mighty dome, statuary had fallen from the walls, rows of seats had been violently demolished. The stench of brimstone filled the air.

That and an aura of death.

The beautiful woman no longer wore her shabby blue dress with the white puffed shoulders. For she had become magically transformed.

She wore a corset, cut it seemed from the Empire's Union flag, which clenched her slender waist and brought her female curves to favour. High-laced boots and black silk stockings and a black silk skirt so short as might only be worn onstage at the Music Hall. Her golden hair flowed in wonderful waves. Upon her head she sported the prettiest pair of ladies' brass evening goggles as might be imagined. And as she stepped through the open doorway, her kiwis bustled about her.

She was no longer Alice Lovell, trainer of kiwi birds.

She was a Valkyrie. She was Diana, Goddess of the hunt.

She was Lady Britannia.
Huzzah!

Upon the stage a gentleman knelt, fussing away at three dogs.

Beside him towered a monster, laughing most hideously.

Alice turned down her gaze from his horror to find herself observing further horrors near at hand.

Before her lay the body of Colonel Katterfelto, with Darwin weeping over it and rocking to and fro. And next to the body, Cameron Bell, his clothes all torn, his right leg twisted, looking the worse for wear.

'Oh no!' cried Alice. 'I am too late.' She rushed to the fallen colonel.

Darwin looked up with tear-filled eyes.

'I am so sorry,' Alice said. 'I felt that something was wrong and so I came. But the time is different in Fairyland.'

Darwin bared his teeth at Alice and stroked at the colonel's head.

'Alice.' Cameron Bell could see this vision, though somewhat out of focus. 'Alice, you must go. Take Darwin, run as fast as you can.'

'You are wounded, Cameron,' said Alice.

'Don't bother about me, I am sure I will think of something.'

There came a sudden cry now from the stage.

'Look there,' called the man who was fussing the dogs. 'A woman and many birds.'

'A *woman?*' The monster fixed its gaze upon Alice. Straightened its shoulders, threw out its massive chest. 'And not *any* woman. It is Alice. Alice at the Palace, we have met before and I have held her slender neck.' Then the monster laughed. 'And still . . .' It sniffed, took in the scent of woman. 'Intact. The blood of such as she nourished me whilst I awaited *this*.' And it held up the hand that bore the ring. 'But now, sweet tender flesh, you will become my Scarlet Woman.'

Alice stood with hands upon her hips.

Magically fearless in the face of such a fiend.

'Scarlet does not really suit me,' said Alice. 'I think that you must die.'

The creature stiffened, then once more it sniffed.

'I smell powerful magic upon you. The magic of the ecclesiastics of Venus.'

'It is the purest magic,' said Alice. 'The magic of a world still pure, untainted by evil such as yours.'

'But I have *this*.' The Beast displayed the ring. 'Given unto Moses on Venus by God. That whomsoever should wear it would become the leader of nations. You are but a foolish girl, but you will pleasure *this*.' And he waggled something absolutely vile at Alice, something which had so far received no specific mention or description and would *not* do, no matter what now occurred.

'That is *very* rude,' said Alice. 'Kill this nasty thing.'

The command was issued to her kiwi birds. And these, it seemed, were now possessed of some of Alice's magic. They tumbled in a shrieking blur towards the evil waggler.

'*Ki-wi ki-wi ki-wi!*' they shrieked, with their beaks all peck-peck-pecking.

'Birdies,' said the Beast. 'What we need for birdies is a gun dog.'

It clapped its horrible clawey hands together. The three French bulldogs of Mark Rowland Ferris merged together before the Fifth Earl's eyes. Merged and swelled and so became that canine horror of myth.

Three-headed Cerberus, guardian of Hades.

'Kill them all, boy,' growled the Beast.

The kiwi birds engulfed the Beast, engulfed the hound of Hell, and there were terrible screechings and howlings and rippings and tearings. The Fifth Earl fled to cover.

Alice directed her birds as would a conductor leading his orchestra through a particularly rambunctious passage. Probably something by Wagner involving a lot of extravagant arm movements. The 'Ride of the Valkyries', perhaps.

At her magical direction the kiwi birds darted about the monster and the dog, pecking here and snatching there and doing something or other around and about. The feathers flew and dog fur too and nasty bits of Beasty came adrift.

Alice's arms moved this way and that, conducting—

A concerto of chaos, carefully controlled.

> A monstrous mazurka.
> A riotous rondo.
> A polka of pecking and pain.
> Bohemian rhapsody.
> Symphonic strategy.
> Ah, such a raucous refrain.

Had the crowd been there to see it, the crowd would not have thrown mouldy fruit and veg. The crowd would have been appreciative. The crowd would have cheered.

Alice flung her hands into the air. The kiwi birds swept

from the stage, returned and fussed about her. Some looked somewhat bent of beak but there were no fatalities.

Cerberus looked more than a little cowed.

The awful Beast did not.

Pecked parts reassembled, the Beast was whole once more.

'You will have to do better than *that*,' it sneered.

But Alice shook her head. 'I would not want my kiwi birds to come to harm,' she said, 'for after all, I now have what I want.'

A kiwi bird raised its long slim beak to Alice. In it was the Ring of Moses.

'What?' screamed the monster. Staring aghast. 'It stole the ring from my finger?'

'It seems to be of value,' Alice said. 'Would it suit me, I wonder?'

The horrible Beast leapt down from the stage. 'Enough of this nonsense!'

As it advanced upon Alice, Cameron called to her.

'Alice,' shouted Cameron. 'Throw the ring to Darwin.'

The monkey now was nodding his head. That ring had cost the life of his friend. He would run as far as Southend if he had to and hurl it into the ocean.

'Oh no you do not.' The Beast was upon them. It snatched Darwin up by his tail and advanced upon Alice.

Alice threw the ring to Cameron Bell.

'And your climbing days are over, I think,' the creature snarled at the private detective. 'Watch now and see what imaginative things I do to this young woman.'

Alice said, 'I *wish* you were in Hell.'

The Beast reached out towards her.

Kiwi birds gathered to protect their mistress.

The Beast breathed Brimstone upon them.

The kiwi birds took to coughing and falling over with their legs in the air.

'I wish you in pieces,' cried Alice. 'I wish you dead. I wish you were bird seed—'

'Bird seed?' queried the Beast. 'I fear that you have used up all of your magic. Were you not instructed how to use it?'

'I wish, I wish,' said Alice.

The monster shook its head. 'There is no happy ending for you,' it said. 'Only pleasure for me.'

And it snatched up Alice by her slender waist and held her high above. Darwin screamed and clawed at the Beast, but the creature just ignored him. It would sate itself upon Alice now, then have some monkey brains on toast for supper.

Cameron Bell crawled painfully across the floor of the auditorium, through rubble, lath and plaster. He was far too wounded to hope for escape. But Cameron sought no escape. He sought only rescue for Alice.

Alice's screams echoed as the Beast ran a forked black tongue across her face.

Cameron edged his way forwards. Not towards Alice. He had another destination. Fingernails broken, sweating pro-fusely, lungs fairly gasping for air, the private detective edged to the Mechanical Messiah.

'Last hope,' gasped Cameron Bell. 'Last hope.'

As the forked tongue sought Alice's more intimate places, Cameron Bell reached the lifeless metal figure, dropped the Ring of Moses into the compartment in His chest and slammed shut the little door.

Alice Lovell screamed in terror.

Darwin gibbered and fought with all his might.

Cameron Bell locked his fingers in prayer . . .

The Mechanical Messiah came alive.

The air seemed as water once again, with a big stone dropped in it from on high. The Beast let go its hold upon Alice and Darwin, turned as its nemesis marched upon it, shining as of gold.

The metal God fought once more with the Beast of Revelation. But now the powers of darkness did not have the upper hand. Alice and Darwin, aided by a number of helpful kiwi birds, dragged Cameron Bell out of the auditorium and into the grand foyer as the titanic conflict raged. Alice did not even dare to peep through the door marked STALLS.

She was comforting Cameron, who was comforting her in return. And Darwin, too, whose hurty-tail was in need of very much comforting.

Within the auditorium, watched by a man and a three-headed dog, neither of which wanted particularly to become in-volved, the Beast and the metal God went at it something wicked.

This was a no-rules, all-weapons match. The winner decided when the other was dead.

The Beast struck hard at the metal God, its clawed fist belabouring the finely muscled body. Again and again the blows rained down, but the Mechanical Messiah, its heart the holy Ring of Moses, grasped the Beast by the throat.

These titans smashed from wall to wall in a frenzy of destruction. The Beast now felt it time to leave and sought to fly away. The Mechanical Messiah dragged it down by a leg and snapped off its nasty little wings. The Beast poked the Mechanical Messiah in the eye. The Mechanical Messiah stamped on the Beast's foot. The Beast gave the Mechanical Messiah a Chinese burn.

'That is not really going to work, is it?' asked the

Mechanical Messiah. And He kicked the Beast in those parts that had not and would not receive any specific description.

The Beast doubled up and the Mechanical Messiah tore the last remaining row of seats from its mountings and beat the foul creature over the head with it again and again and then again again.

The Beast struggled up to its nasty lionish feet.

'You cannot kill me,' it said, 'for this is not Your time.'

'Then neither is it yours,' said the man-made God.

'I am always here,' sneered the evil one, 'in one form or another. This planet reeks of corruption. Its scent is delicious to me.'

The Mechanical Messiah viewed His enemy. 'These people are not evil,' said He. 'You might seek to make them evil. The brutal lives of some will make for brutal people. But I have seen love here. You will bring no more sorrow to these people.'

'And how will You stop me?' asked the Beast. 'Will You beg me to leave?'

'I will force you to leave,' said the Mechanical Messiah. 'I will take you away from this world. Together we will leave this place. And all the worlds where men of different races walk. The worlds that swing about this sun. You do not belong here and nor do I. It is not My time, but neither is it yours. I will carry you with Me. Together we will fly across the universe for ever.'

'No!' cried the Beast. 'I must have my vengeance.'

'You must come with Me!' said the Mechanical Messiah.

61

here was a mighty crash and then there was silence.

Alice dared to peep around the door. Dust rolled in as a grey storm, but the war was clearly over.

She spied the Fifth Earl of Hove. He was still upon the stage and patting once more at the heads of his three French bulldogs.

'They are gone,' said he, in answer to Alice's unasked question. 'The metal man took the beast. Flew with it through what is left of the ceiling. He said that together they would fly for ever across the universe.'

Alice stared up to the broken dome. Beyond, a clear night sky showed tiny points of light. One of them the planet Venus. And was that too a shooting star streaking away from Earth?

Alice made a wish upon it. Just to be sure, as it were.

But Alice was not magic any more. The magic had flown away with the Beast and the beautiful golden God.

Cameron Bell dragged himself back into the auditorium.

'It is done,' he said.

'Almost.'

Cameron Bell stared towards the stage.

476

Mark Rowland Ferris stood upon it. Somehow during the mayhem he had managed to acquire Colonel Katterfelto's ray gun.

'You cannot leave,' said the Fifth Earl of Hove. 'That would be a very bad idea.'

'It is over,' said Cameron Bell. 'Give it up now, if you will.'

'Oh no.' The young man shook his head. 'The creature has sown the seeds. The country is on the brink of war. I can succeed. My plans are not altered.'

'And so you will kill us?' asked Cameron Bell.

'Kill you? Yes indeed.'

'And what about our bodies?' It was a strange question, but Cameron chose to ask it. 'What about when our bodies are found?'

'That is a very strange question,' said the Fifth Earl. 'But your bodies will not be found.'

'Why not?'

'*Why not?* Because I will put a torch to the place. It has been nothing but trouble anyway. I will burn it and your bodies. I will collect the fire insurance. I might build a coffee shop here. I believe they will be very popular in the future.'

Cameron Bell nodded thoughtfully. 'Could I ask you to do me one favour, then?' said he. 'Just tell me one more time, loudly and clearly, your plans for this theatre.'

'Are you mad?' asked the young man on the stage.

'I am hoping *not*.'

'Then I will indulge you. I intend to *burn down this theatre*!'

And with that said, he pointed the ray gun right at Cameron Bell.

And with that *done*, fire descended upon him from above and he went the horrid way of Harry 'Hurty-Finger'

Hamilton, Smelly Charlie Belly and Master Makepiece Scribbens the Brentford Snail Boy.

In a great big burst of flames.

Then gone.

Alice looked at Cameron Bell. 'You knew that would happen,' she said, 'but how?'

Alice and Darwin assisted Cameron Bell. They struggled, as he was a heavy man, but eventually they pushed their way from the ruined Music Hall and out into the street beyond. In the company of a flock of kiwi birds and three French bulldogs that Alice Lovell had taken into her care.

'We have survived,' said Alice. 'Thank God that we have survived.'

Policemen leapt from many hiding places.

Sergeant Case called out to the survivors, 'I arrest you all in the name of the law,' called he.

62

here was some unpleasantness.

The kiwi birds and the three French bulldogs did not take kindly to being herded into the rear of a Black Maria. But order was eventually drawn from chaos.

Cameron Bell was carted off to hospital to have his broken leg set and encased in plaster. The following day he was visited by Sergeant Case. Who did not bring chocolates or flowers.

Cameron Bell had a lot of explaining to do.

Happily the Mark Seven Patent Ferris Audiophonicon had survived the holocaust intact. It made for interesting listening. The voices of Mr Bell, the Fifth Earl *and* the Beast issued most distinctly from the wax cylinder.

'Extraordinary,' said Sergeant Case when the playing was done. 'But all most unsatisfactory.'

'But, if handled with care, that recording can earn you much praise and the return of your rank. This is the first-ever recorded criminal confession – you will earn yourself a place in history for it.'

'*I* and *not you*?' asked the sergeant. 'It is your voice and not mine upon that cylinder, extracting the confessions, as it were.'

'Naturally I will testify that I was employed by you. I am sure you can shift some funds into my bank account, should anyone care to check.'

Sergeant Case rolled his eyes, and nodded with his head.

'I will further testify that it was *you* who rescued me from Scotland Yard when the mad Chancellor blew up the building seeking to destroy me.' Cameron Bell smiled upon the sergeant.

'You have an answer for everything, don't you?' asked the sergeant.

'Especially when it comes to saving myself from death at a rope's end.'

'Quite so. However—' and here Sergeant Case took out a packet of cigarettes, Ferris Extra-Mild, and lit one without offering them to Mr Cameron Bell '—all of this does *not* explain the death by fire of Mark Rowland Ferris. In the identical manner to the Music Hall bill-toppers. The cases *you* were originally called in to solve. The cases that still remain unsolved.'

'I solved those cases yesterday,' said Mr Cameron Bell.

'Then how come the Fifth Earl died the same way?'

'It was either him or me. He intended to shoot me.'

'I can understand how he felt,' said Sergeant Case. 'But who killed him?'

'The murders at the Electric Alhambra were not the work of a man, but of a machine. A marvel of the modern age.'

'A machine?' asked Sergeant Case.

'It is called the Harmonising Arithmetical Logisticator – a most sophisticated mechanical nexus that governs the internal running of the Electric Alhambra.'

'HAL,' said Sergeant Case. 'Oh no, you are wrong. I have

seen that machine with my own eyes and heard it speak. But its speaking was just a trick, designed by Mr Babbage to fool Lord Andrew Ditchfield.'

'I wonder whatever happened to *him*?' wondered Cameron Bell, who knew a loose end when he saw one. 'But I regret to tell you that Mr Babbage was fooling *you*, in order to protect his machine. I visited it yesterday. HAL and I came to something of an arrangement.'

Sergeant Case did shakings of the head. 'Let us say I was to believe you, that this machine actually thinks for itself. Why did it kill the Music Hall stars, and why Mark Rowland Ferris?'

'It is, as I have said, a most sophisticated piece of mech-anical apparatus. Mr Babbage schooled it to play chess and to appreciate good music. Classical music being the veritable music of the spheres. A music of celestial harmony. The Harmonising Arithmetical Logisticator found itself night after night having to endure the banal songs of Music Hall bill-toppers. I mean, have you ever heard Smelly Charlie Belly's song?'

'I have,' said the sergeant. 'You flatter it by calling it banal.'

'Precisely, and the Harm–HAL, if you will, got fed up and took to wiping out the performers in the name of high art.'

'And the Fifth Earl?'

'He threatened to burn down the theatre. He was standing right onstage when he did so. *Twice.*'

'Twice?' asked the sergeant.

'Well,' said Mr Bell, 'he was also threatening Alice and me with a ray gun. I had to make him say it twice, in case HAL had not heard him the first time.'

'It won't do,' said the sergeant. 'It just won't do.'

'It will have to be made to do. Trust me, when I give

evidence I will make all the pieces fit and you will take all of the credit.'

'And I should trust *you*? If you were *me* would *you* trust *you*?'

'I have no wish to be hanged,' said Cameron Bell. 'Believe me, you can *really* trust me this time.'

The private detective put his hand out for a shake.

The sergeant paused and then the sergeant took it.

'A happy ever after, then,' said he.

63

hree months later, the Electric Alhambra reopened.

Alice Lovell was topping the bill.

The Harmonising Arithmetical Logisticator had been completely rebuilt.

Cameron Bell had sent many red roses to Alice's exclusive dressing room, into which he had somehow failed to gain access. He had also purchased seats in the Royal Box.

With Cameron sat Darwin the monkey, looking most dashing in top hat and tails. Major Tinker in his dress uniform. Commander Case in his. Commander Case's wife was also in the box and she was being bothered by the Queen's physician, Joseph Carey Merrick.

Her Majesty would not be there this evening, because *somebody* had humorously prescribed her a rather strong laxative.

Someone else who sadly would not be there was Colonel Katterfelto. The old soldier had been buried with full military honours. And awarded a posthumous Victoria Cross for his services to the Empire and his fight against the Beast.

Many had turned out to see his coffin go by on a gun carriage. The British Empire knew how to honour a hero.

'I shall ask her tonight,' said Cameron Bell, popping the cork from vintage champagne and splashing it into outheld glasses. 'I have not seen her for months. I have been writing my book. I have kept my word with Commander Case and he will be the hero of it. My publisher assures me that it will be a best-seller and that I will be able to retire from the dangerous business of being a private detective upon the proceeds. I have purchased an engagement ring and tonight I will ask Alice to marry me.'

'Jolly good show,' said Major Tinker. 'Hope it all works out.'

Darwin held out his glass for champagne and whispered to Cameron Bell. 'Are you really sure about this?' he asked.

'Of course I am sure. I will finish my book. She and I will be married. And she and I will live happily ever after.'

'But what if she says no?' asked Darwin.

'Well,' said Cameron, 'she might. And if she does I will just have to make the best of it. I will return to what I know best. Being a private detective. There are still a few London landmarks that I have not yet destroyed.'

Darwin made a face of alarm.

'I am only joking,' said Mr Bell. 'But if Alice says no, I *shall* return to being a private detective. I understand that Commander Case is presently baffled by something he will only describe as "the biggest case ever".'

Darwin made a thoughtful face. 'Have you ever considered taking on an assistant?' he asked. 'Or a partner?'

Cameron Bell viewed Darwin the monkey. 'Are you applying for the post?' he asked.

'I am sure it would be a very big adventure,' said Darwin.

Cameron Bell reached over and tousled the monkey's

head. 'If Alice says no,' he said, 'I will return to my profession and you will be my partner. It is a promise.'

Darwin the monkey grinned.

He had gained access to Alice's dressing room. And *he* had caught Alice in the arms of a tall, dark, slim and handsome fellow. One of the jugglers. Alice had referred to this handsome fellow as her secret admirer. And sworn Darwin to secrecy.

'I think I might take to the wearing of a deerstalker hat,' said Darwin, the world's first monkey detective.

THE END

Alice Lovell died in 1979.

Her son Ernest (1917-2010) was the inventor of the *Deanox Process*, which produces the world's finest iron-oxide pigmentation used, amongst other things, for the colouration of asphalt. The pink of the Mall that leads to Buckingham Palace is a testament to this modest man's genius.

His granddaughter is married to the author.

THE ORDER
OF THE
GOLDEN SPROUT

THE NEW OFFICIAL
ROBERT RANKIN FAN CLUB

12 Months Membership consists of . . .

Four Fantastic Full Colour Issues of the
Club Magazine featuring:

Previously unpublished work by Robert Rankin
News
Reviews
Event details
Articles
And much more.

Club Events @ free or discounted rates

Access to members only website area

Membership is £16 worldwide and available through
the club website:

www.thegoldensprout.com

The Order of The Golden Sprout exists thanks
to the permission and support of Robert Rankin
and his publishers.